A Beautiful Decay

A Beautiful Decay
A NOVEL

Karan Madhok

ALEPH

ALEPH BOOK COMPANY
An independent publishing firm
promoted by *Rupa Publications India*

First published in India in 2022
by Aleph Book Company
7/16 Ansari Road, Daryaganj
New Delhi 110 002

Copyright © Karan Madhok 2022

Cover photograph © Volodymyr Melnyk | Dreamstime.com

The author has asserted his moral rights.

All rights reserved.

This is a work of fiction. Names, characters,
places, and incidents are either the product of the
author's imagination or are used fictitiously and any
resemblance to any actual persons, living or dead,
events or locales is entirely coincidental.

No part of this publication may be reproduced,
transmitted, or stored in a retrieval system, in any
form or by any means, without permission in writing
from Aleph Book Company.

ISBN: 978-93-93852-09-0

1 3 5 7 9 10 8 6 4 2

For sale in the Indian subcontinent only.

Printed in India.

This book is sold subject to the condition that it
shall not, by way of trade or otherwise, be lent,
resold, hired out, or otherwise circulated without the
publisher's prior consent in any form of binding or
cover other than that in which it is published.

For my parents

ONE

Suno now, listen to me: I thought about Papa when it happened. About his ballooned rosy cheeks, his thick square moustache. About his commanding voice from the head of the dinner table, silencing every other sound in the room. It's strange, but you must believe me: the mind works in un-fucking-controllable ways. You can't plan your last thoughts—that last taste on your lips, that last flash of colour. Death is so random, yaar. One minute you are sitting tipsy in the comfort of a noisy crowd, sipping beer, eating a cheeseburger, watching playoff basketball; the next minute your head is a mangled pile of shit. Red blood on your orange T-shirt, blood on your red meat, and blood on the fries, a suitably coloured replacement for the ketchup that you, too embarrassed of your foreign accent, never requested from the bartender. Red on the fat brown face of the friend whose life you possibly just saved.

And I ask myself, behenchod: you didn't think you were going to die, did you? You didn't think that your last meal was going to be this succulent beef in the company of your heathen Muslim and gora friends. In truth, I fear that autopsy more than whatever void that awaits. *Thin brown-skinned youth with a bushy unibrow shot dead in Northwest D.C., with a mouthful of delicious cheeseburger and the stench of sweaty armpits. As a saving grace, at least he wore a fresh new pair of Nikes.*

Yes, that's me, that same kid who, after spending over three years in this country, still smelled like he had jumped fresh off that kela boat. That same young man who is now disintegrating into a fresh corpse, meat splatting on medium-rare meat.

And him? He was the same wild-haired man whom Hamid had confronted some twenty minutes before the fatal shot. We named him Wildhair, for the long blonde hair that fell down to his neck, spraying out in different directions, criss-crossing and spider-webbing within itself. It seemed as if each dark-yellow strand had a consciousness of its own.

'Go back to your country,' he had said before he pulled the trigger, and at least fifty other faces—black-brown-yellow-white-blue—turned towards him, because half the people in that bar probably had a different country to go back to, even if they preferred to continue sitting right there watching NBA basketball and dipping onion rings into mustard sauce in the United States of Fucking Amreeka—theek hai?—thank you very much. Wildhair's 'go back to your country' was meant for Hamid, of course, and it was all so ridiculous because I was definitely more likely to fly a few thousand kilometres back to India than Hamid was to return to see his family in Bedminster, New Jersey.

Hamid. Oh, he had a million expressions on his face after that shot: fear and anger and panic and sorrow. But it's fine, let me tell you, he needn't worry about me, yaar. It was as clean a death as I could have hoped for. A half-second of the absolute worst pain you could imagine in the forehead, where it felt as if someone had turned up the temperature to a few thousand degrees, and another half-second of the searing heat rushing down to my heart. And then: numb.

The last flashpoint left were the senses, which were paused in time forever at the moment I went from Vishnu Agarwal, the twenty-one-year-old, breathing, drinking, laughing, hot-blooded young man who couldn't pronounce his V's differently from his W's, to a stinking, bleeding, about-to-shit-its-pants lifeless object. Those temperature valves? They descended to freezing point within seconds. Extreme hot to extreme cold. Mummy would say, in her voice that was the most delicate balance between affectionate and irksome: Beta, you're going to catch a cold.

Yes, those senses, they lasted a little longer, and so did the needling sound of screams following the gunshot, and 'Vishnu!' from Jess who always said my full name, and 'Viz' from fat-ass Hamid, who had a rare moment of stress in his voice. I heard a rush of boots thumping against the floor and then felt a dozen pairs of hands on me. I still had the taste of meat and beer in my mouth. And, *suno*, it felt hot; I have told you that already, haven't I? And then cold, but the cold didn't last too long before all of those senses froze into an eternal end. OK. Tata. Bye-bye.

And after that, only the memories remained. I swear, those memories, *kasam se yaar*, they are real. Memories of every moment before the final moment.

In Varanasi, my hometown, the ashes of a cremated body are immersed in the Ganga River, supposedly allowing the soul to pass from one realm to the next, or so those fraud *sadhus* around the *ghats* tell every sucker ready to believe anything uttered in Sanskrit. But my expertise is JavaScript, not scripture. I understood death more in simple binary terms: passing over from 1 to 0, yes to no. And somewhere in the eternity between that switch going from 'on' to 'off', I began to have memories that lay ahead of me too, memories without me, of moments where the senses stopped, but something—*behenchod*, how can I explain it?—something like an imprint of the future remained.

It was, or still is, something beyond time. *But listen, Vishnu,* I say to myself. *It's all in your name, so this shouldn't be a surprise, should it? You're part of the goddamn trimurti of gods. The trilogy of creation, destruction, and everything else in between. Act like it, at least.*

I don't know where the rumour began, but there is a misconception that your life flashes before your eyes when you die. *Nahi, nahi.* What you see is *every* life flash before your eyes. You see every consciousness at every point of its experience. In that instant, I knew why that waitress with the cornrows stared longer at Hamid than she did at me. I knew the names, addresses, and favourite TV shows of all the fifty-three revellers at Lucky

Luke who witnessed my death. I could see Rishi bhaiya out in California insisting co-workers call him 'Russ'. I knew that, despite my best hopes, Mr Palpreet Singh in the white Maruti would never walk again after that accident in Delhi. I knew the name of the Indian engineer from Vadodara to whom Wildhair lost his job last year. I knew why we were all here. And why I was going away.

The *real* challenge of this moment isn't to imagine and understand everything, but to parse it and filter it down to what is truly relevant. To separate the connections that count from the malware of memories bombarding every thought, to draw a map from A to B and translate the entire Ka Kha Ga. From those dancing bears I grew up watching on Cartoon Network, to Papa in the passenger seat of his old Maruti, driven away from the riots in Muktigarh, to Wildhair and his handgun. Ah, fuck. It all matters. All of it.

The riots changed everything, but Death—*the capital 'D' Death, the Bhayanak Maut*, which hunted down wet-bloused girls in Hollywood movies—had a way of figuring out its own balance. And so, here ends the known human life of Vishnu Agarwal, born near Ayodhya, raised in Varanasi, shot in Washington D.C., soon to be cremated back in Varanasi, and resurrected as a roach to haunt your favourite hamburger joint, because all that gluttonous cow eating is definitely going to keep me rotating through a few extra cycles of reincarnation before achieving moksha.

*

'Go back to your country,' Wildhair shouted. Some people spilled their drinks; some froze chewing on their French fries midway. Wildhair held the handgun in front of him, and later, some of the media would report with horror at how easily he was able to carry it into Lucky Luke. Others would marvel with pride that, despite the tragedy that followed, the little weapon worked perfectly, with a firm, comfortable grip allowing the shooter accuracy across the crowded distance of the bar.

Dekho, how his face flushed fiery red. I remembered those red cheeks instantly: fifteen minutes earlier, he had been sitting in my place by the bar table when I returned from the bathroom between the second and third Yuenglings. I had walked into him having an argument with Hamid and Jess. He wore a white sweatshirt, unzipped from the middle to reveal a red T-shirt, and a pair of grey trackpants that looked a couple of sizes too big on him. The red on his T-shirt matched the crimson spread over his pale face. There were rows of creases on his forehead and extra rolls of skin under his chin. He was in his forties, maybe late forties, perhaps even as old as Papa.

He wanted my place.

Hamid said something to him first, which I didn't hear over the crowd. Jess had a hand on Hamid's shoulder. If Hamid sounded a little meek in the moment, Jess, of course, was not one to remain quiet.

'Scuse me, sir,' she said, and it impressed me how she managed to sound both polite and rude in the same stern voice. There was no fear in her, even if she was dressed—as usual—as the coldest person in the room on a midsummer night, in a full-sleeved, cream-coloured D.C. Tech hoodie. Nahi, nahi, Jess was not a book to be judged by its insulated cover. 'Our friend has this seat,' she said. She saw me wading through the crowded bodies. 'Vishnu,' she called out.

She had awoken something in Hamid, too, so when Wildhair didn't budge, Hamid spoke up louder. 'Yo, you gotta move. That's my boy's seat.'

'Fuck off, Mohammad,' Wildhair slurred back at him.

Then, a tense stand-off at the bar. Fight or flight. Flight or fight. *Fuck off, Mohammad.* The words stung us, pricking into our skin. Even if, less than two years ago, President Gaandu-face had snuck into the White House a short drive down the road from us, adding a lot more distasteful masala in these conversations between cultures.

I'm always surprised at the capacity of human instinct; my delicate reaction to this situation was to douse the fucking fire. 'Guys, suno,' I said. 'D…Don't worry, I…I don't need a seat. It's okay.'

Wildhair looked at me and raised a curious eyebrow. It was my accent, I was sure. Between Hamid and me, Wildhair had been addressed by two brown-skinned young men, and they sounded drastically different from each other. Hamid had the extra New York twang when he spoke, a little natural, a little exaggerated, flowing with casual braggadocio to match his dreams of emulating every mid-90s Biggie Smalls record. Mine was closer to the Great Western Fear of that indecipherable foreigner: a pinch of Apu from the Simpsons with shades of ISIS recruitment videos mixed with CNN's Fareed Zakaria's almost-polished-but-there-is-still-something-off enunciation. *Do not worry, I don't need a seat*, I heard myself say, like a cartoon convenience store clerk.

'No, Vishnu,' said Jess. Her voice wavered a bit. She gulped and then continued, 'This is your seat. Don't worry. *He* will move.'

Gingerly, Hamid moved an inch closer to Wildhair, and I realized how physically imposing my friend could look to an unsuspecting stranger. He was the same height as Wildhair. Both of them loomed two or three inches over me, and I was almost six feet tall myself. Wildhair's nose flared, and his eyes were firm and deep blue, and his eyebrows were a rich shade of blonde, so blonde that they almost disappeared in camouflage against his forehead, a combination of light object on light background that would have been an instant sin if I had designed it for an interface myself. I looked closer to see that the hair on his arms was bleach blonde, too, as he stood with those arms and his muscles tense. But Hamid was still bigger, wider, and even if it was all baby fat, those loose T-shirts gave an impression of greater strength.

'Please move,' Hamid said. Jess nudged close to him, and

he used the support to speak out with extra confidence. 'Please move, *sir.*'

Wildhair took a deep breath and then exhaled 'Fucking Mohammads' under his breath. He took a few extra seconds to make his decision, a dramatic desi soap opera of emotional pauses, until he grunted 'Urghh!' and bounced up, lifted his beer off of my coaster, and left my seat.

'So, who was that wild-haired guy?' I sat back down.

Jess breathed a sigh of relief. Hamid had the casual swagger in his pose again. 'Urghh!' he impersonated Wildhair's final grunt. We saw him leave. Soon, he was swallowed up by the hordes of cheering crowds as the second half of the game began on the TV. We ordered another round of drinks. I asked the bartender to put it on my credit card tab.

That card, that credit card; it remained with the bartender. That silver and blue beautiful swiping sliding swishing sustenance for my existence abroad. The bartender never gave it back, so when the shot went off, that card was somewhere behind the bar, either sliding through a machine or waiting for my signature in a thin, black receipt book. That would be fine; someone would find it, someone would get it back to Hamid, and in a few days, Hamid would cancel it. I had lost the card before, of course: at a karaoke bar in Chinatown and at a concert in Alexandria. A few hundred dollars went missing each time, which annoyed Papa, but it always made its way back.

That card. It paid for cold sandwiches and Cheetos and cases of beer from Safeway and it linked with my apps to buy new T-shirts and jeans and the iWatch for Jess on her last birthday and my new Nikes, too. It worked in healthy tandem with my other card—the debit card—that made the wonderful *fluff-fluff-fluff* sound as money revved up inside ATM machines until the crisp, fresh-smelling faces of famous dead white presidents stared sombrely back at me.

I preferred the card over cash. It was light, simple, eternal.

There were no numbers that came back around to me every time I swiped and paid and flashed and plugged it in. A couple of oceans and a few extra continents away, from a bank somewhere in South Delhi, a bill was mailed a few hundred more kilometres east to Varanasi, and the credit was fataak se settled and paid, and a bank account somehow topped up, and I didn't ask questions because the answers were too complicated, or too boring, and Papa just took care of things.

The last time my credit card had gone missing, however, on that night in April at the karaoke bar, I made a long-distance call home to ask Papa for a new one. He missed my call, and then, I missed his callback. The next morning, I waited for the inevitable, my heartbeat racing because I knew what he thought of me. *Absent-minded chootia.* I dreaded his voice. 'What happened?' he asked when we finally spoke. I tried to sound as sad as I could, and I knew he wasn't convinced, but kasam se, he was ready to call the bank in Delhi immediately. He told me to wait, to check again, to retrace my steps. 'Where have you been drinking Vishnu?'

'You shouldn't be drinking too much, Vishnu,' came my mother's voice. I sighed, because I thought she should instead invest her concerns complaining to Papa about the same thing, but that was another issue for another time.

You know, the mind is capable of unbelievable things, and even the haziest of nights can sometimes get clearer with conversation, and later that day, I spoke to Tapiwa the African Prince in our kitchen, while he ate Froot Loops without milk, and after I made yet another phone call, there it was—yes!—safe in the hands of another bartender in another corner of D.C. That silver and blue, limitless swiping relief. I had it back.

But on my last night, suno, that card wasn't in my hands. The stoic bartender made sure to be polite to our group every ten minutes or so. I was going to tip him extra, as usual. I always tipped extra, 25, sometimes even 30 per cent. It was overcompensation for how I looked, and how I sounded, out of a need to be accepted into the bartender's tribe, among American White People and Black People and Latino People and Indian People like Hamid. It was my desperate attempt to make my generosity overcome my accent. It's something that I had always done in this country, and somewhere between South Delhi and Varanasi, the accounts handled themselves.

I was tipsy and munching on the Luke Burger, the most delicious item on the Lucky Luke menu, and perhaps it made complete sense that my last meal was this forbidden meat. I could write Chitra Kathas and bulky Russian novels on excuses I told Mummy and Papa for why I wanted to come study in America; or say, perhaps I did it to follow Rishi bhaiya, my estranged elder brother, the prodigal son. But maybe a simpler reason was that, behenchod, I just loved the food. I got my first taste six years ago when my parents brought Sakshi didi and me to New York. I walked around the city looking sullen, too old to be on a family vacation, but fortune doesn't wait for age, does it? Papa had money now, and he needed to celebrate, to simmer down after the stifling heat of the riots back home, to travel to Western countries and buy Mummy colourful Juicy Couture tracksuits that she was definitely too old for. And here I was, impatient while my parents tried to experience their first chance of a carefree youth. I looked away from Mummy duck-waddling through crowds near Times Square and Papa taking selfies with faces of celebrities he recognized on billboards behind him.

'That is that famous Black singer, hai na?' he asked with childish enthusiasm I had never seen back home. 'Sakshi, you are always playing this music. What is her name?'

'Beyoncé, Papa,' my sister mumbled.

'Beyonss, yes,' he replied, and popped his moustachioed face, without smiling, in front of the camera. 'That one. Let's take a photo with her poster.'

No, I kept my head low, buried into new the iPhone Papa had bought for my fifteenth birthday, embarrassed among the thousands of strangers striding past us.

But then, while taking a break from the humid afternoon sun in midtown Manhattan, we stopped for a quick first taste of firangi McDonald's, and, what can I say, yaar? Kya baat hai! It blew me away. Beef so real that it took me twice as long to digest it than the McChicken sandwiches back home.

∽

My third pint glass was a little over half empty when we heard some commotion on the other end of Lucky Luke. I heard loud shouts—not cheers or exclaims in reaction to the game—but sounds of panic. I looked up from my bar stool, and so did Hamid and Jess, and so did the other people who leaned on the wooden high bar table next to us, people out on dates or in celebration with groups of friends, or those who only wanted to drink alone and munch on the complimentary popcorn. All of us looked at the source of the ruckus coming from the doorway into the bar.

'Stop him,' a woman shouted.

'Somebody, stop him!' a man shouted louder.

It took me a few seconds of semi-intoxicated realignment to recognize him. 'Wildhair?' Hamid asked behind me, and I nodded. It was him, the same man, with tentacles for hair, those blonde eyebrows, that white sweatshirt, and that beefy frame that made him look like an out-of-shape professional wrestler. Yaar, I have watched my share of pro wrestling—samjhe?—and that man, he had one of those faces. A full, angry face, which now flared into a deeper shade of red. In the tense blur of that instant, the long, swinging hair behind him created an optical illusion, as if there were two extra heads on each of his sides, and each extra head had more heads trailing behind it, like the ten-headed Ravana, but instead of a Chandrahas sword he would soon reveal a Ruger LCP, which in his unshaking right hand could do glorious damage at this range. He was pushing through people. Some of them pushed him back, others scolded with high-pitched voices. His cheeks were redder than his T-shirt, red as blood.

It all happened in a matter of seconds, the last moments before all of my time halted, flowing into this new unmoving infinity. There were more men—tall and wide and all proportional in size to Wildhair—crowded around him, pushing him away and back out the door. Wildhair threw his arms out at them to create space. He smashed his forehead against the head of the man directly in front of him and the man staggered back. There were a few more exclaims of men or women, or amorphous sounds that could belong to either sex or both.

Human instincts kicked in. Fight or flight. Two men jumped towards Wildhair, and other patrons at the bar turned backwards. In a wave, those seated around tables stood up and pushed their chairs back, and in turn pushed back more people seated around more tables, until all of them had moved several feet back and closer to us at the bar. A small sea of heads ducked low, in near-perfect unison, towards the ground.

Then there was a crashing sound like shattering glass, and a man's scream, or a woman's scream. There was the sound of a fist connecting with flesh, and something dramatic happened in the game on TV and the commentators shouted, but the noise in the bar drowned them out.

Dekho, see with me now: this is what I saw. With a laboured grunt, Wildhair pushed the bodies off of him, and there was a clearing between him and our group. Or more specifically, between him and Hamid. Wildhair unzipped his sweatshirt to reveal his little semi-automatic, and somebody shouted, 'He has a gun!'

Some bounced away from him, and some even closer. But he had his clearing, and he couldn't be stopped. I swear to you, yaar, there was something in him, some true motherfucking dedication. What else can I say? 'Go back to your country!' he shouted, and he pointed, and he shot, and in the same infinitely long instant a new wave of pushes and shoves and punches submerged him, but no, they couldn't stop the bullet. There was no *dishkiyaoon!* sound effect like in old Hindi movies. Just a loud, short bang. First, it simmered on my eardrums; then, it burned in my head.

In my computer science classes, we were taught in increments that the smoothest operations are actually built upon micro-moments rushing with rapid speed from one to another. The finished product might look like perfect flow, but the backbone of the programme is a meticulous ticking from one command to the next.

In this instant, suno, there were no commands, no ticking, no incremental decision-making algorithm. There was just space between Hamid and that bullet, and in that space, in the same unbroken flow of time, there appeared my clear, wheatish-brown, oily forehead. And when the bullet hit me, I knew everything, I told you that before, no? I knew Wildhair and I knew his name. And then there was red, and then there's this.

There's Papa.

'Go back to your country!' Wildhair shouted, and so I did. I flew forward into time and eastwards around the globe, looking for the India I never found in America, and to the family that was waiting, and to the father who made me who I was. And who I wasn't.

Papa was standing on the shores of the Ganga at the Manikarnika Ghat, overseeing my body as its last remains were charred by flames. It had cost nearly four lakh rupees for him to bring what remained of Vishnu Agarwal back to the city where he lived, and it was mandatory for him to do so, because there was no way that Mummy was going to allow my soul to be released somewhere in international waters. It had to be here, by the muddy banks of the river in Varanasi, next to the very kund that was built by—who else?—Lord Vishnu.

This is the story that the boatwallahs in Varanasi tell wide-eyed gora tourists tripping on bhang so they believe in the exotic and the immortal, too: the story of Vishnu creating a kund, where

Goddess Parvati and her consort Shiv—the greatest, or at least the most fabulous of all our gods—took a bath together, where Parvati lost her earring. Somewhere in this process, the holy threesome inadvertently created the city, and thus, the whole goddamn universe. Viz was back here now, Viz the Vishnu, who was now supposed to be switching realms for promised moksha somewhere on the other end of the river.

Behind the dense, black smoke rising to the skies from my funeral pyre, Papa fixed his face, straightened the lips below his black moustache, and looked as impassive and unmoved as he possibly could. The Doms, who were the only caste of people entrusted with cremation—cursed and blessed to be the last line of humanity between the realms of maya and atman—spoke to Papa from time to time, and Papa responded to them with confident jibes. He had negotiated the terms of cremation out here on this ghat before, for other relatives. He understood the city's business of death.

You are a big man in this city, the Dom said, and Papa nodded, *Yes, yes, we know that*, and he knew that they were right to charge him extra for my cremation, but they were being ludicrous at this point. *Sixty thousand? Who were they kidding?* A couple of Papa's employees from Bhagwan Beads stood beside and behind him, supporting his claims. He told the Dom his final offer was thirty, but the man refused to go lower than fifty-five, and finally, both sides settled for fifty.

Papa was dressed in white kurta pyjamas, and the brightest flash of colour on him was a red tika on his forehead. He had shaved his head clean bald for my cremation, looking like one of those enlightened gurus by the ghat. This new look worked to his advantage because he only had a few sorry twigs of hair left up there, anyway. He stood still, as straight as he possibly could with his arms down in front of him and his hands joined together, his eyes attempting to focus through the haze of the pyre's smoke. Soon, the body on the wood began to cook evenly and persistently over the fire. They had anointed the dead body with ghee to further ignite the flame. The burning flesh didn't perturb Papa even as its aroma infused with the smells of the river, carrying the scents of the city's sewage and shit. Papa's two hirelings took a few steps away from him. One of them was Happy Singh, who wore a red-and-gold turban instead of his usual blue to mark the sad occasion. The other was a scrawny, pointy-nosed driver whom Papa called Chhotu even though it wasn't his real name. Both gave him his space. Papa stood alone.

Mummy wasn't there with him. She and every other woman at the cremation had to wait about fifty metres away from the ghat on the stone steps up in a red Shiva temple that overlooked the funeral pyres and the river from a safe distance. Mummy, being Mummy, had fought at first, insisting that she deserved to see Vishnu the body become Vishnu the bowl of ash, but a priest reminded her that 'Ladies must be kept away from such things, please madam, it is sensitive.'

So many people here call the Ganga their mother—Ganga Maiya—and believe that, like a good Indian mother, she would clean up her children's mess, that she would cleanse us of our filth and our pollution. But the children grew up, and the filth grew out of hand, with chemical plants and textile mills and overflowing sewer lines and the stench of the dead and the living, and our mummy was sullied to a point of no return.

My mummy had been looking on with swollen eyes as they carried the body chanting 'Ram Nam Satya Hai' through the gullies—the narrow bylanes of the city—and now, those eyes had begun to water; and I know her, and I know that she can be a little overdramatic about things, and there wasn't a single Hindi film where I had seen her leave the theatre without shedding a tear or two. As the body burned below, black smoke rose up the ghat and reached out to the open corridors of the Shiva temple and stung her eyes, but by then she had already been crying in a gushing waterfall, and those tears, kasam se, were real.

Down by the body, however, those weren't tears that Papa was now wiping off his chubby face; it was sweat. A few ghats away, the sounds of bells and conches rang out, signalling that evening's call to the river to pray: the Ganga Aarti.

Across the riverbanks, farther than any of their mortal eyes could see in the dusk, there were a dozen human corpses—men, women, children, and the unregistered—floating whole and unburnt, bodies of those too poor to afford a proper cremation. They would, like me, become a part of this river's pollutants, part of all the organic and inorganic material that our realm was leaving behind, and no matter how much of a price Papa paid for my final rites, I knew that all our fates were destined to be the same.

And this is how I departed, how all of those spirits released at this shamshan ghat depart. We become fire and fire becomes smoke, and the smoke pollutes the atmosphere and becomes the air you breathe, and you breathe us all in, until we pollute your lungs, too, and we seep into your bloodstream, and we become a part of you, and we never leave.

The sun had set, but it was still a humid summer night, and now Papa had begun to sweat out of his bushy eyebrows, too, through the hairy spot between his eyes that nearly connected the two diverging bits into a unibrow, below his red tika. Saala, didn't I say I had those eyebrows, too? Same genes, behenchod, what do you expect? Sweat poured down Papa's forehead, but he showed no other sign of weakness or strain, and for an overweight man nearing fifty out here in this human kitchen on a hot North Indian evening, that was certainly an impressive accomplishment. Soon, Happy Singh and Chhotu moved away to watch from the chai shop on top of the ghat steps, and the Doms got busy with another body, and the former Vishnu Agarwal was all but ashes. But Papa stayed a little longer, standing all by himself in silence, with one hand in his pyjama pocket, where he kept his yellow sapphire gemstone, and he swirled it around in hope of a past that could never be unturned. And I knew then that he thought about me, his son, and about how my life had been wasted, and about whom he could blame for it all.

The body was fully burnt now, and in the end, one of the Doms stabbed at the head with a bamboo stick to crack the skull, and they say it is done to release the soul, if there was such a damn thing, and when it happened there was a terrifying crunch in the hot night, and Papa, at a safe distance, shivered a little.

TWO

Papa had requested the Doms for sandalwood for my cremation. 'Only the best quality for our son,' he said, hoping that the wood's creamy, milky scent would overpower that sharp, sizzling human flesh. But, of course, it didn't. There was too much of my body to get through. Around him, there were hardly any others who could afford chandan, sandalwood, on their pyres; but in that unstoppable flame, it didn't matter if my cremation had cost five hundred or fifty thousand. Our ashes were indistinguishable in slightly different shades of grey.

But the fire had always kept burning. Inside a small temple above Manikarnika Ghat, the local Doms preserve a flame that has remained lit for centuries. Every body ever burned, they claim, is lit with this eternal flame. Mummy's father—my Nana—was burned here, too, by the same never extinguishing fire, and decades from now, this is where Papa's body will lie when my niece is old enough to weep for her grandfather.

Papa insisted that there be no change in his schedule after my death, at home or at work. He berated Mummy when she insisted that they bless and wash the house. The only attention I got was the newly framed eight-by-ten photograph they installed on the wall outside the kitchen, enlarged from one of the passport photos I had left behind. It was the only picture of me they could find which showed my full, clear face. That photo was taken at one of the visa offices in New Delhi, from the time I had dirty, long hair, and faint scars of my teenage acne which had refused to fade away. I wasn't smiling.

Mummy had the photo framed and perched on the wall, and she adorned it with a fresh yellow marigold garland, and placed two criss-crossing agarbattis in front of my departed face. Some of the eggshell-white wall paint behind this photograph had begun to peel off, small slabs hardened and detached to reveal the ugly, reddish disfiguration of brick behind it. The painted interior near the entrance to our home was suffering the same fate, as was the paint on Mummy's makeshift home temple. *It's a sign of moisture, sir,* the contractor had told Papa months ago, *or maybe the paint was painted over a dirty wall. I'll send someone to clean it all up in the afternoon.*

But no one had come that day, or later in the week, and Papa watched the paint chip away, tracking the daily decay. Now, there were spots of mould forming on some of the walls, too, spreading into small, sickly pools of yellow behind the chipping paint. Even the most glorious home, Papa knew, eventually loses to the ravages of time.

'We'll fix it ourselves,' Papa told Mummy. It was dinner time, on the night my body was cremated. 'That chootia contractor will never send his fellow. Get us some paint and a brush and we'll just have to fucking do it with our own hands.'

'Hmm,' Mummy said.

Then, silence. Fingers tearing roti, mouths chewing paneer.

The silence was to Mummy's relief and Papa's irritation. He enjoyed the sound of his voice and the wide-eyed interest of an audience. Mummy had been his faithful companion through his thicks and thins, through the risky move from Faizabad to Varanasi, the land disputes, the riots, Rishi bhaiya's departure, the trips abroad, and Sakshi didi's unnecessarily expensive marriage… she had always been by his side, allowing him to be the loudest voice at the table, and only offering her criticisms when he half-listened.

But she was not in the mood tonight. She ate silently and sighed loudly between each spoonful of dal. A part of her hoped that he would notice her silence, that he would ask her how she was feeling. *Kya hua? What do you want?* But he never did.

She was extra deliberate, tearing her roti into smaller and smaller pieces. She always sat on his left at the table, with her back facing the wall, and her eyes on him and on the kitchen door beyond him, from where Himanshu the cook rushed out with steaming hot rotis every few minutes. Papa, of course, sat on the lone seat at the head of the table, perpendicular to Mummy so that he could choose to turn to her on the left if he wished, or look straight ahead at the empty seats when he wanted to avoid eye contact. His was the only seat that had extra cushioning.

The table, capable of comfortably seating twelve people, stretched from one end of the dining room to the other. The majority of those seats had remained unused, chilly without the warm embrace of a human butt. The new place mats that Mummy had bought in Malaysia had still not been taken out of their original packaging. The place mats, along with Mummy's unused bone china plates—imprinted with elaborate white-and-blue dragon designs—sat gathering dust in a cupboard behind Papa's seat, next to where he kept the sealed bottles of foreign Scotch bought duty-free from the airport. They were all visible through the cupboard's glass doors, doors that were only opened when Mummy needed to bring out her little Ganesh statue and agarbattis on days when dinner was to be preceded by prayer.

Usually, Mummy prayed only to herself, muttering rote-memorized Sanskrit verses without understanding what they meant. Usually, I sat next to her, on her left-hand side, a good distance away from Papa. On his right was that cold empty seat, cursed and mostly untouched due to the shraap of family departure, for it was originally where my elder brother, Rishi bhaiya, was chosen to be placed. But Bhaiya had left home and he wasn't coming back, and this we all knew, and Papa promoted Rishi's twin—Sakshi didi—up to his spot, and when she got married and a new man came into the family, the seat became his. But

Sakshi and that new man—Mohan—lived in Indore, and they rarely visited, too, and coincidently, at the time of my death, my niece fell ill with chickenpox, and Didi chose to stay in Indore instead of flying to Varanasi for my cremation.

At the dinner table, Mummy ate with a spoon. Papa ate with his hands and made loud smacking noises with his mouth, adding an occasional burp in tribute to Himanshu in the kitchen.

Himanshu was a good cook, you know? But saala, let me tell you, he had nothing on Mummy when she decided to get her paratha-hands rolling. Her parathas, which she cooked in a tawa drenched with desi ghee, were always a little crispier and tastier than Himanshu's. Nowadays, she only cooked on special occasions, like the last time I visited Varanasi over Christmas vacation from D.C., nearly six months before I was shot, when it was winter; that smoky, smoggy, North Indian winter.

'How many parathas will you eat, Vishnu?' she shouted from inside the kitchen, while I waited impatiently in my seat. I was avoiding eye contact with Papa, who sat at the head of the dining table. He was gazing intently at his phone, scrolling through messages with one hand, while he tapped his fingers on the table with the other.

'Just one, Mummy,' I shouted back at her. 'Not that hungry.'

'I'll make you two,' she said.

'Mummy....'

I heard sounds of steaming pressure cookers and slaps of roti on the chakla and the whir of the exhaust fan. Then came that first sizzle of something frying, followed by the sweet musty smell of cooked potato.

'Have two,' she shouted over the noise of the exhaust fan.

'Why are you two screaming at each other?' Papa snapped without looking up. 'Be quiet, Vishnu.'

'Shankar, what about you?' Mummy asked. 'How many parathas?'

'Aloo parathas for dinner?' he turned around towards the

kitchen door. 'When was the last time you entered the kitchen, Pushpa?'

'You come in here,' she said. 'At least learn how to make chai for yourself.'

'Leave it, leave it,' Papa answered.

Himanshu rushed out a minute later with a perfectly bronzed, stuffed-to-its-edges aloo paratha—the surface bubbling with a thin layer of ghee—and laid it down on my plate. I immediately tore off a bit. It was warm and crispy, and by the second bite, the soft pieces of potato and bread squished into a delicious, comforting taste. The taste of home itself.

THREE

There is something strangely subdued about the sound of a gunshot. Nahi, you must understand, I don't mean that it was soft or muted. But when Wildhair's gun spat out that hot, speeding bullet, it wasn't like the movies. It was low-pitched and piercing, a forceful needling clang. For that one instant, everything else became a vacuum and Wildhair's bullet penetrated forcefully through. Wildhair dropped his weapon when he saw my body drop, and then he collapsed weightlessly to the floor, too, as if all the air had escaped from his body.

It grew considerably louder after the shot; the *clang* echoed in a chamber within itself, bouncing off the walls inside my head with nowhere else to go for the rest of time. Behenchod, I'm sure I would have heard that echo for the rest of my life even if the bullet *hadn't* killed me.

But, of course, it did. Nine-and-a-half hours ahead of me, Papa's phone rang early in the morning. He slept through the eight loud rings, ignoring the droning alarm and the beeping light. While he slept, on the other side of the world, I had already heard my very last ringing, and then, the bullet's slightly anticlimactic *boom*.

Another hour had passed before he finally woke up to the news. It was Uncle Monty from Virginia. Even in the chilly air-conditioned insulation of his bedroom, Papa began to feel hot.

'But why...' he muttered into the phone, feeling a burning sensation in his chest, that feeling of something pressing down on him.

'We don't know Shankar bhaiya,' Uncle Monty said. 'Some crazy man just came and he…and he shot him….'

'But why…?'

But, of course, Papa didn't hear the answer. When I was alive, I had never seen his determined, serious face lose composure; but this morning, he seemed to be melting under the weight of his years, of his life, of the pain of the riots that he had never allowed to bring him down. Now, that face fell and those lips quivered. He was sad, sitting alone in the darkness of the early morning, while Mummy softly exhaled in sleep next to him, and no one was there to witness him.

I like to think that, at this moment, we shared the same headache: mine pierced through the forehead with the sweltering heat of that shot; his troubling him from another night of heavy drinking and the sudden realization of tragic, permanent loss.

Eventually, he shook Mummy awake, and she knew something was wrong when she saw his horrified, wide eyes in the shadows of the room. He gave her a hug and held her tight, feeling colder in the air-conditioned environs. 'We did everything for him,' he said. Mummy had never seen her husband like this. Eyes red, cheeks swollen, shoulders trembling, words choked by his own breath. She hugged him, shouldering his heavy weight, ignoring the strain it caused her smaller body.

That night, he drank again while Mummy sobbed by the dinner table next to him. 'Why…' he asked, speaking only to the decomposing molecules in the air, but Papa wasn't articulating the correct question. No, yaar, he wasn't asking why Wildhair killed me, nahi. His 'why' was rhetorical, a question to the predetermined entropy of time or to whatever deity he chose to believe was controlling his fate, to the astrologers who had given him false promises and whatever stroke of luck that seemed to have stroked me the wrong way. *Why*, he was asking without words, *would a father outlive his son?*

Papa, you must understand, had been secretly obsessed with

his own mortality. The riots of 2010 had exposed him to more death than he cared to keep account of. He chose to gloss over the specifics, to register the tragedy in summary rather than its particulars, because each time he remembered a name, it stabbed him in the inner lining of his stomach. He couldn't take it.

～

In April of my last year alive, half a world away, I had lost my sleek silver *swishing-swashing* credit card for the second time in D.C. When I called Papa in Varanasi, he was out roaming the grounds of the factory, unreachable due to the faulty mobile phone towers in the area. He wouldn't have heard his phone ringing anyway, what with the steady stream of noise pollution coming from outside the factory walls. There were too many distracting noises inside the factory as well. Generators rumbled out rapid fire rounds of machine gun bullets. Sometimes, Papa heard the occasional clang of a hammer on steel. And the traffic outside the gates was the usual discordant symphony of horns and beeps. I realized I could try calling him again when he was back home, unwinding in his air-conditioned room, drinking a glass of ice water, or perhaps even whisky on ice, because he was never nicer than when he was a little ulta-seedha—you know—topsy-turvy.

Papa was short and stout, and when he smiled, he revealed the reddened molars in the corners of his mouth, which were rotting after years of chewing paan and gutka. I failed to connect with him that day, but as he walked around his factory with Happy Singh, rubbing a pinch of gutka into his palm, he was thinking about me. More specifically, he had in mind the idea of my life after him: in his office at the Bhagwan Beads factory on the dusty outskirts of Varanasi, he called his lawyer and Happy Singh to discuss how his family would continue after him, to discuss my future inheritance, not realizing, of course, that it would be him passing on the burning logs for my cremation to the Doms instead of the other way around.

He tended to sweat a lot, spending the summer days drenched, sweating out of every pore in his body, just like I did. It's a curse, yaar. Unless you are going to stay in air-conditioned rooms and cars all day, there is no respite for our jungli hairy masses in these North Indian summers.

Papa wasn't one to stay safely confined within the comforts of an air-conditioned lifestyle, though. During the height of the hot season in May and June, when the tar on the roads melted and thousands died of heatstroke, Papa would walk fearlessly in the searing summer around the factory. Enduring the loo of the hot summer, he visited shitshow villages in eastern Uttar Pradesh, where craftsmen wound molten glass around metal wires, sliced and polished the heated glass under an even hotter lamp, drew elaborate mosaics, and created little pieces of decorative jewellery, to be eventually sold at checkout counters at gas stations in bumblefuck towns in Middle America. It was during one of those summers that he had purchased Bhagwan Beads, staking his claim on an arid piece of land on the outskirts of Varanasi, and over many more summers, built it into one of the biggest factories in the district.

And then there was the summer of the riots, where the ground boiled hotter than those heated lamps, hot as the fucking sun. Much blood was spilled, but nahi, it wasn't his: Papa left with reddened skin, surviving the catastrophe with little more physical harm than the worst tan of his life.

I don't know if his skin had always been darker than mine, or if it was a result of years in that direct, blinding sunlight, but Papa was now permanently afflicted with that tan, and his hardened face and arms had become an unnatural mixture of brown and red, a rosy shade that seemed to glow whenever he got furious or excited or drunk or saw a plate of samosas.

That formerly arid ground, where the new Bhagwan Beads factory now stood, was still perpetually covered in dust. Papa seemed to love the dust: he walked with an extra spurt of energy when at the factory, patches of sweat blooming in the armpits of his Lacoste polo shirts.

So, this was another day, when he had on a plain navy blue Lacoste, complete with a tiny crocodile stitched over where his heart would be. A carefree stream of sweat flowed from his armpits and down his hairy back.

'Haan, tell us again, Happy Singh,' Papa walked rapidly, daring the manager to keep up with his pace. 'The Delhi company was giving us that polishing machine for...how much? One point four lakhs each, no?'

'But Shankar sir,' Happy Singh trailed him, 'this one is more modern, sir. New Chinese technology. Centredoodle force.'

'Centrifugal.'

Now, suno: Papa liked Happy Singh because he was a lickspittle, ready with encouragement and agreement at all times. Papa also trusted him with the accounts because he, like Papa, was born in Ambala. Happy Singh became the unofficial foreman at the new factory, and soon, was named the floor manager, and even when the riots happened, it was Happy Singh—his consigliere—in his blue turban who stood steadfastly by Papa's side in the blinding heat.

'Centrifugal machine,' Papa repeated. He retrieved a white handkerchief from his pocket and wiped the glistening perspiration off of his forehead. 'Happy Singh, suno, the China machines are... how much...two lakhs each?'

'One point nine, Shankar sir,' Happy Singh said, droplets of spit spewing from his lips.

'One point nine,' Papa finally stopped walking and turned around. They had covered the full circumference of the factory ground—an hour of gruelling exercise around nearly 25,000 square metres of land—until they returned to the front office area. Believe me: there was nothing to see outside brick walls of the factory building, except for parking space and trash piles. Across the street from the back entrance of the factory were the heaps of trash that emptied out into the gutter, which in turn emptied into tiny streams in tunnels that eventually ejected into our holy Ganga Maiya. There was a constant metallic, burning smell around the factory, but it didn't bother Papa. Over years of acquiring property, he had made it a habit to circle his land, moving like a territorial beast, braving the inclement weather and environment with pride.

By the time they circled back to the main gate, the air-conditioned air was seconds away, and Happy Singh, sweating and breathing heavily, was eager to get back inside for a glass of refrigerated cold water.

'Do you know how much that's going to cost us?' Papa said. 'Those Chinese are trying to make a chootia out of you, Happy Singh.'

'No, sir, no Shankar sir,' Happy Singh huffed. His forehead was damp with sweat under the edges of the bright blue turban on his forehead. 'Kashi Beads already got some. It is not a bad deal. These centrigoogles are much better machines than the Delhiwallah's, sir. All the companies are moving to the Chinese.'

The Chinese, he knew, were indeed taking over the beads business, not just in Varanasi or Gorakhpur, or Gwalior or Kota, but all over the country; sach mein, even all over the world. The machine-made options were cheaper and faster than men, men who sat in humid, dark rooms, blowing beads into new shapes as if each piece was a work of art. Men who worked for Papa, men who were prone to sickness and disease and emotions and beliefs and rights.

'Hmm,' Papa grumbled and grew silent.

These days, he was often prone to these silences filled with quiet ruminations. Even as Bhagwan Beads became the top exporter from all of Purvanchal, and he had enough money to go on holidays to Athens and New York instead of Khajuraho and Nainital, and even after he built us his dream home over an acre of new land in Varanasi, where he installed generators and electric geysers to ensure we never had to bathe in cold water again—even then, the ruminations grew graver, the silences ever louder.

No, the riots had changed something in him forever. Sometimes, when he closed his eyes in these moments, he could still feel the particular late afternoon sun on the farm in 2010, still hear the moans of the young man by the handpump, still smell blood and death in the air.

FOUR

The lawyer, Sud, had a sharp, angled face, and his chin seemed to be pointing perpetually to the documents in front of him. 'Sir,' he said. 'All the Bhagwan Beads properties will be passed on to Madam Agarwal, and so will the flat in Westoria Heights. When your younger son—Vishnu—turns twenty-one, he will be entitled to the factory, the workshops, your Varanasi residence, and the Delhi office. The handicrafts store will go in your daughter's name.'

Seated opposite him, Papa listened intently, one forearm pushing his weight down on the glass top of his desk, the other hand in his pocket, fingers touching his sapphire gemstone. In moments like these—moments when consequential decisions loomed ahead—he could manage to keep his facial expressions unchanged, refusing to let go of his usually enthusiastic command of the room, refusing to be anything less than the loudest voice. But his fingers rotated the gemstone in his pocket with growing anxiety.

When Papa couldn't find penance in his daily work, he turned to astrologers who recommended he carry a sapphire gemstone, a stone so precious that he refused to have it manufactured or crafted by anyone at Bhagwan Beads. He chose to believe that the gemstone should come from somewhere more mystical, some source that he couldn't understand or explain to himself. He visited an astrologer at Dashashwamedh Ghat and handed him wads of cash. The astrologer comforted Papa with his sage eyes and the three stripes of white tilak, resembling the Adidas logo, on his forehead. Then, the astrologer handed the cash to his asssistant, and his assistant ordered the Rajasthani gemstone for Papa from JyotishLuckStore.com, and Papa was temporarily satisfied.

That day, Papa completed his round of the factory with Happy Singh before the lawyer arrived, sweating under the hot afternoon sunlight. 'Okay, chalo, let's go inside,' Papa finally said. 'It's too hot, Happy Singh. Ask someone to bring us a glass of ice water.'

⁂

I carry no mass in this vacuum of my lifeless ether, but I continue to carry my memories. Haan, I can still remember every detail of this office. It was furnished wall-to-wall in blinding white, with white cushion covers over the chairs. All the furniture was painted white, too. On the wall behind Papa's chair were two portraits with marigold garlands hanging over them: a painting of an all-blue baby Krishna playing a flute while approaching a pot of homemade white makhan; and a photograph of Papa's papa—the Dada I never knew—taken a few years before his death, sitting cross-legged on the grass at his farm on the outskirts of Ambala. The office, like every room in the factory, seemed imbued with a light smell of wood chips and oil.

The lawyer, Sud, was already there, waiting. Papa sat down on his white leather chair behind his white desk, and Happy Singh and Sud sat on the chairs opposite him. Another one of Papa's subordinates, whom he also called Chhotu, walked in quietly to hand them all glasses of water.

'Namaste Sudji,' Happy Singh gasped as he tried to recover from the heat outside.

'It is only you, sir?' Sud asked Papa. 'Madam is not here?'

'No Madam. No children. Only us, sit, sit, Sud. Suno, Sud,' Papa said to the lawyer, 'We are going to order samosas. Do you want a samosa? What about you, Happy Singh? Chhotu!' Papa called out to the thin, scrawny young man who stood by the door. 'Chhotu, get us some samosas from that shop across the road.

Get eight or nine and get some for yourself too, samjhe, you're the thinnest person we have ever seen. Isn't he, Happy Singh?'

'Yessir, Shankar sir.'

The lawyer took out three folders from his bag containing legal documents. On a plain sheet of paper, he began to list—in pencil—all the properties that Papa owned. On top of the list was Bhagwan Beads Limited, and underneath it, the lawyer added the address of the factory in Varanasi; secondary workshops in three other villages; our home address, which was in a different part of the city but also legally under the company's name; the commercial office in New Delhi; the Bhagwan Handicrafts store in Central Delhi; and the apartment on the fourteenth floor of the Westoria Heights township in Noida.

Soon, Chhotu returned with a plateful of samosas. Papa grabbed the fattest one of the bunch and took a hurried, hungry bite.

'Eat, eat,' he said pushing the plate towards Happy Singh and Sud. Morsels of aloo and spit spewed out of his mouth as he spoke. 'Don't be a Saddy Singh, Happy Singh. It's bad for our blood sugar, too, but sometimes we just feel like having a samosa.'

Happy Singh didn't need further convincing. 'Okay Shankar sir,' he shook his head from side to side, like a pendulum. Behind his beard, he stretched out his thin lips wider in a nervous smile. As he chewed, crumbs fell on his sweat-soaked shirt.

Sud pushed the documents towards Papa, who saw my name printed at the bottom, with a string of my inheritances and their current values next to each entry.

'You, Sud,' Papa said. 'Have a samosa.'

Suno, one time, at 2 a.m. at a pizzeria near the D.C. Tech campus, hungry after a drunken night, Tapiwa the African Prince told me about some dead Frenchman from the 1700s who was obsessed with food. This man, Tapiwa said, truly believed that a person is what they ate, and that I was a few slices away from stretching into pepperoni-pocked dough. We laughed about it but listen to me—Papa really was becoming what he ate. Over the years, his face had taken the lumpy shape of a potato, bloated with fat, uneven protuberances under his chin. The only sense of order on his face was that moustache, which sat like an old-fashioned black comb over his lips, making him look like a brown-skinned Mr Potato Head.

(Maybe I should be glad that I didn't live long enough to look like a lump of dough like him, because that was surely my inescapable destiny, wasn't it? Same genes, behenchod.)

The lawyer overturned a smaller stack of papers on the table so they were the right side up for Papa to read.

'Okay Shankar sir…. But, Shankar sir…?'

'What?'

'Your elder son? Ri—'

'Bas, bas, this is good, it's good,' Papa responded with a mouth full of samosa. He dug into a drawer under the desk and fished out a black pen. 'Eat, eat something, Sud,' he said as he quickly leafed through the pages. 'Arrey, don't you want to be healthy like our Happy Singh here?'

The lawyer sat with his back straight and watched Papa sign the papers, flipping the pages over with a swift snap each time Papa added the final dot under his name.

'We are done, Shankar sir,' Sud said, and offered Papa a celebratory handshake. 'I only have to get this notarized now.'

Papa held on to Sud's hands a few seconds too long, squeezing the lawyer's tiny fingers in a firm grip. 'Don't be late, Sud,' he said, and finally let go.

Papa only told Mummy about it when he got back home that night, waiting for Himanshu's dinner around the dining table in the large, empty hall. Over the faint sounds of dishes being scrubbed in the kitchen, Papa's voice echoed, even when he spoke softly.

'No, Pushpa, no, you don't need to worry,' he said. 'Arey yaar, you women and your khich-khich! Your inheritance is secured. We will take care of things. Don't you worry, okay?' Papa drank a glass of Bagpiper whisky with soda, while the expensive Scotch gathered dust in the cupboard behind him, and explained the breakdown of the property in the case of his demise to Mummy. He reassured her once again, 'No, Pushpa, don't you worry! Your name and our name is the same, samjhi? All in the family. It's no big deal, you understand?'

Mummy nodded and offered him more mattar paneer, even though they both knew that it contributed to his escalating blood sugar. Papa resisted at first, but with Mummy holding a ladleful of the ghee-laced dish halfway between the bowl and his plate, he succumbed to the temptation and nodded his head in agreement.

'Just a little bit. No, okay, that's it. Have to watch our sugar, Pushpa. We both have to watch our sugar.'

Haan, Mummy needed to watch her weight, too. After Wildhair's gunshot, however, her body rebelled: she dropped kilograms at an alarming rate, and floated around the house weightlessly. She became a zombie—speaking in monosyllables, sobbing from time to time.

One day after my death, alone at home in the afternoon, she opened the glass cupboard in the dining room and uncorked one of Papa's bottles of duty-free Scotch. She stared at the bottle: at its tall, curvy shape, at the amber hue, at how it felt cold to the touch. She wiped the dust off the bottle with a kitchen rag and put it back in, then locked the cupboard.

The next day, alone again, she returned to that amber bottle, unscrewed the cap, and poured herself a small peg. It tasted strong and bitter. Mummy had never had a drink before, except for mistaken sips from Papa's gin glass which she had assumed was water. Now, she sipped the Scotch slowly, nursing it with love, as it went warm down her throat.

A few days after my death, Sud the lawyer showed up, and

Mummy broke down in hysteric shrieks when she saw him, realizing the irony of Papa leaving a will for a son who had died before his parents. She cried in dissonant, loud wails in the presence of Sud and Himanshu and the guard at the gate, in broad daylight next to the Mercedes parked inside the gates of our home, covering her face behind a red sari. Papa asked her to calm down and stop embarrassing him in front of his employees.

FIVE

Some beads are made by winding molten glass around a metal wire, before being sliced and polished. Some are made by lampwork where the same wound bead is heated over a lamp. Sometimes, long-drawn glass canes are fused into the beads to give them colourful, ornate designs, making mosaics over its surface. It is unbelievable, actually, how much work—man and machine—goes into the creation of each little piece. The process can get even more intricate and expensive, with beads made of leaded crystal glass, or the beads that have zigzag chevron patterns. Didi's childhood favourite were the millefiori: beads made with layers of colourful glass fused and melted, then cut along the cross section where patterns would emerge on the surface. Every twentieth November—Didi's birthday—Papa ordered Happy Singh, who in turn ordered one of his subordinates, to make a new millefiori necklace for her, and even though we all knew it was coming, Didi would always act surprised and wear the necklace all the way through to Christmas.

The beads had become Papa's obsession, and he had hoped I would obsess over them, too. He wanted me to be invested in the process of their creation, in the effort that went behind achieving the end result. When I was younger, several years before the riots, Papa had driven me to one of the small villages on the outskirts of the city where his craftsmen worked, making shapely art out of hard pieces of glass. We entered a dark, stuffy room, where two of the craftsmen sat on both sides of a burning, hot lamp. One wore a white vest, the other was bare-chested. Streams of perspiration flowed down their thin, hairy chests.

The men stood up when they saw Papa, like we stood at full attention when the principal strolled into our classrooms. Papa nodded at them and they greeted him with namastes, heads bowed low. 'Haan?' he asked. 'All good? You guys are working hard?'

'Yessir, Shankar sir,' said the one in the white vest.

'Yessir, Shankar sir,' said the bare-chested one.

I gulped, suddenly feeling out of breath in the terrifying, human oven.

'What's your name?' Papa asked the one in the vest.

'Lakshman, sir,' he answered. He had a squeaky, high-pitched voice and a murmur on his lips, as if extra, silent words followed everything that he said out loud.

'Lakshman,' Papa repeated the name, in a tone that suggested mild curiosity. I knew that, an hour later, the name would mean nothing for Papa: Lakshman, Lakhan, Lalit, jo bhi. But in that moment, Papa saw this man, identified him, realized him. 'How long have you worked for us, Lakshman?' Papa asked.

'Sir, just eight months, sir. Both me and Kareem,' Lakshman said, pointing to the other man, the bare-chested one, 'we both came from Jalalpur.'

They spoke in a thick accent, Hindi fused with Bhojpuri. It was an accent I had to strain to understand, but Papa seemed to have no problem, nodding along, catching each word.

'Jalalpur?' Papa asked. 'There was a workshop there also?'

'Yessir, Shankar sir, nearby Jalalpur. Sir, we have been doing this job for generations, my father before me, his father before him. We have always been glass-blowers. Kareem's father, too.'

Kareem didn't speak for himself, and he didn't look at Papa, either. His face was plastered with soot, and he stood with his head hung low, arms folded submissively as he faced my father. I could see how his hands jittered, tall, bony fingers fiddling among themselves, anxious to get back to work.

'Go on, then,' Papa nodded, breaking the spell, allowing the men to sit down. We stayed around, however, watching them work for a few more minutes. I watched them blow into the glass tube, turning it over the heated lamp until they had morphed it into new shapes, a small act of daily evolution.

Finally, Papa turned around and so did I; he put a palm on the small of my back and ushered me back out—out to the white gleaming afternoon sun. 'This is an intricate business, beta,' he said to me. 'You can bend the glass into any shape if you heat it enough, samjhe, Vishnu?' he asked again.

'Yes, Papa,' I nodded. Yaar, I would've given him any answer that pleased him, any that satisfied him and left him content with the belief that perhaps I had learned something from the experience. I just wanted it to end. *Why was I even here?* I wondered, in that village far away from civilization, a hot box filled with electric flares and sticky perspiration.

Papa, however, looked immaculately comfortable in the setting. He held more conversations with the manager outside and the other karamcharis in grave detail, asking about their jobs, attempting to understand their minute art almost as well as they did. Someone offered him a cup of chai, freshly made from the village buffalo's milk. He looked at me and raised an eyebrow.

No, I shook my head. I watched him with a mixture of admiration and annoyance. Work was work. *Kaam ke pehle aur kuchh nahi, Vishnu*, he used to say, a sermon to never prioritize anything over his work habits. It was this sermon—this work ethic—that took us out of Faizabad, from the small apartment to the mansion, and then, abroad.

I was far lower on his totem pole of priority back then, carved much below his work, and Mummy, and Rishi bhaiya. And yet, at that young age, I accompanied him wherever he asked me to. I wanted to be exactly like him, and also nothing like him. I hated his dedication to work, and I failed to keep up.

I could no longer stand there, in that congested, hot room. I ran back out to the dusty open expanse of the village. Papa followed behind me, laughing out loud; a little overheated, but otherwise unshaken by the experience.

He rarely laughed that way again, boisterous and carefree, unconcerned by the judgement of any observers, uninterested in any other opinion. That laugh ended after the riots. After Rishi bhaiya left home. After I left, too, and never came back.

'What did you learn today, Vishnu beta?' he asked on the drive back home, as I sat in the passenger seat, fiddling with the cassette player.

'Nothing,' I shrugged without looking up.

'Nothing?'

'Did you bring Rishi bhaiya here, too?'

'Your brother has been to all our manufacturing units, you understand? All the factories and all the offices. But he can't do it alone. You have to learn the family business, too.'

The car hit a bump on the road, bounced up and jiggled, and bounced back down. I could hear the engine groan. I groaned, too.

I pressed play on the cassette player. Drumbeats and lasers and a deep bass voice hollered 'Hmmmmmmmm!'

'I don't want to come here again,' I whispered under the music.

'I didn't hear you,' Papa looked at me, then back at the road.

'I said,' and I cleared my throat. 'I don't want to come here ever again.'

SIX

Kareem was born not in Jalalpur, but in Firozabad; he was eight when his father first took him to the factory, in a slippery, humid godown filled with sand, water, and shards of old, recycled glass. Abba showed Kareem a large, metal machine, a complex pulley system that stomped and crushed and moulded the material over an anxious, hot fire.

Other children were there, too, older than Kareem, younger than him, girls and boys. Young Kareem made a friend, two years younger, but two times bolder than him. Yusuf spoke in a squeaky voice. He had short, quick legs, scurrying around like a little terrier dog on the factory floor. Sometimes Kareem chased him, sometimes he didn't.

Then, one day, when chasing Yusuf among the crowd of busy older men, Kareem heard a scream. A shrill pitch at first, followed by a dense, painful growl. It was Yusuf. He had slipped and landed on a burning furnace. Glass and sand and water and his right hand. Third degree burns. Palm reddened and charred, wrist turned pink, then white. Layers of skin peeled back.

Yusuf never used that hand again, and never returned to the factory floor. Kareem now spent time outside the factory, collecting smooth shaped stones in the dirt, petting stray dogs, inhaling the dusty air. He decided never to step close to an open flame again: whether it be the fiery machine inside the factory, the cooking chulha over which his mother flipped rotis at home, fireworks at the walima after a wedding in the neighbourhood, or bonfires at the Hindu festivals. Later, when his father began to do lampworking, Kareem would observe only from a distance, half in fear, half in admiration, wondering how Abba could twist and turn and turn and blow and finish without a single mistake. And then, Kareem would gradually begin to imagine that he might be able to overcome his fear and maybe one day follow in his father's footsteps, gain the confidence of being so close to the fire, to the pain and the heat, and, instead of fearing it, create something new and beautiful.

'We're artists,' said his Abba with a smile. 'You'll be an artist.'

Years later, after his family moved to Jalalpur, Kareem worked odd jobs—when jobs were available—under the command of a rotating set of new masters. He served under a butcher, a bricklayer, a car mechanic, and it was in the latter's workshop that he met another young man—Lakshman, a Hindu—who spoke with a squeaky voice, one that reminded him of his childhood friend, Yusuf. Kareem told Lakshman about his past; Lakshman shared his story with Kareem, too.

'And you've worked at a glass factory before?' Lakshman asked.

'I didn't work. My father worked.'

'Same thing, no? You must have learned everything.'

'And he was a glass-blower, too, my father,' Kareem added.

'Good,' Lakshman flashed a wide smile, teeth stained with paan masala. 'I have a job for you.'

Suno, now if I was telling you a fairy tale, I would tell you that Lakshman helped quell Kareem's fear of fire and flame with a special prayer to Agni himself, that he lit a havan and found a pandit to chant a few magic spells—Sanskritized Harry Potter—and suddenly, it was all over, and Kareem found himself the next morning blowing glass, swallowing lit fire sticks, and walking on burning coal.

Chal hatt, behenchod. That's not how life works. Kareem already had an inherent skill from years of observation, and just needed a little more 'experience on the field to master the craft of glass-blowing. And in Lakshman, he found a friend who didn't question him, or push him, or expect anything but his company. 'Just come to the workshop,' Lakshman said. 'It pays well. And we both need the money, don't we?'

They did—especially Kareem, who had lost his father to pneumonia the year before, and was now left to provide for his mother and unmarried younger sisters back in Firozabad. And, so, with timid steps forward, Kareem stepped close to the flame again in the workshop. Time passed, and each day, he got better and better; until the fire wasn't fire to him but just another tool; until the tool wasn't a tool any more but just another limb, an extension of his self, as natural as the hand he ate with, the hand he used to wipe his ass, the hand he used to shake hands with Lakshman at the end of every workday, before they went home on their separate ways.

They would meet again in the workshop the next morning, and then again, and again, until they weren't in Jalalpur any more but in a village on the outskirts of Mirzapur, where they spent their days making beads—pink and yellow and amaryllis and azalea and opaline and dahlia—for my father.

Mummy had a habit of placing those small, colourful spheres—beads from Papa's factories—in unexpected places around the house. 'It is the fruit of your father's labours, bacchon,' she told us once, back when all three of us would sit together in front of the TV set, *Shaktimaan* playing on screen. 'It's good fortune—nahi, it's good gratitude—for us to celebrate these fruits.' The beads would end up in a large decorative glass bowl in the middle of the dining table, or used to create intricate, colourful patterns inside the glass paperweights that sat next to Papa's desktop computer at home, or in Didi's make-up kit, or in my Iron Man pencil box. Even when I moved to D.C., I kept finding beads in random places around my room: a red and white one in my shaving kit, a turquoise one in the inner pockets of my laptop bag, a yellowish one with a chevron pattern in the side pocket of the blue jeans I wore to Lucky Luke on the day I died.

They collected the bead in a plastic pouch with the rest of the evidence and Uncle Monty shipped it back to my mother a month later.

SEVEN

'Aloo parathas for dinner?' Papa had exclaimed. Mummy had made for me the crispiest, greasiest parathas I have ever had. Didi was home on vacation for a few days from Indore with her family. She and her husband, Mohan, sat at the table shivering in three layers of warm sweaters, even though Varanasi winters were a fucking beach compared to the snowfucked temperature depths of the American northeast.

I smirked as I ate that night, unbothered by Papa's irritations and Sakshi didi's shivers, enjoying the last ever aloo paratha of my life. My week-long trip was coming to an end; the morning after, I would fly to New Delhi, and the day after, back to America. I was determined to make the home cooking count.

Papa sat at the head of the table, funnelling down his second whisky-with-soda, or maybe his third; yaar, I wasn't keeping track. Mummy and I sat at one end and Sakshi didi and Mohan at the other. I have already told you, haven't I, my dost, that Mohan occupied the seat that Rishi bhaiya had left vacant, all those years ago? But we didn't talk about Rishi bhaiya any more; my sister's marriage had ensured that my brother's seat was now occasionally occupied. There was a new man in the family, and a few times a year, Papa could count us up to five again.

That night, Papa told us about the new safety regulations that were affecting his manufacturing units in villages all around the district. Mohan listened with both elbows on the table, and an earnest look in his eyes; it was difficult for me, however, to pay attention. For years, I had heard Papa speak so much about his work that the sound of his voice had been reduced to a hypnotic hum, like the whirring of the air conditioner in the summertime, or the never-ending blares of car horns in traffic outside the gated confines of our home.

'You see,' Papa was looking left and right between us. 'These regulations are going to slow things down. We can only have the karamcharis in the villages work two or three hours now, and the temperatures in lampwork workshops are going to be lower, too.'

'But Papa,' Sakshi didi asked. 'Why don't we build them nicer workshops? Change our safety standards?'

Papa smiled slightly and reached over to pull her cheek, like he used to do when she was young. He had grown a lot more affectionate towards her since her marriage—it was, as if, she was a child to him again. 'No, beti, it's more complicated than that,' he said, and then turned to Mummy. 'Our little chweeti daughter has grown so old now, hasn't she?'

'Nooo, Papa, don't say that,' Didi said. She giggled, and for a brief second, was possessed by her earlier self, too, dropping her roti to give Papa a spontaneous hug. Physically, she had changed very little since her marriage and motherhood, boasting the same light green eyes and friendly round face I remembered growing up with. But to Papa, her new roles of a young wife and mother were a never-ending surprise.

'Beti...our daughter,' Papa said to her first, and then turned to Mummy. 'Can't believe you are so old now. We remember when you were this high,' he placed his palm a few inches below his chair, 'and all you wanted to do was run down to the colony and play cricket with your brothers.... Uh, uhm...she was a pucca tomboy, wasn't she, Pushpa?'

Papa wiped a gravy stain from his lips with his shirtsleeve.

'Oh ho,' Mummy complained. 'Use a napkin, Shankar, you're so filthy.'

'Anyway,' Papa said, now looking past the women at Mohan, who had continued to silently smile throughout the family interaction. 'What were we telling you? Oh yes, the lampwork. Vishnu, are you listening? This is important. Those craftsmen will build a union again, like they did before…like 2010. Right now, it's a good thing that so many of them are in many different villages. But today, every chootia has a phone. Everyone can connect. Everyone is too smart for their own good…. It's going to cost us, samjhe? But, you know, it's a good thing, a very good thing. Safety is the first and most important. You see Mohan? Vishnu, you see? Vishnu, do you remember that time we took you to the workshop near Mirzapur?'

I had one eye on my phone and another on my plate. 'Mirzapur?' I asked without looking up.

'Yes, do you remember? We met those glass-blowers. The women made you a small chain with the beads.'

'Oh yes. Of course, Papa.'

'Mohan, you should come with us, too,' Papa continued. 'They make these chains to go with your gemstones. They will give you one. Vishnu, where is yours?'

I swallowed a bite and answered slowly, too stubborn to match his energy. 'It's here…somewhere, Papa.'

'What colour was yours—do you remember? They gave us a yellow one. You know, Mohan beta, yellow is our lucky stone colour. We bought a new, big stone from the jyotish later, but those ladies knew our lucky colour.'

'Mine was red, I think,' I said as I took another bite. 'Or maybe orange. I think it was mixed: half red beads and half orange.'

'That's so great,' Papa said. 'So great. Oye, Himanshu: one more whisky. You know, before we purchased Bhagwan Beads, we had nobody in those villages. Now, do you know how many people we have employed?'

I didn't answer. 'You've told us, Papa,' Didi said. 'There are now thousands out there, no?'

He didn't look at her. Himanshu dropped three ice cubes into the glass sitting beside Papa, which made a sizzling sound when

he followed it up with a shot of Bagpiper. And then more soda.
'We want to hear from Vishnu,' Papa took a sip.

I looked to my left, at the curtains that ordained the far end of the dining room, curtains that Mummy had bought from Lucknow a few years ago, with intricate designs of red dragons fighting against green ones. I followed Himanshu's brisk, thin legs as he rushed away from the table and into the kitchen, moving as soundlessly as he possibly could. I looked over at Mohan, who was scooping up sabzi with the paratha between his fingers, making a chakravyuh of circles revolving like an inferno on his plate.

'Vishnu?' Papa asked.

'I don't know, Papa,' my voice was soft, hesitant. 'Di-Didi said, no? Hundred? A few thousand?'

'Why don't you show your chain to Mohan.'

'Later, Papa.'

'Vishnu,' his voice suddenly grew stern. He was looking at me—me alone—as if for a few brief moments, we were the only ones at that dining table.

I dropped my phone and looked up. 'What did I do now, Papa?'

'You're not listening to anything, Vishnu.'

'I am, Papa!'

'Vishnu, this concerns you, too,' he said, chomping on the aloo. 'This is *your* business after all. Think about your future.'

What future? Time tended to come to a standstill at home, to a time before America, even before Delhi. Something about being there, next to Mummy, in the comforts of home where I didn't have to do my own laundry or wash my own dishes… yaar, it made me feel as if I could crawl back into my shell and be my younger self again, a self who wasn't expected to make plans for the future, when I wasn't expected to be anything more than what I already was.

I sighed, desperate to finish eating, ready to get up and go back to my room. 'Aah! I'm listening to you. You are *always* talking and the rest of us are *always* listening.'

Papa smiled, but I had seen this face before. I knew him—it was the type of smile that meant the opposite of what it pretended to be. It was a threat, his way of forcing some calm upon himself before the inevitable explosion.

'How many days have you been back from Amreeka?' he asked.

I wiped some gravy off my chin, making a mess on the back of my wrist. 'Mummy, can you hand me that tissue box?'

Papa put an arm in front of Mummy, stopping her in her tracks.

'How many days, Vishnu?'

I knew the answer, but I stammered and delayed, hoping against my better judgement that the delay would calm him down. 'Twelve…twelve days, Papa.'

'Twelve days,' he said, and now he repeated louder to Mummy. 'Twelve days, Pushpa. And do you know how many of those days he has visited the office? Come and seen us where we work? Given Happy Singh a call to ask how the business is doing. *His* business? He's just spending our money drinking, eating, loafering, whatnot abroad. Chootia still doesn't listen to anyone. Remember when he lost his credit card? And even after all that tamasha in Delhi, he didn't learn. Laaparwaah, careless child.'

Mummy placed a hand on Papa's arm. 'Let it go, Shankar,' she said in a soft voice. 'Those Delhiwallah problems were so long ago.'

I was suddenly invisible in front of him, as if I was already a spectre floating through time, observing and witnessing the moment without being a part of it.

I floated back in time. Back to my first flight to New Delhi alone. I was fifteen and had fought and rebelled my way out of home. I was going to stay with Mummy's brother's family, like Rishi bhaiya had, and I was desperate to start a new school in a new city where no one knew me, to be away from Papa's gaze.

Papa had given me thirty thousand rupees in cash—pocket

money for my early escape—on our way to the airport. At security check, while armed guards patted me down and inspected my ID, Papa shouted something from behind, but his voice simply ricocheted away along with the rest of my past outside the metal detector. As soon as I got through, I cranked up the music on my headphones and didn't look back. Only when I boarded my flight did I realize that I had misplaced the cash. I couldn't remember where. It had disappeared—khallas—into the humid air.

Papa never let me forget it. I was the careless one in the family now, the absent-minded chootia, the one who couldn't be trusted, the one who wouldn't pay attention.

Back at the dinner table, Papa was still talking to Mummy about me. 'That is the problem with our children, Pushpa—they don't understand their privilege, you know? They don't understand that we can't sit here in this city at a big dinner table ordering aloo parathas, playing on expensive phones, speaking this fancy-shmancy English, having beer and meat and whatnot drug things in foreign countries, without actually understanding our work. They have no work ethic.'

Mummy moved up closer to Papa to press up against his shoulder. 'Achchha, okay, Shankar, it's fine, let's just enjoy the few days we have, the family back together….' She shot a glance at Mohan, the relative newcomer to our gathering, and turned back to Papa again.

'No,' he brushed her away, until she backed off to her own space. 'Our kids need to learn the value of hard work. They are old enough now. He looked at me and immediately lassoed me back into the room, 'Vishnu is our only son, you know? Who will take care of the business after we are gone? Rishi won't be here again. It's all on you, Vishnu, samjhe? Pushpa, you know what the problem is?' He raised his voice loud, so loud that even Himanshu's clanging in the kitchen quietened down. 'The problem is that we didn't smack him as a child. Just a few good thappads would have done the job. But we didn't. That's why

now he is a spoiled, badtameez boy.'
'Shankar, that didn't work with Rishi, did it?'
'Don't say his name here.'
'Papa,' I said. 'Why don't you call Rishi bhaiya?'
'You shut up. Useless child. That boy...he abandoned us over just a little bit of trouble. But you think you can make a fortune without trouble? You think you can spend dollars and...and not worry about where the next aloo paratha will come from? Do you even know the cost of aloos in the market? Trouble is a part of success, you understand? This is the only way this country works.'

Papa's hands were shaking; he rubbed the nails of the fingers of his opposing hands against each other, grating them together to calm himself.

I wished my brother was here, absorbing the barbs hurled towards me, sharing my pain. But I was alone in the moment, a glacier, frozen but melting. My shoulders slumped weakly in front of Papa, and my eyes were unable to look back into his. I glanced quickly at my sister—the offspring denied consideration in this conversation—and saw her purse her lips at me. My voice shrank in his presence; my words came out in a stammer.

'Papa...I...I....'

Papa licked the grease off of his thumb and his index finger, making a mess as he did it. Even as I averted my eyes, he kept gazing steadfastly at me. Then, he turned to Mohan.

'How is that construction business going, Mohan beta?' he asked, smiling, but still simmering under the new tone of his voice.

Mohan was only four years older than me, but we seemed decades apart. It was that side-parted hair, those collared formal shirts that he wore on every occasion—shaadis, parties, family dinners—or perhaps it was the weight he had put on in the three short years since he had married my sister.

'It is good, Papaji,' he replied, his voice crisp, slicing cleanly through the dense air. 'The second township in Indore will be ready to sell by March—latest, April. You know Papaji, you were talking about those safety standards, no? Same problem for us. Now all of those labourers need hard hats, and we've had to invest in more pulleys, and they have placed regulations on working at night, too. Can't get any work done in the country like this, right?'

Papa nodded and turned to his glass for a sip. His drink was finished. 'Himanshu, yaar,' he shouted in the direction of the kitchen, 'bring us more ice!' Then Papa turned back to Mohan. 'Regulations, regulations. Those chootias need to learn. Someone always has to suffer. Can't get any work done if someone doesn't suffer, samjhe?'

Papa turned to me and repeated himself. 'Your brother would deny it, Vishnu, but you must understand. Someone always has to suffer for you to sit here and be comfortable, use that new phone, study in a big college. We have told you this before, haven't we? Your comfort is someone else's catastrophe, you understand?'

'Yes, Papa.'

But I didn't understand then, and now, as I try to piece this all together, I wonder—to whose catastrophe did I owe my comfort? Who suffered for my security? Why did Rishi bhaiya leave?

EIGHT

When he was a child, Papa's parents passed away from diabetes-related ailments in Ambala—his father of a heart attack and his mother of kidney failure—and he had since been raised in Faizabad by his uncle. Uncle Narender owned the Ram–Rahim Guest House, a small and dingy hovel near Faizabad Junction, and Papa had his own bedroom at the end of a dark corridor on the second floor. Papa's small window oversaw the other buildings in the neighbourhood, tightly packed like jagged tectonic plates. None of the buildings were higher than three storeys. Further down the street, where Papa's ears followed the sounds of traffic honks and bicycle tinkles, was the vegetable market, always smelling like a mixture of petroleum and spices.

The corridor outside his room had no windows and no lights, and at night-time, it got pitch dark. Little Papa was not afraid: he trained himself to master the long journey through the second-floor corridor with his eyes closed, skipping over floor mats on each side as if they were imaginary landmines, talking to himself about his adventures well into his teens. Guests began complaining to Uncle Narender that they could hear what sounded like a chudail's whispers in the night, mistaking Papa for a banshee haunting the dark hallways. Uncle Narender installed a solitary bulb on the wall outside Papa's door to illuminate him back into the real world.

The guest house was usually frequented by some pilgrims that visited the Babri Masjid in Ayodhya nearby, and others who showed up to protest at the same mosque. Uncle Narender was a man of business and didn't discriminate. But, by not taking either side, he had chosen to balance on a thin, lonely wire, and his tolerance in the matter proved to be a financial misstep.

Papa learned early that it was futile to try and make everyone happy. Ram or Rahim? Halal or sattvic? Masjid or mandir? The guest house soon went out of business. In Uncle Narender's final days, the rooms were only rented out by the hour, and Young Papa spent days in his bedroom at the end of the corridor pretending that the sounds of transactional love he heard through the thin walls were actually sounds of pain.

Then, Uncle Narender died, and when Papa married Mummy and brought her to Faizabad, he was the only one left to inherit the failing business.

Mummy first met Papa for a seven-minute conversation supervised by Mummy's mummy—my Nani. Papa was there alone. Mummy was twenty-one and he was twenty-two. He was thin with long arms and long legs, a sharp nose and beady eyes and thick eyebrows, and yes, that fucking unibrow between his eyes. She was fair with smooth skin, and wore a green salwar kameez. He wore a light-blue shirt that was missing a button halfway down the placket; the hems lay uneven once the shirt was buttoned up. He sat awkwardly next to Mummy in a small living room in Nani's old house in Delhi, with his hair drenched in Dabur Amla hair oil. Behenchod, he looked just like me, except that I had inherited Mummy's rounder face.

Mummy was wearing the same hair oil, actually, and Papa immediately identified its wet, fruity smell. His hair was oiled down into a side-parting. The first thing Mummy noticed was his restlessness. His hands busily brushed a tuft of hair on his head and pressed it down; in stubborn resistance, however, it always rose back up.

She thought he was handsome despite his somewhat unkempt appearance. She liked how thick his square moustache was, a dense black blob over his upper lip. In return, he liked the innocence of her face, the baby fat on her cheeks that made her look a couple years younger than she was.

'Your hair smells nice,' he said and smiled.

Nani read their every move, spoken and unspoken, deciphering their body language to predict their compatibility for the rest of their lives. Papa shifted his weight from his left knee to his right and then back to the left. Mummy sat frigidly with her head bowed low.

'Yours, too,' Mummy finally said, without looking back at him.

They got married five weeks later, and Mummy moved with Papa to Faizabad.

Balancing expertly on his right, Shiv lifts his left leg and bends it in the air at a sharp 'L' angle—his devant—in a graceful, ballet-like, 'Attitude' pose. The cosmos will be created and destroyed to the rhythms of his command. He spreads out four arms as if he's DJing at his own party, with one hand playing the damru and dropping the beat, another wrapped up by a snake under his command, a third providing the burning flame, the strobe light for his dance floor, and the fourth hand resting in front in gaj hast mudra, looking like an elephant trunk, inviting all onlookers to share his yogic bliss in the moment. Thin strands of his hair whirl wildly behind him like background performers. All of time and history stop for his signal. He isn't Shiv any more; he's Nataraj.

And he's ready to dance.

This is more than Shiv the yogi, or Shiv the destroyer, or Shiv the house husband, or Shiv the Neelkanth with poison stuck in his blue throat, or Shiv the lord of bhang who is tripping balls across time and space, or Shiv the midwife, or the intellectual, or the merciful, or the merciless. Nahi, nahi, this is Shiv the performing arts graduate, burning up the dance floor, with superpowers in each graceful move to glissade over the arrow of time, twirl it into a cycle, to put all the reality of maya and atman into a loop: birth and death and genesis and apocalypse. He teases Time, seduces it, makes love to it, conceives it with the Biggest Fucking Bang to start a new timeline, all over again.

Suno, this dude doesn't exist. Or at least, he doesn't exist in the same reality I used to inhabit. He's as amorphous as Darth Vader or the resurrected Messiah, even though all of them are said to possess some form of that same Force. He's humanity's confusion, our concentrated effort to place a metaphysical symbol—a metaphysical man—in that precarious space between our conscious now and our dark forever. Between life and death. We don't know what keeps the drumbeat going or what lights the universe's dance floor, so we create our own Nataraj to dance us in and out of existence, our own Allah in charge of the celestial bodies swimming in galactic dust, our very own enlightenment story to chase. Because behenchod, what the fuck else is there?

There are no gods here: there's only my consciousness, and the burden of every perceived reality that ever existed, and all of eternity to ruminate.

And then, somehow, in this eternal moment between life and the blank abyss of death, I see him. Or I see him seeing me. Or I see through his third eye. We are now the same fictional being. I dance with Time, too, waving around my iPhone instead of a damru for the background beats, shoulder-bobbing like the rappers Hamid impersonates, too cool to actually engage my limbs into a more flexible posture. I'm not Nataraj but I'm Vishnu, allowing Shiv to destroy and create while my own consciousness preserves and continues.

We meet between our foreheads, where Shiv has his third eye—a chakra—the wormhole into parallel universes and the pasts, presents, and futures. There are women dancing in the ancient acropolis at Dholavira and androids rhyming shers at a mushaira, earning waah-waahs by an impressed human audience. Haan haan, I have my chakra, too: the bushy spurt of hair between my eyes, the unibrow I inherited from my Papa and tried so feverishly to trim and shave out of shame during my short lifetime, though it always grew back. Same genes, behenchod.

NINE

There were no guests in the twelve available rooms for the first three weeks of Mummy's marriage. This was her honeymoon, haan, their lonesome stay in this vacated khandar. They had all the time they needed to spend with each other and nobody but a cook and a maid to disturb them. When the staff left in the evenings, Papa and Mummy fell into each other's arms, convinced that their young lust was love, convinced that they would make it through their financial struggles as long as they had each other.

Even when there was no one to serve, Papa loved to walk around the guest house, open the door of every empty room, smell the damp sheets and the mouldy bathrooms, stroll to the kitchen where the stovetops gathered rust, and sweep the dust off the staircases himself. Even when he had little work, he looked stressed, with the warm, red face of someone who had been keeping himself busy.

Mummy spent her empty days sitting behind the reception desk, wearing kajal around her eyes and red nail polish that had a cheap, chemical smell. She would read the names and addresses of visitors who had stayed at Ram–Rahim in the past. She purchased small stone idols of every little god-thing that could possibly be relevant in their lives: Shiv and Ganesh and Ram and Lakshmi and Durga and Hanuman and Vishnu. She had brought along a steel prayer thali from home after the wedding and began to pray each morning, adding a gentle incense fragrance around the guest house. It still wasn't enough to mask the untraceable smell of dead rats emanating from somewhere below, but Papa was glad because the new additions added some much-needed colour to the drab establishment.

Mummy was more religious than him in other ways, too. She didn't drink alcohol and didn't eat meat. She was always ready to starve herself for a cause: on Mondays for Shiv, during Navratri for Durga, and on Karva Chauth for her husband. During her fasting days, she made a habit of chewing on the new ballpoint pens Papa had brought for the reception desk, turning the plastic end of each pen into a moist mess.

'Stop it, Pushpa,' Papa would say, rushing past the reception as if he had been called somewhere. 'We can't keep buying new pens for you.'

During the fourth week of their marriage, a young man with crossed eyes finally walked into the guest house. Mummy perked up instantly, happy to help, excited to take his details and address and hand him a rusty bronze key to the best room available. That cross-eyed man was the only customer at the guesthouse that month.

Soon, Papa couldn't afford to pay the cook in the kitchen, so Mummy took over the job of making tea and simple vegetarian meals, but nobody came to eat them. The maid who cleaned the rooms quit soon after, and once the rooms began to gather dust, Papa felt less motivated to walk in and smell the disintegration. The yellow walls in some of the bedrooms began to peel off. Mummy spotted a rat in the kitchen one afternoon, only to discover that the room right below—Room Number 8—was harbouring a colony of a dozen little scurrying rodents nibbling on the damp carpet.

Mummy slammed the door shut and shrieked so loudly that Papa rushed down.

'We need to sell this place, Shankar,' she said.

'What happened?'

'Now, Shankar! I don't want to spend another second here. We need to leave.'

But the next morning, four men showed up at the guest house, asking for two rooms. By afternoon, six more men walked through the door. It was a small miracle. The protests down at the Masjid were picking up again. There was hope, yes, Papa thought. The guest house could be saved.

The next week, Papa paid a majdoor from the railway station thirty rupees to paint over the sign at the entrance. He had decided that, being close to Ayodhya—the holiest of cities, the very kingdom where Vishnu's own avatar Ram was born and had reigned—he needed to pump up the religious pomp a little. Mummy, too, wanted something more exclusively Hindu, something that sounded like a dozen ringing bells, something that ignored the secular in place of the sacred.

So, they killed Rahim. It was now only called Ram Guest House. They stopped cooking meat in the kitchen, which made Mummy happy, and Papa decided to become a vegetarian, too. When a mob of three hundred men came into town that weekend to throw rocks at the Masjid and threaten to tear it down, Papa accommodated dozens of them at the guest house overnight. Their battle with the Border Security Force went on for three whole days. Some came back shot with rubber bullets, some scratching their eyes because of the gas, but all in high spirits, and all alive. Papa and Mummy worked late into the night ensuring that their rooms were cleaned, their sheets were changed, and their dal was hot and spicy.

At 2 a.m., Mummy dragged herself back into the bedroom, tired but smiling after seeing the collections of the day. 'We need to bring the cook and maid back, Shankar,' she said. 'We can't do this alone.'

The staff returned. A year passed and business continued to improve. Papa bought a new scooter for himself and Mummy got to spend cash on colourful bangles in the bazaar. The number of guests stopping by Faizabad Junction increased exponentially. Mummy would ask all these men to sign their names and registers at the reception. She would read their information to herself when she was alone. They came from all parts of the country, from Gujarat and Bihar and Haryana and Rajasthan. Under 'Occupation', they all listed themselves as kar sevaks—volunteers for the cause.

One cold December morning, in the second year of their marriage, Papa told Mummy who was running the reception that he was going to ride the scooter to Ayodhya.

'It's going down today,' he said, with his face glowing red with excitement. 'You stay here. It will be safe here. Something big is going to happen.'

All the kar sevaks had left earlier that morning, and so had hundreds of others staying in other guest houses and ashrams around town.

'What's happening, Shankar?' Mummy asked.

'You stay here,' he repeated and, with the bounce of an excited young boy in his step, bounded out of the guest house.

The traffic got worse the nearer Papa got to the Masjid. This day had come after much anticipation. The Ancient Chariot Man had ridden his rath all over the country as if he was a mythological warrior himself. A thousand other enraged souls were also present at Ayodhya to bring down the mosque. Papa had to park his scooter a kilometre away and walk, rubbing against hundreds of sweaty, screaming, jubilant, blood-thirsty protestors.

Some of them were carrying trishuls, spiky tridents that Papa had only seen inside Durga temples. He felt a sharp chill run through his body, making him shiver. Some carried bows and arrows. Most wore some type of orange or saffron insignia—armbands and headbands and scarves or shorts. A few brushed past Papa, bumping hard into his back, apologizing with a brief hand gesture, and then running ahead into the rumbling chaos. Papa even recognized a couple of his own lodgers, carrying trishuls and smiling wildly.

He was excited to be there, haan, but he kept his distance; he was there to watch. Across the street from the Masjid, while men climbed over the useless bamboo fence and into the mosque's compound, Papa found a cocoon next to a streetside bhelpuriwallah, an old man in a dhoti pushing his thela. 'How much?' Papa asked, and the man put up a single index finger. Papa gave him a one-rupee coin and got a little newspaper cone filled with the crunchy pieces of puffed rice. 'Add some more red chilli, old man,' Papa said.

In the cacophony of sounds, there was suddenly a short boom—a firecracker had gone off. Papa followed the sound back to the direction of the Masjid. Then, there followed a direct attack, a shower of stones and bricks, at the mosque. Very soon, more of the crowds who had united in the large circle outside the monument surged past the few policemen standing guard and into the mosque's grounds. Time seemed to stand still for Papa in the chaos that followed. He didn't know where the minutes went, shifting him forward into the future at an ever-accelerating pace. A group of men made it all the way to the top of the Masjid with shovels and hammers and axes and rods, and some had heavy ropes that they carried up to the top, and they began to strike down the stone dome. Some of the men were young boys. A cheer erupted when the first cracks appeared. Then, more strikes. And more cracks. They destroyed it with the same glee that temples and mosques and churches had been destroyed by tyrants in the past, a vicious playlist on infinite loop, one that had been replaying for centuries. Then the dome imploded, and some of the men slipped and fell, and in reaction, more men screamed and shouted.

'More red chilli, old man,' Papa turned back to the bhelpuriwallah and repeated. 'Why are you being so stingy?'

It took a few hours and then the deed was done.

Meanwhile, back at the guest house, Mummy walked into Room Number 8 on the ground floor. You know, yaar, the one with all the rats. The maid had come to her crying, complaining 'Hadh ho gayi, madam', that there was no way she was going to clean that room. Mummy decided to take on this task herself. Papa had never shown interest in saving something once it had become uninhabitable. She knew that Papa only wanted to see the rooms that looked good and smelled good and ignore the one rotting from the inside. So, on the day that Papa was out in Ayodhya watching the mosque being demolished, Mummy walked down to the bazaar to buy a small achaar-sized bottle of rat poison and traps. She kept all the curtains drawn and the lights off, refusing to see the room's true colours under a brighter glare.

She covered her face with a dupatta, hopped and skipped over scurrying creatures in the darkness under her feet, and poured out the entire bottle in all four corners of that cursed room. She laid the traps strategically with small morsels of the previous night's roti to entice the rats.

The operation was an overnight success. The next afternoon, while sweeping up the brown rodent corpses in the dark, she puked a little into her mouth in reaction to the unbearably horrifying stench in the room's still air. She ran outside into the corridor but there was no respite. She could smell rotting rats everywhere.

Soon, *every* smell made her feel queasy: old bedsheets, fresh tomatoes in the market, and even Papa's Dabur Amla hair oil.

She was pregnant.

Papa smiled at the news. Then, his face fell.

'Arre baap re baap, how are we going to do this, Pushpa? We still don't have money. We have to refurbish this entire place and pay the staff and make sure we have food in the kitchen. How are we going to do this?'

There were riots around the country when the Masjid came down. Bombs exploded in Bombay, followed by fires, followed by stabbings and gunshots. People were killed in Ayodhya and Faizabad, too; but now, these were not the type of customers coming to the city for an overnight stay.

Hard times hit them once again. Ram Guest House turned into the khandar it had been in the early days of my parents' marriage. Its name was now common enough: there were hundreds of Ram hotels, Ram electricwallahs, Ram temples, or Ram hair oil companies around the city. The guest house became one of a crowd. It lost what had made it *it*. Samjhe?

The bedsheets collected mould and the window panels fell apart. One day, a man from Varanasi checked himself into the disintegrating property. He was terribly old, with a crusty and cracking face, like the wall paint in the room he was assigned. He was in town to visit the grounds where that mosque had been demolished over the rumoured once-demolished temple—the Janmabhoomi—but also to let his proposition be known far and wide. His business, he said, had no heirs: his daughters had been married off and he never had a son to pass on his name. The man told Papa that he was looking for buyers for his property. 'Would you be interested, young man?' he asked Papa. He was desperate to ensure that his Bhagwan Beads factory in Varanasi would have a future, that a lifetime of his work wouldn't go to waste.

Chootia we have no fucking money! Papa thought to himself. But in those days, before he was rich and powerful, he could ill afford to openly rebuke a stranger. So, he provided a more polite rejection. 'We can barely afford to keep the water running here, saabji!' Papa folded his hands together and said, 'We can't even dream of any factories or businesses right now.'

The guest house seemed to be their only option; they weren't qualified to do much else with their lives. Papa's father had had a government job at Ambala's Electricity Board, rubber-stamping papers and running after senior officials for their signatures; all Papa wanted to do was the opposite of what his father had done. He didn't want to wear glasses like his old man and lower his eyes in the presence of senior officers. Papa skipped college and got a job working the assembly line in a textile plant. But he also had to serve as his boss's peon, samjhe? He had to run for chai and massage the boss's crusty feet when he was ordered to do so. He had to walk with his shoulders hunched down to look shorter than he actually was. He was the type of young man whose name he would forget later in his more successful life, whom he would call 'Chhotu'.

He quit his job. He didn't have money, but he had pride. *We are the son of an educated man*, and he appointed himself Uncle Narender's assistant manager at the Ram–Rahim Guest House.

When his uncle died, Papa knew that, at least, he would have some property to his name, and that alone would help him find a suitable bride.

Mummy didn't go to college, either. Her parents chose her brother.

TEN

Papa was always the first to be up every morning. The local Jal Nigam had decreed that water would be released in the basti from five every morning; Papa had to not only monitor the filling tankers with the kook-roo-kooing roosters every morning, but also switch off the taps after a couple of hours to ensure there was no overflow. Accidents had taken place occasionally. Water had been wasted.

So, even when he was better placed to hire some help for these menial duties, and even when he moved on and away from life at the guest house, from Faizabad to Varanasi, he couldn't reconfigure his body clock. Five minutes to 5 a.m., morning after morning, decade after decade. Sleep made him impatient, and he would quickly get on his feet to start the new day.

Mummy usually woke up later and started her day by lighting an agarbatti in the prayer room beside their bedroom, filling her lungs with the smoke from the incense and the smell of marigolds before breathing in the morning air outside.

Papa's routine didn't change even the morning after the cremation, after the Dom cracked the bamboo stick into my charred cranium. It was a Sunday, his day to be alone and away. He was up early and on his feet in his Lacoste polo shirt and his black sandals. He sat behind the wheel of his smallest car and drove himself less than ten minutes to Assi Ghat near the Ganga, a few kilometres away from the ghat where my ashes had been scattered.

Papa parked near the ghat and then walked five minutes on

the stone-cobbled path—avoiding the piss and shit of monkeys, dogs, cattle, and people; passing by the leathery-skinned baba who sat below the small marble temple in his orange robes with a trishul; passing by the morning chaiwallahs and the hollering boatwallahs—and then counted forty-eight steep steps up and away from the river to find his favourite spot under the peepul tree on the rooftop over Tulsi Ghat. He crouched down on the cement rooftop, ignoring the white splats around him which could be milk offerings to the gods or pigeon shit, pulled up the bottom of his shirt, and sat down. He sat by himself, took a brief moment to lift the corner of his pyjama leg to scratch a dark-red rash on his ankle, and then relaxed to watch the sun rise in front of him, its orange hues washing over the dirty river below. The river reflected the sun back to him in shades further strained and coloured by the dust in the air.

It was beautiful.

I had never seen him like this, in isolation, in a moment of lonely silence, where no one recognized him and no one was around, and there were no ears to hear him if he spoke. This holy river, even the polluted parts that were saturated with chemical dyes and the city's sewage, never failed to bring him a crumb of peace. He preferred to be alone, in fear that Mummy might read his thoughts through his eyes. From the river below, he listened to the gentle splashes of the boatwallahs' oars dipping in and out of the still Ganga water, and he allowed himself to float, too.

Papa sowed the first cells of my existence when he was twenty-seven years old, impregnating Mummy three years after Sakshi didi and Rishi bhaiya were born. He revelled when the doctor at the Metro Nursing Home in Faizabad told him that 'It's a boy!' He cheered, because he now had another seed he could mould into a man just like him, a seed that would one day have his own seed, and the grandson would plant more seeds, and so on and so forth, keeping Papa's genes alive long after his death and offering him his immortality.

He had high hopes for Rishi bhaiya and I. Girls, he believed, became wives once they were married off, and that he would one day lose his daughter when she moved on to continue someone else's gene pool. But not his sons. Even if Bhagwan Beads failed and his properties were razed to the ground and long after his body was roasted into dark grey ashes down at these ghats, he would have us as the tether to the future. *What else could I leave to the world*, he thought, *but my sons?* Without Vishnu, without Rishi who would be there for him?

A flurry of bell chimes sounded from the ghat below, ringing through his body, shaking him alive, reminding him of himself, of his mortality. He stayed still, rooted to the spot long after his butt became sore on the temple's stone rooftop, for ten more minutes.

Soon, the sun rose higher. More bells rang for the morning call to prayer, and it got a little warmer, too. At the bottom of the steps, half a dozen young children appeared—boys and girls—each of whom carried a candle on a small leafy plate to offer to the river. They had come looking for Papa, and once they saw him, they waved. He nodded back at them with a stern face.

Behind the children stood Bhola, one of those multitasking henchmen, who had been a Chhotu for years until Papa finally learned his name. Like every Sunday morning, Bhola had ridden his scooter from the other side of town to greet Papa at the ghat. Like every Sunday, he had helped Papa arrange for a community breakfast.

Bhola was thin and lively, an active and energetic man in a lethargic city. He was older than he looked and wore tight T-shirts to flex his newly carved biceps. Papa liked him because he showed the same zest no matter when he was summoned for an odd job.

While Bhola waited by the river, Papa prepared himself for the most strenuous part of his day: getting back up to his feet. It had to be done somehow, and Papa, that stubborn old man—saala, the root DNA of *my* stubborn genes—knew that he had to do it alone. With considerable effort, he lifted the heavy weight of his upper body, feeling crushing pain in his ankles and knees, and he groaned, and behenchod, he did it. He got up. Walking down was always going to be harder on his knees than walking up, but he soldiered on, turning sideways as he descended the narrow steps to keep his balance, until he eventually reached the children.

'Namaste Shankar uncle!' a little girl shouted gaily. She had thin, black hair that had turned orange in the daily mud of the city. The other children mimicked the girl. 'Namaste uncle!'

Papa nodded at them again but didn't reply. He avoided looking down at their faces. He never wanted to distinguish between them, never wanted to learn any of their names.

Instead, he turned to Bhola. 'Aur bolo?' he asked. 'Any news?'

'Good morning, Shankar sir,' Bhola joined his hands together in greeting. Bhola knew, of course, of the tragedy in the family—the whole city knew—and his optimism was a few degrees dimmer this morning, his smile just a little less wide than usual. 'Everything is good, sir,' he said.

Papa and Bhola led the way, and the children followed behind them. They turned into one of the thin gullies that opened out of the ghat, and soon, they were walking on cobbled stones carpeted with excrement from multiple species of inner-city dwellers. The ancient, decrepit homes around the gullies shaded them from the warming sun. They passed by stray buffaloes and children riding recklessly on bicycles. Scooters *beep-beep-beeped* past them, too, and chaiwallahs hollered their morning greetings. The gully was narrow enough for Papa to stretch both hands and touch the walls on each side if he wished. Some of the younger kids trailing behind him tried to do so, but their arms fell short by a few inches.

The children were loud and excited, but Papa didn't want to hear them, so he fished out his mobile phone and dialled a number, any number: first, a contractor for the new office wings being constructed at the factory; then, a contact in the Delhi office who liked to wake up early; and next, Happy Singh. Papa took himself out of the moment.

They reached a sharp turn beside a Hanuman temple, which opened into a crowded street. Out there was a small stand that made Papa's favourite kachori in the city. The kachoriwallah was a chubby, dark, moustachioed man in an unbuttoned red shirt. He waved at Papa with one hand while stirring the large frying pot in front of him. The kachoris bubbled in the hot oil, looking juicier, let me tell you, than even a meaty Luke Burger.

'Almost ready, sir,' the kachoriwallah announced. Papa nodded his head and a few dozen little children with their thin arms and torn vests gathered around him and the large pot. An onslaught of passing traffic honked and motored its way past them, zigging and zagging in organized chaos. Papa kept his head low, and even though every passing cyclist, rickshawwallah, and hatchback driver knew who he was, he preferred to pretend he was operating in anonymity.

Salivating, Papa bit into the first fried snack. He nodded his head from side to side and grunted 'hmmm', which was his version of a five-star restaurant rating. He reached into his pocket and handed the kachoriwallah a five-hundred-rupee note, and then nodded at Bhola.

'Theek hai, Shankar sir.' Bhola said, 'I will take it from here.' Papa nodded goodbye in the vague direction of the children and left. Within seconds they had forgotten about him because another kachori was ready, and Papa was back in his car, driving himself home.

Mummy was awake, waiting for him at the dining table, the red tika in the middle of her forehead a remnant of her morning prayer. Her cheeks looked shrivelled after another night of troubled sleep. There were dark circles under her eyes, so dark that they stood out drastically over the light brown shade of the rest of her face. She had been crying.

'Let's have breakfast,' Papa said.

He sat down in his chair at the head of the table, and Mummy followed him to take the seat by his left.

'What are we going to do, Shankar?' she asked. Himanshu rushed out of the kitchen with a paratha for each of them.

Papa took a bite and liked the warm taste of the paratha so much that he began to stuff his mouth as quickly as he could.

'What are we going to do, Shankar?' she asked again.

'We have to meet Happy Singh about some new contractors today.'

'Shankar....'

'And Pushpa,' he added, 'we forgot to tell you. Next week, we have to go to Delhi, for a few days to check on the store.'

'Shankar....'

Papa swallowed another mouthful and told Mummy about the sales reports from the handicrafts store in Delhi. Mummy watched him eat and heard him talk but didn't touch her own food.

A hundred years ago, the mayor of Tokyo gifted Washington, D.C. three thousand cherry trees. The trees crossed the oceans to get to the American capital, and landed at the Tidal Basin, where they have since flourished once a year, every year, even in an alien habitat, garbed in their finest light-pink and white blossoms.

Sometime during my second year at D.C. Tech, just as the frigid snowy winter subsided to make way for a pleasant North American spring, Jess insisted that Hamid and I head down with her to the banks of the Potomac. Tourists thronged the area in thousands and took selfies. The slight earthy smell of fresh mulch wafted in the air. We moved away from the larger crowds next to the water, and crossed the road towards a smaller, quieter garden with five or six cherry trees. On that cold yet sunny day, I watched with lazy curiosity as Jess strolled from one tree to the next. Occasionally, she would lean in closer, extend one of her hands in fingerless woollen gloves, and touch a flower petal, gently, as if she were petting it.

Hamid, meanwhile, had wandered away towards a different tree and planted his heavyset body underneath the branches, allowing the sun to make beautiful shadows on the grass under his feet. He was inanimate, smoking a cigarette in silence.

'They're beautiful, right?' Jess called out to us. Her voice came out cartoonishly high-pitched, full of childlike excitement.

I shrugged. 'They're just trees, yaar.'

Hamid, still immersed in his stoned zen moment, didn't answer.

'It's so funny, isn't it,' I said. 'People go crazy to see something that can barely stay alive more than a few months. Kya bakwaas!'

'They're beautiful.' Jess looked up at me. 'Vishnu, they're beautiful because they go away. Because they have an expiry date. I...I can't believe you can just bring a tree from Japan, something from a completely different environment, and plant it here. And it grows just the same.'

'Well,' I said, 'I'm sure it's not exactly the same.'

'Huh,' Jess turned her back to me and walked slowly around the tree. 'Not exactly the same, that's true,' she said. 'But this city makes them into their own thing, doesn't it?'

ELEVEN

After spending sixteen-and-a-half hours squeezed in the middle seat of the middle row of a giant, smelly airplane—this Vishnu's personal Garuda—I landed in Washington, D.C. for the first time. Or, to be more geographically specific, I landed at the Dulles Airport in Virginia, outside the city. I got to my feet to take down my bags from the stowage bin even before the plane came to a complete halt on the runway. An airhostess barked at me to sit back down, but in my excitement, I could barely keep myself fastened to the seat. I wanted to rush out and see this country, to breathe its clean air, to walk on its dust-free earth.

Washington has half the population of Varanasi, but as the taxi took me deeper into the city—passing its glowing green parks and giant white monuments—I felt that I had gone from a village to a metropolis. That pleasant fall evening I pulled my suitcases into the escalator and got out on the fifth floor of Saxon Hall. There was a smell wafting out of the kitchen, something sharp and abhorrent and herbal and delicious.

It was in the kitchen that I would soon become familiar with all the other dwellers on our floor: Andrew, Tapiwa, and Hamid, who perpetually had a joint in his mouth while rolling a second between his fingers. There were three other students from the sixth floor who sat around the table—one guy and two girls; all tall, white-skinned, and blonde, with bluish-green eyes.

'Hey, there,' said Tapiwa. He had a pimpled face, with deep, dark skin, and a head full of curly hair. In a matter of days, we would randomly declare him our very own African Prince. 'The ornament of a house is the *new* friend who is joining us,' he said. 'You in room 5?'

'Yes,' I said, and slid my thin frame in front of them. There was no place to sit around their little round table, so I stayed on my feet. 'I'm Vishnu.'

'How do you say that?' one of the girls asked.

'Vish-nu,' I repeated.

'Wizhnu.... Is that a "W" or a "V"?'

'Like the Wizard of Oz?' asked the other girl.

'The Wiz!' the boy declared. He stood up to shake my hand. 'Sean,' he said. 'Sean Stockton. Double-S.' He took his seat again between the two girls. He was bald with a shiny pale head and a light, red beard over his cheeks.

'Umm...' I looked at all of them again, taking in the various shades of their skin intermingling around the same round table of strong-smelling weed. Suno, in America, I would later learn to be more careful about noticing the different colours. But on my first day there, behenchod, what else was I supposed to do? I came from a country where most of us fell along a spectrum of shades of brown. Here, suddenly, was a mini colour palette in my very own kitchen. Super Black. Black. Light Brown. White. White. Almost Translucent White. I, for the first time, was conscious of *my* colour, but I wasn't yet afraid of its consequences. I felt my skin, darkened by an unshaved stubble of black hair on my cheeks, and I saw them see it, and I saw them ignore it. The fifth floor—with Andrew and Tapiwa and Hamid and Gokul and I—would soon turn into an international confluence of darker human palettes, all bonding in the common gas chamber of marijuana smoke and computer engineering.

Well, all except for Gokul, of course, who didn't smoke or drink and had moved in earlier that day after living in a different hall for the first year of his master's degree and who, after seeing the stoned sammelan of foreigners in the kitchen, said a curt namaste and locked himself inside his bedroom to nap.

One of the white girls—the taller, paler one—smiled at me. 'That's a cool name, Wiz,' she said.

'You want a seat?' one of the guys stood up, his voice a husky cough filtered by clouds of smoke. 'I'm heading out.'

'Sure,' I said.

He was taller than me, and the curly Afro shining like a halo over his head added an extra six inches to his height. 'Andrew,' he offered his hand.

'Vishnu,' I offered mine. Andrew patted me on my back and stumbled out of the kitchen.

Hamid turned to me when I sat down, a mischievous gleam in his stoned, red eyes. I would see those eyes again and again during our four years of friendship, until my last night—our inevitable reunion at Lucky Luke, my inevitable choice to save him.

'Viz,' he said. 'Take a seat man. You smoke?'

Hamid was high on the day we met. He carried his own stash of weed from New Jersey along with the usual clothing and bedsheets and heavy textbooks.

He was high on that night at Lucky Luke, before Wildhair's shot.

Before I ordered the third round of drinks from the bartender calmly floating from one end of the bar table to another like a fucking Jedi, before I walked into the restroom, *behenchod*, before all of that, I was the first to arrive at the bar. I got there seven minutes before Jess and twenty-two minutes before Hamid. I had spent my time staring at my phone, double tapping photographs of old friends on Instagram whom I would never see again. Jess walked in looking apologetic and hassled, and I said, *nahi nahi, it's okay, where's Hamid?* But he was late because he had stayed back at the Saxon Hall kitchen to smoke a joint, his second of the evening.

He was high on the first day of class in our first year and still managed to ask Prof. Eckstein the boldest question of the afternoon at the end of Intro to Computational Thinking, when she handed out our course syllabus: 'But how are we going to stick to schedule after the robots enslave us?' Some other students in the large amphitheatre had chuckled and sniggered, and I thought that the professor was going to lose her mind, but instead, she just smiled and replied: 'We'll make amends to our algorithm. Don't worry.' Instead of getting in trouble, behenchod, he basically became her favourite for the rest of the semester, so that every two weeks when he raised his hand to offer an opinion in class, she ignored all the other students to point at him and say in her croaky voice. 'Yes, Hamid, please enlighten the rest of us.' Even when I wasn't quite certain any more if he was high or not, I accepted that it was safe to assume that he probably was.

The first time we had a *real* conversation was when I knocked on his bedroom door looking for some help in our Java programming coursework. 'Just a minute,' he coughed after an elongated period of silence; I could smell weed from underneath the crack in his door. Hamid finally opened the door, dressed in a loose T-shirt that hung low around his chubby neck, and a pair of loose-fitting trackpants. Behind him was a messy little bedroom with no bed; against hall rules, he had sold his wooden bedding for extra cash and instead slept on an inflatable mattress on the floor. He had put up bedsheets with trippy, colourful hues—blue and yellow and magenta and pink—all over his walls. He had a framed photograph of the Notorious B.I.G.'s *Life After Death* album on the floor, leaning up against the wall on his far side. He had a red yoga mat stretched out on the floor like a mini cricket pitch next to his inflatable mattress.

Both of us had turned seventeen over the summer before college, but Hamid looked much older than me. He was fully formed, with beefy wide shoulders, a hairier face, and a glint of experience in his eyes.

'Slumdog Chaiwallah!' he would say, greeting me at the door, or 'The motherfuckin' Viz!' he would holler when he saw me sitting alone in the cafeteria. He sat opposite me while I ate a cheeseburger. He poked a couple of unsolicited gluttonous fingers into my tray to help himself to my French fries. 'Drop some wizdom!' he shouted when he saw me, seated on the green grass in front of the Sophia Monument—the giant marble statue dedicated to the Greek goddess of wisdom—in the central lawn of our D.C. Tech campus. 'It's the fuckin' Viz-ard of FOB!' He smacked me on my back when he overheard me ordering a plate of fried chicken at the Fried or Die takeaway shop where the young woman at the counter was struggling to understand my accent.

Fried or Die was two blocks away from Saxon Hall, but the fried oils in their kitchen produced an enchanting, spicy smell that wafted up to our open windows and infused itself with the smell of our sweet skunky weed, creating an irresistible cocktail every evening. Hamid and I began to shell out on the four-dollar-ninety-nine meals multiple times a week. Hamid spent too much time at Fried or Die, or trawling restaurants and bars from D.C. Tech all the way out to the National Zoo, and it was at the zoo where he liked to walk around alone, studying the zebras and the nocturnal animals' habitats. Occasionally, he would even take a coursebook with him to a bar alone, order himself an Old Fashioned bourbon, and do some reading.

Hamid was a smart guy, samjhe? When he was young, his parents tried to get him into the Indian–American spelling bee cartel, but his heart was never in it. At eleven, he found his cousin's stash of hentai comics; at twelve, he lost in the preliminary round of the New Jersey Bee for misspelling 'beleaguer'; by thirteen, he smoked his first cigarette in the parking lot of an outlet mall in Bridgewater after school. Now, he was the type of guy who often didn't even need textbooks to learn. He would yawn and stretch in class, leaning back in his seat as if the subject bored him. But when I would see him in the computer lab, casually troubleshooting through JavaScript while he ate burritos and dropped crumbs on the keyboard, I knew that he retained everything, that he could learn on the fly. Asli, practical knowledge.

'You Indian, bruh?' Hamid said the first time I talked about home. 'Sweeeet, me too!'

I rolled my eyes. For Hamid, 'Indianness' meant learning a couple of yoga positions and asking for a chai tea latte at Starbucks. Nahi nahi, he had little connection to his ancestral home. His father, he told me, came to America from Lucknow in the '70s with a hundred dollars in his pocket to do something in the tech industry 'before there even was such a thing as tech, you get me?' Mr Senior Hamid made a shitload of money and produced a chubby gangster-rapper-wannabe offspring who wouldn't have been able to tell a Lucknawi biryani from a Hyderabadi one.

And when I couldn't keep up with Hamid's pace and needed help, I turned to Gokul. Good ol' vegetarian, teetotalling, cricket-loving Gokul Ramnarayan from Hyderabad, that graduate student with two jobs and an accent so thick that he made *me* feel less desi.

My first impression of Gokul had been wrong, samjhe? When I saw him trudge across the corridor, ignoring us while we smoked joints in the kitchen, he looked like the perfect studious Indian boy, with side-parted hair and that *dum-di-dum-di-tam-thank-you-come-again* accent, a walking-talking machhar-chhap woman repellent. Nahi yaar, I didn't even want to be seen with him. The first time we came face to face, introducing ourselves as co-Indians, he immediately asked me about the cricket scores from the other side of the world, and my face fell in embarrassment. I panicked and giggled nervously, afraid to look like what they called a *fob* in front of my new American friends. But Hamid stepped up and grabbed Gokul by the shoulder. 'Yes, yes, India won today, right?' He surprised both Gokul and me. 'That Virat Kohli is a ruthless motherfucker.'

It's hard to explain, yaar. My country is a hundred countries. A thousand. We live in different realms of the same bubbling soup, each boiling at a different temperature. And if our temperatures didn't match, we would have little to do with each other. Gokul and I spoke different languages at home and ate different foods, and he earned a scholarship to come to the US, while my father was rich enough to pay for my education. But eventually, it didn't matter. In America, we fit into the same sub-folder. Non-whites > Indians > Indians from India. We were both here, and suddenly, conversations that wouldn't have happened in India were now possible in Amreeka.

'Come, come, please come into my room, Vishnu,' Gokul said the first time I knocked on his door. 'Welcome, welcome. You are enjoying Washington? It's a good place, no?'

Gokul was usually dressed in dull green or grey sweaters and scarves, like a grandfather on a hill station holiday. But in his room, in his comfortable abode, he was stripped down to look as casual as possible: a pair of long-shorts and a white baniyan—a sleeveless vest that unashamedly flaunted his small, dark shoulders and long arms. His face was flat and oily, scarred with remnants of teenage acne that refused to age with the rest of his body. He welcomed me with a warm, full-toothed smile.

His room was an uncluttered, dark chamber. He kept his windows drawn close at all times, illuminated only by the brief glimmers of sunlight during the day, and a lone table lamp on his desk at night. Apart from the usual bedding and wardrobe, he had few other belongings: an old, fat laptop from the medieval ages of computing sat on his desk and a small wicker basket of loose change—pennies, nickels, dimes, quarters, and even rupees—was on his bedside table. Taped to his wall was a newspaper cut-out of a famous Telugu actor—Nagarjuna—standing on a mountain somewhere in blinding white trousers.

'So,' Gokul asked. 'You said you wanted help with the Robotics class?'

'Yes, yes, Robotics,' I said. 'I can't understand that professor's accent yaar. All that *yaay shaayy payyy*.... He talks too quickly. Didn't you take some classes with him before?'

'Why don't you get the notes online?'

'Behenchod, have *you* ever understood his notes online?'

Gokul turned red at my language. 'No, don't worry,' he said. 'What is the problem? Let me see if I can remember anything.' He wasn't very helpful, but it didn't matter to me. I was here, and in my unmanageable early sense of America, it was comforting to have someone who spoke in a similar accent and didn't judge me when I stuttered with my own.

Over the next few weeks, Gokul showed me around the library and computer labs. I spent two hours at the Safeway where he worked, just dragging my feet across the colourful products on display, exclaiming to myself in disbelief like *Wow, people eat this stuff?* The cereal aisle was the holy Mecca, with everything from healthy GoLeans and boring granola flavours all the way to chocolate drizzled sugar flakes and evil cartoon characters on the Count Chokula box, and Flintstones bouncing over Fruity Pebbles and of course, Tapiwa's favourite: Froot Loops. Later that day, Gokul took me to Georgetown and waited patiently in the Nike showroom while I bought myself a pair of Jordans. He helped me navigate the lines on the Washington Metro. Then he took off my training wheels and I began to ride the trains alone.

One day, when I attempted to scan my metro card at the entry machine, it took an extra second too long to respond, and I tried again, and again, until a line stretched out behind me, some grunting, some coughing, some talking among themselves, all shooting their passive-aggressive frustrations at me. The light on the machine finally flashed—*beep*—and I exhaled. I rushed through, walking away from the masses as quickly as I could. At the platform itself, I tried to jump into the train before allowing people to exit, and, once again, no one said anything. The polite silences of the commute in D.C. were more unbearable than a simple 'bhosadi-ke, wait!' would have been back in Delhi. I felt immensely alone, standing in a crowd as the train moved forward, and although nobody was looking directly at me, I felt as if I was under the cold glare of some overseeing American overlord. I sneezed, and a half-dozen strangers responded by passing on their useless blessings, and when I looked up an instant later, the faces behind all those voices had disappeared into the crowded atomic structure.

While taking the Red Line during rush hour one day, I stood too close to a pretty, caramel-skinned woman who seemed to be in her mid-thirties—I hadn't yet been trained in the American value of personal space. When the train started moving, the sudden jerk made me lose my balance and stagger closer to her from behind, softly hitting my chest against the back of her brown hair, which was fragrant with faint vanilla shampoo. The train swayed from side to side, and I held on to the grab handle above to find my footing again. I was desperate not to fall. When another sudden stop hurled me too close to her again, the vanilla-scented woman turned around with a look of annoyance on her angular face and said, 'At least buy me a drink first.' I backed away immediately, retreating to a colder space between a different group of people under the bright light, and focused on the train's rhythmic oscillation instead of answering her back.

This was my first winter in America, a winter that put into proper perspective my former complaints of those cool, foggy North Indian nights. There was no lenity in D.C., with temperatures that felt uncomfortable both in Celsius and Fahrenheit. The sun set early and rose late, and when the semester ended for a short holiday break, it became easier to simply stay indoors. Hamid had gone back to New Jersey for the winter. I spent the cold afternoons in the dark of my heated bedroom, streaming high-definition porn on my computer with internet speeds so fast that the *anticipation* of graphic sex got me feeling more tharki than the porn itself. Back in India, with all of the sanskari blockers on our web, my life had revolved around those gol-gol loading symbols on the videos, tortuously forcing me to withhold my impatient erections. But in Amreeka—kya bolen yaar?—my imagination outpaced my intellect, leading me to lonely spaces at light speed before reality could even catch up.

TWELVE

Hamid's first girlfriend was Shaista, a Hindu girl he had met on the spelling bee circuit. They were both twelve years old. She lived two towns away and they only crossed paths in the regional finals. Shaista was the smartest girl he had ever met, and he used to call her 'External Memory Bank' because that's how well she could store information. They flirted over ice cream floats at the end of the tournament and promised to keep in touch. Over the summer, they exchanged dozens of emails, most of them long essays about the other friends they had made on the circuit. Then, they wrote about each other's parents, and they discovered that their families—despite coming from different religions—had a lot in common. Both their mothers watched Indian soap operas in the evenings, stories about women who could turn into vengeful snakes when provoked. Both of their fathers rooted for the Indian cricket team over any other sporting loyalty they could've ever had in America.

It seemed like they were going to be rooted together, competing to spell correctly all the way up to their multireligious wedding vows. But at the regionals the next year, Shaista told Hamid that she'd started seeing someone else, another Indian–American Hindu boy who had made the nationals of the National Geographic Bee in D.C. which, Shaista explained, required more critical thinking and global general knowledge than the well-spelled circuit.

It had nothing to do with his religion, he was told. Her father had a lot of Muslim friends at the gas station, she said.

Hamid had two ice cream floats by himself that evening. On the other end of the globe, in Varanasi, I was living a starkly different life. My parents had no expectations of early academic success. Out of a classroom of forty-five, I always finished somewhere between twenty-fifth and thirtieth in the rankings. Mummy was happy as long as I didn't fail. I ranked at a career-best twenty-first one time in Class 6, and returned home, floating on my feet as I hopped off the school bus, with my report card in hand. Mummy hugged me and ordered besan-ke-laddus from the neighbourhood halwai. When Papa returned home later that evening, he gave me a pat on the back. 'Good job,' he said. 'Twenty-first? Good job. Your sister is a topper, you know that, right? Next time, do a little better.'

But Class 6 was my academic prime; I never returned to the lofty air of above average marks again. In New Jersey, Hamid began to smoke weed and still excel in class, and he coped with his break-up with snacks and desserts and an incredible memory for Cartman quotes from *South Park* that made him into a relatively popular kid in junior high. He was friends with everyone, always wearing a relaxed smile on his face. Meanwhile, in Uttar Pradesh, my teens began with me losing interest—in *everything*. I didn't care about school, or my father's job, or playing cricket as much any more, or hanging out with Dhiraj, or the comics I used to read. And later in Delhi, I was even more distracted: by friends, by Aastha—the only girl I ever dated—and by this safety net that assured me that, no matter how much I failed, someone would be there to make sure I succeeded.

So, when our paths crossed just as we had legally become adults—Hamid and I—we bonded not because of any similarity in character or experience, but, perhaps, only by fluke of geographical proximity. He was only a few doors down, and all I needed at that age was company and regular joints to smoke. In Hamid, I had found both.

He was, I realize now, the closest friend I ever had.

Suno now, don't be surprised by this. I had been uprooted, not just from my physical home bases—Faizabad to Varanasi to Delhi to D.C.—but in lifestyle, too. Less cricket and more PlayStation. Fewer trains and more flights. Bhojpuri accent to Delhi-speak to American slang.

Long before Hamid, however, before I extended my hand to Dhiraj on the cricket pitch, before I was boasting of twenty-first place, before I had anyone else, I had Rishi bhaiya.

There was a time when Bhaiya and I did everything together: antakshari over our favourite film songs, book cricket with his social studies textbooks, TV at the neighbour's place.

Our favourite day of the year was Holi, when Bhaiya and I would rush to the rooftop of our Mehmoorganj apartment building, fill up balloons with coloured water, and throw them at unsuspecting passers-by. When we did occasionally get into colour-wars with others in the neighbourhood, Bhaiya always served as my shield, making sure he took the brunt of the watery punishment, while I got home relatively safe and dry.

It was on one such Holi day, that, after we washed off the intense blue dye smeared over both of our faces, Papa decided to take the two of us out to the ghat. 'Only the boys today, Pushpa,' he told Mummy at the door. 'Boys day out!'

Mummy had no desire to join us, but Sakshi in her twin ponytails, fumed, giving Rishi bhaiya and me an unforgiving glare, as if leaving her behind had been *our* decision.

Everyone was in a festive mood by the ghat that afternoon, some enjoying a much needed day off, some high on the spirit of the festival, some high on the spirit of the bhang thandai, dragging their chappals over the stone steps with goofy, blank looks in their eyes and orange smears of colour on their cheeks. The bhelpuriwallahs were selling bhelpuri, the golgappawallahs were serving golgappas, hawkers were selling yellow balloons and pink cotton candy and shiny silverware utensils.

'Follow us,' Papa said, as we left the parked car and walked into Assi Ghat behind him on foot. Papa was in a good mood that day. All three of us had changed into pristine, shiny white kurta pyjamas. Mine was a little too big for me, and Rishi bhaiya's was a little too small, but we didn't mind. I looked around at the crowds and the colours and heard the music from the temples and smelled the clean aroma of the usually smelly river, and then, excitedly, I looked at my brother. He was smiling, too, taking it all in.

'Come, both of you,' Papa said. 'We will show you our favourite spot.' He was quicker on his feet in those days, chubby but not fat, with strong knees that didn't creak or groan going up and down the ghat steps. He motioned for us to follow him up the steep rise to that famous old peepul tree at the Tulsi Ghat. He pointed to our final destination on the rooftop, and Bhaiya ran up ahead, racing to be the first. I tried to keep up, but the steps were too wide for my small strides. Papa arrived second, and I was last. Bhaiya grabbed my hand and pulled me up to the rooftop, by the tree. A few other drifters were already here, hanging out by the far side of the rooftop's ledge, letting their feet dangle in the air, looking out at the river or, maybe, at nothing.

Papa led us to an unoccupied corner and crouched to sit on a low platform. Rishi bhaiya and I followed, sitting on either side of him. 'Good for us boys to come out here, isn't it?' he said. 'Look, look. Look at the Ganga. Beautiful, isn't she?'

'She' was fine, I thought. A little overcrowded, a little noisy with all the motorboats gurgling by, a little polluted with unidentified floating objects popping up from time to time. But I wasn't as cynical then as I am now, you understand? Papa was in a good mood, in a mood to talk to us. And his mood was infectious.

'Do you know, Rishi,' Papa said, still looking ahead at the river, 'that it was at this very spot, five hundred years ago, that Tulsidas wrote the Ramcharitmanas.'

'What's that?' Rishi bhaiya said.

'Who is Tulsi?' I asked.

'Tulsidas,' Papa said. 'He was…' Papa sighed. 'He was a writer. Poet. He sat here, on this spot, and wrote the Ramcharitmanas. Basically, the Ramayana that you read today, it comes from him. The original was in Sanksrit, and he translated it. Did you know this?'

'I don't read the Ramayana.' Rishi bhaiya said.

'Abey hatt! Nalayak!' Papa playfully slapped Rishi on the back of his head. 'They don't teach you Ramayana in school?'

'I don't read it either, Papa,' I giggled from the other side.

'Abey!' Papa exclaimed again. Then, he continued, 'You need to read up some of our mythology, you understand? Both of you. History of your city, your culture. Look, look below, you see all those people taking a dubki in the river? You see why people come from all over the country…all over the world… to take a dip here?'

'They're idiots, that's why,' Rishi bhaiya giggled and moved away, anticipating another little slap. He bounced up to his feet and laughed louder. 'They're idiots and don't understand how dirty the water is.'

Papa was pointing to a group of elderly women in the water below, just by the part where the stone steps descended into the Ganga. All of them were wearing saris, letting their clothes get drenched by the water's polluted blessings. One of them, an especially grizzled lady who seemed to creak and croak with each movement of her limbs, brought her palms together in prayer to the river, bowed, and dipped her head underwater. A few seconds later, she rose back up.

'Nalayak,' Papa muttered at Rishi bhaiya under his breath. 'Useless chootia. You don't understand how much this means to people, praying here.'

'Like Mummy?' I asked. I moved to squeeze in closer to him. I felt a familiar warmth, accompanied with that old smell of fruity hair oil and aftershave.

'Like Mummy, yes,' he said.

'Do you pray, Papa?'

Papa sniffed. He put an arm on my back, and then looked back at my brother, standing behind us.

'What do *we* need to pray for?'

Suno, suno, time is muddled up here. Nahi, I don't mean to tell you that time was changing directions, but for me, it was adding dimensions. My story isn't so simple—samjhe?—where one event happens per one moment in time on a single, thin arrow. Nahi, nahi, the arrow moves forward on the x-axis, while the y-axis stacks up higher, too, hitting multiple points that happen simultaneously towards an uneven crescendo.

THIRTEEN

Jess was dressed like an Ewok when I first saw her.

It was a party at Maya's, Hamid's girlfriend at the time. It was Halloween—which, yaar, how can I explain it—reminded me of those fancy-dress parties we used to have as kids at Little Blooms School, Varanasi, but with alcohol and short dresses. At Maya's house, there were men dressed like scary clowns, women like Wonder Woman, and a whole group of doctors and nurses without pants. Maya wore a full bodysuit like those blue alien giants from *Avatar*, with a fake tail that, by swaying her hips, she swung behind her every time Hamid crossed paths with her.

Jess was covered head to toe in a brown bathrobe with a hood over her head. I tried to bury my accent as much as I possibly could when I said my first words to her.

'Are you supposed to be Chewbacca?'

She was in a corner of the large, noisy room, all alone, looking down at her phone, thumbs hastily scrolling on the screen, smiling at something. It took her a second to realize she had been spoken to, and her fair face blossomed into sudden rouge. 'No!' she replied with what I would later learn was exaggerated annoyance. 'I'm an Ewok. Can't you tell?' she said and pointed to the ears that sprouted off the sides of her hooded head.

'Oh,' I replied. '*Return of the Jedi*, right? I don't really remember....'

Her mouth gaped open in shock. 'You don't remember?'

Nahi nahi, I had to get this right. In front of me was a pretty girl with glowing skin and eyes that appeared green from some angles and blue from others, and she hadn't yet scrunched up her face when she had heard my awkward Apu voice. No, I wasn't going to make a bhujia out of this situation. You know how us desi boys get when white girls say two words to us, right?

She examined my outfit, too. I was in a white Karate-gi, dressed like the Karate Kid, feeling that the only way I could find my place among this strange culture was to become even stranger. Around my thick, tangled, long hair, I had tied a martial arts headband that I found in an artefacts store in Chinatown. 'Far out,' she said of my costume, and I nodded along.

She smiled. Her thin and rose coloured lips parted to reveal her teeth, and immediately, she put a furry Ewok glove in front of her mouth. I would later discover that she had done this since childhood, since the days she was forced to wear braces over her misaligned teeth, when bits of meat stuck between the silver metal. And even after those teeth were adjusted and fixed, she was never quite confident about her smile.

People walked past us and the party grew to thirty or forty people. People I recognized and new faces all blurred into one, and I couldn't hear much of the music except for a soft trumpet tooting behind my ears. The lights were low in this corner, a dark shade of orange. Behind Jess was a poster of a blue Venus symbol, with a raised fist extending from the cross into the circle. She leaned against the poster and talked, and I moved in closer to listen. She spoke softly, almost in a whisper, but with a commanding tone, and I had no choice but to lean in to catch every syllable. She finished sentences abruptly short, without wasting any words. Later, I would learn that she operated with this economy of movement in all aspects of her life: how she used her words; how she bit into her sandwiches; how she kissed.

'Are you from D.C.?' I asked.

'No. I just moved from Vermont a few months ago.'

'Yeah? How far is that?'

'Seven hours,' she moved her head side to side. 'Give or take.

Depending on the traffic. You?'

'Not much further,' I said. 'Twenty, twenty-five hours. Give or take any on-air delays, transit, lost luggage. And traffic.'

She laughed again, and again, she covered her mouth.

Suddenly, I felt a heavy weight behind me, pressing against my shoulder. It was Hamid.

'Here you go,' he handed me a can of cold beer. He moved up beside me and glanced at Jess.

'Thanks,' I took the can, and I pulled up the pop tab to open it, but the moment I did, a spray of beer shot out, spraying my neck and my Karate-gi, too. Hamid had shaken the can before handing it over. 'Oh shit,' I said, and turned to see him laughing.

'Got you again, Chaiwallah.'

'Motherfucker,' I replied, and quickly took a sip. I looked up to see that Jess was grinning, too.

'And I know what *you* are supposed to be,' Hamid finally pointed at her. 'Ayun! Ayun na maganda!'

Jess clapped her head back and broke out in hysterics. 'Yes!' The hood fell back off of her head, revealing a mop of straight, light blonde hair that came neatly down just a little below her shoulders. I could only watch her amusement in silent confusion.

'Hi,' Hamid extended a hand towards her. 'I'm Hamid.'

'Jess,' she answered and shook his hand, and then she shook mine, too. 'Jess,' she repeated to me.

And I realized, behenchod, I hadn't even told her my name yet. 'I…' I stuttered, yaar, like I did in front of Papa. 'I'm Vishnu.'

'Viz, the motherfucking Wiz!' Hamid bellowed and slapped my back. He was dressed in a shiny red suit and decided at that moment to shake his round body from side to side, clicking his fingers in a silly little dance. Jess giggled again.

'How do you guys know each other?' she asked.

'Oh, this little guy?' Hamid wrapped an arm around my waist. I nudged him away with my elbow. 'We're neighbours—Saxon Hall.'

Her eyes suddenly lit up. 'Oh, I was in Saxon recently. A

friend of mine threw a party, and you won't believe it, someone almost set her curtains on fire. One of the idiots there—'

'Hold up,' Hamid grabbed her wrist to interrupt her. 'Are you talking about Luka's place?'

'Yes!' Jess shrieked. 'Were you there?'

'Oh shit, I left early,' Hamid laughed and tossed his head back, 'But I heard they had to bust out the extinguisher....'

Hamid moved an inch closer to her, and I moved an inch further to the right, getting squished between his frame and the wall. He was in his element. Hamid was the only one of my friends at D.C. Tech who got invited to such parties. The rest of us on the fifth floor at Saxon Hall—where the residence advisers had lumped me together with other computer engineering students of almost every colour in America—spent more time playing our Xboxes than stepping out into the uncertain city nights. We sat in the common kitchen of the hall which smelled of weed and rotten bananas. Under the light of a single, yellow bulb, we smoked joints, ate Cheetos, and tapped furiously on our control buttons.

Earlier that night, Hamid had rolled up into this kitchen, carrying the largest bottle of vodka he could find, which he thumped down on the kitchen counter.

'Let's go,' he shouted and snapped his fingers together in the air, raising us up from our seats. 'Still not ready?'

I put on my costume and added a couple of extra sprays of deodorant under my arms. Tapiwa the African Prince, stepped out of the bathroom with double splashes of aftershave on his acne-infested face, and put on a full-sleeved, denim-collared shirt he had been saving for a special occasion. 'Some men may be snared by beauty alone,' said Tapiwa, 'but none can be held except by virtue and compliance.' Andrew Justice, one of our other neighbours on the fifth floor, had spent all day in his blue-and-white pyjama set. He put a jacket over his pyjama top, and he was ready.

Only Gokul wasn't interested. Gokul Ramnarayan, my fellow desi fish-out-of-comfortable-waters in America, didn't drink or smoke or play on the Xbox; he actually used the kitchen to cook dinner, making microwaveable pasta dishes and carrying them to his bedroom to eat alone while he studied or streamed Indian television on his laptop. He was a master's student at D.C. Tech, of a mysterious age somewhere between four to twelve years older than the rest of us, busy with other preoccupations in his life.

'Come on, bitches,' Hamid repeated to the rest of us, 'let's bounce.'

So, we did, walking in the chilly night through the city down to Maya's place, a couple of shots of vodka down our throats and a thin joint of weed passed around between the four of us. Maya lit up when she opened the door for Hamid and shouted a hoarse 'Hey babe!' to him over the music in the background. The rest of us followed him inside, quickly jettisoning each other to shoot off in opposing directions in the crowded apartment.

Soon, I had seen the Ewok I liked. A few minutes later, Hamid had seen her too.

Jess told me that she was a literature and language major, and then she said she was on a pre-law track. I nodded along, more interested in her delivery of words rather than the words themselves, samjhe? From the corner of my eye, I saw Hamid on the dance floor, continuing his fat jiggle, while Maya danced opposite him, moving slowly with her eyes closed.

Soon, my eyes got a little blurrier, as if I was seeing life through the foggy windows of our car. I was sitting between Rishi bhaiya and Sakshi didi, while Papa drove and Mummy sat in the passenger seat and the outside world looked distorted through the rain, hazy and harmless. Then I heard Papa's voice, and I wasn't sure if it was from my childhood or from earlier that year, or if it was something he had never said at all but I *imagined* he would say, and he told me: *Chootia, don't be careless out in Amreeka, okay? Stay away from anyone who looks suspicious!* I smiled to myself because I caught a glimpse of the Ewok again. As I was topping off a shot of vodka into my cup in the kitchen, she rushed up to me, looking distressed.

My blurry eyesight sharpened into focus. Her hood was off and her blonde hair was flowing down her shoulders. 'Vishnu,' she said. I was elated she had remembered my name. 'My earring! I lost one of my earrings somewhere.'

'Oh really, where…? Okay, tell me what happened,' I slurred back. 'You know, I'm really good at finding things. I have a sharp eagle eye. Indian eagle.'

'My earring,' she said, and showed me her right ear, in which she wore a small, gold, Minnie Mouse stud. 'I was showing it to someone earlier and it must have fallen off. I can't find it anywhere.'

'Where did you drop it?'

'I don't know…' her voice trailed off.

I fantasized that I would be her saviour that night, that I would find her lost Minnie Mouse stud, and be rewarded with a kiss, and I would have a story to tell my friends back in the kitchen. But behenchod, by the time someone turned on the next song, I was distracted again. Jess went to another room, and I was pushed elsewhere, thinking now instead about the squeaky *chip-chip* sounds the soles of my new basketball sneakers made when I walked across the sticky floor of the apartment. I drank some more vodka and the red punch that Maya was serving. Tapiwa the African Prince got his hands on a few more cans of Budweiser and I drank those, too, and I got more talli, and it was a Friday night, and I was happy.

But somewhere between drinks, I saw Jess again; my blurry vision cleared for an instant, and there she was, standing next to Hamid in the corner outside the kitchen door where I had first spoken to her. Hamid touched her right arm and pointed to the kitchen, and she threw her head back and laughed.

I felt a sudden weight on my entire body, like something had climbed on top of my shoulders and was pushing me down. My knees wobbled and my feet felt clammy inside those sneakers. I turned away from them and walked past a group of girls all dressed in blue-and-yellow overalls like animated Minions; I walked past Tapiwa the African Prince, lying with his eyes closed on Maya's couch. I needed to escape that loud house music; it thumped in my head, spaceship sounds without any lyrics, a *swooooosh* followed by that heavy bass *thud-thud-thud-thud*. It was too much, yaar, I needed to get out.

Maya's apartment was on the third floor of a row house near Dupont Circle, with a glass door on the opposite end of the kitchen, across the living room that opened up to a tiny balcony. I pressed down on the handle, slid the door open, and stepped out into the chilly air, immediately scolding myself in Mummy's voice, *Beta, why didn't you bring a jacket tonight?* When I closed the door behind me, it almost muted the spaceship music and I was ekdum alone, and it felt good. Out here, it was a quiet, dark night, shrouded from the moon by red maple trees, without a soul around. Down below, the streets were sprayed with dead leaves discarded by their mother trees.

I collapsed down on the cold floor of the balcony and sat with my back against the wall, legs folded one over the other, pucca Indian style.

There was a *whoosh*, and the loud music spilled out of the room and hit my throbbing head like a gust of wind.

'Sup Viz?'

'Hey,' I looked up and saw Hamid's smiling face. While I could barely keep my eyes open, he was beaming widely.

'What you doing out here, bruh? You missin' all kinds of ass in there.'

'Nahi, it's nothing yaar,' I tried to smile. I wanted to ask him about Jess, but there was a troubleshooting voice inside me, anticipating errors before they could unfold, and I decided to hold

back. 'Nothing,' I said. 'Just needed a break. I hate that tatti music.'
'Oh whatever, yaar,' Hamid laughed, switching between accents. 'Dude, it's fucking Halloween. Just *look* in there!'

He pointed at the other dancing young bodies through the glass panels. It was dark, except for a small lava lamp at the far end of the room. From the outside, all I could see was a small room packed with tiny bubbles, shimmering, repelling, and bouncing. Jess was nowhere to be seen.

'You know—I was talking to that girl. That white girl. I know you....'

'What?' I said with exaggerated surprise in my voice. 'Who...? There are so many white girls here.'

'Okay,' Hamid reached over and put an arm over my shoulder—but this time, the heavy weight felt more like a blanket, insulating me against the cold evening. 'But you know you can trust me, right?'

'Yes,' I said, and then I stood up. 'Of course, yaar.'

But in my head, I blamed him for *stealing* her and I blamed myself for letting it happen. Why was he always more comfortable around women? He never needed to think twice, and that vela attitude made it easy for him. He was always in one relationship or more, off and on and off, some casual, some a little more than casual, but none too serious. White Girls, Black Girls, Desi Girls, Korean Girls, European Girls on exchange programmes. And Maya. He even dated a girl in a full niqab in his second week in D.C. Tech, boasting that he was the only man on campus who had seen her face. I knew Papa would have killed me if I had ever dated a Muslim—slaughtered me right in front of a Shiv temple, and not even done a clean halal job of it.

But I was never as confident as Hamid. I needed alcohol to loosen up, to be my asli self, to shut out my own voice of fear and self-doubt—saala-behenchod-don't-do-it!—just to be able to have any form of decent conversation. Or I needed to be high, a couple joints of Malana Red permeating that sweet skunk into my lungs, before I would shed my inhibitions, before I could speak without hesitation, speeding past the roadblocks I'd set for myself. That's how I had met Aastha.

∽

In Delhi, I had once been friends with Sanjeet. Have patience yaar, you'll hear *his* story soon enough. But it was at Sanjeet's place, in Delhi—two years before my first flight to Washington—where I first saw Aastha. I was sitting with my back leaning against the beanbag on the floor when she walked in through the door, following close behind the heels of her friend Twinkle. I poured two glasses of Kingfisher beer for the girls. Twinkle nodded as she accepted her drink, and then began scrolling through her phone absent-mindedly. Aastha swirled the glass lazily in her hand and looked at me for a longer moment.

Sanjeet put the music on in his bedroom. A blast of trance. 'Chalo chalo, you guys are just sitting here being complete bores? We smoke now?'

My friend, this was some pure shudh stuff. Straight from Malana in the Himalaya, thick with flavour, a particular moistness I could taste even through the joint. The charas subtracted my senses. My vision blurred and my skin felt numb to the stifling heat in the room. But the most fantastic of the sensory edits was sound. Yaar, the trance music suddenly felt amplified and funnelled as if it was being delivered in a vacuum straight from the speakers into my eardrums. In what felt like an eternity of real time seconds, I was able to separate each component of the track—the thumping, kicking bass syncing with my heartbeat; claps sweeping over the bass that made my shoulders flinch; lasers whooshing in through one ear and out the other, and then back and forth causing interstellar warfare in my head.

Oh, fuck.

We spoke, I'm sure, but I hardly remember what was said.

Words poured out of my mouth, unrehearsed and unfiltered. Aastha crept close to me and gave me a kiss, my first asli lip-on-lip kiss with another being, and I marvelled to myself that waah yaar, a few years ago, I couldn't even hold a girl's hand unless it was my sister. Our kiss was simple: one lip on another lip. I opened my mouth just a little, following her lead.

Papa had always warned me that Delhi was too big and complicated—*not a city but a maze, samjhe?*—but I realized soon that he was wrong. He was a small-town rich man and a big city nobody. He felt like a fish out of water when he visited the capital. But to me, it came easy. I learned the metro routes and schedules and haggled fearlessly with autorickshaw drivers. I knew how to find my way to Aastha's home on the west side of the city. We went to see the newest Hollywood films and shared the same tub of popcorn extra-sweetened, just the way she liked it. I had seen Sanjeet buy a bracelet for one of his girlfriends, and, without asking if she would like one, too, I decided to get the same for Aastha. It had a gold rim and tiny, smaller rings that tinkled softy when she moved her hands. Her wrists were so thin that I feared the bracelet would slip off.

One time, we snuck into the Hard Rock Cafe and, after we drank tall glasses of Long Island iced tea, she kissed me right there in public. As we sat on the barstool under the yellow backlight, I felt all eyes in the bar on us, and imagined that they somehow knew my family. But instead of being daunted, behenchod, I got even more excited.

It was the summer of '69, sang Bryan Adams out of the speakers. 'Oh wow!' she perked up and said, 'This is *my* song!'

I pretended to know the lyrics and sang along with her. 'Hmm...hmm...hmm...hmm...fingers bled.... Hmm...hmm... hmm...hmm...sixty-nine....'

'Ah, typical Vishnu,' she said, sipping her drink after the song was over. 'If it's not a desi song, you're not aware, isn't it?'

I moved my stool closer and slithered a palm to feel her

slim waist over her thin, cotton T-shirt, and my hand quivered as I squeezed her gently there, but she suddenly stiffened up and became ice cold. 'Later,' she said and pushed my hand away. That 'later' was postponed indefinitely.

Less than two months after that first kiss, Aastha decided that she was bored. She stopped answering my calls, or reacting to my posts online. I spent all day looking at her photos online, refreshing each page to see if she had posted anything new. I would see pictures she took of pasta carbonara before eating it, or of her holding a friend's Pomeranian in her arms with a wide smile on her delicious face. And then, photographs with another man, who wore tight T-shirts and a beaded mala around his neck. *A new boyfriend?* With every photograph, she looked fuller, blooming into her body at a faster pace. I imagined them kissing each other, and I imagined his hands on her breasts, and behenchod, I couldn't imagine any more.

One day, I followed her. She was meeting him in Hauz Khas Village, and on that cold winter afternoon, I found the restaurant—Yeti—from where she had posted a photograph of untouched, steaming hot momos. It was crowded there, with hundreds of young people on the pedestrian only narrow path, walking into dozens of little bars and restaurants on either side and taking photographs of each other at the mouth of tiny gullies cutting between the buildings.

When they finally stepped out, I saw Aastha in a red sweater and dark shades, walking with the man under the heavy smog that envelops Delhi every winter. I blended into the heavy pedestrian traffic to follow them. The air was polluted and thick, and it made me feel safely concealed. They walked past the shopping area, and through the gates that opened into the old monument. A number of other young couples found their way in here, holding hands and hugging, all under the protection of the ancient domes, thankful to the Archaeological Survey of India for providing a hideaway from society's prying eyes.

Aastha and this man stopped in the middle of a corridor in the pavilion. The man took Aastha into his arms, and she looked around to ensure they were alone. Even the heavy smog that separated us—its low visibility that shut down the international airport and provided a layer of stealth in these cold winters—nahi, it still wasn't enough. She saw me.

Then I saw me, too. I saw how I looked with my long, dirty hair, wearing the black sweatshirt that I had slept in the night before, and I smelled the tobacco on my breath and experienced the lazy drooping of my eyelids, and I was exposed nanga. Fully naked.

I turned around and ran, up a column of stone steps, back out through the old ruins, back to the market street of rich, young Delhiites who were drinking and mingling and laughing. I didn't think. I ran.

Aastha and I never spoke again, and nearly six years later, when she heard about my death on social media, and then saw an online video of the frantic blinking lights outside Lucky Luke from ABC7 news, she called and told her friends about me and posted a photo of us together which she had previously taken offline. We were both sixteen in that selfie, and she was making a duck face while we waited in line to watch a movie at the multiplex. I was wearing the same black sweatshirt in the photo.

FOURTEEN

At Maya's Halloween party, later that night, when Jess had left and the music had died down to soft rock, and nothing but empty beer bottles lined the walls, I found it. Jess's earring. It was in the folds between the couch where Tapiwa lay snoring.

The following morning, I woke up groggy in the Karate costume and opened my computer, and on the connecting thread of common friends on the internet, I found her. Jessica Barnett. I messaged her with a photograph of her earring, and less than ten minutes later, *ting-ting* she pinged me back on my phone. A day later, she suggested we meet at the big bookstore on Connecticut Avenue, where she came dressed in a green turtleneck sweater and spent time hovering by the Mystery shelves. I assumed it would be okay to invite her to a Sri Lankan restaurant across the street for lunch. She said yes.

She had never eaten a papad before, and her face lit up when she took a bite, with morsels of the fried snack flying out of her mouth and on to my plate. 'Oh my gosh, I'm so sorry!' she covered her mouth, smiling while she chewed at the same time. She brushed her hair back behind her neck and nodded. I wondered then, yaar, if she knew why I wanted to spend time with her. That I had already begun to think about kissing those pink, pencil-thin lips and rubbing the bristles of my unshaven cheeks against her smooth white face.

Nahi nahi, I took a breath and leaned back while she ate. She was here for her earring and some papad with her masala dosa. Nothing more.

It was a Monday afternoon, and there was nobody else in the restaurant. I watched her fingers tearing small fragments of dosa, carefully filling them up with the spicy potato, and dipping her concoction into the sambar like I had taught her, and I could hear myself thinking in Papa's voice that *Waah, even these firangis know how to eat with their hands!*

When she held my lifeless body three years later, she ran those fingers through my hair, carefully avoiding the pool of blood that now formed on one side. I marvelled at how she continued to hold herself steady, hands calm like a surgeon's even in that most distressing moment.

⁂

Rupert is tucked between the Taconic Mountains and a few miles shy of the New York State border. It is a quiet town, embraced by thick, lush woods under clear blue skies. Jess could be alone here. Matlab, not completely alone—her parents were upstairs—but alone enough. She could contemplate the loss. She could switch off.

Over four years ago, Jess had left someone behind here. Justin was tall—a few inches taller than me—with floppy, brown hair and a flair for quoting jokes from *Arrested Development*. Jess, however, was too big for this town, too curious about the rest of the world to stay with Justin alone. It was a curiosity that Justin never understood, and—*sach bataon yaar?*—I never considered, either. Justin's idea of adventure was driving his friends to the interstate bus terminal in Albany. Jess wanted to go snowboarding down Mammoth Mountain, teach English in Japan, and hike in Nepal. By seventeen, she already had a faint idea of what she wanted to study, and why she needed to leave town to do it.

And so, she applied to D.C. Tech, far enough from her hometown to be unbothered by it, but close enough to keep her tethered to her past.

Now, she sat on the sofa in the basement, wearing a pair of *Game of Thrones* socks, thinking about me, long after my murder. She recalled the sound of my voice, the hesitation in my accent, the feeling of my coarse palms, the warmth of my arms when I'd hugged her.

And then, lying there on the squeaky floor of Lucky Luke, it was all gone. Cold and lifeless. She couldn't un-smell my dead body, couldn't un-feel the sudden weight of my arms, almost impossible for her to lift.

So, she sat at her parents' home in Rupert, silent. But, at some point, even to the most disciplined of grief-Ninjas like her, temptation was only a remote control away. There was Netflix and Hulu and Amazon Prime and YouTube and HBO Max. There were sports to watch, variety shows to consume, celebrity gossip to lap up. And there was the news, of course.

She flipped to the news, and immediately regretted her decision. In front of a boisterous crowd, two old men stood on stage—Santa Gol Gappa and President Gaandu-face—holding each other's hands. The crowd cheered louder as they walked down the aisle, united in unholy matrimony, Mogambo and Voldemort available as a special two-for-one offer under the blinding lights of the same multipurpose stadium in Texas. While they marched, the news ticker under them continued uninterrupted with mundane sports results, as if there were no objections to this union, as if they were all choosing to forever hold their peace.

Jess switched off the TV and settled back into her couch. Nahi, nahi, she wasn't angry; she just wanted peace. She reached out to her ankles and pulled down her socks and then pulled them back up. She remembered me again, and she remembered my death.

∞

In the weeks after I'd first met her, I swam with Jess in uncertain waters. We sent each other emoji-filled texts commenting on our entire days, about professors and Star Wars characters and plot twists in our favourite TV shows. No hearts, however, or kissing lips, and definitely no eggplants. Every time I was even tempted to send a yellow kissing face I settled for a yellow face with tears of joy.

Then, for the second time, I introduced her to Hamid.

He had just stepped off a five-dollar discount Greyhound bus from Jersey, and despite the journey, he beamed with fresh energy when he saw us through the automatic glass doors at Union Station. I had offered to see him at the station for lunch when he returned; Jess had offered to come along with me.

Hamid looked at her with a glint of half-recognition in his eyes, as if they had been long-lost lovers from a past life, carrying a faint connection in their atman without any memories in their current reincarnation.

'How was the trip?' I asked.

Hamid eyed Jess for an extra half-second before turning to me with a smile. 'It was great,' he said. 'Met another one of your countryfolk, Viz, y'know? Another Indian student from our D.C. Tech. Fresh off that curry banana boat, bruh. This woman—she sat right across the aisle from me.'

'Theek hai,' I shrugged. 'So what?'

D.C. Tech was filled with my fellow countrywomen and men. Back in India, the university sent representatives to rich-kid schools in the biggest cities, with fantasticated advertisements on hoardings and in newspapers with slogans like 'Global Excellence in the Capital of the Globe'. The campus attracted Indian engineers and programmers and MBAs and medical students all wanting to be the future Doctor Whatshisname Gupta on CNN, informing us about which of the world's leaders were showing signs of dementia.

'There she is,' Hamid pointed behind him. Beyond the transparent automatic doors of the station, an Indian woman descended into the scene atop the escalator. Decked in a green salwar kameez with a bold, red bindi on her forehead, dragging behind her a blue wheeled suitcase, she was a tiny explosion of colour in the blandness around us, where everyone else had toned themselves down to white or black or various shades of grey. She was small and thin, however, a delicate, underfed calf in a station full of rampaging American bulls.

She saw Hamid, and in a sign of recognition, smiled, flashing a set of uneven upper teeth that protruded out of her mouth like musical notations.

'Hey,' Hamid said, and then looked back at us. 'These are my friends: Vishnu, Viz, he's from India, too. Like you. And Jess.'

This was an awkward spot for our gathering, in the middle of heavy foot traffic, with people walking to the local or intercity buses, or the Amtrak trains, or the metro, or from one to the other. Boots stomped and sneakers squeaked against the clean marble floor. The spacious station was a grand hall of marble, the Taj Mahal of transport hubs, a monument made in honour of the passage of men and women a hundred years ago, and now restored as a shopping centre with body butter being sold close to hot buttered biscuits. Behenchod, suno—to me, 'train station' meant Mughalsarai and Varanasi Cantonment and Paharganj in Delhi. This was a different world, yaar, with automatic doors and decorated walls and high ceilings arching over the sky, and a million little places to eat and shop, placing American humanity in its naturally comfortable confluence with capitalism. The main hall of the station was a sprawling Roman veranda, somehow transported from those renaissance paintings directly into modern-day U-S of A. There was no stench of that terrible outside world: no piss, no tatti, no air that felt heavy with lead. Only the smell of Bojangles fried chicken wafted up from two floors below where we stood.

'Hey Viz, didn't you hear me,' Hamid said. 'I said she's from India.'

I looked back at the woman, unsure if our shared nationality was suddenly supposed to translate into shared camaraderie. *How* old was she, even? I wondered then. *Five years older than me? Fifteen?* Why would I be expected to talk to this woman just because we were in a different country together?

She stared at me with deep, dark eyes, and I could feel her attempting to read me.

'So, you're in D.C. Tech, too?' Jess asked.

The woman answered with the same polite, unwavering expression. 'Yes, we're here for an MBA.'

Her accent transported me back to Delhi and to the voices of a million other people—young and old and men and women—who chanted those three magical letters 'M' and 'B' and 'A' as if they formed the passcode to Ali Baba's cave and all the treasures of life.

She nodded and then turned back to me. 'Where in India are you from?'

'Oh,' I stuttered, looking around the station, and kya bataon, I was suddenly uncomfortable. I was here trying to fast track my American assimilation, you see? I spent most of my time with Hamid and Jess and rarely knocked on Gokul's door any more. But this woman here—this stranger—had a look in her eyes, a sort of X-ray vision, where she could see me nanga, and then see beyond me. She knew what I was and what I was trying to run away from. She was a sudden glimpse of my past, and I worried that she might reveal a secret of my Indianness to my new American friends.

'I'm from Varanasi,' I said, only whispering the four syllables of my city's name. I was embarrassed in the same way I had been when friends in Delhi had asked me the same question, afraid that my archaic hometown would push me back into time in their eyes.

'God's shithole,' Hamid added.

The woman ignored his jibe. 'That is very interesting,' she said, and her accent suddenly attained a stronger tinge of the Hindi Belt, of a place a little too close to my overpopulated part of the nation. 'What a beautiful city. We are from nearby only then.

Well, not so near, but near enough. Our family is in Ranchi.'

That voice. It was mesmerizing. Sach mein bataon? She had a look of experience in her eyes, of something mysterious. I saw her carefully compute each word, each action, every smile.

'Oh, is that far from Vishnu's city?' Jess asked.

'Not too far. Our husband used to be from Gorakhpur, actually. But we moved to Ranchi when he got his promotion, after we had our boy.'

'Your boy?' I said.

'Yes, yes, Aakash, our son,' she said, widening her smile now, speaking louder.

'Here?' I asked. 'In Washington?'

'No, no, he's in Ranchi, with our husband. They couldn't come with us, you know, but we have to do our studies. We have family here, too. Actually, when we met your friend Hamid, we were just coming back from New Jersey.'

'Hmm,' I said.

'Well, it was nice to meet you all.' She turned to leave. I realized that I had held my breath and grown tense, and I exhaled when she rolled away with her suitcase.

'What was that woman's name?' Jess asked Hamid.

'I don't remember,' he chuckled. 'I just know that she reminds me of all of my mom's friends.'

I laughed nervously. 'Mine, too.'

'I call them all "aunties".'

'Me, too.'

'Hey don't you worry, Jess.' Hamid smiled. 'I remember *your* name. Jessica. Jessica Barnett of Rupert, Vermont. I won't forget you so easily.'

If he was trying to make Jess blush, Hamid failed. But they did exchange numbers that day. When we left Union Station, I thought I had left that Indian woman behind; who is ever going to see another person on a campus with some twenty thousand students? But nahi, the world was a lot smaller, samjhe? Just a few weeks later, all of our kundlis realigned: Jess had convinced me to walk with her to the National Zoo, and unbeknownst to me, had called Hamid to meet us there, too. The three of us were on a break from the animals, drinking beers and eating extra-buttered popcorn at the outdoor diner in the winter sun, when we saw that same woman stroll past us—all alone—at a leisurely pace, dressed in a white salwar suit with a bright green scarf around her neck and shoulders.

'Yo, it's Auntie!' Hamid hollered. I giggled but stiffened in my spot, worried that any movement would attract her attention.

'Shhh.... Stop it, Hamid!' Jess snapped.

When I had first heard Jess speak to him, her voice had exuded a real sense of annoyance. But this death has given me the chance to binge-watch my life, and I see now that her plea was only half-hearted; that she, too, was amused by Hamid, and she had another beer at the zoo that Sunday afternoon, and began to laugh with amused little snorts when he made fun of a tourist with a fanny pack, or when he imitated a primate in the cages, or when he imitated my accent.

A week later, Jess and Hamid linked up to march down to the National Mall area to take part in a Black Lives Matter march. I chose to stay home, recently rewarded by what Andrew had advertised as the most potent weed he'd discovered all year. ('Dostoherbsky, they call it,' Andrew had said. 'It'll have you seeing double.')

'Dude...don't be a bitch about it,' Hamid said, trying to convince me to join him and Jess in the march. 'Come on. Put on a fucking pair of sneakers. Let's go.'

I coughed and shook my head. 'Got that new ganja, bro.'

'Are you sure? Do you have anything better to do today?'

I was tempted, of course, but ultimately, unconvinced. Sometimes, I was ready to be blown like a stray piece of nothing by the breeze—the breeze of my friends, the winds of my circumstance—but sometimes, I could be stubborn. That little bit of Papa in me, hai na? And if I'd decided I was going to stay in the kitchen and smoke, then I was going to stay in the kitchen and smoke the Dostoherbsky.

'We'll miss you there,' Jess said. 'This is a big deal, you know? It's a new revolution. It's a big moment for *all* minorities, you know?'

'All minorities aren't the same,' I shrugged. 'It's not that simple.'

'Ah,' she tutted. 'You know what I mean.'

'I don't feel like a minority. Where I'm from, Jess, you should see—everyone looks just like me.'

'Well. Where *I'm* from—this country—most of the people look like me. But that doesn't mean I'm happy about how things are, am I?'

I rolled my eyes. I knew she was right, of course. America hadn't been exactly what I had expected. Theek hai, I hadn't yet suffered any type of all-caps racial TRAUMA—all that was to come later, courtesy Wildhair. D.C. was mostly a liberal and friendly place, carrying with it little baggage of the racist, backwater America that we'd seen selectively broadcast on global news in my part of the world. And yet, I felt myself swallowing my words when I heard my own accent at the cash register in any supermarket, embarrassed suddenly of the voice that had been boisterous back in my homeland. I found I was shrinking into myself in large crowds of people outside my immediate circle of friends, hoping to be ignored. I found myself hardly locking eyes with people on the street or in the metro, afraid that they would see my colour before they saw me. It was a new feeling, not something that overtly troubled or depressed me, but was always an itch, a slight discomfort, a loss of voice that I wouldn't regain until the wheels of the jet I was on touched down at the smoggy New Delhi airport and a plane full of unembarrassed Indian uncles and aunties would clap to celebrate their arrival back home, letting me know that I had landed in the safety net of my privilege.

Only once in my young life had that privilege been tested in India, the night I was jailed, the night with Sanjeet in the driver's seat. Our karobar. And then, at eleven the next morning, I was free, and that shameful kahaani came to its logical conclusion, and even with the inefficiencies and uncertainties of law and order in my country, life was back to normal by dinnertime.

You see, where I'm from, people like *me* have no great reason to fight, no reason to march, to take to the streets. My Amreekan friends just couldn't understand this, you know? To them I look like your typical, brown-skinned, computer-fixing-wallah who worships a million gods and smells like a mixture of agarbatti and onions. But, behenchod, where I'm from, I am the equivalent of the all-powerful rich white man. I am innocent until proven guilty. I am the majority. Male and Hindu of a high caste, with fair and glowing skin that every face-whitening skincare product promises in my country. And rich. Achchha, I wasn't rich, but my father was. You know what I mean, don't you?

In a city like Varanasi—where policewallahs came to Papa's office for chai and prasad and adjusted their moustaches and remained standing until Papa decided to sit down—no, people like me didn't need to protest. And achanak se, with a mere shift in time zones and longitudes, I was suddenly supposed to feel oppressed?

☙

By the end, I was mostly alone. Even as it got warmer during my last spring, I continued to feel cold in my bedroom, aching for another human body to be nestled into mine. It was always cold in this country. I was spending each night alone, joints of Dostoherbsky and square-cut roach paper scattered around the ashtray, while I buffered porn at the speed of lust, wasting my chip-chipe seeds over naked bodies of strangers online.

And on one such night, lonely and restless, I decided to go

out for a drink.

Nahi yaar, I didn't go with Jess, whom I hadn't spoken to since our only kiss, which had managed to both excite and disappoint me, a mixture of salt and sweet like that Haldiram's khatta-meetha snack I had found at the Patel Brothers grocery store in Hyattsville. Nahi, I didn't go with Hamid, and Tapiwa the African Prince refused, too, 'You dambe!' he shouted, 'We have finals starting on Monday, what the fuck are you doing?' He spent his evening vacillating between his books and our Xbox controller. Nahi, Andrew wasn't with me either; nobody ever knew where Andrew was. And Gokul, saala, of course *he* wasn't there—he didn't even drink.

Nahi I went alone. I had nobody, I was unseen, invisible, as if my presence—or absence—didn't matter. I had turned twenty-one, was about to graduate, and behenchod, I wondered, *What have I done with my time in this country?* Nahi, I couldn't let it end like this. I was too impatient on that Friday night. I took my wallet and that reacquired swishy-swashy unlimited credit card, and my phone, and I went out.

It was one of those basement clubs on H Street, in a recently gentrified corner of Northeast D.C. with new apartment constructions in progress and a Whole Foods three blocks away from the aggressive darkness of the park across the street. It was one of those clubs where I felt like I had entered an ashtray, clouded by smoke almost as thick as the Delhi winter smog, but smelling like a toxic combination of tobacco and weed and something chemical. It was dark except for a single, faint white light on the ceiling which provided just enough luminescence for me to see the shadows of some people on some other people. It was a space too small for the hundred-something bodies crammed within, and it was perfect because the whiskies were just four dollars a glass. And when the bass dropped for the next song—yaar, those speakers were too large for a space so small—shit, I knew I was in the right place. I got drunk in a room full of strangers and found myself somewhere in the middle of those bodies, seeing new faces but feeling waists and shoulders and arms and stomachs bumping against me, and I felt warm and comfortable.

Behenchod, of course I didn't know how to dance properly. Nahi yaar, I just swayed my body from back to front and side to side, grooving to the rhythm, and only bobbing my head, because I was afraid I would lose my balance if I flailed my limbs too ambitiously. I was starting to perspire out of my overactive sweat glands, so much so that my white shirt was now drenched in disgusting dark hues, so much so that the wettest parts stuck to my body and allowed my chest and my back to offer a light brown glow from the inside. Somebody stomped their feet over my white Air Jordans but, suno, it didn't matter. I didn't care any more. When I saw the next man's Nikes, yaar, I fearlessly, drunkenly, stomped back.

The songs changed to a slightly slower hip-hop beat, and with my eyes lowered, I slowed down, too. I teleported, omnipresent like an imagined all-powerful god hovering across the club, flying away to Saxon Hall, to my lecture halls, to Raghu maama's balcony in Malviya Nagar, to my bedroom in Varanasi, to the fields of Muktigarh. Now suno, you might not believe it, but in the crowded anonymity of this club, I found myself getting into a pose I had never attempted before. Balancing on my right foot, I kicked my left leg up and held it suspended in front of me. I spread my arms out behind me and moved my wrists side to side, as if I was providing my own beat. In the wave of other dancing bodies gently pushing and tugging, I felt myself float into the centre of the floor, right underneath that solitary light. Thin strands of my hair bounced behind me, silver beneath the light. Near the end of the song, when the second chorus gave way to the bridge, a woman sang seductively and painfully, and I reacted by bringing a palm in front of me in appreciation for the voice bumping through the speakers. Nahi yaar, I wasn't Vishnu any more. Nahi nahi, I was…I was….

I was sick.

I felt violence brewing in my stomach and I lost that perfect balance. My limbs fell back into position, my legs lost all their strength, and I crumpled down. I put my palms flat on the ground, feeling the sticky wooden panels of the floor, and then that floor throbbed back with the reverberation of the bass and a hundred pairs of dancing feet. Soon, one of those feet, or to be more specific—someone else's Limited Edition Air Jordan Vs—mistakenly kicked my face. And then I went blank.

Maybe I had stayed awake for the next few hours, or maybe the blurred kaleidoscope of lights I saw were just a dream, or perhaps they were visuals produced and presented for my exclusive viewing. Suno, all I knew for sure was that, when I opened my eyes again, there was a fucking tube attached to my forearm and a strange movement *inside* my skin, of my veins throbbing and pumping as if still dancing to the beat of the speakers at that club.

Nahi, I wasn't at the club any more. I had lost a few hours, maybe five, maybe more, and I was in this beige room lying on beige sheets and with a bright white light shining ruthlessly over me, and men and women in all-white uniforms pacing back and forth. One of them—a young white man with a Hollywood-perfect jaw and eyelashes that fluttered with confidence—came by my bed and smiled, clipboard in hand.

'You're fine, young man,' he said. 'You ever had a hangover before?'

It didn't take them long to detach those tubes from my arm. I was still dressed as I had been the night before: dirty white shirt, slim light-blue trousers. I checked my pockets and breathed a sigh of relief because I still had all my belongings on me. Even that motherfucking credit card.

They discharged me after just another hour of rest, and as I stood at the reception, signing documents, and paying without insurance out of my Papa's hard-earned, currency-converted rupees, I heard a slightly familiar voice.

'It's been hurting us all weekend,' her comforting Indian accent rolled off her tongue, suddenly giving me delicious memories of home. 'Like, you know, fireballs in our forehead.'

'It'll be fine, ma'am,' came another woman's reply. 'Just take the prescribed pills after your next meal, and then again before going to sleep. You should be fine.'

'But,' the first voice insisted. 'What if it's a migraine? What if it's something worse?'

It was Auntie, yaar; that same woman whom Hamid had met on his Greyhound from Jersey to D.C. three years ago, that woman we had seen walking around alone at the zoo. Here she was, alone again. Even after all this time, she looked almost the same as I remembered, in a timeless place of some age between twenty-five and forty. Small frame, round face, curly hair, and those deep, large eyes.

'It will be fine, ma'am,' the nurse repeated, and walked away from her to the beat of frantic, busy steps.

That same woman. Yes, she was in a pink salwar kameez, with a red silk dupatta over her shoulder, a red bindi on her forehead, red lipstick, and a small set of colourful bangles clinking on her forearms, looking like a bride on the way to her own shaadi.

'Hello,' I said.

She looked up at me with those large eyes, surprised that someone had addressed her. But in the next instant, a flash of recognition passed over her eyes, and they brightened up to see me.

'Oh, hello. We've met before, haven't we?' she asked.

'Yes, yes,' I said, taking my time to answer, as if I was trying to recall a scene that was already crystal clear in my memory. 'At the Union Station. My friend, he....'

'Yes, yes, Hamid. That was his name, wasn't it?'

'Yes,' I agreed, and I smiled.

'Yes, yes, good,' she said, and put her arms in front of her body in a defensive stance.

'I'm Vishnu,' I said. Behenchod, my head was still buzzing

from the previous night, and some more feet clanked against that busy hospital floor, and someone clicked a ballpoint pen, and someone scribbled violently on a piece of paper, and there were a few more white coats brushing past us, and she smiled back.

'We remember,' she answered. 'Our name is Jyoti.'

'Are you...are you okay?'

And for the first time, that pleasant formality slipped from her voice. She moaned, swung her head to the side, and then brushed some hair off her face. 'Oh, we're fine, fine. Only these headaches we've been getting, you know. Bad migraines. Always happens during exam time, no?'

Later that same day, Jyoti would reveal to me that she had no shortage of these migraines; that she puked often, spreading her arms around the toilet seat, that she drank multiple cups of decaffeinated green tea in an aggressive bid to relax herself, that she gave herself migraines worrying about the next migraine.

She invited me back home. We were out of sorts—she, troubled with a disorienting pain in her head, and I, hungover and smelly and trampled on from the night before. But it didn't matter. We were both a little sick and more than a little Indian, and when she offered to make khichdi for breakfast, I smiled and brightened up. I hadn't had khichdi since I was a sick child, on those groggy evenings in Varanasi when no other food felt appetizing going down my gullet. I could taste the warm, wet rice on the tip of my tongue already. 'That sounds great,' I said.

'We used to make khichdi for our son all the time, whenever he got sick,' she said as she drove. I sat in the passenger seat beside her, looking at the road ahead, careful not to stare at the bit of fair, exposed skin below her neck and down to where her kameez covered her bosom, revealing just the tiniest hint of her cleavage, and bas, let me tell you, that's when I started to feel something. Her hands gripped the steering wheel tight—a little *too* tight, I thought—and on her left hand, on that fourth finger, she wore a thin yellow ring with a small diamond stud.

'Oh yeah,' I remembered. 'Your son.'

'Aakash is eight, now. He turned eight last month.'

'Oh, yeah?' Haan, I still avoided eye contact. 'How did, umm…. How did you celebrate?'

'We wished him on Skype. Luckily, we were able to get a good connection.'

'Oh. Cool.'

At the next exit, she slowed down, driving extra cautiously, and slowly inched her car rightwards to the deceleration lane. It was a grey, overcast Saturday morning and there were no other cars on the road. She breathed hard to concentrate on the task ahead and exhaled when she made it out of the highway.

'He's tall, so much taller than when we last saw him,' she said, speaking in a quivering voice. 'Probably gets it from his father.'

I didn't know what to say, so I said, 'Yes, kids grow quickly, don't they?'

'Aakash has grown so fast. We haven't met in nearly two years.'

It was a handsome name, Aakash, I thought. I imagined him as one of my own childhood friends in primary school in Varanasi. Maybe someone like Dhiraj. Someone who read comic books and watched Cartoon Network and conjured up his own animal superhero squads with breathless excitement.

On her dashboard, next to the car's air conditioner vents, stood a small Krishna figurine. It was all gold, with one tiny leg bent in a stance over the other, and holding a flute up to his mouth. Above this figurine was a gold pendant, hanging in mid-air from the rear-view mirror, with an image of a man I immediately recognized: one of those godmen from India, with a sharp nose, long black hair, and a smile on his face.

'Do you know Guruji?' she caught me looking.

'Oh, yes, of course. My mother has portraits of all types of babas and gurus around the house.'

'We have been to his ashram, down in Bangalore,' she said. 'It was a wonderful place, let us tell you! So much peace and cleanliness. And every evening we got together for a satsang, and the best part, oh, let us tell you the best part—the haldi milk afterwards! It was fantastic.'

'That sounds cool.'

She stretched her right hand up to the pendant to fondle it between her fingers. Then, she moved that hand towards me. Gently, she squeezed my collarbone.

'Our husband—he never liked having any images of Guruji around our house. But now that we're here alone,' she glanced quickly at me with a nervous smile, 'we can put them wherever we want, can't we?' Her bangles tinkled when she moved her hand back.

I smiled back too, trying to mask the sudden humming under my skin. Behenchod, meri gaand phat rahi thi. I felt uncomfortable in the seat, stifled by the seat belt holding me in so tight.

'Our husband says it's all a fraud,' she continued. 'But it's not a fraud, is it? If so many people, millions of people, have been touched by Guruji?'

'Uh-hmm,' I nodded. *Touched, behenchod.*

'Even here in America, there are so many bhakts, you know? It's good to have something like that here. We feel we can be so lonely in this country. With Guruji, we never feel that way.'

I looked out my window. The clouds above had gathered closer together, making the morning sky heavier, darker. It would rain today, ekdum for sure, I knew.

'We are so far,' I said.

'So far from home.'

I didn't pay much attention to her home, yaar, except glancing at a green garden gnome that looked like a Christmas elf as I walked in through a red door. As soon as she closed the door behind me, she pressed her body against mine until I could smell the faint waft of jasmine from her hair, and it ignited a memory of the chameli shampoo that I had smelled on so many women on the Delhi Metro, and I put my arms around her, and she put her arms around me so that the bangles on each forearm rubbed against the sides of my stomach. She tiptoed to reach up to my face and put her lips on my lips, and I kissed her back. She was wearing thick, red lipstick and it tasted sticky and wet and delicious. She could smell the grime on my skin and my clothes from the night before, and taste my stale whisky breath, but suno, she didn't stop. Neither of us noticed when that red silk dupatta fell off her shoulders.

With one hand she took off her open-toed sandals. A thin, silver payal glistened around each of her naked ankles. For a brief second, I imagined how Jess would look with those anklets over her *Game of Thrones* socks, but Jyoti rose to kiss me again, this time with even more desperation, and then I didn't think of Jess any more.

I was already naked by the time we reached the bedroom. For years, I had anticipated this moment and feared how I would react, but when she kissed me again—this time with a slight hint of violence as she bit my bottom lip—I forgot all concerns. I didn't worry about that stench from my armpits or the close proximity of my hairy eyebrows or whether the little jawan unleashed from my pants would be ready for his duty. With tremulous hands, I ripped open the ribbed Durex condom packet purchased years ago from the Safeway where Gokul had worked. She turned on some music, a soothing classical Hindustani track, and the livening sounds of sarod and sitar washed over us. Then, it took her a few long seconds to pull that pink bottom down her thighs. She was thicker from the waist down than I had expected, and I giddily placed a palm on her creased, plump butt in anticipation. With the kameez still on, she lay down on her back and smiled up at me. I know now yaar—sach mein, believe me—that she had thought about this from the first moment we had met at the Union Station. She wrapped those arms around me again and pulled me in. I groaned lightly, and she groaned after me, and I could feel that smooth ring around her finger as her cold hands rubbed against my back. The beat of the music accelerated in pace, the vocals and sitar got louder, and we sped up together to the percussion once the tabla started up.

And then I fucked her.

And then she fucked me back. She fucked me with spite, and I know now that she thought about her husband in Ranchi—about how he could never make love without breaking into a series of wild, throaty coughs, and how he touched her with his rough palms and how his beard pricked against her sensitive, smoother skin. I would be him for a lovely, short instant; I would be in love with her. Then, the next track kicked in.

We wouldn't see each other again. This was good enough. This was all we needed. This was utter paagalpanti.

She spread her thick thighs to make space for me. It was my first time inside a woman since I had got out of one. We made unloving love on her neatly made bed. We switched positions so she was on top of me surveying her room—the clean white ceiling, still lifes of fruits on the wall, and framed photographs of a happy family on vacation in Nainital.

And then, from within me, I felt a surge of the end, of a sharp pain that would allay my heartbeat, that would blank my senses. And then, numb.

It's the numbness I feel now, an instant after Wildhair's shot took the last of my life out of me. It buzzes behind my ear like a bee, and at first, I ignore it, but then I realize that it's not just a buzz; it's an alarm, a cry. I follow it until the sound gets louder, until it takes me back in time, before Wildhair took out his gun, before I met Jyoti at the hospital, before I came to America, before the riots when Papa watched blood spill in his name in Muktigarh, before I played street cricket with Dhiraj near the Mehmoorganj house, before I rocked on Papa's lap as he made the decision to move to Varanasi, before Mummy let me out.

Mummy was dying. She had felt pain when she gave birth to the twins, and they say that the second birth is supposed to be easier than the first; but nahi nahi, on that hospital bed in Faizabad where the big-lipped doctor man seemed to speak in casual slow motion, Mummy screamed and shouted. It was a hot summer afternoon, and the windows were open. She was sweating. A dusty Usha fan creakily revolved in circles on the ceiling above her. She worried that the fan would come unhinged, that it would fall and slice her up. Her back ached. She was twenty-seven years old, but on that maternity bed she felt as if she had lived a thousand lifetimes. She dug her nails into the sides of the bed and pulled up the bedsheet, tearing through the seams.

And for a brief moment, she went numb, too, and she too followed that buzzing alarm, until she met me—nahi yaar, not me the soon-to-be-crying little baby, but me, the recently deceased twenty-one-year-old—and she recognized who I was, and I looked back at her light green eyes and that fair, young face until she understood what my life would be and how it would end.

The buzzing ended. The big-lipped doctor brought her back to Faizabad. I came to life, and Mummy saw me once again.

'You've had a boy,' said a doctor, a statement of fact rather than a celebration. Mummy exhaled to herself. She knew Papa was outside, pacing back and forth in the corridor, nervously waiting for this news. She knew he would be happy. He had always wanted another boy.

FIFTEEN

For many months after my death, Mummy would sit in my bedroom clinging to the scent of a past that was slowly vanishing from that dusty room. She would quietly begin drinking in secrecy at noon, and stop by four so she could sober up in time for Papa to return from work. She was miserly with the Scotch, ensuring it lasted as long as possible. Papa hadn't yet noticed the half-empty bottle as he preferred the cheaper stuff for daily drinking.

Mummy twiddled her thumbs over my Xbox controllers, laid my T-shirts on my bed and rearranged them in a neat stack. She spent hours staring at my desktop computer screen, which had a background wallpaper image of Ranbir Kapoor and Nargis Fakhri from *Rockstar*. She wore the same clothes she had woken up in—her white-and-pink nightie that fell loosely over her shoulders and reached all the way down to her ankles. She sat on the beanbag in front of the TV for a while, and then shifted to the leather chair by my computer, rolling it across the room on its noisy castors. She sat with the lights off and curtains drawn. Only a thin sliver of white sunlight cut across the room.

Once daily, at the height of the afternoon when she felt lethargic because of the summer heat and a heavy lunch, she would dial my phone number—my US phone number—just to hear it go to the automated 'out of service' message. Papa had stopped the payments to my silver credit card, which in turn, had ended the automatic monthly payment for my phone service; but yaar, Mummy didn't care. She sat on the edge of my bed and called. She listened, and once or twice, when she was sure none of the household servants were outside my bedroom eavesdropping, she said 'hello?' at the first hint of sound, only to remember that the discouraging voice of the robotic white woman on the dead line wasn't me. Mummy cleared her throat with an exaggerated groan. Death does a lot of things to erase your presence, but it doesn't completely rub you out, especially if the death was newsworthy like mine. Everyone from the *New York Times* and CNN to the local Bethesda literary magazine tried to find a +91 number to connect with my parents in India; but for Mummy and Papa, it helped to be a few oceans away from the tamasha in Washington. The only one who ever got through was a journalist with a nasal voice from the *Washington Post*, and even then, Mr Postwallah gave up when he realized that Papa's English was too difficult to understand over a distorted phone line. Papa had learned the language from television and his 10th-pass education at Faizabad's Lovely Flower Public School. When Papa didn't understand the reporter's accent, he would resort to cryptic, quasi-philosophical English phrases he had picked up from junk WhatsApp messages that his friends forwarded among themselves.

'Life is a cruel thing and this death is even more cruel thing,' Papa told the reporter. 'You understand us? Please, okay, do not be calling to us any more, okay? Life and death are cruel things, but death is more cruel, okay?'

And no, the Postwallah didn't call again, but he did write a beautiful investigative report two weeks later, and in the process, taught me that my death was about much more than my death. The feature photograph on the Sunday edition's centrefold was of me, smirking slightly, around the cherry blossoms in D.C., the same photo that was used at the service in my memory at the Church of the Epiphany. But in the sidebar was an image of Wildhair, not the one with the aggression of a rakshas as I had seen him, but a Wildhair of the past, wearing a crisp, white-collared shirt and a red tie, with his short, neatly gelled hair, sparkling in a deep dash of blonde. The photo was provided by his previous employers from their HR records. His shoulders slouched slightly. He had blue eyes, and he looked at the camera like any of us would; uncertain if he was holding the pose right.

His name was Mark Tillerman, and his official job title at PotoSystems (before he was laid off just a week after his forty-sixth birthday) was 'Information/Content Supervisor', but his real job was staring into a computer screen at dozens of pages of code, sometimes hundreds of them, and looking for small errors in JavaScript. He supervised nobody but himself, and that worked well for him. He sat on his swivel chair in a corner cabin and farted when his stomach rumbled because he knew no one was around and he took forty-minute naps after lunch on his desk, but those were encouraged by the company. He occasionally cracked open a beer on the evenings when he was asked to stay extra hours, without the extra pay; he felt he deserved a hoppy refreshment. His eyes hurt from staring into the bright screens and his wrists ached from typing, and even the ergonomic mouse pads the company provided couldn't ease the pain. The beer helped, though.

And when he went home every evening, Mark drank some more beer as he leaned against his kitchen island, and ate cold spaghetti that his wife had made straight from the family bowl, while his wife and daughters sat in the other room watching TV, and occasionally they nodded and greeted him, or asked for his help when the toilet flush stopped working or the dishwasher's door was jammed in hard and needed a man's strength to be opened. But mostly, he was ignored, and he went to bed on the couch that his family had vacated, while his wife slept alone in their bed a floor above; and he wondered if this was it—if this was his life, if this was his liberty, the pursuit of happiness, vagerah.

He was fired from PotoSystems some years after this, but Mark Tillerman found a way to stay connected. He was no chootia, samjhe? He had created a shadow username before they removed his account. He used this email address for all his accounts, including his blog, and logged on to the PotoSystems servers whenever he wished, even from the basement of his dilapidated home on the outskirts of Bassett, Virginia. He added a VPN to his home computer and re-routed his internet access through Berlin or Tokyo. When blogging, he only used a secure browser, to ensure his connection was bounced several times around the world before it stuck.

One night, he heard a voice from the bedroom above. It was his wife, giggling, and he knew she was on the phone with someone, and he knew what he felt deep down in his gut was true, but what he didn't know was that this was the night that would soon change his life and drive his family away and leave him alone and battered with jammed-up dishwashers and clogged toilets, and one day far in the future, lead him to murder.

Papa would wonder, years later, if Mark killed me as a form of punishment, a retribution for Papa's own sins, for the circle coming around full chakkar, for the karma Papa occasionally believed in, when he had time to remember. It was the reason why he donated to local NGOs in Varanasi or bought kachoris for street kids by the ghat. He wondered if Mark killed me because of that division between us, the division of our bestowed identities—American and foreign, white and brown. Did he kill me, because I wasn't *me* to him, but a symbol for my entire race of people? He killed me without knowing what my own father had done to those who looked the same but believed in different gods, or how he treated those that had the misfortune to be born something other than the caste of his privilege. Of our privilege. Mark killed me without knowing of the fortune Papa had amassed. Not that it mattered. I could've had a barren bank account or gold credit card (Platinum? Diamond? Palladium?). Nothing mattered, except for the matter of my last breath, and where he'd left me, blasted and bloodied and breathless. Dead.

No death, it seems, can escape the addition of a political annotation, as if every human life means something more than, simply, *life*—as if I was suddenly a symbol for every victim and every trend, as if my life was now less meaningful and subsequently more useful. In India, where fifteen thousand people die a day and fifty thousand are quickly born to replace them, the cycle never stops, and we become accustomed to the future casually replacing the past. But in America, I learned that my death was about guns, and the rise of Angry White People, and security at drinking establishments, and minorities under threat, and the general cloud of viciousness under President Gaandu-face, and about how a barely diligent innocent foreign student like me—Vishnu Agarwal, twenty-one, of Varanasi, India—bore the brunt of what Mr Postwallah titled the 'Entropy of Modern America'. I was, he said, the symbol of a new civil war. Suno, after nearly four years of getting it wrong, it took my death for me to finally, truly, become American.

Do the dead dream?

Do their nightmares trap them in a hellscape resembling home? Do they hear their own voices scream out for attention across the dinner table? Do their fathers and mothers and brothers and sisters remain deaf to them, until the screaming throats go hoarse, until the dead shrink away, further and further, now mere toddlers, hardly able to communicate without cries of pain, and further, until they are mere blimps in the grand scale of time and space, god particles, non-existent?

Do the dead have anything worthy to say?

SIXTEEN

During my first three weeks at D.C. Tech, Papa and Mummy called every alternate day from Varanasi with cautions and concerns about America, right before they went to bed, while I sat nine-and-a-half hours behind their time in the afternoon, answering their queries about vegetarian restaurants in D.C. and where each of my new friends was from. It was Mummy, of course, who had most of the questions, while Papa sat beside her on the bed in his sleeveless baniyan and short-shorts over his hairy thighs, scratching the itchy spot on his feet, watching *Comedy Nights with Kapil* or angry news anchors debating the day's latest sansani headline.

'Mummy, I got a call from Rishi bhaiya yesterday,' I said.

'He called you? From where?'

'Where else? California.'

Papa, on the other end, could sense the shift in direction of the conversation. 'Your uncle, Monty chacha,' Papa came on the line, 'you know he once got such a big scare at the Burgerwingwallah restaurant in Washington. Vishnu, don't you remember hearing that story? You must be careful. And visit your Monty chacha, okay? Virginia is very close to you. Okay? Visit him.'

I avoided my uncle. His suburban mansion felt as if it was further than flying back to Delhi. I hadn't seen him since I had arrived in D.C. and didn't plan on visiting him—I had left India to *leave India*, I told myself, and my Uncle Monty represented something that reminded me too much of home.

Instead, every weekend, Hamid, Tapiwa, Andrew, and I ventured out into the city to find new bars to explore. Gokul didn't join us, working all night at his Safeway check-out counter. And for a whole year, I remained in that trance, brain khallas, drifting from Intro to Computational Thinking to Intro to Programming in Python, intercepting fat, weedy joints between Hamid and Tapiwa and back to Hamid again, playing basketball at the Sports Hall, and watching live cricket online next to Gokul, where we secretly shared a moment of desiness that we would never be able to explain to our firangi friends. When I was out, I ate beefy cheeseburgers without guilt and pizzas and burritos and spicy red noodles in Chinatown, and, of course, the occasional butter chicken whenever a familiar accent called out from a food truck. Every weekend, I drank heavily, sometimes at grimy dive bars in Shaw that were cheap and didn't ask for IDs, sometimes at karaoke bars in Chinatown, and often at Lucky Luke near Dupont Circle where we watched sports, drank beer, and ate burgers until our stomachs demanded we puke it all out, until our systems rebooted so we could do it all over again the next day.

When the hangover subsided and my mind rewired itself, I spent Sundays at Jess's apartment in Tenleytown, with Jess and Amanda and Hamid; but never with Jess alone.

As time passed, I saw Jess closer, zooming into her, and I saw her flawless image a little less pixelated. I had begun to see her blemishes, her imperfections, the moles on her skin, random red spots on her neck, a nose that was a little too crooked. She had one of those uneven faces where the chin took up a disproportionately large space and her eyes and mouth all looked cramped on her face. As more time passed, I began to love those imperfections: the little eyes, the crooked nose, the spotted skin.

The summer after my first year in college, I flew back home to India, slept in the afternoons in air conditioning during the hottest hours of the day, and played *Heroes of Warcraft* on my computer after my parents fell asleep. When I returned to D.C., Jess invited me over to her place. It was the first time I was there all alone; bas she and I, no roommate, no other guest. 'Leave your shoes by the door, Vishnu,' she said, waving me in.

Her home smelled like her santra-scented bodywash, and fresh, buttery popcorn. We sat on her couch, covered in a tattersall brown and red design, snacking on popcorn while ignoring the news on CNN on the TV. She was wearing two differently coloured socks, each with an emblem of House Targaryen from *Game of Thrones*. She shivered and allowed me to move closer to her. She smelled fresh and fruity.

'How was home?' she asked.

'Fine.'

'Did you travel around India? I read a book about world railways over the summer…and there was so much about India…and….'

'Didn't travel. Just Varanasi—for months. India is really big, you know? Flights are long. Trains even longer.'

'How long will it take across on a train—east to west?'

'I dunno, yaar,' I said. 'A few days.'

'Far out. I gotta visit. And we'll go on a long train journey.'

I imagined Jess sitting next to me on the top berth of a sleeper carriage, sharing the same green Indian Railways blanket in the winter.

'Cool,' I said.

Suno, I couldn't think about those trains without smelling them. The smell of samosas and diesel. The smell of urine, and not just ordinary household susu urine, but acidic piss, something that smelled fresh and fermented at the same time.

I smelled a time past, a midnight years ago, when I was at the Mughalsarai railway station with Mummy and Sakshi didi. I stopped to use the one-rupee-per-piss toilet, and yes, that susu smell was there: festering, disgustingly foul and acidic. Despite having already paid the bathroomwallah a coin, I held my bladder and ran back out.

That night in Mughalsarai, Mummy, Sakshi didi, and I sat on a bench for hours under a tube light on a dark railway platform—a woman with her head covered with a green chunni, her teenage daughter wearing shorts too short for her mother's liking, and her adolescent son shifting from one leg to another, desperately trying to distract himself from his bursting bladder. We waited for the train to Delhi, which was running two hours and forty-five minutes late.

In the dark, my eyes couldn't focus enough to see the unlit ends of the platform, at the dozen men, women, and children who slept shivering on top of Hindi newspapers spread on the floor, covering themselves with more pieces of crinkled newspapers. It was too dark for us to even look below the bench and the cracks in the cement, where colonies of giant rats scurried about, nibbling on garbage.

Papa wasn't with us. A few hours away in a small village outside Varanasi, the riots were about to begin.

'It's no big deal,' Papa had said. 'These chootias just want to create panga, small troubles, samjhe? I'll deal with them. Don't worry, I'll deal with them.' But he knew it would be safer for his family to spend the week with Raghu maama—Mummy's younger brother—in Delhi.

The riots that year changed everything, and after 2010, Papa ensured that we never had to take those trains again. We flew everywhere we went: Delhi, Singapore, and New York, until the day I boarded that direct flight to D.C. alone, to the new world where I made new friends. Where I met Jess.

She stretched one of her legs towards me, and I grabbed her foot pretending to examine the red dragon on her sock. Feeling ticklish, she giggled and instinctively kicked back.

Dekho now, I'm going to tell you about a time on the same couch, in the same room, but a time without me, a vision I can only see after Wildhair's gunshot opened me up to infinity. It was a time when Jess extended her socked feet out and didn't recoil. It was Hamid, yaar; Hamid had been here, all alone with her, with popcorn and colourful socks on a small sofa for two, but they watched a basketball game instead of CNN, and Jess wore a loose-fitted, navy Washington Wizards jersey over her sweatshirt. When she felt cold in the heated indoors, Hamid had rubbed her ankles above her socks, and then, one by one, taken them both off to rub her naked feet. She looked at him and smiled.

When I touched those socks, however, unaware that Hamid had already slithered up the same body, she pulled her legs away.

'Tell me about Varanasi. Isn't your father, like, the richest man there?' She smiled.

'Second-richest.'

'Who's number one?'

'This guy. Vijay Malhotra—he owns a hospital.'

'Ooh, nice,' her eyes twinkled. 'Maybe *he* has a son in D.C. Tech, too. Sounds like a real catch. Lots of money and free healthcare.'

I snorted.

'And your mother, what does she do?'

I shrugged. 'Nothing. She sits at home.'

'Does she cook?'

'She used to. Now we have Himanshu.'

'You guys have a personal chef? Wow, you *are* rich. Does he make biryani? I had biryani once at that restaurant near H Street. It was wicked good.'

'No,' I shook my head. 'He makes dal, chicken, roti, things like that. You need to go to a Muslim household if you want *really* good biryani.'

'Oh....'

'We're Hindu.'

'I'm sorry—I didn't know it was a religious thing.'

I laughed. 'No, no, not like that.'

'Hamid's a Muslim,' she said.

'That would really confuse my mother,' I said. 'If she knew I had a Muslim friend in America.'

Jess straightened her back and looked straight at me. 'Really? Why?'

'What would your parents think?'

Jess paused and considered my question. 'I...I don't know, really. But...I guess they would be fine with it. They hate the president, so they'll love anything he hates.'

'My parents are old-fashioned,' I chuckled. 'And I know that, Mummy told me, after that mosque went down in Ayodhya, things changed.... Papa was there...and....'

'So, you guys don't eat beef and those guys don't eat pork. What do you eat together?'

'Chicken, I guess. Fish. Mutton. Everyone eats that. Except for the vegetarians.'

'Like me,' she said.

'Yes, like you.'

Even though the volume was low, we were suddenly interrupted by frantic, rising sounds from the TV. A scene in some European city. Stone-paved paths and gothic churches. Smoke bombs in the air and paramilitary troops. A curfew and a manhunt. Two ever-rising numbers on the ticker banner at the bottom of the screen—one for the dead, one for the injured. Jess straightened up.

There had been a bomb blast somewhere in Paris, at a concert, and then a shooting at a cafe, killing some people, and now the terrorists were on the loose. Then, the screen split up into three panels: one with the continuing live shot of the scene, one with an angry TV anchor, and one that displayed passport photographs of each of the terrorists. Brown men, sharp noses, big beards.

I rubbed the rough stubble around my cheeks. I knew what Papa would have said if I had been back home. *Shave that face if you don't want to look like one of those Mohammedans,* I could almost hear his voice from the other side of the world. He would watch the news and tsk under his teeth. *Kaat dena chahiye sabko.... All these chootias deserve to die.*

I looked over at Jess, who was now engrossed in the news.

'This blows.'

'Fucking murderers,' I said. 'And look at the news. The media highlights them like they're some sort of heroes.'

I heard Papa's words in my own voice. I heard the echoes of the phone calls he had made in the past, the way he trumpeted the news in his own angry tone, the times he mentioned the mosque that was destroyed years before I was even born. I wanted it to go away—his voice. I wanted to shut him up, but even in the imaginary conversations we had in my head, I couldn't dare say anything back.

Jess turned to me. 'What do you mean? The media?'

'I mean…these guys are murderers.… Yaar, if it was me that gets killed, I want the news to show *my* face. Not the behenchod who killed me.'

'Heh,' she said, a half-laugh, half-snort. She wasn't chatty any longer, and soon, the only sound in the room was the monologue of numbers and warnings on screen. Jess angled her body away from me. I panicked, yaar, and my brain, you know it went into troubleshooting mode, with the anti-virus software scanning the system to find out where I had made the error. I told myself it was because of the news, but saala, that doosri voice of reason told me it was because of me, and then there was a teesri voice of paranoia, and it screamed *CTRL-ALT-DEL* on repeat, hoping to restart this whole night.

SEVENTEEN

'You're early,' Jess said. She was dressed in a loose, red sweater, one size too big for her thin frame.

Suno, two years had passed now since that Sri Lankan lunch with her, samjhe? Two years of buttered popcorn and angular limbs and smiles that lingered longer than I had expected. She texted me every day, and she touched my shoulder to get my attention instead of calling out my name. After two years of patient penance, tonight was finally going to be my night. Eight months ago, I had bought a packet of Durex ribbed condom from Gokul's Safeway and begun carrying it in my wallet, just in case, for the right day. I had waited long for a night like this, and although Jess never fully committed to me, I believed that we had a spark at the end of a slowly burning long fuse, finally ending in a firework ready to explode.

So, of course, that evening, I was early.

She left the door open for me and turned around, walking back inside with forceful, determined steps. The apartment was a mess. Shirts, dresses, and underwear were laid out to dry on her clothing racks and wall heaters. The plastic table in the middle of her room was covered with stacks of disposable plates filled with leftover food. Without saying a word, she went to the kitchen sink and started scrubbing a large cooking pot.

I took off my new pair of sneakers and stepped in. 'Did you…did you have a party?'

'Amanda,' Jess said softly without looking back up. 'And her fucking friends.'

I put both hands in my jeans pockets and waited. I looked around her apartment. Framed photographs of snow-peaked mountains sat on the floor, leaning against the wall.

I picked up a cushion off the floor and sat on the couch, then turned on the TV to the news without sound.

After a half hour of silence, she was finally done. She nudged my feet off of her end of the couch and sat down.

'Are you okay?' I asked. Her body, even from the distance, felt cold. She sat straight, without relaxing back into the cushions.

'Amanda...' she said.

'Ya...?'

'And all of her friends, too.'

'Hmm....'

'And your fucking friend, too.'

'Who?'

'Hamid,' she said. 'He's a bastard.'

'Ha-Hamid?'

'Yes. That bastard.'

In public, Jess and Hamid had mostly kept a friendly distance. Sometimes, Hamid joked about how she nibbled on her peanut butter and jelly sandwiches, and at other times, Jess rolled her eyes when he broke his Ramadan fasts, getting drunk on Sunday afternoons and overdosing on gyro-meat sandwiches.

But dekho, they also shared their private moments. I hadn't seen him visit her apartment every other week, seen her nuzzle his neck, and seen how he gently rubbed her back making concentric circles like an Ayurvedic masseur. I hadn't seen them kiss, seen Jess giggle nervously, or seen Hamid grow serious and quiet to ensure he didn't say the wrong thing and spoil the moment. I hadn't seen her cry in front of him when her sister-in-law miscarried. And I hadn't see him sliding her socks off.

Now, with me seated beside her on her couch, she didn't speak again, and time passed, and finally bored of our silence, I thought, chhoro, and decided to leave. Jess got up to see me out the door.

'Hey,' she said, and suddenly stepped close to me, and for a second, I smelled that citrus santra smell, this time slightly diluted with the lemony scent of the dishwashing liquid. 'Thanks for coming.'

'Nahi, nahi,' I said, trying to sound casual, 'no problem.' Behenchod, I know now that I should have said something more, thought more with my head than my frustrated laddus.

'Hamid,' she said. 'He got back with Maya. You knew that, didn't you?'

'He did?'

'Did he say anything about me, Vishnu? We were just fooling around or whatever, but, still…' she stopped and composed herself.

My head spun. I let the fragments fall into place and arranged all the data in the right folders.

'I do-don't know anything.'

And suddenly, Jess threw her arms around me and sobbed. I could feel her breath on my temple. Her body, pressed closer against mine, and I panicked and tensed even more.

'Jess,' I said. 'I…I think….'

And before I could say anything more, she pressed her lips against my lips, and behen-fucking-chod, we were kissing. We were kissing. My mouth on her mouth. I tasted her tongue gently glide against mine, and it sent a little electric spark down my spine. I tried to respond with my tongue, but instead ended up licking back awkwardly, so much so that, quicker than it had begun, it was over.

'I'm sorry, dude,' she pulled back. She reached across me to open the door, and shit, yaar, what else could I do? I walked out.

I walked home alone on that cold January night, bundled under multiple layers of sweaters, a warm woollen beanie, thick gloves, and a large overcoat, still shivering. My face was the only part exposed to the extreme chill, and the taste of Jess's tongue hovered for a long minute on my drying lips. I pursed those lips together, trying to preserve the feeling for as long as I possibly could.

EIGHTEEN

Look at him at his desk, his blonde hair a tangled mess, his forehead flushed pink. In front of him was a computer screen, turned down to the lowest possible brightness so he could work without needing to squint too much. Those deep blue eyes, firmly locked in place, stared into that screen. His thick fingers typed furiously without making a single spelling error. He rarely paused to breathe, but when he did, his breaths came heavy and laboured as if the air in his lungs was clamouring to escape through his windpipe.

He paused typing for a moment and exhaled.

He needed a drink. The time on his computer screen read 11.52 a.m. but he decided he had waited long enough. Fuck it.

He grabbed a cold can of Budweiser. The letters on the can read 'America', a special edition release for the election year. He pulled the tab with a satisfying *pop* and *sizzzzz* and took his first sip of the day. He had a rule to wait until noon before his first drink; but saala, who the hell was going to stop him from starting a few minutes early? Who was going to stop him on *any* day?

Fuck it.

He was happy in his drunken anonymity, lost in the millions of pings of servers tunnelling him to random corners of the earth. At his happiest, he was also at his most enraged, clicking and scrolling and typing in a state of meditative, controlled anger, with beads of sweat forming on his forehead. He believed this anger brought out his best work.

On his blog, Mark called himself 'The Watcher'. He scoured

the internet and social media for stories that inflamed him, and in turn, he further amplified these stories to his followers. He shared links of an underground trafficking ring that provided underage minors to satisfy the most grotesque desires of powerful celebrities. He commented on YouTube trailers for major superhero film releases, convinced of an international conspiracy to sedate the youth with fantasy.

On weekends, he set out on drives around the suburbs. As The Watcher, he posted photographs and videos of dark-skinned strangers playing cricket in random neighbourhoods around the state, and of families in malls further up in Northern Virginia and D.C., women in saris shopping at Costco, and women in hijab dropping off their children at public schools. Sometimes he posted audio files of secret recordings he did of Uber drivers with thick foreign accents. Under each posting, The Watcher typed his comments, his outrage at how these men smelled of garlic and radish, at how he distrusted any woman who felt the need to veil herself, how he couldn't believe America was getting overrun by those who could barely pronounce English words the correct way. *Speak AMERICAN*, he wrote.

His trump card, of course, was the PotoSystems server, off which he copied all the data under non-Biblical names in the employee list. There were a whole lot more Venkataramans and Khans and Huangs and Pereiras than he remembered. He didn't post these details publicly, but he kept an eye on them. He had learned, by then, that the darker faces could come with more familiar names, too, like Fernandez or Joseph or Thyle—he had to be more careful, he knew. He followed some employees and their families around Indian or halal grocery stores, annoyed by the smell of cumin and that chatter of *vandamana ramananam adracadabra whatever the fuck that is*. Occasionally, he even found himself following Egyptian families into the driveway of a mosque and Malaysian families into Asian food emporiums.

But idhar wapis aao—on this day, he posted a video taken

from a shaky camera phone, capturing a Sunday afternoon cricket match in the suburbs. Below the video, he wrote: *These curries here playing sticks and stones. This is a family place. Family first.*
People commented under The Watcher's comments. Updates popped up in real time from followers and fellow bloggers, other mostly anonymous men with vague usernames like 'RedFever' and 'Christmas Is Here To Stay'. Some mocked the men in the video for looking weak and defenceless. *Vegetarians!* Some said that they probably kept their women locked away. *ISIS Sluts!*

Mark, The Watcher, lifted a leg and furiously scratched his right ankle. He took a sip of his beer and burped, then leaned forward into his keyboard again. *Family First*, he repeated. At his most dedicated, he would be too engrossed in his task to be aware of his own self; if he could smell his trackpants, he would know that they smelled of piss. There was a faint puddle of old urine staining the floorboards below him.

As a father of two daughters, he wrote, *as a husband, a family man, this is not what I want for my country. This is not a country of curries.*

He opened another beer and looked at his bare ring finger. He still had a fleshy indentation at the bottom of the finger after sixteen years of wearing that ring. His finger had grown thicker, and there was a distressing rash appearing all over his body, his ankles, his upper shoulder, the insides of his thighs, and the interdigital folds of his fingers. He finally removed the ring and put it away, in a drawer along with a photograph of his two daughters and old birthday cards that he only reread in a half-conscious state, whenever he awoke from a drunken dream in the middle of the night.

Sometimes, his dreams were vivid, surreal, and he saw strange shapes and foreign figures, and sometimes, those figures appeared in front of his eyes when he was awake too, like creatures from augmented reality, like Pokémon GO characters but in darker, human forms. They always seemed to be threatening him, his life, his home, even the family that wasn't *his* to protect any more.

He knew which window in his bedroom above provided the best vantage point for a panoramic view. Sometimes he could see self-augmented forms in this panorama, too, out in his backyard or sneaking behind his Dodge Challenger. He knew that in the drawer on the other side of the bed was a handgun available for easy access. He knew the closet in which he kept his other gun, the AR-15. Sometimes, he dreamt that he was shooting out of his bedroom window, and imagined that he was out in dry deserts on the other side of the world. He ordered the As Seen On TV Tac Glasses with night vision and kept them in another one of his drawers. Once, he had a vivid daydream sitting drunk out on his porch, in which he had blown a terrorist's face clean off before the man could even finish chanting 'Allahu Akbar'.

When the right time came, Mark knew he wouldn't hesitate.

NINETEEN

Winter nights could get bitterly cold in Varanasi, especially during the nights when we could not afford to have more than that one brown blanket that Rishi bhaiya and I had to share. We took turns with the blanket, one night each; but, of course, I could not stop my elder brother from snatching it away all for himself.

Thud...Thud...Thud....

'Stop it Bhaiya,' I mumbled, eyes closed, limbs spread out wildly, as if I was stretched on the mat in a compromised kabaddi position. 'I'm trying to sleep.'

On the bottom bunk of the bed, underneath me, Rishi bhaiya was wide awake, as he usually was at this time of the night. He had already complained to Mummy about it; he shouldn't have to go to sleep, he argued, at the same time as me. He was older, he reasoned, and should be allowed to make up his own schedule and to watch TV next to Papa. But Mummy was strict about such things at home—sleep times, TV times, prayer times—and didn't budge.

So, instead, he was on the bunk below, restless, warm under the brown blanket, and wide awake. He had a tennis ball with him, the one with which he played cricket, and he was practising his spin throws against the plank of wood underneath me that separated our beds.

Thud...Thud...Thud....

'Bhaiya, please...' I moaned. I wrapped my arms around myself. Full-sleeved shirt and pyjamas and a vest, and still, not warm enough.

'Bhaiya, please…' he mimicked me in a squeaky voice. 'You sound just like a girl…like Sakshi. "Please!"'

'*You* sound like Sakshi,' I retorted. 'You are the twin. Twins with a girl.'

'Oye, shut up, Vishnu. I'll break you, okay…. I'll break you like…I'll break you like Mummy tears up her rotis. That's how she eats, doesn't she? In small small pieces.'

I giggled. 'No, I'll break you,' I said, my eyes still closed. 'I'll break you like…Dhiraj broke his arm that one time.'

He laughed. This was our little game—his and mine—one-upping each other with the fiercest threats.

'I'll break you like Papa broke the car door last year.'

'I'll break you like…I'll break you like Hanuman broke the mountain.'

'Ooh, good one,' he said, sounding genuinely pleased. I swelled with pride. 'I'll break you like…like…like, in *Dexter's Lab*, when he breaks the thermometer, *crash!*'

Now, I laughed out loud, imagining the moment in full animation. 'I'll break you like…' I said, calming myself, 'I'll break you like a dam.'

'A dam?'

'Yes. A dam breaks and the water floods.'

'Where did you learn that?'

Rishi bhaiya had a fluctuating voice, dipping up and down between fearsome and friendly, between serious and jovial, sometimes in the same breath. When I was excited—like I was now—I frothed inside my mouth and sprayed a little saliva when I talked. But Bhaiya's voice was clean even in its fluctuations; no mumbles, no gargles, no stray saliva wasted.

'I'll break you like an earthquake,' he said.

'I'll break you like Shaktimaan broke Jackal.'

'I'll break you like Superman breaks Shaktimaan.'

'I'll break you like a big building.'

Rishi bhaiya had stopped throwing the ball. The only sound

in the room, then, were our whispers, slowly ascending in volume as we verbally jostled back and forth.

'What building?' he asked.

'Any building. Like the buildings in America.'

'I'll break you like the masjid.'

'What's that?'

'The mosque.'

I stopped giggling, confused. 'What mosque?'

'They broke a mosque, don't you know?' he said. 'Many years ago. When Papa was in Faizabad.'

'Why did they break the mosque?'

'I don't know. I wasn't there. I wasn't even born.'

'How do you know then?'

'Papa was there, you idiot. He told me all about it.'

Rishi bhaiya had a copy of the latest *Manorama Yearbook* under our bed; he knew all the facts.

'Don't call me "idiot". I'll break you….'

'Like what?'

'Like the mosque!'

'No,' he said. 'I already said that. Think of something else.'

The mosque came down in 1992, four-and-a-half years before I was born. There was a before and an after, even though the before was infected by the plague of the aftermath, too. And there were infections of violence a little earlier before those earlier times. And there was camaraderie before that, and some dushmani, and some dosti, and a hundred years, or five hundred, or more, of back and forth, between the rulers and the ruled, the perpetrators and the victims, the murderers and the murdered.

TWENTY

Ram was the seventh avatar of Vishnu—not I, but the god Vishnu—and Lakshman was a big bhakt of Ram—not Ram's brother Lakshman, but Lakshman the glass-blower in Papa's workshop. And as all good devotees, Lakshman looked forward to his favourite deity's big day—Ram Navami—every spring, and for all nine days that led up to this festival, he would show up lethargic for work as he fasted all day and ate all night. 'You wouldn't understand—it's an important custom in my family,' he told Kareem in their stuffy workspace, seated inches away from each other, sweat pouring from their sticky armpits and chests and belly buttons and thighs. Kareem lit up a bidi and they passed it between each other. 'The vrata is important, okay? Makes me weak during the day, but for Ram—anything.'

Kareem coughed and laughed. 'You think *I* won't understand? You're talking about nine days. Have you ever done a full month? A full month of Ramadan with no eating while the sun is out. Now *that* requires devotion.'

'Yaar.... But at least you Muslim-log can eat meat at night. It gives you strength for the day, doesn't it? In my household, we don't even touch egg for the whole nine days.'

Kareem took a puff of the bidi and tutted. 'Nahi, bhai. It's not about the meat or egg or fish or sabzi. It's about the farz, you understand? It's a duty. You perform your farz, and that is all the strength you need. What do Hindus call this...this sense of duty?'

'Dharma. It's all about our dharma. The food...the food is just a small thing, you know?'

Kareem laughed again, flashing a full set of teeth in the dark room. 'Only for a big man is food a small thing.'

Then, Lakshman laughed, too.

'Haan. Your farz, my dharma,' he said.

The bidi was almost finished. Lakshman pressed it close to his lips, and then saved the last puff for Kareem.

'Can you call Hindus to your house for Eid?' Lakshman asked.

'Will you eat biryani? Chacha-jan makes the best mutton biryani outside of Lucknow, you know.'

'I'll eat anything you offer, yaar.'

Kareem extinguished the bidi on the side of the brick wall and flicked it away. Lakshman took his place opposite the flame. Break time was over.

TWENTY-ONE

That shot changed everything. I was there and then I wasn't. Hamid and Jess gave separate police reports and returned home: Hamid to Bedminster and Jess to Rupert, back to the comforting embraces of their families. For some time, neither of them turned on the news, and both of them ignored insistent calls from Mr Postwallah for his piece about my death.

But ruko, I'm getting too far ahead now. Let me float back half a year, back to my last winter on this good and lovely planet earth. Our mostly equilateral love triangle was shattered into three disparate tangents. After Jess told me about her and Hamid, I didn't hear from her again—until my last night on earth. The cherry blossoms returned, and Jess went to see them alone this time, once again petting the flowers delicately as if they were her endangered offspring.

I spent the winter in a self-imposed quarantine, partly in reaction to the freezing cold weather; partly, because of all the assignments that had piled up by now, months before graduation. I would see Hamid in the hall and walk away, avoiding his eyes—there was always an excuse of upcoming coursework and exams now. I stayed at my laptop locked inside my bedroom, all alone, or in the white soundless computer lab in campus, shuddering after multiple shots of espresso until late into the night, typing away HTML tags and diagnosing JavaScript errors.

Hamid, who was one of those chootias who could ace a test completely without any strenuous preparation, never stressed about exams. That winter, he grew a goatee that circled over his lips, around his mouth, and down around his chin. He drove to Baltimore with Andrew every weekend and the two of them sat by the harbours smoking weed and talking about Nietzsche or *The Wire*.

Eventually, winter thawed into spring, and some of my anger melted away. On a Tuesday evening, I sat at the kitchen table next to Tapiwa, scrolling through pages of code on my laptop. Tapiwa scooped up Froot Loops without milk, reading Shakespeare pressed up to his nose.

Then he slammed the book shut.

'Done?' I asked without looking up.

'I can't believe it's over,' he said.

I smirked to myself. 'Read something else, then.'

Tapiwa shook his head. 'No, it's not the same, brother.'

'What?'

'I can't believe it's over.'

'How are you.... How are you feeling now, bro?' I asked. He rarely spoke of home any more; it had been two years now since Tapiwa had lost his mother to a sudden stroke, two years since he'd shared his regret at not flying home to Harare for the cathedral service.

'What does the cathedral have to do it, huh?' he asked. 'People die and they just die. What's the point of looking back, huh?'

This had been his capital-A-Atheism phase, while the rest of us—me and Hamid and Andrew and whoever else we spent our time with—were going through *We-Don't-Really-Give-a-Shit-Ism*. Yet, from my distance, I could only witness the small sorrows that Tapiwa faced—the sorrow of a deadline missed, the sorrow of a good book's final sentence.

'Do you know who Yvonne Vera was, Viz?' he asked.

I shook my head.

'Time is as necessary for remembering as it is for forgetting. Even the smallest embrace of pain needs time larger than a pause; the greatest pause requires an eternity, the greatest hurt a lifetime. A lifetime is longer than eternity: an eternity can exist without human presence.'

He looked up at me, his eyes meeting mine, expecting a response, but I could hardly react.

'All I need is time, my brother,' he said. 'I'm young. I have time. We all have time, don't we?'

The door swung open suddenly, and Hamid burst in, a familiar, energetic smile on his face.

'Get up bitches, get up. You aren't gonna spend the whole year in this fucking kitchen.'

I raised an eyebrow. 'What?'

'Let's go. It's three-dollar Corona night at Cat King. We gonna get fuuucked up, bruh.'

I looked over at Tapiwa, and he smiled with his chapped lips. Tapiwa had been the silent data router between Hamid and I, keeping our networks connected even when there was a glitch in our friendship. When Hamid burst in, I saw the instant brightening of Tapiwa the African Prince's eyes. The glow on his pimply, dark face. I knew he was intrigued. Suno, it had been so long since we had left the campus, that this random invite on a busy weeknight seemed like the most appetizing idea we had heard for months.

I resolved to myself not to talk about Jess. That was the beauty of our deciduous youth yaar, of our friendships—nothing could be concrete and every emotion was malleable. It was a programme constantly refreshed and updated.

'Chalo,' I said. 'Let's go.'

There was a gargantuan archway with Chinese characters and golden dragons outside the Gallery Place metro stop, and oxen and monkeys painted on the crosswalks, and food from China and Japan and Korea for maximum Asian effect around the basketball arena. But sach mein bolun? Chinatown in D.C. was only a half-hearted effort. It was like any downtown in any city anywhere in the First World, eventually blurring into a singular groggy haze after a few drinks.

After a few drinks at Cat King we stumbled out of the club. I stopped on top of the stairs and took a moment to catch my breath as the noisy night traffic rushed past us. I put my arms on my knees and bent down, lowering my head and eyes to focus on the concrete below. 'Viz's getting old, brother!' Tapiwa laughed, 'My brother, "Age isn't how old you are but how old you feel!"' I put a middle finger up to him, but in my head, I was thinking yaar, shit, I'm becoming just like my father. I had seen him suddenly wobble on his feet on the drunkest of nights after meeting his friends at the Varanasi Trader's Union. If my father saw me now, however, he wouldn't see himself; nahi nahi, he would just shake his greasy face in disappointment.

I stood up straight. 'Let's keep going!' I announced.

We walked slowly on the crowded pavements of the brightly lit city, remembering our earliest days together. Hamid put an arm over my shoulder to put me into a headlock. 'The motherfuckin' Wiz!' he said, and all my early hesitation at hanging out with him evaporated. I shoved an elbow backwards into his soft stomach.

'Abey, get the fuck off,' I laughed. 'Get off, behenchod.'

Outside, on the busy cross street, hundreds of other young people walked and sang out among themselves. The cars honked angrily, briefly reminding me of rush-hour traffic in Delhi. I heard the sounds of happy percussion being played to the rhythmic beat of our footsteps, or of our pulsating heartbeats. Next to the big, decorated arches that formed the gateway into Chinatown, there were a number of older men who sat on the pavement playing fast-paced jazz, drumming on upturned blue buckets, using the lids of trash cans as cymbals to punctuate their rhythm.

'What's next?' Hamid moved off me and playfully punched Tapiwa on his shoulder. 'Karaoke?'

'No, no,' I protested. 'I'm too hungry, yaar. Let's get some food.'

'Shut up,' Hamid said and turned to Tapiwa. 'Yo, Prince! You?

Tapiwa, who could barely keep his droopy eyelids open, smiled widely across his pockmarked face. 'I'll do whatever, man.'

'He'll do whatever!' Hamid slapped a fist into the air and led the way. We walked over to General Song's Chicken, a crowded Chinese restaurant in a basement that led up, via a winding, dark stairway in the back, to a well-hidden karaoke bar. At the top, the stairway gave way to deliriously bright lights. In a space no larger than our Saxon Hall kitchen, there were fifteen, or maybe twenty other young people, all staring at a common screen and cheerily screaming out the lyrics to a song by a boy band from the '90s. Their out-of-tune, high-pitched voices merrily polluted the air. A disco light sent dots of colour revolving around the room.

There was a loud, trumpeting sound over the speakers, like the shankh conch shell blowing in Hindu epics before the start of the day's battle, and then the heavy bass kicked in, followed by a cheer before some new masscult hit of the day. Heavy bass and rhythmic ringing bells and slow-paced emo rap. Tapiwa and I shouted past each other over the loud music.

'I'll get the drinks,' I announced. 'Beer, everyone?'

'No, no, Viz,' Tapiwa protested. 'It's my round.'

Hamid put an arm over both of our shoulders from behind. 'Let Viz get it, Prince,' he slurred. He turned to me and winked. 'This is your thing, isn't it, bruh? Go buy it for us. Don't be shy.'

'What do you mean? What's my "thing"?' I pushed off his arm.

But I already knew, haan haan, I knew the answer. This *was* my thing. My *swishing-swashing* card that made up for everything else I lacked. I couldn't get the girls or grades or friends like Hamid, and I would always be an outsider in his country, but *this*...this was my thing. I could spend, I could buy.

Hamid pushed me gently on my back. 'Just get those beers, bitch.'

So, I did. We carried our respective pints and squeezed through the sweaty dancing, jumping bodies into the centre of the dance floor, hoping to spread our elbows out for some breathing room. A Michael Jackson song came up next on the screen, and Tapiwa the African Prince screamed and raised a bony fist in celebration.

I laughed at him, and Hamid—perhaps the most drunk of us all—began to swing his arms around wildly, splashing his beer all around him.

Midway through that song, a group of loud, cheering gora boys, all in matching tight T-shirts that barely seemed to contain their bulging muscles, snaked their way through between us, pushing us backwards as they parted the sea of bodies to march on to the other side of the floor. They were our age but looked bigger, beefier. In the sea of colours, all of us meshed into the same shade. Hamid was red, sweaty, and drunk, and so were those white boys. Hamid watched them walk past, keeping an angry eye in their direction.

Behenchod, I should've seen it coming.

A few minutes later—and it couldn't even have been that long because the same MJ song still played on the speakers—the group of boys prised us apart again to cross the floor. People were dancing wildly and there was no room to back up. The boy in the front was wide-chested, with short, silvery hair, and he carried a tall glass of beer. Hamid, in a split second of paagalpanti, purposely leaned forward, so his shoulder struck that silver-haired one's shoulder, and it sent him off balance a little. He quivered and the beer slipped from his hands. The glass seemed stuck in mid-air for an instant, battling helplessly against gravity, until it came crashing down, sending broken glass and beer flying in all directions. In another second, everyone in a large radius around the crash bounced backwards, away from us.

A loud crescendo of exclamations broke out over the music. Two of the other gora boys stepped in front of Hamid, facing him aggressively with their chests puffed out. Somebody pushed me hard from behind. 'Hey!' I said.

'Stop stop stop stop' came the panicked, breathless voice of the bartender over the crowd.

'You wanna die you piece of shit?' the wide, silvery-blonde one said to Hamid.

'Fuck you gon' do?' Hamid answered back. His voice was easy, almost frighteningly casual. 'White trash piece of shit. What the fuck you gon' do?'

Yaar, this was too much for that Big Silver one to take. Suno, I can see his thoughts now. *Now,* I know everything about this stranger. Big Silver came from South Virginia, where his father and stepmother owned a lumberyard, and they lived in a large country house with picket fences and had a saltwater fishing boat that they took to Chesapeake Bay every few months for family get-togethers. He was in Washington to visit his cousin Bart—also in the karaoke bar that night—and the last thing he expected was for someone like Hamid to disrespect him.

Tapiwa grabbed Hamid's hand. 'Hamid, hold up, brother. Hold up.'

A bouncer appeared behind Hamid and pulled him back. He was a wide-shouldered man, who wore a black leather jacket and a frown on his face. I moved towards Hamid and the bouncer, and so did Tapiwa the African Prince, and I inadvertently bumped my hand against someone else's drink, and it spilled with a sound of crashing glass behind me. 'You motherfucker!' a girl shouted. The MJ song ended, and someone queued up a slow Disney ballad on the big screen.

I can show you the world.... Shining, shimmering, splendid.

'You—you three.' said the bouncer in a low baritone voice. 'Out. Now.'

In a drunken haze, the three of us made it down the dark stairs and back outside to the sidewalk of Chinatown, full charged with adrenaline. My eyes blinked at the blinding car headlights and colourful signboards. From around the corner, the percussion of drumsticks on buckets continued, throbbing at a faster pace, multiple beats per second *dum-di-di-dum-dum-dum-dum-dum.*

And then I heard a voice call us from behind.

'Heyou! Your name is Ham-eed, right? Isn't that what your

black friend called you? Ham-eed? We ain't done yet, boys. We ain't done yet.'

It was that silvery-blonde one, leading the rest of his group—three, nahi, four more—behind him. The silver-haired one was the biggest of them all, but they all looked hatta-katta and athletic as if they were American football players or giant wrestlers.

'Hey Bart,' silver-hair turned to his cousin and smiled. 'Do you know what they call a Muslim with a ham on his head?'

Bart began to laugh in short, hesitant spurts. He was thinner than Big Silver and stood behind him. His pink face bobbed under a blue backwards-facing baseball cap.

Silver-hair answered himself. 'Ham-Head!'

Hamid looked at me, eyes screwed in disbelief. He didn't know how to respond.

But Big Silver wasn't done. 'Wait, wait, I have another one,' he gestured with his hand to quiet his friends. 'What if you put *another* ham on his head?'

They laughed again. It was a moment—kaise samjhaon, yaar?—where all of our decision receptors were switched off. We were drunk and angry and free. They stood in a straight line opposite us, shoulders firm, arms tensed. There was an invisible Line of Control dividing the two sides, and for a second, we were all waiting for the first one to stumble forward and break the tension.

Bart couldn't wait for the punchline this time. 'More-ham-head,' he said and broke out in hysterics. 'Mo-ham-head.'

The punch came out of nowhere. That Line of Control was infiltrated. In a swift instant, Bart's laughter stopped. He moaned and stumbled back. His cap fell off his head and, losing his balance, he fell to the ground.

Above him, Tapiwa stood in a fighting stance, fists prepared to hit again.

Dekho yaar, it happened in increments. One thing leading to another. One and zero, zero and one. I see those few short seconds as they slowly disintegrated into the chaos that followed.

Big Silver pushed Tapiwa the African Prince, who was shoved aside weightlessly. His face hit the pavement. *Thud*. Hamid formed his chubby fingers into a fist and let loose a string of punches on Big Silver's side and shoulders. Two more of Big Silver's friends, who had been quiet so far, pulled Hamid up and flung him aside. Hamid stumbled and landed on the grass on the sidewalk. Traffic continued to zoom past us. Other pedestrians, without interfering, quietly walked around the brawl.

I stood frozen.

And then someone struck me with a mighty blow on the back of my neck, and I felt a stinging jolt that suddenly awakened my entire body to the pain. The drumbeats continued. In pure blind instinct, I swung a fist in a semicircle around me, slicing through nothing but the night air. Sach mein, let me tell you, I had never been in this situation, samjhe? Not in the playground at Little Blooms School, not during all the adventures with Sanjeet in Delhi, and of course, not during the riots, when I was far away in a train, from the massacre that was to follow. Nahi, this night was my first brush with real violence, because all I had known until then was shooting at pixelated motherfuckers in *Call of Duty*. Fight or flight, yaar; and surrounded on this pavement outside the karaoke bar, I had nowhere to fly to, so I fought back. I swung at Big Silver and staggered. My fist connected with someone else, and when my knuckles hit his jaw, I immediately felt another sharp pain reverberate from my right hand down to my wrist, hurting me perhaps more than it hurt him.

That second surge of pain powered up my sensorium. The street bubbled with a smell of urine—acidic, fresh urine—mixed with the sharpest smell of skunk unlike any weed Hamid had ever rolled before. I felt cold again, not like the cold of the winter, but enough of a breeze to give me a sudden shudder. I heard manic, desperate sirens, swirls of rotating sound hurtling towards us *vyoon-vyoon-vyoon*. The police were here. I was at once back in Delhi, back in the passenger seat of Sanjeet's Santro, back in the crowded jail cell that smelled of feet and sweat and piss. It was that night all over again, it was my life in a whirling loop of bad karma.

I opened my eyes wider and the picture sharpened, and there were bright yellow lights and blue uniforms, and I was lying on the ground separate from Big Silver and Tapiwa the African Prince and Bart and the whole rumble was suddenly broken into desperate bodies *flipping-flopping* in their corners.

The last thing I remember was Hamid, who had somehow scurried out of the brawl and was running wildly up the block. I couldn't believe he was leaving us behind. 'Yo fatass!' I called out to him, but he was long gone, out of hearing range.

He wouldn't have heard me, if at that moment, I had decided to tell him that my brief feeling of cordial dosti for him had evaporated into the night breeze. That I hated him again, that I had hated him for months since Jess had told me about them, and that up to my last days, I would continue to hate him. And without him, without Jess, without anyone who knew me well enough on this entire hemisphere—barring my long lost brother, who hadn't known me for years, either, had he?—what was I to do here? Who would understand me in Amreeka? Who would translate me?

And then I pictured Papa, and I wondered what he would think, and that's when the real panic kicked in, and I heard Papa's voice spitting at me between bites of samosa, and I bit my lip and closed my eyes.

TWENTY-TWO

There had been no arrests that night. A tall, blonde policeman questioned me and let me go. Tapiwa the African Prince was with me, but somewhere in the blur of the drunken night, we had started to walk in opposite directions. As I walked home, I passed out. When I finally opened my eyes, I was lying on my side on cool, wet grass, and all around me it smelled fresh—like the forewarning of warm weather to come. I saw a giant erect pillar penetrating the sky on the horizon, and, when I turned over, a bulbous dome on the other. The Washington Monument and the Capitol. My ears still buzzed from the previous night's Michael Jackson hollers—*Sha-mone!*—and from the swirling police sirens. I remembered Hamid leaving me behind.

I looked up at the blue, oh, perfectly blue sky. Blue like the crayon I filled up in the skies in every KG-class drawing. Blue and clean, unblemished by the greying pollution of the world I had grown up in. The sky always seemed to be the deepest blue in Washington, as if professionally photoshopped, and complemented those perfectly cotton-white blobs of floating clouds. Yaar, this sight was normal to those who were from here, those who never looked up because they already felt elevated above the rest of the world...but I could lose track of time mesmerized by that blueness. Around me, tiny creatures scurried and chirped, squirrels and groundhogs, and robins that hopped over the blades of grass before taking flight. In India, the fattest little critters were the rats of the night, nesting in millions on railway tracks and feasting on the mountains of infested urban garbage in every city. In

Washington, even the rodents of the city seemed harmless, even those fatass pigeons, plump and healthy, flying around the perfect skies, shitting down their blessings over the rest of us. I stayed still for a few minutes basking in the warmth of the morning sun. I suddenly remembered the policeman who had patiently asked me my age, which I had exaggerated by a few months 'Twenty-one', and he simply said 'Be careful now.' He patted my back and let me go.

I checked my pockets and found that I still had my phone and my wallet; but missing from my belongings was that good ol' life-giving *swishing-swashing* credit card. *Whoosh*, it had disappeared. I panicked and looked around in the wet grass. I fished out my phone to call the karaoke bar, but it was closed.

I needed to call Papa back home, much like I had done whenever I had got in trouble in Delhi. I could hear his voice. *So irresponsible,* he would say to me. *Absent-minded chootia. You have absolutely zero value for money.*

Sach mein bolun? He was right. How was I supposed to have any of this mysterious value at all? Papa grew up in a different time, yaar; but for me, such things didn't matter. Nothing mattered if you have money in India—not an eight per cent increase in petrol prices; or the rising cost of onions and tomatoes; or college students committing suicide because their marks did not match the expectations of the competitive job market; or farmers committing suicide because of mounting debt; or even a government announcement in the middle of the night stating that your currency notes were useless *namasteyji thankyouverymuch.* The entire country went nuts forming serpentine lines outside the banks, but Papa figured a way out of it. If you're rich in India, you always figure a way out.

Back at Saxon Hall, on the fifth floor, I stopped in the kitchen. It was dark, except for a few beams of sunlight streaming in from the two high windows opposite the entrance. The TV was on, and there was Tapiwa the African Prince, slumped comfortably on a couch, clicking on his controller, playing the newest *Halo* on the console, too engrossed to notice me. Next to him was Andrew, dressed in his usual pinstriped pyjamas and vest, silently watching the screen.

'Yo, Prince,' I said.

Tapiwa paused the game and turned around, and so did Andrew a few seconds after him.

'Yoooo Viz,' Tapiwa the African Prince gave me wide smile. 'You made it.'

I sat on a plastic seat behind them. The remains of the previous night's dinner were strewn around the table: empty cups of instant noodles and unfinished cans of Coke.

'Where's that fatass?' I asked.

'Hamid's not with you?'

'He left after…' and a faint memory of the blue police lights came flashing back again, '…after the fight.'

'I know, brother,' Tapiwa turned towards me. 'Shit…I bailed on you, too, afterwards, didn't I? Sorry about that. It got wild.'

I nodded. It was okay. Sach mein, it was fine. I could have stayed here last night, sitting in this same kitchen, studying with Tapiwa, undisturbed. Now I remembered—if Hamid hadn't shown up, we would have stayed here, probably just a little stoned, just enough to help us concentrate without rendering us useless, and worked on our theses, instead of being out in the streets like we were fucking freshmen again. And where, behen-ki-chod, was that fatass now?

'Do we have something to eat?' I asked Tapiwa.

'Sure, sure, ya man, I know there's some more ramen here.'

'No, no, I mean, something else man. I'm feeling sick. You still have some Froot Loops?' I asked.

'Hey man,' Tapiwa leaned closer. 'Is something wrong?'

'No, no.'

'What's up, brother?'

'It's fine,' I insisted. 'Just need something to eat.'

'Viz. What's up?'

I sighed. 'Yo, Prince, I lost my card again.'

'Oh...fuck.... Nah, don't worry, brother. Just call and cancel. Did you call and cancel?'

'I think it's at the karaoke place. Or outside, on the pavement. Or when I stumbled and walked.... Yaar, I don't remember the walk at all. It's all blank. I don't remember where I went. Papa will be so mad. Papa will fucking kill me.'

'Nah, brother, you don't need to worry,' Tapiwa laughed. 'It's just a card. No big deal. It comes and goes, you know. We all lose it.'

'You don't know my Papa.'

Tapiwa looked at the paused game on the TV screen, and then back at me. I finally locked eyes with him again—his big, bright eyes—and I knew that he, too, probably had a Papa or an Auntie or someone back home in Zimbabwe—a 'King' or 'Queen' to his 'Prince'—who had helped him make it here, someone who was counting on him, someone who had invested in his dreams, someone that he had to make sure to never let down.

'He doesn't think much of me, Prince,' I said.

I needed to brush my teeth. My breath still smelled of beer. I was still drunk from the night before.

'Listen, that's no big deal,' Tapiwa cleared his throat to speak in a deeper voice, his voice of quotation. '"Few sons are equal to their fathers; most fall short, all too few surpass them."'

'Is that some fucking Zimbabwean proverb?'

'It's the *Odyssey*.'

I laughed.

'Just cancel that card,' he said. 'It'll be fine.'

'How will cancelling the card solve anything?'

'What do you mean? Cancel it. Get a new card.'

'It's my *card*, Prince,' I heard my own voice crack. Nahi nahi, how can I explain it? I was suddenly feeling a surge of emotion within, samjhe? Like when on the first night I met Jess, Hamid deliberately, vigorously shook a can of beer before handing it to me. And when I pulled the tab, behenchod, I opened the can....

'It's my card,' I said. 'What will I do without my card? I'm a tourist here. An outsider. I don't even belong here. How will I pay for things?'

'What are you talking about, Viz? It's not that big a deal. Cancel and....'

'Don't you remember what they all said yesterday? The stuff they called Hamid? Those fuckers outside General Song's Chicken?'

Tapiwa sighed. Did I have to say it out loud, behenchod? Could he not understand what I was talking about? That fight had got ugly. Tapiwa would understand, wouldn't he? He had probably heard things before, racial insults far more degrading than I could imagine. I was trying to articulate what had been haunting me since I opened my eyes on the dewy grass this morning.

Tapiwa pressed his lips together and nodded

'They were crazy,' he said. 'Fuck them.'

'I mean...' and now I shifted a little on my seat, because I realized that in all my years of knowing Tapiwa or Hamid or Gokul or Jess or any of the black and brown and white and pink and whatever friends in America, I had not once spoken to anyone about those colours. '...It was bad, wasn't it?'

Tapiwa smirked a little, as if half-amused by my concern. 'Sure.'

'So, Viz,' Andrew finally turned around. 'Took four years, but you made it to the Unites States of Fucking America. It's been a long time comin'.'

He had a deep, baritone voice, not quite Morgan Freeman narrating the story of your life, but deep enough to send a bass effect around the kitchen. It seemed to be a juxtaposition of sorts, carrying a heavy weight in the way he said 'fucking' but also jumping over the words lightly, like a pebble skipping over a still lake.

He stretched his pyjama-clad legs out in my direction.

'I heard what happen to you all last night,' Andrew said. 'That shit was terrible. But why are you even surprised? It's nothing at all. That's what this country is. That's what this country does.'

'But here?' I said, 'in D.C.? I didn't expect....'

Andrew got up to his feet. He walked towards the kitchen counter behind him and flicked the switch on our shared kettle—it was Gokul's, but it was all of ours, samjhe? Then, he fished out a cup of instant noodles from the cupboard above the counter and peeled the top open. He placed both his arms in his jacket pockets and strolled next to the counter, waiting for the water to boil.

'Motherfucker, there are parts of this country where I can't even sit at a fucking Starbucks without people thinking I'm there to start something,' Andrew said. 'And somehow, you expect to be treated like a—whatchu call it?—a fucking "maharaja"? Damn, Viz. How long have you been here? You don't get to start complaining yet. You can be the king of your little village back home; but in America, the darker you are, the darker it gets.'

The water bubbled in the kettle behind him, *bubblingbubblingbubbling* till the little machine went *klat*—a short, violent snap.

Andrew poured the hot water carefully into the little plastic cup and then brought it to me. 'Eat something,' he said. A spicy, warm smell filled up the room.

He was right, of course. I had fallen into a comfort zone here, high on the clean oxygen of Washington, excited by its mighty structures, seduced by its limitless possibilities. But after nearly four years, I had begun to notice the haze again, where I was alone on the cold metro, where I would always be a foreigner who looked, talked, and smelled different. Where I would never think in Fahrenheits or miles or pounds or nickels. Where no amount of practised accents and slang could change how I spoke.

Where I could never be home.

But where, indeed, was home? Ever since the riots, I had been a stranger in India, too. Papa had a front lawn that kept the pollution and population of the city away from our doors, and car windows that kept us insulated from the scooter drivers on the streets, and airline tickets that ensured that we would never ride in those exposed, shared train coaches again.

Haan, I was a pardesi back in India, too—a foreigner in my own land, uncomfortable in the dusty outskirts of Varanasi, or the traffic jams in New Delhi. I was among the percentage of a few of my countryfolk who could afford to create a Parallel India of our own that uneasily fit over the real country.

I had now flown multiple times, USA to India to back, Washington to Delhi, Delhi to Washington, one foot in each land, but without a seat in either one. Kabhi here and kabhi there but, mostly, kahin bhi nahin. Nowhere at all.

I blew on the noodles, waiting patiently till the soup grew a little colder, before taking a timid sip.

∞

Most of my fellow countrymen in Amreeka were like Gokul—aspiring engineers who topped their small-town board exams back home, coming from families who could barely afford to buy them a computer; and now, they found themselves halfway across the world, wearing plaid full-sleeved shirts and combing down their eager eyebrows, threatening to fix your printers, take away American jobs, and launch the next big start-up that would change the world or make them billionaires or, at least, secure them US citizenship.

And sach mein, that is what it's all about then, hai ki nahi? Every small step to ensure that their next generation is born not in B-tier cities in Telangana or Bihar but in white-washed suburbs in Texas or Illinois. They want the education first, then the job that follows, with that ever-elusive H1B working visa, then a green card, and then citizenship. Somewhere along the way they hope to lure in a good Indian wife—who would otherwise be way out of their league—to start a good desi family, speak with a bastardized new accent, and complain that all those *other* minorities were causing too much of a mela en route to their own American dreams.

That is the life Gokul wanted, and he worked his fucking ass off for it. One day, yes, he will get that green card, although diplomatic and political drama will keep him a few years away from full citizenship. In the midst of all that, he will briefly return to Hyderabad to meet all forty-six members of his extended family and get introduced to his future bride. She will seem shy at first, but they will soon begin to bond over aloo bondas, and he will start a family with her in Frisco, Texas, and after a few years together, she will shatter his expectations of a submissive Indian wife, find a job in marketing, and tell him to cook his own goddamn biryani.

And if he really is lucky, then he will find his American utopia not in Frisco, but in California, just like Rishi bhaiya did.

Rishi bhaiya, saala, I still haven't told you much about him, have I? Chhoro, forget everything else I've said—*he* is the reason that I wanted to come to America. Rishi bhaiya, my elder brother. He was the one who did it first. While I was still in my early teens, he paved the path—he got his master's degree, locked in that H1B, and as soon as he made it in Silicon Valley, got bumped into one of those exceptionally fast lanes for his green card.

Ruko, ruko, let's rewind a little. Before America was Delhi, and before Delhi was Varanasi, and before Varanasi were the riots, and for all of my short, barely lived life, I believed that my brother had left the family—left Papa—to escape the stain of those riots, to purge himself of the stench that would stick to the rest of us, a stench that would emanate off my burning body on the cremation pyre along with the aroma of camphor and smoke.

But in the moment of my death, I'm pulled even further back in time with my brother, and so I know that the riots weren't the inciting incident of Rishi bhaiya's departure, but the final push. It's as if I'm seeing through my brother's eyes now, wearing a VR headset that shows me Papa's index finger pointed in our direction, the weight of expectations on Bhaiya's young shoulders, a promise—no, a threat—that *beta, one day YOU have to run this business*; and *beta, you hardly seem interested in our work*; or *beta, when will you ever shape up?*

So, he left. He left the city, and then, the country.

Bas, uske baad kya hona tha? Rishi bhaiya had never planned to look back home—he was tall, fair, intelligent, and had a million-dollar future ahead of him. Top-notch matrimonial material. Every Indian parent's model child; but ever since he had stormed out of Varanasi, the only parents he answered to were Raghu maama and Sharmeen maami in Delhi. Childless themselves, Rishi bhaiya had filled their empty nest—and, later, so had I. Bhaiya, after moving to the States, soon made them into proud step-parents, by getting engaged to a US citizen, a second-generation Indian Hindu, who fasted for him on Karva Chauth and knew how to drape her sari for formal occasions. Back in Delhi, Maama and Maami celebrated his engagement by shoving motichoor laddus into each other's mouths. Fireworks went off across their colony in Malviya Nagar. Badhai ho badhai, said the neighbours, citizenship to ab pucci hai. Rishi beta is almost American now!

As per Rishi bhaiya's request, my father wasn't invited to the party. As per my father's request, my mother didn't attend, either.

His celebration was truly glorious, deserved and earned after years of lonely toil abroad. Back when he was still a student at the University of Pennsylvania, Rishi bhaiya rarely wasted time. He kept a busy schedule between his classes and part-time jobs, and allowed himself no more than a single beer every alternate Saturday at the Irish bar off-campus. After getting his master's, he bought himself a 2004 Mitsubishi Galant, and while driving the I-476 to New York for a meeting one time, he saw something peculiar that nearly made him spill his latte on the new leather seat cover. In the approaching darkness of dusk, there was a short, elderly Indian woman—complete with blue sari and a yellow marigold in her hair—standing alone next to a broken-down minivan on the side of the road, furiously typing into her cell phone.

Usually he didn't do this, but Bhaiya decided to stop. He swerved right, changed lanes too quickly, and parked on the shoulder behind the minivan. The auntie—because every Indian woman who is considerably older than you is an auntie, hai na?—looked like she needed help, and Rishi bhaiya would later admit that he would have never stopped had she not been one of 'our people'. She had a flat tyre and was waiting for roadside assistance, and since it was getting dark, Bhaiya offered to wait with her. He was well-built and soft-spoken, and she immediately felt safe with him. She was excited at hearing his Hindi, even though her mother tongue was Malayalam, and they would have scarcely understood each other if they hadn't settled on English.

'Thank you, beta,' she said, and Bhaiya replied in mock shyness, 'Auntie, it's okay, I'm only doing my duty.' She asked him what he did for a living, and he replied that he worked in software development. 'Good,' she answered, and told him she had a nephew working in San Francisco who could help him out. 'Sure,' Bhaiya replied, and thought to himself, *I'm sure this Random Auntie knows someone in San Francisco who can help me. Why not?*

But as it turned out, she wasn't exaggerating—that Random Auntie had a Cousin Sister whose Son-In-Law's Younger Brother had indeed worked for Yahoo! in California, and was now launching his own app. On one of those second Saturdays after a beer, Rishi bhaiya decided to send this guy a message, and a week later, he was in his first meeting with the founder and CEO of SkipMode in Sunnyvale.

Soon after Rishi bhaiya was hired, SkipMode went public, and for a three-day news cycle, they were the talk of Silicon Valley. It was here that he met Nikki, and within a few years, moved with her and their infant daughter to the twenty-eighth floor of a two-bedroom apartment. They spent their weekends at potluck parties with other young Indian couples. Nikki was born and raised in Chicago and now worked at SkipMode with him. She wore Cubs jerseys to work and had more friends than he did, but he didn't mind that.

Before all of this, however, before he had met Nikki, before SkipMode and California and that Random Auntie on the I-476, while he was still a student at UPenn, Rishi bhaiya came back to Delhi for a long summer break. It was his first trip to the motherland in over two years. Of course, he had no intention of visiting Papa and Mummy. But one of his first chores was to drive to the domestic terminal of the IGI airport to pick up his little brother, who walked out with three heavy bags, with a sweaty face, ashamed of having recently lost thirty-thousand rupees at the airport in Varanasi.

Me.

∽

'Bro! What's up?' Rishi bhaiya waved at me outside the airport. He stood straight, smiling, with the priceless confidence of a young man who was about to make it in America, for whom all this tension-vension of an Indian life was now just a temporary inconvenience.

'Hi, Bhaiya,' I extended my hand to shake his. I hadn't seen him in four years, and he looked taller and beefier than ever before, and even had a faint trail of facial hair growing on the edges of his fair face.

He slapped my hand away and instead pulled me in for a hug. I hugged him back, tighter.

'How was your flight?'

'Bad, Bhaiya,' I shook my head. 'I think I lost a lot of money before departure. Haven't stopped worrying about it since.'

He nodded his head and pried the luggage cart away from me.

'Don't worry bro, such things happen. Chalo, your maama-maami are waiting for you. You still love aloo parathas, no?'

'They're the best,' I smiled.

'How's Sakshi?'

'She's good, Bhaiya,' I said, still beaming in his presence. 'She misses you a lot.'

'I miss her, too, Vishnu. Does she still chatter all the time? *Bak-bak-bak-bak*'

'No, no,' I smiled. 'She's better now.'

I was waiting to see if he would enquire about our parents, or show any signs of nostalgia for home, for our childhood, for that Mehmoorganj house, for our cricket games in the gully, for the bicycle rides we took through traffic to catch matinee movie shows, for the stale popcorn and eclairs at the theatre.

But he didn't ask.

'Wow, Vishnu,' he said as he walked towards the car. 'I can barely even recognize you! All these pimples popping up, huh? Who's the big man, now?'

I had left Varanasi after Class 10. I was still a good student back then (sach mein!) and scored a percentage that was good enough to get me admitted to Delhi Modern School for my eleventh. Papa and Mummy had frowned at my decision, but I was stubborn, yaar, I didn't back down. Rishi bhaiya had charted this path—against their wishes, of course—and I was determined to follow it. I had enjoyed my holidays in Delhi before that, the capital with its multitude of malls and pretty girls and fast-food restaurants. Finally giving in, Papa said, chalo theek hai, and said I could live in Delhi with my Mummy's brother's family: Raghu maama and Sharmeen maami.

As he drove, Rishi bhaiya complained about the traffic, and said he was still struggling to get used to left-hand side driving after cruising around American suburbs in his Mitsubishi. 'It's complete peace there, Vishnu.' He spoke with an authority in his voice I didn't remember him having, 'Not like the uthal-puthal here. Look, look at that,' he pointed as an autorickshaw closely avoided hitting a scooterwallah ahead of us. 'How do people even drive here? And it's so noisy. I feel like I'm always going to die, no?'

No, I thought, because, how was I to know what was good driving and what wasn't? Delhi at least had *some* traffic rules; Varanasi was a complete shitshow, where the only law was to give the fat cows their right of way. For me, Delhi's controlled chaos—road signs, traffic lights, the occasional cop pulling over a speeding driver—was already a major leap ahead in human civilization.

But I was too impressed by his stories to interrupt him. He spoke about meaningless things with passion, like Starbucks lattes and Yelp restaurant reviews. He told me about the unpolluted air and the wide-open spaces. 'We know nothing here, Vishnu,' he said. 'We know nothing about space. You only went to New York, no? It's so crowded and filthy there. No, bro, you need to see the *real* America. It's empty, no kidding. So few people. You could drive for hours and not see another human being. It's a trip.'

He told me about the time when his car was rear-ended in Philadelphia. He made a complaint, and the perpetrator was fined, and insurance paid him some money, and that was that— end of story. Bas! It was simple, he said. It didn't matter if the person behind him was a crack addict or the president. Laws were laws, no?

I nodded. It all seemed so fair and just to me. So clean. By the time we arrived at Raghu maama's flat in Malviya Nagar, I had already begun to envision my future. After finishing Class 11 and 12 in Delhi, I, too, would go to America. I, too, wanted long drives without the noise pollution of honking traffic, and to drink black coffee every morning. And behenchod, those burgers, too, in a nation where humans were finally above cattle in the food chain. I wanted his life.

Nearly two years later, when it was time to apply for college,

I chose computer engineering only because I thought it would be the easiest path to follow in *his* footsteps. Study what he studied. I definitely wasn't looking forward to growing old walking around overheated factories in Varanasi like Papa did. I only had Rishi bhaiya, samjhe?

Sakshi didi called that evening to ask about the flight, the weather in Delhi, if I had eaten dinner at Raghu maama's place yet, if I had eaten my vegetables. She didn't need to mention the lost thirty thousand; she knew I had already heard from Papa about it.

'How is Rishi?' she asked.

'He's good. He's looking so...so big. So old.'

'American food, no?'

'Maybe Mummy and Papa and you can come to see us?' I said. 'All five of us. Just for a week, two weeks maybe?'

There was a pause on the other end of the line. Didi, hardly ever at a loss of words, seemed to have suddenly lost her voice.

'Papa won't come,' she said finally.

'Maybe...maybe we can come to Varanasi then.'

Didi sighed. 'You're old enough to understand things, hai na, Vishnu?'

Perhaps I was, I thought, or perhaps, *understanding things* was less a matter of age, and more a matter of choice. I would be no wiser at eighteen, or twenty-one, or in my personal forever.

∽

Didi? Kya bataon.... Sakshi didi had been instructed early in her life by Mummy that, *Suno, you don't need to worry about your career, samjhi? We'll find you a good husband.* No, my sister never had a chance; while I drifted further away, she had been instructed to stay in the confines of our hometown. When she was admitted to that famous arts college in Pune, Papa pulled her cheek lovingly and said, 'Beti, you're our favourite, we can never let our daughter go so far away,' and forced her to study at the local Ravidas Mahila Inter College. She had to attend her classes diligently and spend time with my parents and get married when she was told to. A few years later, she stood solemnly under the weight of the glittery silver make-up on her wedding day, watching her husband-to-be dance wildly with his baraat and march forward with a brass band, and she wished she could dance with them, too. I was part of that jubilant baraat, a little drunk, moving my awkward, skinny limbs to the band's classic Bollywood music, mouthing along to 'Saat Samundar Paar'. And a few weeks later, I was back in the United States, blowing up Papa's money halfway across the world, living a life that would never be available to my sister.

But all that happened later. Back when I was only seeing dreams of America, my plan to follow Bhaiya was flawed: I had underestimated how much work would actually be involved. Suno, I had only spent a few months with him in Delhi before he returned to his ongoing American dream. I didn't understand how he earned his money, what he did for those Starbucks lattes and gas for his Mitsubishi.

Nahi nahi, unlike him, I didn't have to think about money. I still had Papa's largesse, and suddenly, Papa had become rich. I chose Washington, or perhaps, Washington chose me, because D.C. Tech gladly accepted the full tuition Papa had agreed to pay. All tens of thousands of dollars.

In Amreeka, I was handed that unstoppable silver credit card, and no fee was too much. I spent my time buying drinks in sticky Washington karaoke bars—yes, dekho now, like the bar in Chinatown on the night Hamid abandoned me. Or at Lucky Luke on the night I was shot.

Suno, Wildhair wasn't rich or powerful. I mean, he *was* powerful cocking his trigger in that moment. But not full-power, samjhe? Not like the power Papa's money could buy in a small city. The power to change laws or at least survive its consequences.

No, on the night I died, Wildhair committed a crime and he was arrested; yaar, it was actually very simple. There were fifty-three witnesses who saw him shoot me. Within minutes of that, fataak se he was locked up. No jhik-jhik, no drama. Apart from that one dead body, of course.

TWENTY-THREE

It is no longer fashionable to speak about reincarnation, not even for those who are hardly fashionable, like my mother. Yes, there was perhaps a time when she was younger that Mummy had enjoyed the idea of the immortal atman, a time when she believed that when her Labrador Imli died, its soul entered the body of another Labrador, and when the second Labrador lived a good life, it got elevated to a horse in its next reincarnation, and then, that horse would become an elephant to be venerated by people like the god Ganesh, and this Ganesh elephant would be reborn as Hanuman, a vanar-warrior that swung from tree to tree with its other monkey buddies, until the monkey's soul would finally be reborn as a human being. This was where our Hindu idea of the life cycle completely synchronized with Darwin's evolution, survival not of the fittest, but of the dharmic. Once human, the soul would rise up the ladder of the caste system—the rungs of which are inaccessible during one's lifetime. If it's truly a special atman, it may even get the privilege of being reborn as a cow—a being ranked above most humans—and on and on, until it reaches true enlightenment or finds a shortcut to the supposedly blessed shores of my hometown, Varanasi. There is a promise here that, as the soul passes the river to the other side, Shiv himself appears and whispers the magical password—the taraka mantra—vocalizing better than most contemporary rappers the complicated flow of these ancient Sanskrit verses, offering freedom from the cycle of rebirth, onwards to nirvana, heaven, etc.

Mummy grew up; the karmic cycle was now an afterthought,

more metaphor than reality, a fable to be good and keep praying, and when her father died of an early heart attack, she lost the desire to track Imli's soul any more.

That was, until Happy Singh, lost for other words to greet Mummy after my cremation, folded his hands and smiled, 'Madamji,' he said. 'At least we brought him back to Varanasi. At least his atman will get some shanti here. His soul will cross the river.'

Kya soul, yaar? Kya reincarnation? When all this is over, there will be no sin or rivers of gold with celestial virgins, no rebirths into any higher forms, samjhe? Maybe I will just return to earth as a squirrel somewhere in the heart of D.C., scurrying around Dupont Circle, a low-level rodent, but with American citizenship, at least.

Mummy had no response for Happy Singh. They were having lunch at the factory, in Papa's office, amid the splash of white walls and upholstery. Now, there was also a photograph of me framed on the wall next to my grandfather's, both of us garlanded and departed, alternating generations of the Agarwal household watching over Papa's desk.

Mummy thought about me that night, and her memories of Imli returned, and she wondered what would happen to my soul, what the rules of karma were if the soul had been let free so far from home, across oceans, in another land with another accent, where they believed in foreign gods that were outcasts to the cycles of her culture. She wondered if the rules allowed my soul to be released in Varanasi at all, or if my atman had escaped somewhere and was lost in transit, never to be found riding the luggage carousel at the Indira Gandhi airport in New Delhi.

What Mummy and Happy Singh and the scriptures and the pandits and any number of self-defined inexperienced experts of the after-death get terribly wrong is that it isn't the individual soul that is reincarnated, it's the dust of every soul, every particle, every neutron and atom that ever existed—or will exist—that bangs and crunches and bangs and crunches and explodes and implodes and starts again, and starts again, and starts again.

This is where I fly to now, past my death and my birth, past the night that I was knit together in my mother's womb in the mouldy, dark bedroom at the Ram Guest House in Faizabad, past my mother's and my father's births, past the time my ancestors crossed over the rough borders of what eventually became my country, past the Neanderthals and the apes that preceded us, past the years the world was covered under ice, before a time when the cyanobacteria added the familiar tint of blue to the skies. I follow the remnants of the first glimmers of light and energy, matter and anti-matter, scrunched into the smallest, heaviest form I could possibly be, floating in the universe's first quarks and leptons, until I opened my eyes to a world beyond the wall of known time and space.

But there is nothing here. It only gets smaller and smaller, and denser and denser, and from there, on to a smaller universe, smaller bangs, hotter space to share with the quarkety quarks, and on and on, an infinite JavaScript loop to crash all functionalities. Ad infinitum, behenchod.

TWENTY-FOUR

Mummy tossed and turned under the covers, tired but unable to sleep. She had been married to Papa for years, but still struggled to get used to his habits. In the bedroom, the bright, white glare of the television pierced through the dark of the night. Papa was watching one of his favourite news shows, the one where a blabbering gadha invited a panel of guests, only to then shout over them. Papa lowered the volume just enough for Mummy, too low for her to understand the content of the rage on screen, but loud enough so that she couldn't ignore the rage itself. Every few minutes, Papa jerked forward to scratch his feet, roughly drawing his nails back and forth across his skin, until his rashes became a deeper red, and parts of his ankles turned crusty and white.

'Lower the volume, Shankar,' Mummy mumbled.

'Haan haan, we'll do it, we'll do it.'

The angrier the host got on screen, the more fired-up Papa became. Tonight's anger was about a protest in Delhi, regarding students who had refused to stand up for the national anthem in a cinema hall. 'These young people are a scar on our country,' the host said on TV. A wedge of unrealistically shiny, black hair bobbed on his head. 'Send them to Pakistan if they can't stand for our beautiful, glorious anthem.'

'Send all those chootias to Pakistan,' Papa echoed in bed.

'Such a beautiful, glorious anthem,' said the host.

'Right, right,' Papa said.

'Oh, ho, shut it off, Shankar,' Mummy nudged him.

'We'll do it,' Papa clicked his tongue in frustration. 'Always with the khich-khich, Pushpa. Go to sleep. Always khich-khich.'

When he wasn't watching this bakchodi on the news, Papa watched comedy shows where contestants tripped over their own feet, and when he wasn't watching those, he watched other news channels that focused on the sex scandals of small-town politicians. Sometimes, he turned on an old movie until the songs finally lulled him to sleep.

'Always with the khich-khich,' he repeated. This was his favourite ammunition in his arsenal against Mummy. He used it when she protested his late-night drinking with the Trader's Union friends, when she complained that he didn't show her brother any respect, when she wanted him to turn the TV off. 'You ladies and your khich-khich.' He knew she hated it when he reduced her concerns to mere noise. It was his checkmate—if she didn't speak out, it would build up inside her to the point of unbearable frustration, but if she said anything, she was being a blabbermouth. Full of nonsense.

Three times during their marriage—three times until my death, that is—Mummy decided to leave him. All three times, she packed up some of her clothes and all of her jewellery and left us to stay with Raghu maama in Delhi. She threatened Papa: *This is it! I am just not happy! This is the last time you will see me!* But Mummy's weakness was that she could never clearly express herself, that she got tongue-tied when Papa used his logic. 'All your khich-khich, again! What did I even do? Tell me *one thing* I did?' and that's all it took to make her stutter. She could not say that it was not *one* thing but a jigsaw puzzle of many little things, you understand? It was his breath, and his habit of drinking late into the night with his friends, and the riots, and how, sometimes in front of their friends, he raised an authoritative hand to silence her—*Chup! You keep quiet* he would say.

She would leave, but she would always come back. It took a week or two, but she always changed her mind. *Those young children*, she told herself. *And he really is a good man who takes care* of his family, isn't he? They had been through so much together. Her kismet, she believed, was to always be by his side. She couldn't even think the word 'divorce' in her mind. *It's not in our culture, no, no: it's only the goras who do the 'D-word'.*

And although she never admitted it to anyone, she pondered going on her own 'Rishi yatra', and follow in my brother's footsteps. When she saw that Rishi bhaiya was serious about staying in Delhi, serious about never coming back to Papa, she told herself that she could do that, too. She could leave Papa and his sins behind. She bought a ticket to fly to Delhi on Tuesday, but on that morning, while packing my school lunchbox, she packed a 5 Star chocolate bar, and decided to miss her flight.

Whenever she returned home or changed her mind, Mummy found excuses to love the things about Papa that actually annoyed her. She looked at him with adoring eyes when he drank his sixth or seventh whisky-soda at a dinner party, smiling at his confidence when he drunkenly slapped his hand on a friend's shoulder and brought his face uncomfortably close to people when he spoke to them. She told herself she liked the taste of his whisky breath at night because he smelled musky and raw, or the paan and gutka he chewed, *Like a real man should*, she thought. And on the nights the drinking got really bad, when he began to repeat himself and stumbled over his words, 'Too much khich khich…khich…khich…frauds and chootias all of them…' Mummy pacified herself in silence. *At least he doesn't eat meat any more*, she thought. *At least he quit smoking.*

Soon, she began to sleep more peacefully next to Papa when he snored. Unlike the rumblings of the TV, Papa's loud, engine-like sounds never bothered her. She had grown up in a small household where she shared a tiny bedroom with her parents and her brother; hearing the sound of someone alive sleeping near her made her feel comfortable and protected. She liked the safety of the snore.

Mummy awoke long after Papa in the mornings, too. No

matter how much he had had to drink the night before, Papa would be up by five every morning. He would bundle up in his shawl and his sandals and take a walk on the stone-paved path in the front garden. Himanshu was instructed to wake up at the same time and keep a cup of chai ready by the time Papa was ready for his morning walk. He sipped chai in the lawn and worried about work, and he would be two cups down by the time Mummy stretched and got out of bed.

'You'll never lose those kilos like that, lazy woman,' Papa would say. As she had grown older, Mummy had begun to worry about her weight. Her stomach was turning into a deep, round vase and she had quickly outgrown the designer tracksuits she'd bought in Europe. She was heavier now than she had been during both her pregnancies.

So, she decided to get up early for some exercise. She put on her salwar kameez and white Reebok sneakers and walked around the garden with Papa. When the walks weren't enough, she purchased a Belly Burner to wear around her waist, hoping it would melt the fat off her body. When the Belly Burner wasn't enough, she began to subscribe to Bollywood Dance workouts on Dish TV to sweat the weight off of her. It wasn't enough.

Papa, of course, had already grown fat by then—much fatter than her. But it didn't matter to him, and whenever he outgrew his shrinking Lacoste shirts, he just bought new ones.

When Mummy was six-and-a-half months pregnant with my elder twin siblings in Faizabad, she called upon a jyotish one afternoon to visit the Ram Guest House. She forced Papa to drop his other errands and sit alongside her for their consultation. To Papa's surprise, this jyotish turned out to be nothing as he expected. He was young, perhaps around Papa's age, or perhaps only a few years older. He had a sharp, angled face, and pronounced dark eyebrows, but in every other sense, had the features of a woman: large eyes, long eyelashes, and full lips. Papa saw that this jyotish wore some colour on his lips, too, not quite the lipsticks that Mummy used, but something to accentuate the curves of his mouth. When he smiled, a blinding white set of teeth flashed at Papa. When he spoke, his voice was soft, welcoming, high-pitched.

'Namaste Shankarji,' he said and smiled. 'Madam has told me a lot about you.'

Papa turned to Mummy and raised his eyebrow. 'What is this all about?'

'Sit, Shankar,' Mummy nudged. 'Rishiji has something important to tell us.'

So, they sat around the wooden table in the guest house's lobby, on plastic chairs, while the jyotish reached out and grabbed Mummy's hand. At first, he studied her palm itself, and traced a finger slowly—sensually, Papa thought—over the lines on her hand. Then, he held the palm over both of his hands and swayed it to check its balance, its shape, its size. He let his index finger trace the length of each of her fingers, starting with the pinkie and ending with her thumb, and in the end, he asked her to form a fist, and peered at the back of her hand at the creases formed between her thumb and index finger. Finally, he let her go.

'Two boys,' he said. 'You're having twins, Shankarji,' he turned to Papa. 'Congratulations—two boys.'

Papa looked between the jyotish and Mummy, raising his eyebrow even higher. He could hardly believe this man's confidence. 'What kind of logic is this?' he asked.

'Uff-oh, Shankar,' Mummy frowned. 'You don't have to doubt everything, you know? Rishiji is one of the most renowned scholars in Ayodhya. Aren't you, Rishiji? Astrology, palm-reading, face reading, tarot cards, everything. Isn't that true, Rishiji?'

The jyotish smiled. 'Yes, madam. It is completely true.'

'Two boys, Shankar,' Mummy said. 'Aren't you happy?'

Papa stood up from his chair, slowly, and took a deep breath. 'It's…it's good news,' he said, almost in a soft whisper. 'Two boys.'

'It's great news, Shankar.'

'Two boys.'

Mummy had twins, a boy and a girl. The girl she named Sakshi after a favourite aunt she had lost in her youth, and the boy she insisted on naming Rishi, after the holy man who had only got fifty per cent of his prediction correct. Papa hated that name, but he couldn't argue with Mummy's demands on her special day. The jyotish came a day later to bless the twins. 'Congrats to both your children,' he said. 'They had such masculine energy, both of them. But no matter, Shankarji—now you have one of each.'

Mummy and Papa had to divide their limited means among four. They rented out the rooms at the guest house to long-stay customers at a ridiculously low rent—students who didn't mind the damp walls or the termite-infested furniture and afeem addicts who slept among the bedbugs, opium pulsing through their bloodstreams all night.

Papa stayed away from those addicts. His own vice was alcohol. He drank when he was happy and drank when he was sad, he drank with his friends, and drank all by himself. At first, he hid the booze from Mummy, but the pretences were soon dropped, and he drank every night before climbing into bed beside her.

Mummy noticed that his snoring had begun to get heavier, that he made strange moaning sounds in his sleep, and if he was mistakenly awoken, he sprang up in bed as if he had been chased out of a nightmare.

'How can all this sharab feel good, Shankar?' Mummy asked. 'Drinking every night....'

'You...you don't know anything,' Papa mumbled, sweating. 'Do you know how much stress we have? We have to feed all of us. We have to feed your twins. Always with the khich-khich. Don't know anything.'

'*My* twins?'

'Khich-khich all day. All that I hear....'

His grumbling turned into gibberish, so Mummy instead began spending the hours before sleep talking to her twin toddlers. 'How are we going to raise you?' she asked the sleeping children. They lay on a mattress on the floor, next to the bed.

'Who are you talking to?' Papa snorted.

'The rats,' Mummy retorted. 'Why do you care?'

Papa crept closer and wrapped his arms around her from behind.

'You don't need any other rodents when you have us.'

The rats had begun to die between the walls and behind the wooden boards of the cupboards. By then, the smell was so ubiquitous around the guest house that it didn't seem unnatural to Mummy any more. That night, with Didi and Bhaiya fast asleep next to the bed, and the little room dense with that heavy, decomposing smell, Mummy and Papa fell into each other's arms again.

'Let's make another one,' Papa smiled at her, kissing her cheeks, and rubbing his moustache against her upper lip.

'And them?' Mummy pointed at the twins, breathing silently in peaceful sleep.

'We love them, too,' Papa said and reached his hand around Mummy's waist. 'But we want another one.'

Mummy smiled and playfully slapped Papa on his cheek. 'You don't know how much it takes to carry *one* of these, do you?' She fell on her back and Papa rolled on top of her.

Mummy raised a hand to Papa's mouth, to shush his heavy breathing. Papa grabbed it and pulled it away from his face. With his other hand, he grabbed her other wrist, pinning her down under him.

'We want another boy.'

Mummy knew he did. From the day Didi and Bhaiya were born, Mummy had seen it in his eyes. He had not got over the betrayal, his promise of being gifted two sons. He had kissed my sister's forehead and danced with her in his arms, but when he sang to her, he used the male declension.

'Kitna pyaara baccha hai!' Papa sang. 'What a lovely child.'

'Kitni pyaari bacchi hai,' Mummy corrected him. 'What a

lovely girl.'

A girl was good, he had said, *Good, good, no problem! But she would leave home one day, she would take another's name, another's family lineage.*

But another boy, Papa's face would light up, *he would be our own, our legacy. Carry us forward even after we are gone.*

Mummy didn't protest. She wanted another boy, too. Not for any excuse of family name or legacies, but because, sometime after the jyotish's prophecy, she had herself begun to feel another boy-shaped hole in her womb, as if my Didi's gender had been a violation of Mummy's faith. She felt uneasy with the dissonance between promise and delivery, unsettled even by the perfect symmetry of the boy-girl duo of her twins. 'Yes,' she agreed with Papa. 'It's only fair.'

The bed creaked, a frail old wooden soul hoarsely calling for help with each of Papa's thrusts. Papa smelled the chameli fragrance of Mummy's shampoo. Mummy smelled the dead rats. And then, Papa was done.

Fair.

That's my Mummy, samjhe? She believed in everyone having their fair share of things. When she was young, her parents allowed her to feed one roti a day to the two neighbourhood stray dogs, and she would take her time carefully cutting the roti apart with a pair of scissors into equal sizes to ensure no dog got to eat even a centimetre more than the other. Later, when she filled up the registers of guests at the reception, she ensured that the information in each box was recorded—name, phone number, address, arrival date, departure date, signature—and even when customers couldn't provide her with all the details, she would guess and fill in whatever she could just to ensure that no boxes were left blank.

She wanted a boy because there was a blank box for one.

I was born on 22 May 1997. I weighed 3.3 kilograms at birth. I was healthy. I cried often.

Bhaiya and Didi had begun to speak by then—and speak often. But around me, Didi grew quieter. She watched me with silent envy being rocked in Mummy's bosom. But she also became more generous, and she gave Mummy the time she needed with me, and later, she didn't complain when her portion of food became smaller.

Papa had decided now, after holding me happily in his arms and doubling up his male pronouns, that enough was enough. That the food portions were not enough to sustain him any more. He had to do something. Something big. They needed to save money, to sell the guest house, to find another business, to move away to a different life.

One day, a former customer returned to the guest house, to Faizabad to visit the Janmabhoomi. It was that ancient man from Varanasi, the same one who had visited the guest house years ago and offered to sell Papa his beads business. One evening, as he sat across Papa at the reception, the man revealed that his condition was getting worse, that he couldn't even piss without exhausting himself half to death every night. That he was desperate. 'It's a good business,' he said. 'I've asked people everywhere, but they don't seem to trust me on this. There is good profit in beads, young man!'

I was there, too, twenty-one months old, nestled in Papa's shoulder, comfortable in the musk emanating from his unshaven cheeks.

This is it, Papa thought. His legs jittered as I bounced gleefully on his knees. Here was an old man almost as desperate as Papa himself. A man who would give him a bargain.

Papa made up his mind. He bought himself a bottle of desi whisky from the theka nearby and drank himself into a happy stupor. 'We're moving to Varanasi,' he announced to Mummy that night. 'We're going to be Banarasis now!' He fell asleep before she had a chance to ask him any questions.

On the train, travelling with a husband who didn't speak to

her, a daughter who plugged the headphones of her Walkman over her ears, an elder son lost in his Chacha Chaudhary comics, a toddler son who wouldn't stop crying, and with four heavy metal trunks containing their lives' belongings, Mummy went onwards to an unfamiliar new city. She burrowed her face into the polyester seat and sobbed. *This was ridiculous,* she thought. Of course, she had wanted to leave Faizabad, too. She, too, had had enough of that place, the smell of death, it's dark and wet corners, the list of names in that register. *But this was not the way.* She had wanted to be consulted, at least. She had wanted to support Papa or to doubt him. She had wanted a choice.

Papa had found a buyer for the Ram Guest House, an ambitious younger property developer in Faizabad who was planning to build a new cinema in its place. The money Papa made in return was enough to pay off the first instalment for Bhagwan Beads. While Mummy cried, Papa couldn't have been more excited about the move. He smiled out the window throughout the train journey and told himself that this would be the start of something big. That he would now be unstoppable.

In Varanasi, he got to work straight away, taking long chakkars around the factory property, planning things, complaining about things, visualizing his future. He inherited the staff and the property manager, including a sullen-faced man named Happy Singh in a light-blue turban whom Papa immediately felt comfortable with. 'But you need to fix your face. Smile yaar, Happy Singh. Don't be such a Saddy Singh all the time.'

All Mummy had, however, were her children and her new home, a small but airy flat in Mehmoorganj. My elder sister hated staying home, and against Mummy's wishes, ran downstairs to play street cricket with the neighbourhood boys. Sakshi had a sharp jawline and pencil-thin lips, and the neighbourhood ice-cream-wallah often mistook her for a boy. She decided to grow her hair longer to ensure that there wouldn't be any further confusion.

Some of the boys made fun of her on the first day she went

out to play with them, but Sakshi didi was undeterred. She practised her pace bowling every evening with a tennis ball. One day, she threw a bouncer with that ball and struck the best batsman hard on his nose, drawing blood and reducing him to tears. The rest of the boys decided to disallow pace bowling altogether. 'There's not enough space,' one of the snot-nosed kids said to Didi. 'Only spinning allowed now, okay? Practise your spinners.'

That snotty runt was named Dhiraj Prashant, and little Dhiraj was my age and my size, and I saw him in the same class when I first joined KG, sitting in the front row across from me. Our makeshift cricket fields were the thin alleyways between the buildings in Mehmoorganj. Even in the limited space, however, Dhiraj was too lazy to run after the ball and appointed himself the wicketkeeper. I disliked fielding, too, and only wanted to play if the other boys let me bat first. After the first few games, I decided that Dhiraj was going to be my best friend, and since Dhiraj didn't have any other best friends, he agreed. 'Pucca?' he offered a handshake.

'Pucca,' I said, shaking his hand.

Dhiraj's father was a professor of botany at the Banaras Hindu University, and on my sixth birthday, he came to our house with Dhiraj to present me with a plastic Batman action figure. Both Dhiraj and I had convinced our parents to buy us Shaktimaan costumes, which we wore for Rishi bhaiya and Sakshi didi's ninth birthday party. Dhiraj wore the black costume, and I wore the red one.

After the cake cutting, Rishi bhaiya, annoyed by the crowd and the noise, excused himself and went to his room to do his homework. Didi, however, danced into the night in her suspenders and denim jeans to 'Koi Kahe Kehta Rahe'. *We are new, so why should our thinking be old?*

One of the neighbourhood mothers at the party nudged Mummy. 'How old is your daughter today?'

'Nine,' Mummy replied with a smile.

'She acts just like a boy,' the woman said.

Later, when all the guests had left and Mummy and Papa lay in bed together, Mummy discovered that Papa—drunk and drowsy—had overheard that conversation.

'She's too old for this now,' Papa yawned, and he turned up the TV. Mummy told herself, *Yes, he was probably right,* and she spent the next hour attempting to silence the television noises in her head, failing to fall asleep.

Didi was never allowed to wear those denim jeans again. Mummy asked her to stop playing cricket, and because it depressed her now, Didi stopped *watching* cricket on TV, too. She matured quickly then, and began to copy the way Mummy dressed and walked in a duck-waddle and spoke with sputtering machine-gun speed. 'Like a tape recorder on fast forward,' Papa said.

Fast-forward some more. We moved from that Mehmoorganj house to the one in Nagwa with the big garden, and one day Didi was told to stop talking too much. She was in her early twenties and a rich family visited us from Indore with their young son asking for her hand, and the groom-to-be—Mohan—drank whisky with Papa late into the night after the women went to sleep. Papa slapped him on his back affectionately.

Then, Didi got married.

Rishi bhaiya had left us by then; he didn't come to the wedding. He wasn't invited.

Dhiraj wasn't invited to the wedding, either. I had stopped seeing him after the move away from Mehmoorganj, and we had little to talk about because he was obsessed with his exam preparations, and I had already seen the skies torn apart by skyscrapers in New York City. I moved away to Delhi and then to Washington, and when I died, Dhiraj wanted to send a note or a message to my family but decided against it. *They probably don't remember me any more,* he thought.

TWENTY-FIVE

In four years in Amreeka, I only met Rishi bhaiya one time.

It was my third summer in D.C., the season of barbeques, swimming pool parties, and girls in bikinis that had stripes over their breasts and stars on their neeche-walleh regions. Rishi bhaiya had flown to Virginia for a meeting. And nearby lived Uncle Monty, our father's cousin, who invited the both of us to his suburban mansion for lunch on one of those hot afternoons. It took me over an hour to get there, a walk, a couple of changes on the metro line, an expensive taxi from the metro station, and a drive into the whitewashed woods, areas segregated from most of humanity, neighbourhoods undisturbed by the unpredictable masala of downtown D.C., the clean and green of America that Rishi bhaiya had, long ago, once prepared me for.

After a few turns into the wrong driveways—yaar, all of these homes looked the same—my taxi finally found my uncle's place, a white and red brick mansion in the middle of this nowhere fucking suburbia. My uncle, with his round belly and slow gait, came out with a smile to greet me. My elder brother—tall, fair, and bespectacled—was by his side.

'You made it!' Uncle Monty said.

'Hi Uncle.'

'Hey Big Man,' said my brother.

'Hi Bhaiya,' I responded. *Big man?* In reality, he was the one that had truly gotten so much bigger. Older. Grizzled grey hairs on the side of his head. Grizzled grey sprouts of beard on his cheeks. Wider shoulders. Fuller face. American Diet. He even looked like he had grown fairer, bleached among the other *gora* compatriots of his new country.

I felt too nervous to look directly at him, at all the history that would arise if we locked eyes, all that we had witnessed together, all that we had spoken about—and all that we hadn't. When I had last met him in New Delhi, I don't think I had still, truly felt the weight of what it meant for him to be away—and be away *all the time*. It had felt temporary back then, this fissure between him and our father, between him and Varanasi, and all of Papa's past.

But now, I understood better, and perhaps, he could sense this understanding, too.

'Come in,' Uncle Monty said. 'We've made a good Indian meal, son. I'm sure you've missed home cooking.'

Uncle Monty lived with his wife and his two daughters, and made a living running franchises of the third-biggest pizza chain in the US, where all of his employees were South Asians, but—he confessed—he never ate pizza himself. 'Only desi food in our home, Vishnu,' he said. 'I never get homesick because I eat like I'm still in India. Try some, try some. I made the paneer myself.'

The paneer, however, was disgusting, and so was the aloo gobi, and the chana masala, and the stiff, cold rotis. But Uncle Monty ate it with pride, as did his family, as did Rishi bhaiya, who complimented the Indian cook in the kitchen at least four times through the course of the meal.

'How old are the girls?' Rishi bhaiya asked Uncle Monty.

'Radha's fourteen. Radhika is twelve.'

'Wow! They must be close chums, then.'

'No, no,' Uncle Monty said with a short laugh. 'Siblings, you know, always fighting over small things. These days all they do is fight for the top bunk of the bunk bed.'

Rishi bhaiya and I inadvertently looked at each other. An entire childhood flashed through my mind, the cold nights, the *thud-thud-thud* from the lower bunk.

'Do you remember the blanket, Bhaiya?' I asked my brother.

'Which blanket?'

'The blanket. That brown blanket we had to share in the winters. You always kept it for yourself.'

Rishi bhaiya shook his head, and turned to Uncle Monty instead. 'Have you heard about the Adult Security Blankets? New start-up, selling two-hundred-dollar weighted blankets, but big ones for grown-ups. Simple concept, you know, but they are all the rage right now.'

From then on, I ate in silence, listening to Rishi bhaiya and Uncle Monty discuss grown-men things, like buying shares and the Virginia property market, and the free-falling value of the rupee against the dollar.

After lunch, Bhaiya and I accompanied Uncle Monty for a walk on the green, well-trimmed grass in his backyard, leaving his wife and daughters behind. It was a cool, windy day, pleasant and relaxing, yet I was uncomfortable.

Uncle Monty nudged Rishi bhaiya and showed him an alert on his phone. Both of them smirked. 'That man,' Uncle Monty said, 'he really has great charisma, doesn't he? Says whatever he feels like. No one else in this country has the balls to speak like him.'

'Nobody does,' Rishi bhaiya agreed.

'He could win, you know. People aren't talking about it, because they're scared. But I think he could win.'

'I'm not sure, Uncle,' Bhaiya said. 'These people are crazy. Do you watch the news? Everything he does, they make it sound like the worst thing in the world. Like, so, he said women in Venezuela look like whores. That's what he said yesterday. Ha! But some of them do, don't they? Every country has that. He's just saying what everyone's thinking. And they make *him* sound like a bad guy.'

'Bhaiya,' I finally interjected. 'What are you saying? He's a fucking cartoon. A complete chootia. How can he—'

I stepped on dead, dry leaves—fallen early before the fall—and heard them crunch under my shoe.

'You're too young to understand, Vishnu,' Bhaiya said. 'Sometimes, you know, the world needs men like him. Someone who says it like it is. Otherwise these fucking…these fucking mosquitoes are going to terrorize all of us. Just like in India. You know, it's the same solution. They need the same solution.'

'Right,' Uncle Monty said. 'The same solution.'

Uncle Monty had a thinner version of Papa's moustache, and a slightly longer face. And suddenly, Bhaiya reminded me of Papa, too. The fear in his voice. Or not fear, but anger—a deep, irrational anger. Papa, too, cursed at invisible forces on the TV as if they were coming to haunt him, to take away his livelihood. Bhaiya just did it in a different accent. Same genes, behenchod.

Uncle Monty lit a cigarette and took a puff. He offered one to Bhaiya, and Bhaiya refused. He looked at me and smiled. I declined.

'Don't be shy, son.'

'No, thanks Uncle.'

I had to get back, I told them, I lived so far away. Rishi bhaiya had to get back to his hotel, too. He had rented a car to get here; I called an Uber.

Uncle Monty waved goodbye and went back inside, leaving my elder brother and I in the driveway. 'I'll wait till your cab gets here,' Bhaiya said.

'Sure.'

'Hmm,' Rishi bhaiya looked me up and down again, sizing me up. 'How long will it take?'

'Twelve minutes, apparently. This place really is in the middle of nowhere, isn't it?'

'I love that about America,' Bhaiya said. 'All these open spaces. You can really cut yourself off from the rest of the world, can't you?'

'You *like* that?'

'You don't?'

I didn't reply. Rishi bhaiya fished out his own phone and stared at it.

'So, how's college going? Are you doing well in your classes?'

'Sure,' I shrugged. 'Not as well as Mummy would want, I know. But I'm fine.'

Bhaiya sniggered. 'Tell me she still doesn't think good grades mean smarter kids.... If only I could tell her how many people in Silicon Valley were failures or dropouts at some point or the other. It's just the Indian system, Vishnu. They worry about the wrong shit over there. Rote-memorizing and percentage marks, that's it. No creativity.'

'It's not that bad any more, Bhaiya. Lots of schools are changing. I went to Modern and they—'

'It's good you came here,' he said. 'It's suffocating back there in India, isn't it? All these cultural expectations, all that craziness. Have you thought about any internships yet? Have you done any already? Start applying soon. I could…I could help with a reference, too, if you need. And all of the tech world is in California, you know that, right? That's where you need to move after you graduate.'

'Bhaiya, are you…are you planning to visit home again? Back to India?'

He shrugged his shoulders, a weak shrug that didn't indicate confidence.

'You should come, Bhaiya,' I said. I sensed the weakness in my voice, too. As if I was saying a memorized speech. 'It's been so long since…since…all that happened with Papa.'

'How long will your cab take?'

'Five…. Now, four minutes.'

'Good.'

We waited in silence until the Uber showed up. I turned to shake his hand goodbye, but he pulled me in for a hug. I wrapped my arms around him and hugged him back. He smelled like Uncle Monty's lunch, bland with a touch of paneer.

'Call me, okay,' he said. 'I'll get you a good reference when you're ready.'

It was the last time we spoke.

TWENTY-SIX

Sakshi was in the kitchen in Indore when she heard the news, one hand holding the phone on speaker, one twisting and twirling rotis over an open flame with a chimta. It was Mummy on the other end, calling her from Varanasi.

'What happened to Vishnu?' Sakshi shouted into the phone. Mummy was speaking with choked sobs. Sakshi wasn't sure she'd heard correctly.

Mummy told her again. 'You should come back to Varanasi, beti. His…his body is…. Your father is arranging.'

'Vishnu?' Sakshi shouted again. 'Vishnu,' she shouted louder. Her maid was noisily washing dishes behind her, utensils clanging in the sink, the water gushing from the tap obscuring my sister's voice.

'Sakshi,' Papa's voice came through the phone. It was gruff and business-like; the voice he reserved for Happy Singh, and his lawyers, and his employees. 'Sakshi, your mother has told you the news?'

'Papa! Vishnu?'

'Haan, haan, beti.'

'Papa, have you told Rishi?'

'Sakshi, we will get him cremated here. Right here in Banaras. We wanted something quick at the electric crematorium—the one in Harishchandra Ghat. But you know your mother, she is insisting on it being done the proper way. And then we can—'

'Vishnu?'

'Here, speak to your mother.'

'Yes, beti,' Mummy said, and sniffled, and her voice was distorted due to electrical interference, and then she cried.

'Vishnu?' Sakshi didi asked for me, as if I was there beside her, as if she knew that after Wildhair's shot permanently destroyed my hardware, my software would still be around for this infinite instant, surviving as a useless echo of my life. I wish I could answer her. Mummy hung up the phone—she tended to do that by mistake, pressing a wrong button here or there when she was distracted. Sakshi didi, speaking to nothing but the stove on the kitchen tabletop, asked for me again. 'Vishnu?'

'Sakshi madam!' the maid said from behind her. 'Madam, the roti, the roti is burning.'

Sakshi didi's hand fell and hung limply by her side. The tongs slipped out of her fingers and fell to the floor, along with the now burnt roti, and Sakshi walked out of the kitchen. She'd lost her appetite. 'Heat up the lunch for Mohan,' she commanded the maid before she left.

Sakshi didn't answer Mohan when he enquired about details. She had no interest in speaking to him yet, or speaking to anyone at all, or discussing with Papa the logistics of getting my corpse across international waters—over the Atlantic? Over the Pacific?—or in arguing over the cremation ceremony—an electric crematorium? A funeral pyre?—or, frankly, getting on the flight from Indore to Delhi to Varanasi—there was no direct connection—stifled for hours with a toddler in her arms and the oppressive weight of sorrow on her head.

She had been to the electric crematorium before, at the Harishchandra Ghat, once upon a time, which now felt like it may have been someone else's life, someone else's memory, someone else's senses, someone else's friendship. Sakshi didi and her friend Vasu—who lived just a gully or two away from the ghat—bunked school on a Tuesday, feeling bored and adventurous as two fifteen-year-old girls are often wont to feel. By the ghat, they climbed up the steps to the crematorium with a sense of morbid fascination. 'It will take an hour or two, that's it,' Vasu told her. 'Body goes into the machine, and nothing but dust comes out.'

Neither was brave enough to walk up to the platform where the families of the deceased waited, but they came close to the steps to watch their reactions. It smelled like wood here, like fire, like wet marigold petals. One of the boys winked at Vasu as he passed her by. 'My uncle,' he said with a cheery smile. He wore a red and blue flannel shirt and a blue handkerchief tied around his neck. 'Who are you here for?'

'Not for you,' Vasu answered, and Didi shrieked out in laughter. The two girls rushed down the steps and away.

'Chalo, let's go,' Vasu said. 'One more thing before we go back to school. I'm going to treat you to the best samosas in the world.'

The samosawallah was just a short walk away, on the corner of a crowded gully populated by dozens of men, their bicycles, and their scooters. Sakshi could smell the steaming hot potatoes, but she heard her mother's voice in her head, and Mummy cawed at her a warning, a message that was permanently installed in my sister's hard drive. *Keep distance from strange men. Actually, keep distance from all men. You don't know the world like I do.*

Vasu, however, walked fearlessly into the crowd, and the sea of men parted to make room for her, allowing her to order.

'Two pieces.'

'With chhole?' the samosawallah asked.

'Of course, with chhole,' Vasu answered.

The men, some holding kulhads of chai, some with plates of samosas, some with gulab jamuns, kept an eye on Vasu, staring at her as if she belonged to some alien species. Sakshi could feel her friend being violated through the protective cover of her school uniform, the white shirt and brown skirt that both the girls wore.

'One for you, one for me,' Vasu said. 'My treat.'

A decade after this incident, Sakshi could hardly remember how those samosas tasted, whether they were truly as delicious as Vasu had proclaimed.

Years passed. Sakshi was married, and I was back home from D.C.; it was the last trip where we'd see each other. She recalled her trip to the electric crematorium to me, and then requested that I accompany her to the Harishchandra Ghat to help her relive her nostalgia. I refused.

'Busy,' I said.

'Those samosas are the best in the world. My friend Vasu, she—'

I put my headphones over my ears. 'Go with Vasu, then.'

But Vasu had been married off, too, arranged to live in another city with another man, and Sakshi instead ended up spending the rest of her holiday in Varanasi in the safe confines of our home, tending to her husband and child, never getting a chance to venture out to the gullies again, to confirm if those samosas were really as good as she remembered, or if it had only been the cocktail of experiences—the thrill of bunking school, the novelty of climbing up the crematorium, the excitement of seeing her friend talk back to the boy, and the presence of Vasu herself—that had satiated her that day.

On the day she heard the news of my death, Sakshi didi called Mummy back, later in the evening, and told her that she wouldn't be able to make it to my cremation. Her daughter, she said, had caught chickenpox.

Mummy sighed. She was silent, but remained on the line, hoping for more words from my sister, hoping for this silence to be filled with a backtrack, a changing of Didi's mind, a change of circumstance.

'Sorry, Mummy,' Sakshi didi said.

'No one's home, Sakshi,' Mummy said. 'Not you, not Rishi. Not Vishnu.'

Then, silence again, a vacuum in the electromagnetic waves that connected the distance between Delhi and Indore. Then, Sakshi heard a soft muffle, a garbling of words, the sound of one language being swallowed by another.

'Sorry, Mummy,' Didi repeated.

TWENTY-SEVEN

It was in Delhi, just as I was about to enter the last of my teenage years, that Rishi bhaiya and I lived under the same roof again for a few months, but we lived very different lives. He had his own friends, and they would sit around old mausoleums sharing cheap cigarettes and dirty jokes, or he would stop by his favourite chhole-bhaturewallah for a late-night snack. It was the last of his days in India, he knew. The end of his desi nostalgia. He would soon return to the States, and he planned to never look back.

By the time he left Delhi, I had already begun to spend more schooldays away from school, often with Sanjeet, a classmate's elder brother, who invited me to play Xbox at his home, taught me how to crumble charas between my fingers, how to roll the perfect cone for a joint, and to ensure that I scraped the black residue off the inside of my nails.

I had forced my way into Modern School in Delhi and out of the stifling Panchkroshi circle around Varanasi. The riots of 2010 were old news now, and Papa had a whole lot of new money. He had already flown us to New York City so we could gaze at the skyscrapers and eat cheeseburgers and take photographs to make Papa's friends at the Trader's Union jealous. But in the process, he had shown me too much of the world, too much to settle for Varanasi, even if, if mythology is to be believed, every goddamn atman in the universe—man, woman, dog, rat, bacterium—is eventually fated to settle for that eternal city.

On weekends, Sanjeet and I bought a crate of Kingfisher Strong beer and drove aimlessly together—him at the wheel and me balancing the bottles in the passenger seat next to him—around Delhi's Outer Ring Road. From the passenger seat, I sparked the joint he had rolled earlier that day and took a puff, and we passed the booze and drinks between each other. This was our karobar. Car-o-bar, samjhe? We haunted the city whenever the sun went down. Late one dark, unstirring night, we almost got caught on our way back, but the policewallahs who had barricaded Hansraj Gupta Marg were fast asleep. 'Move the barriers out of the way!' Sanjeet commanded me. I skipped out of the car, and pushed the wheeled barricades to the side. The two policemen dutifully snored on their stools.

Sanjeet spent much of his day at the gym, while I often sat alone, until late in his apartment, sometimes surrounded by a revolving cast of his friends who came to sit and smoke and drink on the beanbags spread around the creamy marble floors. There was no furniture in the living room. It looked bigger in its vacuity, with high ceilings and that lonely, empty feel of a house where people had recently moved in, or were about to move out—a house that wasn't a home.

One hot, humid evening Sanjeet unwrapped a brown paper bag to present me with a small bomb of a gift, wrapped inside shiny aluminium foil. His face lit up with a wicked smile, the smile of goondagardi. We were alone in his empty living-room, sitting on beanbags, drinking bottles of mineral water, melting in the heat under the slow-moving fan.

'What's this?' I asked. The gift was warm and soft to the touch, and then, the smell hit me. 'Is it...?'

'Fresh from the US Embassy restaurant. You can't get good beef like this in Delhi easily, you understand?'

Two warm buns, holding between them a slab of gorgeously dense meat. Cow meat just *felt* heavier, didn't it? There was a certain strength to it. A maternal strength, a weight of responsibility.

'Thank me, bhosadi-ke,' Sanjeet said with a mouthful, spitting out a small piece of bread. 'Your father never bought you a cheeseburger, did he?'

'My father is a vegetarian.' I took a bite, and suddenly, felt warmer in that already hot room. It was like the gods of fire and fury themselves had set the furnace ablaze. I could feel beads of sweat on my forehead, trickling down the sides of my cheeks as I took my next big bite.

'Well,' he laughed. 'Then that's extra reason to be grateful. Eat up before the Cow Army catches you.'

'Fuck,' I said. 'This is good.'

'Uh, huh.'

'They are allowed to make this in Delhi? The embassy?'

'Of course,' he said. 'It's the Americans. They can do whatever the hell they want—you know that!'

'Yaar, I wish we could just get over this cow business here, too, you know? Just let people eat what they want to eat.'

'Abey, that will never happen here,' Sanjeet said. 'People love cattle too much. They love cows more than they love people.'

'But why, though? They're just fucking animals.'

Sanjeet shrugged. 'So are we. You have to draw the line somewhere, right?' With his wrist, he wiped off a small cheese stain off the side of his mouth.

'Ya, but Americans eat all the beef in the world.'

'And what makes you think the Americans are the gold standard? Saala, be a little patriotic, why don't you? Don't backstab Mother India like that. She has given you everything. Do you want a drink?'

He got up to his feet.

I smiled. 'Whisky?'

Sanjeet pulled out a bottle of Scotch from his kitchen cupboard and fetched two glasses. 'Have you ever wondered why they're so violent,' Sanjeet said, pouring the drinks. 'The Americans.'

The Americans? What did I even know about the Americans back then? What do I even know about them now? Those drinking-water-straight-out-of-the-tap Americans, those only-wiping-never-washing-their-ass Americans, those believing-in-abstract-ideas-of-justice Americans. Nahi, I knew nothing.

'Violent?' I straightened my back against the beanbag. 'All I see are the stoned hippie-types. Varanasi is full of them.'

'Haan, haan. They are both. Some won't even hurt a fly. Won't even hurt an enemy. Gandhiji types. And some are bloodthirsty animals. Just like us, isn't it? But for them, it's in their diet, you know? All the red meat they eat. It jams them up.... It makes their red blood even redder, you know? Gets them all fucked up and shit. Ready to shoot anyone, anywhere. Plus, they have all the guns there, too.'

Sanjeet handed me a glass—neat, with no ice, no mixer—and one for himself. I took a sip and scrunched my face, feeling the bitter taste go down my throat.

'Where the fuck do you get your information?' I said with a snigger. 'Red meat? Some of the biggest assholes I know are vegetarians.'

'But isn't it strange, Vishnu?' Sanjeet suddenly dragged himself closer to me, 'Isn't it strange that there is a *their* right and *our* right? That we kill people for eating beef here and they eat beef with pride and joy over there? People are religious in both countries.... Someone has to be wrong, right? Not everyone is going to end up in heaven, isn't it?'

'Unless they have different heavens and hells for everyone. One for Indians, one for Americans, one for the Chinese.'

'One for the whites, one for the blacks, one for us. Yaar, I think about it a lot,' said Sanjeet. 'After death, you know. Jannat or svarga or heaven. Or just...just nothing. Lots and lots of nothing.'

I laughed and took another bite, already feeling full just halfway through the burger. Years later, my stomach would get more accustomed to beef, so that I would be able to easily gorge on a full cheeseburger—sometimes double-pattied, too—with little problem. But that evening, I was still a novice; my only previous experience had been at the McDonald's in New York, on that trip with my family. I was going to need a lot more practice.

'I don't think about anything, yaar,' I finally replied. 'If I die, I die. Who cares, hai ki nahi? And I might as well eat as many real cheeseburgers as I can before that happens—and in America, too, where they do it properly.... You know, my brother, Rishi...? He lives in America. And, bro, the stories he has about that place! Sounds fucking fantastic. Bas, I can't wait to go again—and spend some good time there.'

Sanjeet grinned and moved farther away from me. 'You need to be more thankful that you are in India, Agarwal.'

'What do you mean? Thankful for this shithole?'

'No, bhosadi-ke. It's easy for people like us,' he gestured at me with his glass in hand, and then took a sip, 'for people like us to criticize, to move out, to move in, to hate India, to leave India, to come back, to do whatever we wish. But do you think you would be special if you were born abroad? Behenchod, have you ever been to a developed country?'

'We visited New York...one year—no—two years ago.'

'Well, if you actually lived there, you know you would be a nothing person, you understand? You have to do your own cooking and cleaning and painting and washing. Ask me—I used to spend my summers with an uncle in Luxembourg. Beautiful place, but all the work is a headache, you know? Jharoo-pochha, sab kuch. In India, people like you and I, we don't have to worry about these little things. We don't have to get in lines to pay bills or see the doctor or break a sweat for anything. We have people for everything here. But in America, you would be just like every other person. Actually, worse than every other person—because you would be a minority there. Second-class citizen. Have you ever been a minority anywhere?'

I shook my head. Many years later, Sanjeet's words would ring in my head in my bedroom at Saxon Hall. I had a sudden fit of homesickness after being away for too long, and had got a photograph of the family—Papa and Mummy and Didi and me, but no Bhaiya—enlarged and printed and framed in a 5" x 7" rectangle. The photo was from a trip we had taken to Sarnath outside Varanasi. We were standing in front of one of those giant phallus-shaped stupas. Papa wore a dark-blue shirt and had tucked it in too tight. Mummy stood between my sister and I, with both of us leaning into each of her shoulders. I had happy memories of that day—of the stupas, the Buddhist temples, the museum, and the egg chow mein we had for lunch.

Anyway, this photograph was framed to go right above my study desk in my bedroom in D.C. But it required one last bit of manual labour from my end—mounting the frame up on the wall. I hadn't thought this last part through. Did I need hammers and nails, or drills and hooks? These were skills in which I had achieved no expertise in Varanasi, one of Papa's 'chhotus' came upstairs and fixed all the fixtures and frames in my bedroom, just as I required. Nahi yaar, I knew somewhere within me that I wasn't even a *real* fully developed man yet, not until I could be one of those men who could uncork a bottle with his teeth or hands or in a swift slap against a tableside. Of course, I didn't know how to mount a picture on the wall, or have the patience to learn it all from a YouTube tutorial.

I left the framed photo on the table instead. And that's where it stood until the day I died.

And yet, Sanjeet's warnings of America—its self-dependence—sounded to me like nothing but unnecessary fear. No chhota-mota challenge was going to stop me from dreaming about my future life. The burger from the Embassy had been so delicious; I salivated at the thought of how good the fresh beef would taste when made by even better chefs abroad, and at barbeque cookouts and baseball games and fancy restaurants and food trucks. I wanted it all.

When I began my final year at Delhi Modern School, Sanjeet moved out of his GK-1 apartment to his parents' bigger condo in Noida. With him so far away, I had no choice but to spend more time with Raghu maama and Sharmeen maami.

Papa hadn't left me with a credit card in Delhi, but he transferred a monthly allowance to Raghu maama's account. Over the phone, Papa warned me to make sure my uncle gave me the whole amount, all the cash, on the first of every month. 'Your mother's family are all frauds, samjhe Vishnu?' Papa coughed. 'All those chootias have no ambition. Nothing. They live in those dirty small flats, and share a single bathroom, chhee! I don't know what ubarkhabar nonsense they filled in your brother's head that he thinks they are *his* parents now. You—you my son—you must be careful, okay? Your maama was a teacher when we first met him, and he is still a teacher. Loafer. Make sure he gives you your money, okay?'

But Papa was wrong. After a whole year of living with the Kauls, I slowed down to their pace. Maama spoke with a soft gravitas that reminded me of my elder brother. He didn't scratch his body in public or spit red paan on every wall he saw like most of Papa's friends back home. He taught sociology at the Sri Krishna College, spoke good English and even better, shudh Hindi, translating each one of the prime minister's televised addresses to the nation for me. When I struggled in my maths class, he offered to help out with the calculus. He read the newspaper in silence every morning, and over breakfast, he sometimes told me about Mummy's childhood, and how they used to steal the neighbour's bicycle to go watch the travelling circus.

I sat with Maama on one of those Sunday summer mornings when the air had already started warming up with the first faint rays of the sun. After he and Sharmeen maami set up piping hot puris to go with our aloo sabzi on the table, Maama told me more stories about my mother.

'We used to be the best of friends,' he said. He had a black, neatly trimmed lampshade moustache over his lips, and wore large, old-fashioned square spectacles. 'I was two years younger, but she was the one who needed taking care of. All the boys in her school tried to get smart with your mother. I had to be protective. It wasn't a good time to be a woman in this city.'

Maami scoffed at him. 'It's even worse now, Raghu.' My aunt had a hoarse voice, weakened by decades of telling elementary school students to keep quiet.

'Yes, yes, it is worse now, but it is also better in some ways,' he said, and then turned back to me. 'You see Vishnu, nowadays, boys and girls in this city are all going to school, and so many girls are going to college, and people are fine with it, and even encouraging it. It's a good thing, isn't it? But back in our day, you know, not many girls went to college. My parents couldn't afford it for both of us.'

He had an economy of movement; his elbows retracted back and forth as he switched between his chai and his breakfast with the least amount of distance and energy wasted. Next to him, Maami picked up the newspaper and unfurled it before her face. 'Here we go again, Raghu,' she said. 'Just forget about it now.'

I waited for Maama to keep talking, but instead, he took another sip of chai. The only sound in the house now was Maami flipping through the newspaper. Their home was on the second floor of a three-storey building, with tiny lanes, neighbours peering into your balcony to ask if you have washing detergent, and a constant logjam for parking space below. Inside the house, Maama and Maami kept their curtains wide open during the day to make the most of the sunlight.

Maami pushed a plate of puris towards me. 'More, beta?' she asked, and I shook my head, *no*.

'So, which college did you go to, Maama?' I asked.

'They chose me.'

'Huh?'

'Your mother could have gone to college, too, Vishnu. But

our parents chose me.'

The neighbours below turned on their car engines. The kabadiwallah's bicycle tinkled by, and then a sabziwallah dragged his cart, hawking onions and tomatoes and seasonal vegetables.

Mummy in college! From my atemporal space, I see a young Mummy clearly, imagining how she would've been at my age, when she walked without the duck-waddle due to her shaky knees. I put myself in her clean polished black Bata school shoes, and see that there was a brief glimmer of selfishness in her. Nahi nahi, I mean the good kind of selfishness. She walked home alone from school one day, clipped off the twin ponytails her mother had braided for her, and told her parents that she had made her decision, that she loved biology class, that she wanted to be a scientist. They laughed at her and affectionately pulled her cheeks the same way Papa would pull Sakshi didi's. *Sure,* they said, *whatever you say Big Girl.*

But it never happened; nahi nahi, there was no college, and no biology, except for the biology of her own body, her womb that sheltered the twins first, and me after, because when she was old enough to be married and raise a family, she did so without complaint.

Now, Mummy's self-determination was gone. She occupied more physical space but tried to keep herself hidden. She encouraged Papa at work, and made sure Sakshi didi got happily married, and called me with words of caution whenever I left home.

Raghu maama lowered his eyes. He stopped eating, too, leaving a half-torn puri on his plate. 'Your mother was the better student, Vishnu,' he said. 'They should have chosen her.'

There was a bit of puri with some vegetables swirling around my mouth, but I waited a moment to swallow.

He reached one hand across the table, and now I know that he saw my mother's large eyes in mine, and he gently squeezed my shoulder. I swallowed the puri.

Raghu maama knew about my American dreams. He could see it in how I had begun to emulate Rishi bhaiya's gait, walking with a sense of casual purpose, never too stressed, but never too relaxed. I watched old American sitcoms and began to speak in catchphrases like those arguing commentators behind the broadcast of NBA basketball games. Maama returned from the market one day and handed me a book where the main character was named after me, another Vishnu, who dies in a stairwell in Bombay and becomes Vishnu the god. The thought of his death depressed me more than I was impressed by his post-mortality, and I stopped reading. Next, Maama offered another book, Anurag Mathur's *The Inscrutable Americans,* convinced that I would enjoy this tale of an Indian college student in the USA, and as I read the book, I laughed out loud at that idiot character's misadventures with gori girls in middle-country America somewhere, and I thought to myself yaar: *Shit, there's no way I'm going to have the same experiences as this fucker.*

I told Papa that I wanted what Rishi bhaiya had. I wanted to go to America, study computer engineering, live in Silicon Valley, design apps, and have future robots drive me around while I basked in those orange Californian sunsets.

'Chootia, you're crazy,' Papa said on the phone. 'Why are you going there for computers when all of those Amreekis got their computers fixed by us? You want to live like Rishi? That boy probably lives in a tiny house smaller than your bedroom, you understand? Go study business, do an MBA, and come back to manage the factory with us in Varanasi. Don't be like him—you understand? He abandoned us. Will you abandon us, too?'

But nahi, I couldn't stay home. I often thought about Dhiraj, my childhood friend, with whom I played gully cricket and Catch-Catch and obsessed over *Shaktimaan* serials. We lost touch when my papa got richer and his papa didn't. Dhiraj stayed back in Varanasi while I came to Delhi. He finished third in the district's CBSE Board exams and was one of the smartest young men in the city.

And yet, he was always going to stay in that city: he was born in Varanasi, he would inhale its dusty air while driving his motorcycle through the gullies, gain a paunch after too many barfis from his favourite mithaiwallah, work there, marry there, fuck there, become a father there, and become a father again and again, get stuck in traffic jams between Rathyatra and Sigra until the 2040s, gain too much weight, get an early heart attack, and then die within the city's holy boundaries hoping to be reborn as a slightly better version of himself in the same hospital he had died in. No, behenchod, I didn't want that. I wanted to get the fuck out.

I could understand Papa's quandary, though. He needed me back at Bhagwan Beads. The riots had made him richer, but they had also aged him by a decade. His real years were in the mid-forties, his body was in the fifties, and each greasy samosa he ate tested the condition of his overburdened heart. He had won the battle over the manual labourers after the riots, but his larger war was against the machines. The slightly older version of me would later learn that making beads through the efforts of those artisans in sweaty workshops around Varanasi was far too expensive. Past the Himalaya that shrouded us from the dangers up north, China had already moved ahead with cheaper and quicker machine-made options.

'Machines!' Papa said.

He knew he would need me one day, maybe a decade later, when I was all grown up and understood how the world operated. He couldn't turn to Sakshi didi, because, yaar, she was a girl, and you think Papa was ever going to trust a *girl* with his business—especially one who would be married off into another family? Nahi, nahi, Papa didn't even trust Mummy with his mobile phone passcode.

'Machines, Vishnu!'

'Papa,' I moaned; my tone became more childish and desperate. 'That's why I should study computers, too, no? Just like Rishi bhaiya....'

As if that's all it would take. I had, of course, wrongly assumed that Rishi bhaiya had somehow just strolled into his American success. Nahi yaar, he was a foreigner in a country where he didn't know the customs, where people didn't always understand his accent, where it was always a challenge for him to get loans, buy a car, rent an apartment, and get a job without getting his H1B, and get an H1B without having a job. When he lit clay diyas outside his Philadelphia apartment on Diwali, neighbours stared at him and wondered if they were Halloween decorations. When he walked outside the Save A Lot with grocery bags, a homeless man called him 'ISIS motherfucker'.

But finally, the day came when Rishi bhaiya got that white-coloured green card, with a faded photograph in which his skin tone looked so fair that nothing but his name could give away his true ethnicity; and he began to watch the NFL and bought himself a 49ers hat; and when he called me in D.C. one time, he chatted about QBRs and offensive pass yards, and I nodded along thinking to myself, *Theek hai behenchod, but can you explain how many runs the batting team made?* He changed his own name—Rishi to Russ—to make Starbucks' baristas more comfortable. After I was shot, he called Mummy to cry together, and even *he* couldn't help but call me 'Viz'.

It was near sunset in the Bay Area when the gunshot rang out in D.C., and Rishi Russ had been invited for a special seminar for schoolkids at Fremont High. He was seated in the backseat of an Uber on his way back home when he got the alerts from India. The chain of communication went thus: Hamid to Uncle Monty in Virginia, Uncle Monty to Papa in Varanasi, Papa to Mummy, Mummy to Raghu maama in New Delhi, and Raghu maama to Rishi bhaiya back in California. Yes, Rishi bhaiya was shocked, and he even cried a little, and the Uber driver generously offered him some tissues, and both of them rated each other a full five stars following the experience.

Suno, yaar, he was genuinely sad about this. Sure, Rishi bhaiya and I—on opposite coasts of America's vast expanse—had barely kept in touch over my last few years, but he *did* care about me, you know? Somewhere deep within him, even in the torn tatters of our familial relationship, was an elder brother who remembered a younger sibling.

Somewhere deeper within him, in an emotion that he wouldn't fully communicate to his wife until the Washington Postwallah's story went viral among the Indian–American community, was the thought that the victim could have just as easily been him. Like me, he had felt safe in a progressive nook of America. He, too, enjoyed the occasional drink (one beer every alternate Saturday) in crowded spaces with strangers in mutual revelry. Like me, his brown face could have been any brown face. Same genes, behenchod.

And in this case, he *was,* indeed, a target of sorts. Suno, Wildhair had lost his back-end computer engineering job in Fairfax to an Indian engineer from Vadodara. Rishi bhaiya, too—a foreign-born shahi-paneer-eating cricket-playing young man—earned a job in the industry as a foreigner. Because jobs are finite (mathematics, hai ki nahi?), one computer-man replaced another. And there were a hundred thousand others, because industries changed, and the jobs in factories and tunnels of sweat and grime were replaced by jobs in white office spaces or in green California parks with free Wi-Fi and unlimited access to kale juice. Yaar, of course, Rishi bhaiya felt responsible.

I was shot and killed that night at Lucky Luke in Washington, and Rishi bhaiya could feel the faint, oozing heat of the cartridge of that .22 LR, too. He could imagine that it was *he* who had been drinking with a carefree smile, breathing in for the last time before there was red and then, there were no more breaths.

'Go back to your country.' Rishi bhaiya heard it echo through the line of communication from D.C. to Virginia to Varanasi to Delhi to the backseat of his Uber ride in Sunnyvale. That night, after briefly weeping in his wife's arms, Rishi permanently died, too, and Russ was born. Yes, he decided, that he wouldn't let his race come between him and his ambitions and the America he so sweetly loved. Russ was angry at Wildhair because Wildhair would have never accepted him as an American. He wanted that American Dream to be his, too, to be seen beyond the colour of his skin. Russ studied for the USCIS test, learned names of early presidents and dates of state establishments. He voluntarily memorized the lyrics of the 'Star-Spangled Banner' and monumental phrases from the Declaration of Independence, believing that he, too, deserved liberty and the pursuit of happiness—and oh yes, life, too.

Two years later, in his first registered opportunity to contribute to his new nation's democracy, Russ voted, as Wildhair had, for President Gaandu-face. He developed a perfect idea of America where only the fittest should survive and every threatening face on the street—even faces that looked like his and mine—should be kept from staining his American ideal. Suddenly, he began to feel like there were too many like him getting those faded-white green cards to enter *his* new country.

And Russ wasn't the only one with that reaction—on conservative news channels in America, beautiful blonde women with bulbous breasts and blue eyes said that my death was a political error, that I had only paid the price for the sins of the opposing party. Then there were others, even blonder, sharply dressed men with slicked-back hair and strong jawlines, who claimed that my death was faked, that it was all a conspiracy, that there was no chance that one man could shoot another, that it definitely wasn't the gun's fault, that it was all propaganda, that perhaps I hadn't even existed at all.

Behenchod. I'm sure I was a warm chemical pool of existence an instant ago, and I'm sure that I'm pretty fucking dead now.

There was proof of me everywhere. That mangled, bloody,

hairy, skinny, shitting body retrieved from Lucky Luke, of course. There were the witnesses at the bar who saw me get shot. Some of them were bruised as they clashed against Wildhair, and some were unfortunate enough to be stained by the blood that sprayed out of my perforated body. Haan ji haan, I also existed in the memory of those who knew me well, or at least, professed to know me online.

The internet was afire with sorrow. The reactions were stronger for one death than all those who lost their lives during the riots in 2010. There were wishes from my closest friends, from Rishi bhaiya, and—behenchod, I already told you—from Aastha, too. Even Papa finally created a Facebook profile a few weeks later to post some photographs of our family, and use smiley-faced emojis inappropriately in captions about my demise. Then, once Papa got a better hang of how to work the site, he began to post photographs of himself all alone, wearing a yellow sapphire gemstone around his neck for Jupiter's blessings. The gemstone hadn't brought him the luck he desired, but it looked great hanging on the V-neck above his hairy chest.

Papa did not believe in prayers, but he did get superstitious when it suited him. After the riots, for example, he built the new house in Varanasi in full accordance with Vastu Shastra. When he began to have nightmares about those riots, he purchased a more expensive, comfortable mattress and changed the direction in which he slept, facing east instead of north. The mattress helped him fall asleep almost instantly, with the shouting newswallahs glowing on the TV in front of him. But the nightmares didn't stop.

That yellow gemstone, however, was his ultimate weapon of self-protection against all ill-wishers in the business and metaphysical worlds. As he had his head shaved by pandits at the ghat, an astrologer told him that he could get all the positive energy of the universe for under 25,000 rupees once he purchased that gemstone. He did; and it worked like the best of placebos, giving him stubborn confidence in his investment. Nahi nahi, it didn't make Papa any less grumpy, or any healthier, or any happier than before, but whenever he failed, the gemstone gave him something else to blame—something in the stars and the planets.

TWENTY-EIGHT

Sanjeet was driving that day, of course, because he never let me get behind the wheel of his silver Hyundai. He drove distractedly; his eyes stared ahead at the road, but I knew that his mind was elsewhere. His parents were forcing him into an arranged marriage, and he only had eight months left of his young life before he had to settle down with the woman his parents had chosen for him. He had only met her twice before, he told me: once at another cousin's shaadi, and the second time at his own roka party, where they exchanged engagement rings. She and Sanjeet didn't have much in common, and he knew that she came from a conservative family that didn't allow her to have onion or garlic or eggs or chicken or beer or whisky or male friends. Sanjeet, frustrated, could only stare at her photographs, imagining what it would feel like to cup her breasts under the salwar kameez she wore to the roka.

'At least she's hot, bro,' he told me. He had one hand on the wheel and the other swiped through matrimonial-site-style photographs of her on his phone. In one, she was wearing a sober dark-orange sari while standing at full attention facing the camera, in front of a white studio background. In the other, she was in a lime-green T-shirt, with blue jeans and sneakers, her long hair tied in a ponytail, and looking a little more relaxed. Sanjeet didn't tell me her name.

He drove around aimlessly, moving slowly to lengthen the pointless evening. This was my favourite climate in Delhi—not too hot, or too rainy, or too cold, or too polluted, or too infested by life-threatening mosquitoes. Just a cool, spring evening when I could finally enjoy the green blooming through the smog. We kept the windows shut, so when I exhaled after taking a hit of the joint we were invariably sharing, the inside of the car was instantly clouded by light-grey smoke.

Our usual karobar, you know? Beer and charas. The concoction was an instant boost for Sanjeet, like some magical jari booti that was now going to set him off beyond the cosmos. Suddenly, he pressed his foot down on the accelerator, impatiently overtaking the slower-moving traffic in front of us. With my next puff, I got a sudden, quick rush up to my head.

As I normally do in these situations, yaar, I checked out. Sanjeet smoked the last of the joint and drove, while I let my neck fall back onto the seat's headrest and closed my eyes, letting the music and the zooming pace of the car hypnotize me. I wasn't asleep, but I wasn't awake, either. I was a passenger, passive as my life moved forward at an exhilarating pace, too scared to get off and find another way, and too comfortable in my seat to actively negotiate the path to my destination. I was just there.

And then we crashed.

I saw it happen, saw Sanjeet's Hyundai hit another speeding car on our left side—on *my* side. Then came that centrifugal force lurching us forward and then sideways, like a rollercoaster in slow motion. I felt my insides plunge, then rise, as if my internal organs were ready to be spewed out in vomit alongside the Kingfisher beer we had been swigging. Then, there was a sudden shift in momentum, and I heard that screech.

Screeeeeee. Behenchod, I can still hear it.

We swerved around in a semicircle before Sanjeet could press down on the brake. The car we had crashed against—a small, white Maruti—could not stop and kept moving forward, only to hit us on the rear again. Another loud thud, and even though the engine was off, our Hyundai turned another ninety degrees.

The Maruti tumbled over us, flipped forward, and crashed

back down on its head. Its wheels kept moving even as the car had stopped, trembling helplessly under the sky.

Twenty-six minutes later, I was lying next to Sanjeet on a stretcher in an ambulance, and next to us was the driver of the Maruti, a Palpreet Singh who had indicated his right turn ahead of Sanjeet, but Sanjeet had ignored it and still tried to overtake him. Later that night, we walked out of the hospital together—me with a small gash just an inch above my left eye, and Sanjeet with a separated right shoulder blade that meant he could not drive for several months. Even later that night, I was taken into the custody of a moustachioed policewallah who drove me to the station. And three days after that crash, I found out that Mr Palpreet was paralysed from the waist down and would never walk again.

When the police questioned me that night—separately from Sanjeet—I told them in a tired, still-drunken haze that *Yes, it was all Sanjeet's fault,* that he was the one in the driver's seat, that he had brought the whisky and the charas and was speeding, that he ignored the Maruti's indicator.

Sanjeet never spoke to me again. Four years later when I was shot and killed, when everyone from Aastha to Papa to barely related mousas and mousis and random classmates commemorated my death on social media, Sanjeet didn't write anything about me. Privately, he told the woman he was now married to that I was a chootia who had it coming to him.

But suno, let me take you back to the night of the crash, theek hai?

The police picked me up and shoved me in the back of their jeep 'Spoiled rich kids,' the policewallah said. 'I'll teach you a lesson.' He had a bushy black moustache and alert eyes. He spoke with scorn in his voice. 'You boys think you can do whatever you want in this city?'

That night, while sitting in the thana cell, all I could think about was Papa. They allowed me a phone call, and I used it to dial Raghu maama, but the policewallah behind the desk, the one who arrested me, snatched the phone from me and told Maama to stay home. 'Come tomorrow morning. After ten. No, after eleven. There is nothing you can do for him tonight.'

Inside the cell there were metal benches where a number of older men sat crossed-legged with sullen, sleepy faces. A middle-aged man in dirty blue trousers and a red shirt shifted a foot off the bench and gestured at me to come sit next to him. I trembled first, then obeyed. The floor was hard cement, littered with red tobacco stains and bidi butts. The smell of cheap bidi smoke hung in the air, but I was determined not to cough.

Among all this filth, I felt embarrassed to be so clean: my face wasn't yet dirtied from the grime of the night. I wore a T-shirt bought from the Calvin Klein store in DLF Promenade Mall and a pair of imported Retro High Air Jordans which I had purchased online.

'Huh.' The man in the red shirt looked at me and motioned upwards with his chin. He had a patchy, badly shaven beard over his face.

'Huh?' I looked back at him.

'Baccha, first time, huh?'

I didn't answer, in fear that my confirmation would make me seem weaker than I already did. I looked away from him, and then I ignored all of them for the rest of that night. Some yawned and made themselves comfortable, staring at the ceiling, studying the darkness with grave intensity, almost as if they could see rich constellations of the night sky. Some fidgeted and shook, stood up and sat down, rolled left on the ground, and then rolled right. One man in a white vest and a white Gandhi topi stared at me, perceiving me through my privilege, and kept staring for hours into the night. I turned away. I pretended I didn't see the men who took out their fucking lunds to piss in a large metal urinal in the far corner of the cell. I pretended to be asleep when a bearded old man was brought in an hour later and pressed up close to me. He smelled of vomit. The old man began to loudly hack in the middle of the night, and it sounded like a hairball was stuck in his throat. The coughs turned into painful, hoarse burps. The man on my other end reached an arm across me and smacked the old man on his shoulder to shut him up.

It was too hot in the stuffy room to sit so close to these strangers, and yet, I wished for a shawl or a bedsheet to cover my body. I felt exposed that night; it was my brief moment in hell, without privacy, pillows, or a Wi-Fi password.

Soon, it got quiet, and a policewallah switched off the yellow light outside, and I only smelled the stench if I paid attention to it, and I ignored the grunts and muffles of my cellmates, and I was too bored to be scared any more.

Maybe Maama wouldn't come to my rescue. I had already had the urge to zip open and add to the mess of urine on that cesspool in the other corner of the cell, but behenchod, I held back. Maybe, I wouldn't hold back tomorrow, I thought. And perhaps I'll be here the next night, too, next to a group of new friends to spit and piss and belch with. Would anyone come for me? I wondered.

Would Papa?

He had always protected me, my papa. Especially after the riots, especially after Rishi bhaiya left us, leaving a void that only I could fill for him. But this...this would be a new, embarrassing low for him. People in Varanasi would know now; they would know that, of the male heirs to Bhagwan Beads, one had become a stranger to the family, and the other, a criminal. Papa would get calls from Vijay Malhotra, the richest man in the city, where Malhotra would ask him with faux concern about the future of his business. Maybe Punditji would call too, and say he regretted offering Papa his help during the riots.

Then I thought of Mummy, and I knew that she would react differently. I knew she would want to call and hear my voice, and then cry a little more, because kasam se sometimes nothing made her more comfortable than a little sorrow.

I was months away from my exams and from college applications, months away from finally realizing my dream of following Rishi bhaiya across to the other side of the world to that beautiful American freedom. Ever since the riots, Papa had made me believe that we were better now, that we had money, that we were above the petty filth of my country, that we wouldn't need to worry about the hypogeal rats in dirty train stations, and never have to spend a summer afternoon without blasting our air conditioners.

But it didn't matter, samjhe? Ultimately, my cellmates and I lived in the same country, breathed the same smoggy air, and no amount of money could filter out the polluted oxygen we choked on, all together.

I *did* eventually sleep that night, and I was so tired that I slept through a revolving carousel of more men being pushed in and pulled out of the cell, and it wasn't until someone jerked me forcefully by my shoulder that I awoke to find myself on the cold bench. My long arms and legs had shrivelled inwards pathetically into my body. It was that moustachioed policewallah letting me know that my Maama had arrived to pick me up. It was exactly 11 a.m.

'Chalo beta,' the policeman said, pulling his trousers up by his belt over his round tummy. He slapped me on my back, 'Get up. Your uncle has taken care of things.'

I didn't ask Raghu maama what he had paid to get me out and clear my name. Papa explained it to me over the phone the next day, scolding me for the embarrassment I had caused him. The police here, Papa discovered, asked for much higher bribes than their small-town counterparts, and Raghu maama refused Papa's offer of paying him back for my mistake.

'You see,' Papa said on the phone, 'We owe that uncle of yours, now. He took one son away from us first, and now, he took care of our second. We will *always* owe him.' Papa asked

Mummy to pray for my future, turned his mattress a few more degrees towards the east, and called on his astrologers to suggest a new gemstone for me.

A bed of chandan, a criss-cross of wood, a charpai for the final rest, brown turning grey turning white. More chandan on the body, pieces of wood crackling and tearing apart, a havan for the departed, a bonfire beyond my time. And sandwiched in between is the frigid, unmoving vessel that was once my body, nostrils stuffed with cotton, wrapped in a white chaddar, a final flimsy cover from the orange flames, big toes tied together to keep the legs straight and parallel, sesame seeds fed into the dead mouth, ghee poured on the skin to add a roasted, buttery aftertaste to the afterlife, and a red tilak on the exposed forehead.

Then, it burns.

Soft tissues contract, skin tears, muscles rip apart, the fat melts, then the organs shrink—the stomach lined with cheeseburgers, the liver damaged with whisky, the lungs blackened by herbal smoke, the heart disheartened—and soon, the joints begin to contract, in a type of post-mortem movement only possible due to the lively flicker of the fire, all until the bones themselves begin to crumble in the heat—the cremation pyre temporarily mimicking the great life-giving sun—until all the colours of my physical form descend into an ashy white, a beautiful decay into eventual nothingness.

TWENTY-NINE

Two days before the riots was a Wednesday—24 March 2010. We finished our classes by noon. Those were the days when Sakshi didi and I took that giant yellow school bus back home every day, where I sat in the back with Dhiraj talking about our favourite WWE superstars, and Didi squeezed in one of the front seats with her friends. Grabbing my backpack and water bottle at our stop, I ran out of the bus ahead of Didi, raced to our building and up the stairs to our flat, making sharp turns as I wound my way up, water spilling from my slightly unscrewed bottle.

I knew something was wrong as soon as Mummy opened the front door. There were dark circles under her eyes. She was wearing her white Reeboks indoors. Before I could even drop the backpack and say 'Hello' she said, 'Pack up, Vishnu. Pack all your things. We need to leave.'

'Mummy! Nimbu pani!' I demanded.

'We need to leave.'

'What happened?' Sakshi didi finally appeared in the open doorway.

'We need to leave, beti,' Mummy said. 'Pack up. Papa will be home soon, and then he'll drop us at Mughalsarai, understand? Pack up now. You won't have time in the evening.'

Suno now, listen to me—I only knew then what Mummy allowed me to know, samjhe? She was my shield, keeping my twelve-year-old mind safe behind her protective kavach. We were going to Delhi, she said, for a week, maybe more. We would see Rishi bhaiya. *Pack all the clothes you need! Day clothes, night pyjamas, chappals, shoes. School? School is off for the next week!*

Chhutthi! I said ecstatically. I'll take my books and pens, and for the maths homework my pencils, cutters, rubbers, scales, protractors, compass. I had my full Iron Man pencil box ready to go. Chhutthi!

Didi, however, deflated my excitement when I asked Papa why he wasn't coming to Delhi with us. We were seated in the backseat of the Maruti Zen, as Papa drove us to the station. Mummy was sitting beside him in the front.

'Don't be an idiot, Vishnu,' Didi said. 'Papa is busy.'

'Don't call your brother that,' Mummy said.

'But you promised, Papa,' I complained. 'The big mall in Gurgaon. You promised we'll go there. What about Rishi bhaiya? You're not coming to see him?'

Papa didn't answer and Mummy didn't say anything either, but Didi took over the reins from them.

'You are an idiot, Vishnu,' she repeated. 'There are bad men here, okay? Very bad men. Papa is taking care of some problems. How are you in Class 7 and *still* such an idiot? Stop watching that fake wrestling dishoom dishoom all day. Grow up, okay?'

'Sakshi!' Mummy said. 'He's still a child, beti; don't say that.'

'He is going to be a teenager soon, Mummy,' Didi shot back. 'He's *not* a child.'

'Silence!' Papa thundered, then followed it up by honking the horn furiously. We got the message. *Silence.*

So, I didn't ask any more questions. Papa dropped us off two hours before the train was due to arrive at Mughalsarai station. He gave Mummy a squeeze on her shoulder and handed her an envelope full of cash. 'Take care of your mother, okay?' Papa smiled half-heartedly. 'You're not a little baccha any more, samjhe, Vishnu? Your sister is right. You have to grow up now.'

I could only nod in reply because I still didn't understand what he meant. His obvious nervousness shook me up. I didn't know who these 'bad men' were, but I knew that Papa was scared—and that scared me, too. We spent many more hours at the station after he left, waiting for our delayed train, smelling the rats and the urine and the smoke, and the people who slept on gunny sacks in the darkest corners of the platform.

⁂

Sakshi didi liked to repeat herself, 'Vishnu, how are you? Are you okay?'

'I'm here. I'm fine.'

'Are you okay?'

Behenchod, I was just fine, thankyouverymuch. I was thirteen and didn't want to be pestered. My sister had a jittery voice, and spoke at the speed of thought. I had long learned to ignore her, and recently, trained myself to not even listen. But now, she spoke slowly, as if enunciating each syllable, in the same way Mummy typed her Google password, one slow letter at a time.

There was no escape from Didi that night. We were all stuck in the confined space of that sleeper coach of the train—Mummy, fast asleep on the bottom bunk, Didi in the middle, and me on the top—and even though we couldn't see each other, Didi could sense that I was lying awake in the dark. It was three in the morning; hour two of our delayed journey from Mughalsarai to New Delhi. Rishi bhaiya had already left, and we didn't know yet that he had left for good.

No matter how much I tried to sleep, the collective smell of the world outside and inside this train—the smoke and the open toilets and the egg curries and the feet of sixty-four strangers who had taken their socks off—kept me tossing uncomfortably, side to side on the cold, hard berth.

Sakshi didi was still a teenager then, years before she met Mohan and was told to marry him. She asked me for a fourth time, 'Vishnu, are you okay? Are you sure you don't want to talk?'

I realized, yaar, that it was *she* who needed to talk.

'It will be fine, Didi,' I finally said, and I knew then that I should probably allow her to speak her mind, to invite a reaction. I turned my statement into a question. 'Hai na? It will be fine, won't it?'

'Yes, yes, it will be fine. Papa said it will be all fine. Don't you worry about anything, you understand? Things like this happen all the time. This is India, hai ki nahi? This is the only way, sometimes, that things get done in India.'

We were in a train coach full of strangers, unknown faces in the dark, all going to different destinations. And it was then that I realized who my sister *wasn't*. She wasn't them. She wasn't a stranger. No matter how much I hid from her in the silence of the night, and no matter how much I would hide from her in the years to come, she could sniff me out. She would know me.

'Will Papa be fine?' I asked, and there was a sincere crack in my voice when I spoke. 'Will he come to Delhi to see us?'

'It will be fine,' she repeated. 'Don't worry, it will all be fine.'

The next morning, we were in Delhi reunited with Rishi bhaiya. Papa called every day, and although he didn't tell me anything, I could tell by Mummy's swollen cheeks that she had soaked up all of the fear into herself.

'Let's go to the mall, beta,' she said. 'Don't worry about anything. Your Maama will drive us to the mall.'

Dekho now, it's this moment, this death, which allows me to know what I couldn't have seen through Mummy's super shield, her kavach. In the summer of 2010, while we walked around the mall in Delhi eating masala corn and Cornetto ice cream, Papa was back home, back in the heat. Happy Singh rushed into Papa's old office with the news, sweating and scared. Four men had broken down one of Bhagwan Beads's workshops in Muktigarh village. Dozens of more men from the karamchari sangh had begun gathering in Muktigarh for a union meeting to protest. They came on buses and bicycles and jeeps.

'Useless chootias,' Papa said.

Papa wasn't surprised that the workers had united, but he was shocked that they had acted so soon. Bhagwan Beads employees—blowers and polishers and glass-cutters and sweepers and painters and the general majdoors who carried whatever heavy load their shoulders could bear—had chosen a leader. Lakshman the glass-blower. The workers had requested Papa for a raise.

Over at his competitor, Kashi Beads, the artisans and majdoors had got identity cards and basic health insurance guarantees, and the glass-blowers in their oven-hot workshops got to wear gloves and eye protection, and the wives of those employees were employed too, painting beads and weaving necklaces while they sat in circles in their villages.

'This is all we want, Shankarji,' said Lakshman. He was a thin man with a scarred, leathery face. Papa recognized him—the determined look in his eye and the proud twirl in his moustache. 'ID cards, sir,' Lakshman said. 'They are the most important thing.'

Papa, however, was wary of identification. An ID card meant that each of them would be counted, that each would have proof of their status, that all the majdoors and village folk could suddenly demand to be treated—*'Treated', he scoffed to himself*—like any other employee. Happy Singh sombrely did the mathematics and reported how expensive the process would be once all the numbers added up.

Now, in Muktigarh, the crowd of seventy-eight unhappy workers gathered outside a dairy farm. They sat on the dirt and grass with their legs crossed, close to the hay and dung, smelling like early spring in D.C. but with the faint foreign smell of chemical fertilizer wafting in the air. Their faces were darkened and hardened by the sun. Standing alone in between them was Lakshman, who led the chants. 'Shankar Agarwal ki Hai Hai!'

Beside Lakshman was Kareem, and the two men raised their arms together, like a referee rewarding the winner of a boxing bout.

'We will not let them divide us!' said Kareem.

'Hindu–Muslim stand together!' Lakshman said. 'Shankar

Agarwal ki Hai Hai!'

'Hai Hai!' the workers echoed.

'Bhagwan Beads nahi khulega!' he said. 'Bhagwan Beads will stay shut!'

'Nahi khulega! Nahi khulega!'

The workers broke into the factory building that night, tearing apart the metal door of my father's cupboard, and set fire to all his documentation: property papers, sale deeds, account statements, and tax invoices. Papa had backups for everything important at home, of course, but this was still an inconvenience, a slap on the face by people who were meant to work *for* him, who were expected to look up to him as their provider. The public act of disrespect ended with a bonfire of the paperwork in the dusty ground in front of the factory gate.

'There was even dancing, Shankar sir,' Happy Singh added.

Papa knew that this agitation would get out of control, that they would soon quit their jobs if he didn't find a solution. They would return to their villages, or join a rival company, or find another industry that paid better. And Papa would be left with nothing, a khandar in the place of a factory.

Papa decided that he had to make a phone call.

'It's me, Shankar Agarwal,' Papa said to the male voice on the other end.

Suno, this is how the past overlaps with the present, where the future folds into the past, making a perfectly holy chakra, all 360 degrees covered. Years ago, one of the men who had written their name in Mummy's register at the Ram Guest House was Punditji, even if in those years—the years before the Masjid fell—he called himself by a different name. This man had fondly remembered Papa's hospitality, up to the night before the great destruction in Ayodhya. It was a big day for him, out on the front lines. He had an unforgettable, lemony-shaped face, with a bald head, and even the Ancient Chariot Man would hear of his leadership amidst chaos. He met Papa again, years later at a mutual friend's wedding in Varanasi. Now, he was known as Punditji, still bald and round, but a rising political force in these parts. 'Your missus made the best roti, Shankar,' he had said, and then, added with a slap on Papa's back. 'Any problem, you call me, okay? There is not a single issue I can't solve. Just call, call this number.'

And when the right time came, Papa called that number.

'It's me, Shankar Agarwal.'

'Shankar Agarwal, who?'

It was a calm voice, both curt and descriptive, giving a command rather than asking a question.

'Shankar Agarwal. From Varanasi. Punditji said that if I ever needed anything....'

A pause. Papa bit into a samosa while he waited.

The voice behind the line changed. This one was softer, but had a nasally after-echo. 'Shankar Agarwal. I think I know what this is about.'

'They are going to tear me apart, Punditji!' Papa's words spilled out of his mouth. 'They are going to destroy me. I will be left with nothing. I need your help.' His voice fell, cracking like a hormonal teenager. He felt as though his feet were sinking into the floor, and he could no longer taste the samosa in his mouth or smell the dusty air surrounding him.

'Slow down, slow down, Shankar,' said Punditji. His calm words didn't match the sharp edge in his voice. It only made Papa more uncomfortable.

'I want them gone, Punditji,' Papa yelped, and then caught himself, realizing that Happy Singh was in the room with him. He cleared his throat and started again. 'I want to punish these madarchods in a way that they'll never dare to disrupt my livelihood again.'

There was a moment's silence on the other end of the line.

'Do you know what you're asking of me?' Punditji finally said.

'I want to cut them all up.'

'You have my blessings. We will cut them all up.'

The voice was seductive and confident. Papa couldn't conjure up a response.

'We know about your problem,' Punditji said. 'Your employees, they are all Mohammedans, aren't they?'

'Not…not all of them….'

'Don't worry, I have people in your district to take care of them. There will be some problems. One or two bodies on this side first. Aur bas, then my people will take care of everything. You show up later, okay. They need to see you there. They need to see who is in command. They need to see who they should answer to. Okay?'

Nahi, Papa didn't know it then, but the wheels were already in motion. By the time he hung up, Happy Singh got a call on his phone. A woman—a Hindu woman—had been raped and murdered and raped again in Muktigarh. *Who else would it be, Shankar sir,* Happy Singh said, *but those Mussulman majdoors, no?*

That afternoon, a glass-blower was murdered in retaliation—the first protestor to speak up in Muktigarh. Lakshman's body lay outside the cowshed, in a white vest and blue lungi. Next to him sat his friend Kareem, his face covered by his coarse, red palms, letting out short sobs. Bare-chested, barefoot.

The riots began.

It was a mini Mahabharat, samjhe, where seventy-seven of those remaining protesting men were surrounded by 214 other men. The protestors carried sticks and thin metal sheets they had crudely cut into sharp swords; their attackers carried shovels and sickles and cricket bats made of Kashmiri willow. The protestors were mainly Muslim and the new men were all Hindu, and behenchod, do I really need to give you the whole damn kahani now? What Papa wouldn't realize was that Bhagwan Beads was only a small spark flickering beside a larger bonfire. Some fought for that temple in Ayodhya and some for the mosque. Some were outraged by cheeseburgers and some by pepperoni pizzas. The rage had been there for generations, dormant, finally visible through centuries-old scars. And in Muktigarh, they wrote another chapter.

One man was killed in a pretty straightforward way, with a dagger to the heart; another got it in the side of his stomach. Another had his throat slit from behind. One was first axed on the back of his knee, in the tibia, and then an axe blade was thrust into his skull. The blade remained stuck in there, you know? Took two men to pull it out. Sach mein, it was some medieval shit.

One man wielded his cricket bat in wild circles, like Dhoni's helicopter shot, until he finally connected with a neck, smashing it. Some men tried to escape into the abandoned school in the village, under the camouflage of the tall wheat plants, to no avail. There were some who were cut across the back and shoulders with sickles. Sweating bodies clashed with each other. Some were stomped down and punched and kicked until they bled to death. Some used stones. Sometimes, the skulls were tougher than the stones and the weapons crumbled upon contact. Sometimes, the skulls cracked open.

Papa arrived in the evening in his old, bright-blue Maruti Zen, with Happy Singh by his side. They parked a stone's throw away, across the overgrown wheat. From this distance, they all looked the same. They had similar hunches in their upper backs, the same black hair dirtied into shades of brown and orange, and they cursed each other in the same language. Papa couldn't tell one side from the other in the dense clouds of dust.

Papa parked the car thirty metres away from the battlefield, where the dirt road ended, across the peaceful rustle of wheat crops. He was in his white shirt, cheeks unshaven, wearing dusty black shoes on his feet. The sky was bluer here, outside the city, and there wasn't as much sound of that loud, honking traffic that had become ubiquitous around our Mehmoorganj neighbourhood.

But he was close enough to hear the barrage of shouts and screams and the thumping of feet and slicing of blades. Suno, I don't have a heartbeat, but I can feel his now. I feel his heart as it thumped on the first day of the riots. It was a rush for him, a fearful satisfaction. This is what it felt like to be alive. It reminded him of that day in Ayodhya, decades ago, when he ate spicy bhelpuri and watched a similar crowd of angry men bring down the Masjid to claim back *their* land, their bhoomi.

Muktigarh was *his* bhoomi, he thought.

Eventually, as the afternoon heat became more unbearable, Papa went back to sit inside his car, baking in its shade. There was a knock on the side of his window. Outside, there were two men, each carrying a local-made katta, muzzles tucked under the waistband of their pyjamas.

'Pranaam, sirji,' the two men folded their hands together to greet Papa. One of them had a pencil-thin moustache and wore a gamchha around his shoulders. The other was lean and tall, with a large black mole growing on the side of his nostril, sprouting out small threads of grey hair.

'Please step out of your car,' said the one in the gamchha. The piece of cloth used to be white—Papa could tell—but had grown brown in the dirt there.

'Wha-what?'

Papa froze in his spot, unable to string together a properly worded response. His eyes were suddenly hazy, as if his vision was blurred by the dust outside.

'This will be over soon,' the man said. 'We are with you. Please come outside.'

Papa took a deep breath. These were Punditji's men. It would be okay, he thought. He opened the door and stepped out. He immediately felt the loo, a gust of heat in the bloody summer afternoon.

'Here,' the man with the gamchha reached inside his pyjamas and pulled out the gun. 'Sardarji told us that you didn't bring your own weapon.'

'My own…?'

Papa had never held a firearm in his life. The katta was cold to the touch, and lighter than he expected it to be. He held it with both hands, palms open, fingers spread out wide, careful not to touch anywhere that would break the little device—or discharge it.

'Yes, sirji,' the man said, and he smiled. 'Don't you want to have a little fun, too?'

The man in the gamchha nodded at Papa to follow them, and obediently, Papa did as he was told. They waded through the wheat field. Both men were built like athletes, six-feet-somethings with strong and broad shoulders; Papa felt so much smaller in their presence.

Papa carried the gun in his left hand, barrel and muzzle pointing downwards. He kept a loose hold over the grip, but then, worried that the gun would fall, he grasped it tightly again. They stepped closer to the action, so that Papa could smell the fresh dung slapped on the walls of huts nearby. He could hear groans of those fallen to the ground and he could see the cricket bats gleaming in the afternoon sun.

They directed Papa towards a handpump at the edge of the village, right where the wheat field ended to give way to a small gutter, flooded with water and mud and blood. A tall, young man was lying here on his stomach, under the handpump, hugging the iron cylinder. He was bare-chested and barefoot, wearing nothing but a pair of white pyjamas. Papa knew he was alive when he heard him whimper.

'Get up,' the man in the gamchha commanded.

At this, the man groaned again, and with great effort, lifted his upper body to rest against the cylinder's hot, grey surface.

Papa didn't recognize him, but he had met this man before. We both had. He had a long face and eyes that seemed to always droop in a morose fashion, disguising his true intentions—happy or sad or excited or frightened. His name was Kareem, and once upon a time, he had been afraid of fire.

Papa could see Kareem's face now. He would've been barely

twenty-five, twenty-six, Papa thought. He had a thin, sharp face and bushy eyebrows like mine. Sweat poured down his golden-brown skin, streaming down both sides of his face to his neck. Those droopy eyelids kept closing, heavy over his eyes, and when his head swayed back and forth, Papa could see a large whirlpool of red on the back of his head, dry and sticky and fully entrenched in the thick strands of his tangled, black hair.

Papa pitied him in that moment. He imagined that this young man would've been innocent if he had lived a different life, if he wasn't here, if he hadn't taken part in this needless protest. *Protesting for what? A waste of time, a waste of life*, Papa thought. *Just another laaparwaah kid. Wasted, wasted.*

I saw this moment, floating up above my deathbed, and I saw Papa look into Kareem's eyes as I did now, nearly a decade later, nearly a generation later, nearly a lifetime later. The grassy smell of the wheat, the wet soil under him, cow dung and diesel generators, spilled beer at Lucky Luke, onion rings next to my cheeseburger and stale, buttery popcorn. Each sensation, pleasure and pain, and heat and cold, from Kareem's death to my own. Then, I drifted, up and away, like wheat husk in the light summer breeze. All that was left now was the future.

The man in the gamchha now looked at Papa, and so did the second man with the big mole. Papa wanted to order them around, to uphold his end of the class superiority between himself and these men. But, with one curve of their lips, they reduced my father to subservience, as if they were now calling the shots, as if Papa was dangling from a lower rung on the ladder, raising his arm up for help.

'Go ahead, sirji,' gamchha-man said. 'We left him just for you. You can finish the job.'

The gun was still in Papa's left hand, gripped tight, warm clammy sweat from his palms all over its cold surface.

By the handpump, there were no tall buildings or trees, or anything to provide shade from the angry sun above. Papa's shadow extended beyond him and towards the young man moaning on the ground.

Papa dropped the gun.

'I...I can't,' he said, and took a few steps back.

'Are you sure, sirji?' the man in the gamchha asked. 'Punditji insisted that you....'

'I'm going back.'

They allowed Papa to return halfway back to his car before one of them shot Kareem.

And time stopped for Kareem as it has for me, and he left behind the cold weight of his body and was reduced to this eternal nothingness, his personal vacuum. His mother wept for him, and his sisters did, too. His childhood friend, Yusuf, was still alive, employed as a cobbler back in their hometown, his burnt hand balancing the weight while the able hand did the work. And when he heard the news, Yusuf, too, visited the kabristan, where Kareem's body was buried in the cheapest plot of land that his family could afford back in Firozabad. And here, Kareem floated away, too, trapped in his own omniscience, seeing my birth and my death in the same instant as he saw his own.

Papa flinched when he heard the shot, and a hot current of electricity went through his body. But he didn't turn around to see. Happy Singh was waiting in the driver's seat, clutching on to the steering wheel as if it was his armour.

I can see Papa, haan, I see him clearly. I see him in the passenger seat of that old Maruti, hand shaking as he wound up the handle of the car window anticlockwise to shut out the dust and the rage from the field outside. This was before the days he could afford a car with one of those automatic power windows, samjhe? This was before he could afford to sit in the back seat while a chauffeur drove him around the city in style in an air-conditioned car. Nahi, it was just him and Happy Singh, and in his hand was an old flip phone, which he held up to his ear to speak to Punditji while he screamed at Happy Singh. 'Drive away! Hurry up! Drive! Drive!'

Outside his car window were scenes that I had never seen before, but scenes which now form the background of my memories of that dusty, sepia-toned North Indian countryside. Men, holding the same sickles that they used to cut grass with on farms, chopped down other men, and spat on them when they screamed, and sprayed the pale-yellow wheat fields with blood. They roared their battle cries, raising their spirits for this yudh. But this was not a war—it was slaughter.

'Drive, drive quickly, Happy Singh,' Papa said, before he turned his attention to the voice in his phone. 'Okay, okay,' he replied. 'It's done.'

They drove away, and when Papa returned home, he called Mummy in Delhi.

'Everything is fine, Pushpa,' he said, but his quivering voice did nothing to pacify her.

'Is it over?' she asked. 'Is everything okay?'

There was a sound of static in the mobile connection, a white noise buzzing like a little bee. It settled into Mummy's right ear and flew across the back of her head to her left and back again. And even though I couldn't hear that buzzing then, I can hear it now. I can feel Mummy's discomfort in her own skin, hear the whispers inside her head. I can hear Papa's whispers, too, and I can feel that he had the strength to tune them out, to silence his doubts, his blame, his guilt.

I climb inside his brain and I give an ear to the voices he ignored, to his place in the madness, to his culpability.

'Almost over,' Papa told Mummy. 'Everything is fine, Pushpa.'

The cricketers at Muktigarh left the field for the night, and the protesting workers used this opportunity to call in reinforcements from nearby villages. Sari-weaving bunkars came from Badhoi. Carpet weavers cycled down from Mirzapur. Rickshawwallahs from Azamgarh. And the next morning, the battle continued in Muktigarh, and there were more fatalities. Just as Punditiji had requested, Papa made an appearance at the ranabhoomi once more—on the field of battle. *They must know,* Punditji had said.

Punditiji had paid the police to stay away, but their payment was only an appetizer. Papa was now in their debt for the main course, and for as long as Bhagwan Beads prospered in Varanasi, he had to make sure that the khaki-uniformed bellies of the local chiefs stayed satiated.

On the third day, men with sickles and axes called upon their god as they lynched and killed. By noon, more than half of the workers and their friends had been murdered. Punditiji's men finally decided to stop the bloodshed when the remaining few alive slumped down among the bleeding corpses on the green grass.

Papa walked through the farm, wading past wheat shoots and overgrown grass, until he saw a heap of dead bodies, and some live ones. There was blood everywhere.

'We're done here, sirji,' said one of the men with the pistols.

'Shankar Agarwal ki Hai Hai!' a voice groaned close to Papa. Someone was alive.

Then, a dagger sliced, a throat choked, a torso thudded down to the ground.

A spurt of blood. Some on the grass. Some on the other pile of bodies. Some on Papa's white shirt.

'We're done here, sirji,' the man repeated.

※

Mummy was my kavach, yes. While that buzzing continued to hum between her ears, she did her best to distract me in Delhi. We went to malls for ice cream, and to Paranthe Wali Gali in Chandni Chowk for paneer parathas and jalebis. Rishi bhaiya stayed home and didn't ask about Papa—he understood everything and spoke about nothing. 'I have exams,' he told us.

Didi and I watched movies at the PVR multiplex and bought

pirated DVDs from Palika Bazaar. And even when we were stuck in traffic with Mummy—all three of us cramped together in the back seat of an autorickshaw—we didn't mind, exhilarated by the dense air of the metropolis. Everything was bigger, faster, better here. How could I ever live in Varanasi again?

Mummy would have stopped me, then, if she knew what was going through my mind, if she knew my restlessness, that I would fight to come back to Delhi, then insist to get on that flight to D.C., then spend years in this foreign country where I would take my last breath. *Tragic,* she would think to herself, *everyone deserves to die in their homeland.*

Haan yaar, if Mummy was at Lucky Luke that night, she would have been my kavach. She would have scolded me for being at the bar, for eating beef, for drinking like my father does. *You need to pay attention, beta,* she would say. *Stay out of the way. Don't argue too much. Remember you're a foreigner there. Be extra careful.*

And I would laugh back at her and point to the man with the handgun. *It wasn't my fault, Mummy,* I would say. And in this ajeeb imaginary scenario, Mummy would be at the sports bar looking overdressed in a blue sari with expensive jewellery around her neck, standing awkwardly among these Americans, and she would be more sad than angry, because truly, she really never got angry at all. Sorrow was all she had.

I thought about my earliest memories of Varanasi, Mummy packing my tiffin box of egg-and-onion sandwiches every day, except for Monday when she allowed Maggi with ketchup as a special treat. I thought about her during my first week in D.C., imagining what she would have been like at my age in a new country, going to class and making friends and spending money on drinks and shoes and not worrying about the Papa she would have to marry one day.

On the day the bloodshed ended in Muktigarh, Papa had told Mummy to stay away a little longer, to not pay attention to the news, to keep the children distracted. She did as she was told. At night, while we slept, she cried into her brother and sister-in-law's arms. Rishi bhaiya saw her, too, and when she went over to hug him, he froze, counting the seconds in this head till the hug was over. *Six...Seven. Eight.*

The newspapers called it Goonda Raj, as in, the Rule of the Mob, a moniker which my home state has worn as a badge of honour over the years. *We survived the Motherfucking Goonda Raj*, we say, *How could anything else on earth possibly harm us?*

The dead bodies were left in Muktigarh for two days, placed in random corners to rot, fusing into the fields like the mosaic beads in Papa's factories. Nobody—neither the villagers nor the kin of those who were killed—came immediately forward to identify and report or retrieve and grieve. The district police finally sent an autopsy and collection force after hearing complaints from the villagers about the stench in the air.

∽

One time, long ago, Papa had told me of the beauty of glasswork. 'You can bend the glass in any shape if you heat it enough,' he'd said. He had made it sound so easy, as if a little bit of heat could give a glass-blower the power to shape and reshape the world in front of him just as he saw fit.

Papa soon replaced the dead employees with new ones, moved into the new factory space for Bhagwan Beads, and got back to work. The ones who were dead were dead. *Kya bataon yaar?*—he didn't see them at all. For him, they were mere shadows of real human beings. Their only agency was how their lives reflected on his. They had no inscapes, no lives beyond what suited him, no backstories.

In computing terms, they were simply dead images, with no URLs linking forward to further information. Papa didn't know about the carpet weaver who loved his aunt's kheer with extra almonds and pistachios, or the painter who was too embarrassed to tell his friends that he watched saas-bahu serials with his wife and actually enjoyed them, or the floor manager who slapped around his son for eating the chicken leg piece without his permission. And he didn't know about Kareem, the glass-blower who had once spent Eid with his closest Hindu friend, and after much coaxing, finally showed Lakshman the ghazal he wrote in his free time, which he had never shared with anyone else.

And now, I laugh; I laugh the accumulated laughter of every cruel joke heard in the brief history of mankind; I laugh until I feel dry, invisible tears streaming down my formless face. From a deep cove of my subconscious, I laugh out of years of suppressed guilt. I laugh for I would never become my father; and I also laugh *at* him, at what he became, at what he did. What he did for me.

After the riots, there was nothing for Papa beyond the surface. No source codes left to examine.

THIRTY

There was a smudge on Papa's white shirt. It was a red mark about the size of a clenched fist, and similar in shape, too. In the chaos of the afternoon, Papa only noticed the stain when he was safely back inside the car, when he was being driven away from the scene of the riots, when he could finally roll up his windows and bring his breathing down to a steady, peaceful pace. He touched the smudge with his index and middle fingers gingerly, and felt that it was still a little damp. *Blood.* He could smell it. He pressed into his shirt but didn't feel any pain.

He exhaled. The blood wasn't his.

Papa arrived home, ran up the dusty stairs of that two-storey building to our old Mehmoorganj flat, unbuttoned his white shirt, and threw it on the floor.

He was alone and felt comfortable pacing around the flat shirtless, unashamedly flaunting his hairy, protruding paunch. Nahi nahi, in those days, he didn't even have much space to pace around, samjhe? He moved from the kitchen to the bedrooms and the bathroom that smelled like a mouldy, wet towel. Then, Papa paced back to the main door to stare at that white shirt on the floor.

Nahi, he would never wear that shirt again. No amount of cursing at the dhobi could completely wash off the stain. No matter how hard he tried, a dark smudge of that fist-sized mark remained on its pristine whiteness. Whenever Papa got that shirt back from the dhobi, he would send it down again. 'Not good enough,' he would say, and every time it was washed, it shrank a little, and then a little more. And then Papa began to gain weight, too, until his waist grew into a wide tube, until he was so big for that shrunk shirt that he finally gave it to the dhobi who could hardly stand the shirt oversaturated with the smell of Nirma washing powder and threw it away.

Papa used to be a thin man before the riots. Achchha, not 'thin' like the men who worked at his workshops, but pretty much in shape, you know? That body mass index was within control. That latent diabetic gene only lurked in the shadows.

But things were about to change—on the last day of the riots, as Happy Singh drove the Maruti Zen away to safety, Papa called Punditji with the news, and Punditji told him he was happy.

'This is a brave act you have done, Shankar,' Punditji said. As privileged and giddy as Papa felt to be under the good graces of such an important man, he couldn't help but squirm a little whenever Punditji delivered homilies in his nasal voice. 'We have shown these monsters that we have the strength of our gods on our side, too. That we will chop off their balls and feed them to their descendants. You have shown them, Shankar.'

'Yes, Punditji,' Papa replied.

'Don't you worry now, Shankar, don't you worry. I will help you with anything you need, you understand? You must not be scared. You have my aashirwad. You have me with you. I'll always keep your belly full, you understand?'

'Yes, Punditji.'

Papa's belly got fuller. Over the next few years, he rekindled an appetite for all the snacks denied to him when he was a child. For lunch in his office at Bhagwan Beads, he ate greasy samosas and fluffy bhaturas with chhole. He gobbled down little idlis at the Kerala Café. He found a kachoriwallah near Assi Ghat which later became his favourite place for Sunday breakfasts. He had gulab jamuns and motichoor laddus for dessert at home after dinner, and ordered kulfis and chocolate ice creams during the summer.

The summer after the riots, while eating samosas drenched in sweet-and-spicy sauce, Papa found a two-and-a-half-acre strip of farmland on the outskirts of the city, and he decided, *Chalo, yes, this is the place.* He made a few phone calls and discovered that the land was headed for legal dispute. It was under the name of an old great-grandmother who was a few blinks away from full blindness. She had three sons by two husbands vying for their share of the inheritance, but Happy Singh and Sud the lawyer reported that they wouldn't be a problem. 'She's poor, Shankar sir,' Happy Singh said. 'Very desperate. Doesn't want to deal with her children, you know? We will get a good bargain.'

Papa nodded his head side to side, happy to hear this news but still uncertain until he could ensure matters for himself. The old woman greeted him, clad in a dirty white sari, with skin reddened by decades of work out in the sun. She was indeed rich in property, but the saggy, thin skin on her bones suggested otherwise. Haan, she was desperate. Papa walked into her hut, and for years later, continued to swear that *he* was the last thing she saw before her eyesight blacked out for good.

'That old lady,' he laughed when, years later, he told this story to his friends at the Varanasi Trader's Union. 'She thought we were one of her sons and she scolded us. We had to tell her, "Nahi, nahi, Auntie, it's us—Shankar Agarwal. Don't you remember? Our lawyer came to talk about your property?"'

Papa made an offer—a criminally low offer—and the old lady accepted. Of course, the case wasn't going to be this simple, jao-khao-khatam-karo, was it? The sons took Papa to court, showed documentation of inheritance from their fathers, and showed bills passed in recent years about protecting farmland from being turned into polluting industry. One of the sons—the eldest and most cunning—even turned Papa's two-and-a-half-acre purchase into a political battle, joining hands with a regional party leader to decry Papa's illegal kabza. Six months after the riots, when Mummy, Sakshi didi, and I were back with Papa in Varanasi, a mob of a hundred angry men sporting red headbands gathered outside our house, waving flags branded with sickles, and carrying actual sickles, too. 'Shankar Agarwal murdabad!' they chanted. One of them had found a photo of Papa, published in a local newspaper after his role in the riots, and enlarged and pasted it on to a large white sheet of poster paper. Another person lit the poster on fire. 'Shankar Agarwal ki Hai Hai! Hai Hai! Hai Hai!'

But none of this bothered Papa. He called Punditji again, who had been elected to the parliament for the fourth consecutive time, and now had the ear of the soon-to-be prime minister of the entire fucking country. Punditji nodded. 'Don't you worry now, Shankar, don't you worry. Your loyalty to our vahini will be rewarded.' Punditji made a few more phone calls, and, just like that—fataak se—the troubles disappeared. The regional party was disbanded when *another* mob—this one dressed in orange—chased away the mob in red. A dozen people were trampled, a couple were killed. Then the smart eldest son of the old lady disappeared into the ether, and his two younger brothers moved to Assam, and finally, by summer 2011, the lady lost her hearing, too. Exceptions were made to property laws in the region for Papa, and more exceptions were made for minimum wages for Papa's employees, since he was able to list the glass-blowers at his workshops as freelance artisans instead of permanent workers.

From the money he saved, he bought a little more land near the airport, and sold it off for triple its value. He turned the original two-and-a-half-acres into what became his home base, the new site of the Bhagwan Beads factory. We moved to the new house in the Nagwa area of the city with a large driveway into the main building and a front lawn that needed two gardeners to maintain. On my fifteenth birthday, Papa gifted me an iPhone, and I smiled with giddy joy because I was the only one in Class 9 with a futuristic all-in-one device that allowed me to send emails, check the weather, and gawk at naked women of every race on earth, all with a simple flick of my thumb.

On the day Papa held a puja to inaugurate the new factory,

Punditji made a surprise appearance, arriving in a helicopter, unsettling the Banarasi dust. Punditji and Papa sat next to each other on the white mattress near the burning havan with their legs folded. Sweat streamed down Punditji's sideburns, over the prickly bits of hair on his otherwise bald head. As always, he was dressed in an orange kurta with an orange scarf thrown around his shoulders, and the fire and the heat made his face look like a dark shade of orange, too. He shook Papa's hand.

The fire was supposed to provide a spiritual cleansing to the new factory, an auspicious start to something new. The destruction of one thing for the creation of another. The wood crackled and contorted for Papa's attention, but Papa was too distracted, talking on his phone, contemplating, moving forward. After the havan, Papa ordered two dozen samosas from a new vendor that had appeared across the street from the factory.

In the years that followed, Papa didn't speak to Mummy about the riots. He didn't speak to Happy Singh, or to his lawyers, or any other chhotus who helped around the home or the office.

Even with Punditji, Papa shared only a silent understanding, a simple nod at the havan ceremony on the inauguration day of the new Bhagwan Beads factory. The fire would cleanse everything, Papa decided. He threw some grains of rice as the priest chanted verses in Sanskrit.

'Svaha!' said the priest. Papa and Punditji and Mummy, all echoed him: 'Svaha!'

My Papa—haan, haan, him—the man who had sweat in the factory grounds and toiled and sacrificed, and for much of his lifetime, suffered. I saw him when I died, and I thought about him at the riots in Muktigarh, that thick square moustache and those rosy, fat cheeks, and they didn't look the same to me any more.

Your comfort is someone else's catastrophe.

We moved to a bigger house, and Papa employed guards that carried guns, and Himanshu to cook instead of Mummy in the kitchen, and he bought a red Honda, and hired a driver so that he could sit in the back seat while he was driven to work. Varanasi is a densely populated city, with over twelve lakh residents all sharing the same narrow lanes on their way to work, to comfort, to prosperity. A holy, chaotic mela in India's most populous state. A city bursting at the seams with more people than its ancient gullies were designed for, where the thin roads of the labyrinthine colonies are now packed with cars of all sizes, scooters, motorbikes, pedestrians, stray dogs, and sluggishly moving cows.

And if, Papa thought from the back seat one day, *at some point on the way in the chaos of this city, the man driving my Honda was to accidently crush a stray on the way, how could I be blamed?* On his way to the new factory, the Honda inched forward in the congested traffic jams in the heart of the city, before the roads got a little clearer in the outskirts. A little less crowded. The journey became smoother. It was summertime and Papa was on his way to work again. He shut the car windows and asked the driver to turn on the air conditioner.

It was eight days after the last throat was slit in Muktigarh that Mummy and Didi and I all took the flight back to Varanasi. I fought for the window seat and was awestruck by the landscape below. Didi sat in the middle seat next to me, and Mummy was by the aisle. She wore a dark, crimson sari with gold-coloured embroidery across its border.

The stewardess was an attractive, tall woman, wearing a large red bindi. She pulled the meal trolley up to our row, leaned over to look at me and asked in a soft voice. 'Veg or Non-veg, sir?'

Wow. She said *Sir?*

'Non-veg,' I said, excitedly.

'Veg!' Mummy corrected me.

'No,' I corrected her correction. 'Non-veg.'

'What about you, ma'am?' the stewardess asked Didi.

'She'll have vegetarian,' Mummy spoke for her. 'Both of us are vegetarian.'

'Sure, ma'am.'

All of us received our little trays of lunch. I tore the silver foil off mine to reveal a chicken roll. Mummy and Didi had paneer.

'You should be careful eating this meat, Vishnu,' Mummy said, after the stewardess had moved on. 'You don't know how they cook it. And with all these diseases going around....'

I took a bite of roti-wrapped warm chicken tikka and nodded. My sister was lost in a magazine, uninterested in her meal.

'Are you not hungry, Sakshi?' Mummy asked.

She shrugged. 'I'll eat later.'

Mummy, it seemed, was persistent to start a conversation.

'What are you reading?'

'Just a magazine.'

'Which one? Show me?' she made Sakshi flip to the front cover, a photo of Beyoncé flashing bare shoulders and bare thighs in a small, violet outfit. Mummy frowned, looked up at Didi, and then at me.

'Don't let your brother have this,' she said.

'Mummy,' I asked. 'When will we visit Delhi again?'

'When your Papa tells us to.'

'Is he going to come with us?' asked Sakshi didi.

'Ask your Papa.'

'Why didn't he come with us this time?' I asked.

Didi rolled up the magazine and smacked me on the side of my arm.

'You're old enough to understand things now.'

'Mummy!' I complained.

Mummy sighed and leaned back. 'Ask your Papa.'

We landed in Varanasi, and Papa looked refreshed when he came to pick us up at the airport. His moustache was a dense shade of black, and his face glowed as if he had just emerged from a relaxing, warm bath. Mummy didn't speak to him on the drive back home.

But she knew. A day later, Papa was back at work and Didi

and I back at school. Mummy was home alone, spending time soaking in the afternoon sun through the cracks in the bedroom curtains, when she opened her Hanuman Chalisa and began to read random verses out to herself.

Ram Rasayan Tumahre Pasa / Sada Raho Raghupati Ke Dasa.
You have Ram's bhakti with you. You are the servant of Ram.
Then she shut it. From a creaky drawer inside her cupboard, she brought out a small, light-blue idol of a dancing Ganesh, put her lips against his round belly, and pressed it hard against her face until, finally, she was able to induce a single tear to fall down her cheek. She promised herself later that afternoon that she would begin an additional weekly fast on Wednesdays, with no solid food until sundown, for the next sixteen weeks.

Still, it wasn't enough to take away that numbing feeling in her forehead, that tiny buzzing bee in her ears. She was feeling a spiritual thirst, and no matter how many meals she skipped and holy water she poured on her Ganesh idol, nothing seemed to quench her. She visited the Vishwanath Temple in the old part of the city, and Sankat Mochan, where she warded off the fat monkeys on guard, and the Durga Mandir for the goddess' warrior energy. Then, she cast her net even wider, visiting the gurdwara for the sangat and sweet karah prasad, and going out to Sarnath to pick up on some of the enlightened vibes the Buddha had left behind a few millennia ago, too.

On the sixteenth Wednesday, she topped off this cocktail of consecration by evoking the highest holy trifecta of her gods. We had another havan at our new home under an old mango tree, with a bald priest mumbling Sanskrit verses seated around a square platform of bricks. The priest lit a sacrificial fire and Mummy asked all of us—Papa, Didi, and I—to come bathed and cleansed, wearing the whitest clothes we could find. We sat opposite the priest who pronounced soothing chants with his thin lips.

Mummy came fully armed. In a row in front of her, before the fire, she placed an akshamala—a garland of small wooden beads. Next to it stood a sudharshan chakra, a golden disc with serrated edges. Finally, there was that ubiquitous lingam, a clay oval column of Shiv's universe-penetrating phallus.

Brahma, the creator of the worlds; Vishnu, the preserver; and Shiv, the destroyer and transformer.

'Fold your hands together and pray,' she instructed me. I folded my hands and closed my eyes and allowed the incense and the smoke and the hypnotic chants to lull me into a mini morning nap. It was better than going to school.

Now, I enter that same moment of hypnosis again, but this time, I pay attention. I hear the verses and look at that akshamala, that chakra, that lingam. I see my life play out in front of that cleansing fire from the creation, preservation, and destruction of the entire universe. Brahma, Vishnu, and Shiv.

Papa, Me, and Wildhair.

Papa got our passports stamped with ten-year American tourist visas before our trip to New York. I learned then, within minutes of having a conversation with the Salvadorean taxiwallah who drove us from JFK airport to Manhattan, that this was a country where everyone could potentially be on an equal footing, where everyone—even me, even this taxiwallah—could have a chance. We spent those summer days walking under the skyscrapers of New York City, marvelling at the animated billboard signs for the latest Broadway release, drinking expensive coffee not from Starbucks but rare local brands that we hadn't heard of. None of us liked coffee, but yaar, it had to be tried, hadn't it? We all got cappuccinos, except for Papa, who ordered an Americano because he wanted to do the most American thing possible. It was strong and sharp and felt like a jolt to the head, taking us all out of our jetlagged drowsiness to continue conquering this grand city on foot.

We sweat in the summer humidity of this great city, and eventually, I landed up at a McDonald's, for the first cheeseburger of my life. Mummy and Papa had no idea that 'burger' by its very definition meant a bonanza of the finest cuts of cattle, and I didn't bother to tell them. It became a joke between my sister and I. Sakshi didi, an avowed vegetarian, didn't eat it herself; she was thinner than the French Fries she settled for, walking around awkwardly as if on stilts. But she enjoyed the conspiratorial moment nevertheless, giggling every time I said 'burger' in front of my parents.

Rishi bhaiya wasn't with us.

When we walked out of McDonald's, I felt changed. I looked up to see a new world, the big welcoming 'M'—the orange arch of capitalism—traffic on two feet and four wheels near Times Square that rushed on without a care, never stopping to wonder if I was the son of the second-richest man in an ancient city in eastern Uttar Pradesh. Flashing images of celebrities and cartoons took up life in a new dimension above us mere humans. We were from Varanasi, which claimed to be the oldest living civilization in the world, and for millennia, it was a city where beauty lay horizontal and close to the earth, to the ground that had shackled generations of people over thousands of years to its unambitious, static dust. A million feet had stepped on those stones back home and a million more were bound to its inescapable destiny. Out here in America, however, the high rises seemed like an elevator into the stratosphere. The gargantuan buildings roared up into space, continuing endlessly, a beautiful vertical escape of hope to all those grounded by problems like gravity and the Third World. *Haan*, my perfect American fascination was born.

Papa and Mummy went to Malaysia the next year, and then to Hong Kong. Papa had begun to wear those polo shirts with the crocodile logo over his heart. He had undeclared currency notes to buy imitation Chanel bags for Mummy, who was quite pleased because she knew that, back in Varanasi, no one would know that the bags were fake.

In Singapore, Mummy walked around in a bright yellow sari, as if she were visiting the Vishwanath Temple in the oldest gullies of Varanasi. They got on a cruise ship from there, where they played the slot machines late into the night, danced like they were decades younger by the swimming pool on board, and deboarded at tiny islands on their way, where Papa drank beer at the beach and Mummy went parasailing, screeching with joy as she soared high up above the water. The next year, they travelled to Europe for the first time, where Papa drank craft beers in Brussels and Mummy strained her knees to walk up to the top of the Acropolis in Athens. Mummy didn't bring her saris along this time, and instead, walked around in trousers or long skirts, with her eggshell-white full-brimmed sun hat, the headgear inspired by a photograph of Jennifer Lopez she had seen in a fashion magazine.

The riots, by then, were old news for Mummy. I moved to Delhi, and then followed in my brother's footsteps to Amreeka to study, and by then, Santa Gol Goppa had comfortably become the prime minister, and Sakshi didi got married, and I had a credit card to spend on whatever I wished in Washington, and Papa paid for it back home without me having to blink an eye, and haan haan, we were comfortable.

There is nothing.

No space, no physical dimensions to stretch from side to side, or look up and down. There are no eyes to see with, and nothing to leer at. There are no sounds to listen to and no ears to hear with. It smells empty and tastes like nothing. It is neither warm nor cold nor anything in between. This isn't heaven or hell or a purgatory or one of the starless rivers that I must cross to be reborn on the other side, or released into a higher state. No Canaan and no Zion. There is nothing higher to look down from, and nothing lower from where to observe the world up there. There is no atman and no maya. There is just all the past and all the future and there is I.

THIRTY-ONE

Eight years after the riots, a stranger shot me and killed me in Washington D.C. Then, I lost the only true home I had had in this lifetime—this body, this vessel, which had contained me as I grew from a nipple-suckling little baby to a beer-guzzling twenty-one-year-old.

I felt my body dry out immediately after the deafening sound of that gunshot, as if all of my fluids had leaked, as if I was the surface of a parched desert, as if I was the gravelly path outside Papa's Bhagwan Beads factory under the fierce summer sun, cracking under the heat. The insides of my eyes—their cruel vitreous humour—yes, that was all dry too, feeling as if the lens behind my cornea had nothing left to float on. I felt no perspiration under my arms or behind my knees. At the very end I felt my lifeless tongue hanging to its side, dry like coarse sandpaper inside my mouth.

I float now, above the body that lies dead in this bar in D.C., in the north-eastern sector of this country, west of the Atlantic about nine-and-a-half time zones away from the city of my birth—and even farther in the winter. Nahi yaar, there is no home. None but this ether.

Suno, I can't even look at that frail, bloody, lifeless body any more, that skinny 5'11", sixty-six and something kilograms of a young man, that baby face that still looked three years younger than what it was, that pointy nose threatening to pull away from the rest of its face, that unibrow, the unkempt knot of long, black hair, that chipped front tooth. Nahi, I leave it all lying there, frozen in its spot, as I am now frozen in time.

Dekho now, there's that bartender, who even on this crowded weekend night of playoff basketball hadn't broken a sweat, who smiled even at the people he hated because he needed every extra tip, who had moved from South Carolina to Washington three years ago because his family would never understand that he had a boyfriend. Haan, baba, a boyfriend. Yes, this bartender was a foreigner here.

And dekho, look at that young woman drinking a vodka sour with a group of friends from her poetry workshop. Look at how she has straightened her naturally curly hair so that people will stop asking her if they can touch it, and how she was laughing right before Wildhair showed up a second time at the bar. Stay with her, and you'll realize that she laughed only to remind the friends in her circle that she was actually *in* that fucking circle. She spoke in random spurts, and instead of making small talk about the weather or the game, she immediately told everyone about her mother's chemotherapy. They all found her a little strange but kept her around because she was pretty and she laughed at their literary puns. Yes, she was a foreigner, too.

There's that old man, who always came to Lucky Luke alone, sat at the bar, ate the nachos-with-cheese, downed three bottles of Budweiser, watched whatever sport was on, and then called it a night. Behenchod, he was a foreigner. That woman with the baby bump, twenty-one weeks pregnant, whose child was going to be a girl, who had allowed herself a glass of wine every week and broken that rule tonight to have her second rosé since Tuesday—yes, she too, didn't belong. That young man, too close to the game on the TV screen, rooting for the Warriors even though the rest of his friends at the round table behind him were Cavs fans; yes, he was a foreigner, too.

And then there was Jess, kneeling on all fours next to my body, golden-brown hair sticking to the side of her face, tears streaming down her cheeks.

Jess had kissed me all those months ago, and she told me she had been with Hamid. She didn't hear back from me after that kiss, and she barely heard back from Hamid either. Hamid had stepped towards Maya and then stepped away again. He stormed into the kitchen to see me and Tapiwa the African Prince. 'Let's go,' he had announced. 'It's three-dollar Corona night at the Cat King. We gonna get fuuucked up, bruh.' And after we stumbled out of the Karaoke Bar in Chinatown, after Hamid drunkenly left me behind, he and I didn't speak to each other either. Jess found out about it somehow and texted both of us a week later. Neither of us replied.

It's not my fault, she said to herself, alone one day in the library, nibbling on her sandwich at the corner table, soaking in the afternoon sun streaming in through the windows. But, deep inside herself, she felt that she had become the wedge between the two of us, and her mind went to crazy places because she had watched the *Gandhi* movie and remembered that Hamid had once joked that she wouldn't be the first white person to come between a Hindu and Muslim.

She had to get us back together, she decided, to make sure that the three of us would remain friends.

Between the spring and summer of 2018, I turned twenty-one, and so did Hamid, and in celebration of both of us being legal, it was Jess—yes, Jess—who messaged us again in the spirit of true world unity, to lay down our arms and squash our beef, and eat beef and drink beer and watch basketball.

'Lucky Luke?' she suggested. 'It'll be just like old times!'

I flinched because I didn't want to be the first to reply, but when Hamid sent back a 'thumbs-up' emoji I quickly followed with the same, too. For everything that had happened, I missed them both, yaar. I had spent years trying to translate this foreign country, but these two had been there the whole time providing me with the subtitles.

Yes, Jess—now sitting there next to my body, feeling guilt for her small part in what was essentially a misfortune of random entropy—was a foreigner, too. We all were.

The gunshot rang *Dishkiyaoon!*, and for seven-and-a-half months, Hamid and Jess continued to hear echoes of that deafening sound. Both left the city. Hamid headed home to live with his parents. He grew a beard that swarmed over his cheeks like a beehive and shaved off all the hair on his head to look like some sort of Chechen rebel. He stopped smoking weed and drinking alcohol and spent most of his nights overdosing on herbal tea and cashew nuts. His parents began to worry when they discovered that, for the first time since he was thirteen, he had decided to fast during Ramadan with them. Finally, it took his teary-eyed mother to convince him to trim some of that facial hair off—'Just to look more normal,' she said—so their neighbours would stop worrying if their son had been indoctrinated by the ISIS or something.

Jess was also back with her parents in Vermont, but she spent the months busying herself, trying to clutter her mind enough so that she wouldn't have time to pause and think. She got a job with a disability rights commission in Rutland, where she spent her days worrying about legal representation for those with developmental disabilities, instead of worrying about me. She was only haunted by my memory during the hour-long drive to Rutland from Rupert, back and forth each weekday, and talk radio became her saviour. She listened to NPR discussions about melting polar ice caps and civil wars in parts of the globe she would never visit. She listened to podcasts that focused on the absolute mundane, including her favourite one that discussed the dying obsessions of humanity, like calligraphy, stamp collection, and VCR repair.

Exactly two hundred and twenty-four days after Wildhair's shot, Hamid shaved his beard to reveal his full, chubby face once again. He smiled to himself and decided to send Jess an email. His words read like they had been written by a grown man twice his age, sach mein! It was the first time he had spoken like Hamid Faizal and not The Notorious B.I.G.'s illegitimate Muslim son. All true from the heart, in the Queen's fucking English. No emojis and no typos. Jess, for a brief moment, wondered if it was really him or an impostor who just happened to know everything about their lives.

'I miss you,' he wrote in the end. 'And I miss him.'

Jess saw the message immediately, but she waited eight minutes before she wrote back. She missed *all* of us, too, she said. She asked Hamid if he would like to visit her in Vermont, at her parents' home. 'It would be nice catching up here', she typed, in a tone almost as formal as his. 'It's quiet here.'

Hamid liked the idea and accepted, and on the day of his drive, he shaved his face clean once again, and when he got to Jess's place she smiled and commented that he had lost so much weight. In the mid-January winter chill, Jess laughed at his sober green turtleneck sweater. 'You look like a real adult,' she smiled and instinctively covered her mouth to hide her teeth. Hamid laughed, too, and to her added surprise, he didn't have a riposte to throw back at her. He was thinking about me, of course, and she was thinking about me, too, but neither of them needed to say anything. *Dishkiyaoon!* It rang in Hamid's ears, and he knew when he faced her deep, green eyes that she could hear it, too.

Jess's dad nodded at Hamid and offered him a firm, coarse palm, which Hamid grabbed quickly because he had heard that her father was the type of man who judged other men by their handshakes. Her mom gave him a warm hug that smelled like eggs and maple syrup, and exclaimed, 'We have heard so much about you!'

Hamid stayed for four days. He and Jess walked in the woods together, and strolled up a small waterfall near Harmon's Mint, where Jess held his hand and made sure he didn't slip on the wet rocks. He said that he would've brought more comfortable shoes if he had known Vermont was going to be full of so much nature, and Jess joked that he could totally borrow her pair whenever he wished. They talked about Jess's job, and Hamid's search for a job, and about what they missed and didn't miss about D.C., and about Fried or Die, but they had both understood, after a look into each other's hesitant eyes, to not talk about me—at least not yet. In the evenings, Jess convinced him to quit his temporary ehed to not touch alcohol, and they drank locally brewed pitchers of beer. In the mornings, Jess's mother made pancakes and opened the back cupboard to give Hamid the special maple syrup they saved only for family get-togethers. Jess winked at Hamid as he ate. 'She must like you!' she whispered excitedly.

On his last day there, while Hamid took a nap, Jess and her mother stood outside the back of their house in the sunny, blue afternoon, each holding a mug of hot coffee, looking up at the woods on the hill beyond their property. Their home was at the bottom of a low green mound, populated by thin white birch trees that looked like giant toothpicks. The closest neighbours were at least a ten-minute walk away. In the shed near the garage, Jess's father made a small racket moving around furniture. There was no other sound except a soft wind howling through the clear sky. *Whoooo*, the wind cried out in the ghostly silence, not as a threat, but like a reassurance.

Jess's mother asked Jess if she was serious about him. 'It's time to move on from Justin, baby.' She said everything with hesitation, trained from years of defensive manoeuvring to ensure she didn't offend her daughter.

'Justin? I moved on years ago, Ma,' Jess said.

Jess's mother gulped and decided to say what she was thinking out loud, unafraid of Jess after a few days of having Hamid over.

'I like this one,' she said.

Jess took a small, warm sip.

'I like him, too.'

THIRTY-TWO

At my cremation, Papa stood a few feet away from the pyre and the Dom. He did his best to maintain a straight face. Mummy was crying in the Shiv temple far up the steps, but of course he couldn't hear her; her muffled sobs would have been too soft for him even if she had been right there next to him.

Despite the number of dead bodies lying on their pyres around the muddy grounds of the ghat, not everyone shared Mummy's sombre mood. It's strange, but the ghats are a place of business, not of grief. People have this mistaken perception about cremations, you know? Death, they assume, must be a downer, *hai ki nahi*? But in Varanasi, the mood is different. Funerals aren't entirely funereal. The rituals of death are a part of life.

It took two-hundred and eighty kilograms of chandan to burn my body. I would have called it a colossal waste of trees for merely one human, but *behenchod*, my opinions of my cremation went unheeded. The wood made a soft crackling sound as it burned. *Nahi*, it wasn't some violent, destructive flame, but a slow disintegration. Amid the ash and smoke and burning flesh and the stink of the river and the faecal remains of men and beasts around the ghat, there was a waft of a singular, pleasant scent—wet marigolds tied in garlands over each body, including mine. There were more marigold petals scattered around marble floors in the half dozen little temples up the steps from the ghat.

Papa took a deep breath and continued to stare into the fire. Soon, the Dom looked away, busying himself with another burning body ten feet away from mine, with another family in need of his services. The air was thick with the smoke from the burning wood, flickering embers popping up once in a while, each taking a quick final breath before getting extinguished forever. Happy Singh looked away too, as the smoke stung his eyes, and beads of sweat dripped down his forehead. He diverted his gaze instead towards the slow-moving Ganga. A stone's throw away were a few young white women—tourists—on a boat, being rowed across the water. The boatwallah was giving them a guided tour of the old city, of the customs of his people. Passing by the burning ghats, the gori women each took out their cameras to photograph the bodies. Immediately, the boatwallah raised his hand up in protest. 'No photo, madam,' he said, and the cameras were instantly lowered. Even from a distance, Happy Singh found this amusing.

Papa, however, did not get distracted. He was determined to see the whole thing through. Suno now, this man—my father—was the same man who joined his hands together in front of Ganesh statues and purchased lucky stones because the astrologers advised him to, but he never paused to think about *why* he did these things. His mind was always elsewhere, worrying about beads, and real estate, and export tariffs, Chinese machines, which of his employees he could trust, and which ones he definitely could not. Nahi, he believed all this bhakti was a waste of time. There was no meditation, no cosmic warm khichdi to comfort his soul, no being 'one with everything'.

But on this day, he stared into the fire, hypnotized by its flames, its power to reduce solid forms into dust, to transform the body of his son into mere ash. He wasn't thinking about anything, sach mein. It was a true form of meditation, his moment of being Buddha under that sacred fig tree. His enlightenment. He was sad, but after two hours of sweating in that intense heat, as my body disintegrated, his sorrow crumbled down into ashes, too.

When he made his way back up the steps later that night, Mummy wrapped her arms around him, but he irritably shrugged her off. 'Not here,' he said.

Mummy tried to goad him into emotion again once they got back home. 'Shankar, we have to plan for the terhvi,' she suggested, but Papa immediately put his hand up to shush her.

'No, Pushpa!' he snapped. 'We know what you are thinking. Thirteen days? That's how long it takes. Thirteen days. Are you crazy? We have work to do. We have to go to office. We have to fly to Delhi next week. You think we have time on our hands?'

'But Shankar…' she protested. It was the tradition in her household, she tried to explain, for the chief-mourner—the soul that had come in direct contact with the Dom, the fire, and the deceased—to maintain a period of social isolation while they grieved.

'No,' Papa said. 'We've made up our mind.'

So, there was no official mourning period. Mummy did place an old framed photograph of me with a garland of flowers in the living room. She lit an agarbatti underneath it, sprinkled a few drops of water, and chanted the Gayatri Mantra. She cried whenever Sakshi didi telephoned her from Indore.

Then, she started to drink the expensive Scotch, and she drank it neat—no ice, no nothing. She would stare at Rishi bhaiya's name on her phone's contact list, but she was too afraid to press the call button.

Soon, the thirteen days were over, and Mummy upgraded to larger shots of Scotch. Patiala pegs. Burning hot comfort.

THIRTY-THREE

About an hour after that gunshot, the Metropolitan Police Department of D.C. organized a bus to squeeze in all fifty-three witnesses of my murder, taking them from Lucky Luke to the police station for a marathon night of note-taking and report-filing. Wildhair was arrested and taken in another police vehicle to a different destination. Nobody else was hurt—I mean physically hurt, samjhe? The police recommended psychiatric help for the witnesses, and thirty-four of them—including that stoic bartender—accepted.

Two weeks later, an interfaith service was held in my memory by a local immigrant rights organization at the Church of the Epiphany in Downtown D.C. Jess provided the organizers with a photograph taken the previous summer in which I was standing near the cherry blossoms with a slight smirk on my face. But she didn't show up for the service herself, and neither did Hamid. Behenchod, they had been through enough to need more reminders of my absence, hadn't they?

The service was mainly filled with angry South Asian–American organizations, random D.C. Tech students, religious leaders from nearby temples, mosques, gurdwaras, synagogues, and of course, from the Church of Epiphany itself, and journalists jostling to construct a positive denouement to a horrific story.

Tapiwa the African Prince was there, and so was Gokul. They met up outside the church and sat together in the middle aisle of one of the front pews. People held up candles and sang songs, and when they began to sing 'We Shall Overcome', Tapiwa joined in the chorus, belting out the lyrics shamelessly at the top of his voice. Gokul recognized the tune, but he only knew the lyrics in Hindi, and even that chootia couldn't stop himself and joined in the chorus, singing, '*Hum honge kamyabab…ek din!*'

Meanwhile, a diplomatic war started online. The Indian foreign minister promised—on Twitter—that every Indian abroad would be kept safe under Santa Gol Gappa's expansive wingspan. President Gaandu-face—also on Twitter—replied in broken English that America was already the safest, most bestest place in the world.

And I admit, it *was* pretty damn good, this country. It wasn't the best—but what was?—and it didn't always keep me happy—but what did?—but I had good friends, and I had distractions, and I had the fifth-floor kitchen in Saxon Hall, and Hamid's Dostoherbsky, and Fried or Die, and despite all the tiny landmines, I had turned twenty-one and somehow graduated before all this hungama put a stop to everything, forever.

I graduated on the weekend before my last weekend. My last week alive. Earlier that afternoon, hundreds of us had put on our graduation robes and received our diplomas on stage in the sports hall at D.C. Tech. I received mine, too, and sach mein, it felt good. Koi kaam ka to nikla, you understand? I wasn't completely useless.

Only Gokul and I were in the kitchen that night, and I wanted to have a drink, and it was Gokul—Gokul Motherfuckin' Ramnarayan—who decided, that he, too, wanted a drink. He had continued to live in Saxon Hall even as he began to work full-time teaching undergraduates at the university.

Aah, and it didn't take more than a single can of Budweiser for him to start glowing with joy.

'It's been nearly four years since we met here, Vishnu bhai, can you believe it?' he smiled, and his cheeks began to turn rosy red. We had turned on the bigger ceiling light, and it gave us an unfamiliar glimpse of a room where we had spent so much time drinking, smoking, and studying over the past few years. Under this new white light, I noticed all the extra space here, all the barren, unused corners.

'We met four years ago,' Gokul repeated. 'Do you remember? We went to that Nike shop in Georgetown that one time. Do you remember?'

I laughed. 'I do...and now it's time to go back.' I began to fiddle with the tab on top of my open Budweiser, twisting and turning it around its base.

'Why not stay here Vishnu? Do a master's degree? Get a job here? There are so many more opportunities!'

I lowered my eyes and kept fiddling with the beer tab until *clink!* it came off.

'I'm going back,' I said.

I spoke in a tone that felt definite, that told him to stop asking me questions that I couldn't answer, questions that I *refused* to think about. I was going back, yaar, because...well, because I hadn't found a real reason to stay here any longer.

'But why, Vishnu bhai?'

'Maybe,' I thought, and then, I lied, 'it's because I miss home.'

Gokul only used his thumb and two fingers to hold his beer, his can never coming into contact with the rest of his palm. Even when he sipped the beer, he did so as if he was drinking a cup of karak chai, savouring it little by little instead of gulping it down.

'Well, I miss home, too, bhai,' his voice staggered. 'But we must change in life, mustn't we? We must grow up.'

'Says the guy who still has Nagarjuna photos taped all over his walls.'

Gokul laughed. 'I can't *completely* let go of home, can I? It's my whole my culture, my family....'

He trailed off into silence. Gokul always grew solemn when he talked about his family, as if he was reverentially talking of a holy kingdom. His father was a retired officer with the Indian Railways in Hyderabad and his mother was a schoolteacher, and he had three elder sisters and four nieces and nephews, and for some reason, it was *his* responsibility now—from the other side of the world—to support all of them. Even before he was employed by the university he was always working. He worked at a sloppy Pakistani restaurant on K Street, scrubbing the large buffet trays after each serving of lamb karahi. After school, he tutored high school kids who made fun of his accent behind his back. He manned a check-out counter at Safeway, made a grave clerical error after which he was demoted to mopping floors, and then worked his way back up to the counters a few months later. And he still never had any money.

Gokul placed his can down on the table and I heard a hollow echo.

'You want one more?' I asked. I walked up to the fridge to fish out another beer for myself.

'No, no, this is enough, bhai. This is enough.'

'You sure?'

'This is the land of opportunity, bhai,' Gokul said, and it took me a moment to realize that he was still continuing the conversation I thought had ended several minutes ago. 'How can you leave this land? Land of opportunity,' he repeated the mantra.

I shrugged and returned to the table. 'Fuck, whatever.' But behenchod, what I was resisting to say out loud, what I was even resisting to *think* about, was that America was only this land for those who fought for the opportunities, those who cherished it, those who were going to make nimbu pani out of their nimbus and all that. Like Gokul.

Me? Yaar, the opportunity had already been gifted to me. I wasn't born into it, but once Papa opened that new factory, once his business took off, when orders came from Germany and America and South Africa and Egypt, when we had enough money to not worry about money, I realized that I didn't need this opportunity any more. I was already comfortable. No, I couldn't be like my brother, who took a stand, who left everything behind, who made it on his own.

When counsellors from D.C. Tech first came to Modern School's international college fair, they had repeated that old slogan, 'You can be whatever you want to be in America'. But behenchod, I already *was* what everyone wanted to be. Where could I go from there?

Gokul was here for a chance to make something out of his life; I had been here to escape the life I already had.

'Are you going to stay here...' I paused, because the next word felt strange, almost like it was spelling Gokul's doom. '...Forever?'

Gokul replied without hesitation. 'If they let me, yes.'

'What do you mean? Of course, they'll let you.'

'This country is not what you think it is, bhai. This country is difficult.'

I couldn't help but laugh. 'But behenchod, you were just here singing praises—'

'It's both, Vishnu,' Gokul stamped his fist on the table with surprising violence. 'It's both. It's beautiful and difficult both, you understand? I can be the hardest working man here, have all of my degrees, and still, I have to take extra English classes to be perfect. You understand this? I have to speak English twice as well as a citizen.... Just for a green card.' He closed his eyes, and then opened them. 'I'll have to get a job that earns me *twice* as much just to stay here. It's a struggle, Vishnu. It's beautiful but it's a struggle.'

'Gokul,' I said. 'Your application...when do you hear back?'

Then his eyes closed again, and he slumped back into his chair, drawing in long, peaceful breaths, surprisingly comfortable under the bright light of the kitchen.

'Behenchod,' I laughed again. 'Wake up.'

When Gokul heard about my killing, he was momentarily paralysed into an inexplicable stillness, his eyelashes frozen in half-flutter, fingers frozen in their curvature, mouth forming a small oval *o,* muscles arrested, and a temporary cessation of the heartbeat.

And when the blood rushed through his veins once more, Gokul vowed never to drink again.

Dekho yaar, my death was only shocking to people like Gokul who knew me because, well, they *fucking knew me*. Hai ki nahi? In the larger scheme of things, it was just another tragedy. All deaths are not equal, because, in our world, all lives are not equal. Some deaths matter more than others. One telecommunication magnate's daughter was worth a hundred poor children dying of encephalitis. The deaths don't become a real tragedy until dacoits in kaala kacchas scale the walls of our own households to cut us up, until there is a riot in our own neighbourhood, until our own family is under threat. In Amreeka, my friends only asked about the Mumbai attacks in 2008 because a bunch of Richie Rais and Prosperous Patels and firangis died at the Taj Hotel. They asked about the one case of gang rape in New Delhi, as if it wasn't a daily occurrence, as if women weren't being abducted and killed somewhere in the country, sometime, all the time.

Many deaths are ignored by history—the everyday tragedy, the flood that uproots hundreds, the pogrom that kills thousands. Maybe it is our belief that, somehow, our souls are eternal, that we have accrued some sort of predestined karma from our previous lives, so we take tragedy with a pinch of MDH Masala. Jo hona hai, ho jaaega, we say. What is meant to happen, will happen. Inshallah, if it's God's will. We are a nation of 1.3 billion or whatever people who absolve ourselves of any responsibility in our short human lives.

I was one of those billion vagerah, too. One among the young programmers in Pune, labourers flying to Dubai, small business owners in Faridabad, starving farmers in west Punjab, tribal women in Bastar, football players in Kashmir, aunties watching saas-bahu serials and eating pakoras in Ahmedabad, uncles joining laughter yoga classes in Delhi, engineers working with multinational corporations in Chennai, aspiring young rappers in Mizoram, Doms at the cremation ghat.

And then there was Palpreet Singh, driving on that spring night in Delhi, whose Maruti had been smashed into by Sanjeet.

Mr Palpreet felt a numbness below his waist, a feeling like nothing could hurt him down there, like nothing was in his control, like he would never feel anything at all.

THIRTY-FOUR

Isko dekho, look at him again. A ping on his computer screen took him on another labyrinthine journey through the internet. It was a link from Norway: serial rapists—all recent refugees—were allegedly roaming the streets, terrorizing quiet neighbourhoods at night. He clicked on the link and another page popped up, and he followed the directions as he was told, and a new page opened up in front of him: an invitation to a political rally. Senator Gaandu-face would be in Harrisburg, Pennsylvania. A couple of the commentators on his blog and communities on Reddit had already made him aware of this event. Mark smiled and took another sip.

He packed a twelve-pack of 'America' beers in his old Dodge, next to the hunting rifle he always kept in his trunk. He placed a handgun in the glovebox in his dashboard, the same Ruger LCP that would one day be the astr of my demise. He had let his hair grow out into wild intertwining long strands that resembled Maggi noodles, flavoured with extra masala.

At the rally, he found himself between a few thousand faces shouting and screaming in orgiastic violence. The candidate, Gaandu-face, stood on the podium far ahead of Mark. His voice cut through the air in the large complex, his little fingers pointed at the crowd as if delivering a threat, and his face glowed orange, the orange of sunsets and fire and Punditji's robes.

Mark, electrified by the anger in the air, watched as Gaandu-face buttered them up with his words, and in the end, declared that the country had to keep out all those who didn't look or sound or smell like him. Mark thought about the foreigners and those willow cricket bats in public parks, and the accents he didn't understand, and he, too, began to chant along.

Dekho, if you were there, you would have probably missed him in that crowd of angry, burly men. But I can spot him now, an individual among the masses. Clumps of his long hair fall like a tangled web onto his shoulders. His nostrils are flared. His biceps seem to pulsate in the white T-shirt that can barely contain his arms. His blue eyes look angry and the whites of his eyes are almost red, gleaming with power. It's as if he has multiplied—he screams like a rakshas, the white-skinned Ravan of American suburbia, his many heads chorusing his rage. When he chants, he realizes that he hasn't heard passion like this in his own voice for years. It excites him.

Two years later, long after Gaandu-face had become president, Mark—who still lived alone, the glow of his computer screen reflecting off his face—got into his Dodge again and went for another drive. By now, he had begun freelancing from home, live-chatting with strangers from across the country who demanded HBO subscriptions or asked for advice on their internet connectivity issues. He had a little more money to spare, not enough to bring his wife back, but enough to splurge on birthday gifts whenever he got to meet his daughters.

So, on that Saturday in early June, he packed up his guns again and left town for D.C. At the National Mall that afternoon, he stood sweating in his trackpants and ate soft-serve ice creams among crowds of tourists rushing past him on their bicycles. Of course, he stopped by to pay respects to Gaandu-face's White House. He was in a good mood that evening and checked himself into a bed and breakfast in Northwest Washington, one of those little places with a white picket fence and porch fashioned to look like a property in the old South.

Later that night, sitting on his bed watching TV alone, drunk after his fifth can of Budweiser—'America' had been discontinued—he received a flagged email on his phone. It was a message from his old employers, PotoSystems. For a brief moment, he wondered if they had made a mistake, if they had somehow included his personal email address in their internal chain.

But nahi, nahi, this email was for him, personally. Dear Mark Tillerman, it began. After he had read the message carefully, he realized that it wasn't from PotoSystems but from a firm that *represented* PotoSystems. He realized that he had been careless—maybe recently, maybe years ago—and they had finally caught up with him. They knew what he had been doing. Maybe someone had reported his blog and knew who The Watcher was. He slapped his knee in frustration: *I didn't even post that much any more!* Maybe someone had seen him taking photographs and followed *him* around. *Who's watching The Watcher?* he thought, and he felt his heartbeat racing. He needed another beer. It was all legalese now. Digital espionage? Court date?

He felt the old itch near his ankles again, under his trackpants. He imagined the faces of those who had replaced him, those accented-English speakers, the same ones that *his* president had promised to keep away from *his* country, who earned so much more and still benefited from the taxes *he* paid and worked on computers *he* was supposed to work on and lived in neighbourhoods where *he* should have been living with his family. No, no, this was completely ridiculous, he told himself.

This wasn't *his* America.

He leaned back against the headboard and slumped his shoulders, slowly slipping as the TV in front of him droned on. Something on the local news. The faces on the screen were a blur.

It wasn't anyone's America. It wasn't the America of Jess in Vermont, or Hamid in Jersey, or Andrew in Baltimore. It wasn't the America that Rishi bhaiya once promised to me, the America of Silicon Valley sunshine where the biggest concern was ensuring that the Starbucks barista pronounced his name the right way. This was the result of two countries unwillingly thrust into one, under the same waving flag and ancient unwavering constitutional rights, under some exaggerated propaganda that Mark and Jess and Hamid and every other citizen had been forced to swallow with the pledge of allegiance in elementary school classrooms. Some made the pledges more sincerely than others did, and some—like Mark—distracted themselves with its mantra as if it was the solution to all of their problems, like the Sanksrit shlokas Mummy repeated with the priests during havans.

Svaha!

Russ—not Rishi—came here with dreams of that American opportunity, and through hard work and luck and brilliance, came through, and one tech-man replaced another, and robots and machines arose to replace more tech-men, and Mark Tillerman, lying on his bed alone in a D.C. bed and breakfast, was one of those men lost in the shuffle of changing times, of a world where everyone felt American, and no 'real' American knew what feeling American even meant any more.

Mark fell into an uneasy sleep, haunted again by his shrunken realities. It was the end of days as he knew it.

So, tell me motherfucker, how would *you* like to die? Would you like to have your brains blown out by a man who had suppressed his anger for years, about to burst out like an over-shaken can of beer? Would you settle for a quick and boring heart attack at an agreeable old age? Would you prefer to drown in your own vomit after an especially belligerent drunken night? Would you go out an innocent victim, blown to bits for the religious satisfaction of some brainwashed terrorist? Or would you like to be that terrorist evoking the name of your deaf god while you blow yourself to bits?

On the day of my death, Wildhair woke up in D.C. with his blonde hair as tangled and wild as ever. I woke up in D.C., too, on the fifth floor of Saxon Hall, too lazy to open my eyes to the bright morning.

But then I remembered that this was the day. Haan, haan, the day Jess and Hamid and I had planned to meet at Lucky Luke for basketball and burgers and beer. I hadn't spent time with them in months. Suddenly, I was able to spring to attention and jump off the bed. *It had been too long,* I thought. *It was time to end all this drama.*

I got to the bar first that evening, and Jess walked in soon after me, and Hamid—who was stoned, of course—showed up nearly half an hour later, and all three of us settled down on the bar stools ensuring that we had a good view of the TV screen. In the noise of the bar, the thin bartender kept calm and composed when he took our order, even when Jess momentarily lost her cool.

'No,' she had to lean forward over the table to be audible. 'I said *no* ice. Vodka-soda-*no-ice*, please.'

The bartender gave her a blank nod and took the drink back. Jess turned to look over at me and Hamid with a frown.

'Chill out, girl.' Hamid said.

'I told him four times,' Jess shook her head. 'No ice, no ice, no ice, no ice.'

'Chill.'

But we knew Jess well enough to know that she wouldn't let a shortcoming—no matter how insignificant—slide. When she finally got her vodka as she liked, she gave the bartender an unhappy glance from the side of her eye, as if she had already lost all confidence in his abilities. *Useless chootia,* I thought in Papa's voice.

The bartender was a stoic presence, floating between requests on all sides of the long table, until he finally returned with a pint of Yuengling for Hamid, and one for me, and a vodka-soda-no-ice-please for Jess, and I asked him to put all three drinks on my tab. 'Fuck you doin', bruh?' Hamid protested, but I ignored him.

'Next one, yaar,' I said. 'You can get the next one.'

Hamid opened his eyes wider and smiled, and then moved his square head side to side like a bobblehead before exaggeratedly imitating my voice. 'Arre yaar you are getting me the next drink dum-ti-dum-ti-dum.'

'Fucking choot,' I said and smiled.

'Last call for Happy Hour!' Mr Stoic Bartender came back with our drinks. Before the rest of them could react, I asked him to repeat our latest order, just in case. 'Put it on my card,' I instructed.

Right on cue, bas, my phone rang, and I expected to see Papa's name on the screen, awake even before the sun was, while I was just getting my night started. He would be alone, I imagined, walking with his chai in the front lawn, or perhaps sitting at his favourite spot in Tulsi Ghat, watching the rising sun.

But it wasn't him, no. It was a local number; the prefix belonged to D.C. Tech. Whatever it was, I ignored it. It was too loud, too busy, too fucking boozy in here.

'Who was that?' Jess asked.

'Nobody.'

'Daddy calling, right?' said Hamid.

'Nope.' I took a sip of my Yuengling and looked away.

'Why didn't you pick up?' asked Jess.

'Here? It's fucking loud in here.'

'Yo Viz,' Hamid put a heavy arm over my shoulders. 'Did I tell you—me and Tapiwa were working on that app? It's for this moment. For shit like this, know what I mean, bruh? You activate it, and your phone just won't ring if you don't want it to. Big Poppa from Varanasi would just get a pre-recorded message. And you call back later. Or don't call at all; fuck do I care?'

'You mean,' Jess said. 'It's an answering machine.'

'No, no. Fuck no.'

'It sounds like an answering machine,' Jess laughed.

I laughed, too.

'No, fuckers,' Hamid sighed. 'It's an app you can switch off and on, you know? With ads and custom messages and pop songs and everything,' he paused; both Jess and I smiled playfully. 'You bozos will be begging me for beer money when the African Prince and I start living our best lives in California.'

'Aww,' Jess reached up to squeeze one of Hamid's chubby, brown cheeks. 'Is Lil Fuzzy Faizal getting frustrated?'

I saw Hamid loosen and melt into her touch. It was a brief moment, but I could sense how they craved it now, how they had been deprived of it for too long.

I stood up and slapped Hamid on his shoulder. 'Gotta take a piss. I'll be back.'

Dekho now, when I exited the scene, Wildhair entered. He ignored the hostess at the door and strolled into the bar, scanning the room for himself. In the happy intermingling of this colourful world, there seemed to be no room for him. He finally saw an empty seat next to Jess and Hamid. My seat.

He was big and beefy, with shoulders bilkul like Hamid's, raised and strengthened over decades of cheeseburgers and strawberry milkshakes, with eyebrows as bleached blonde as the rest of his skin, and long, fearsome hair pointing in random directions around his head and shoulders. He had concealed and carried with him a can of Budweiser, and he snapped it open.

He hovered close to my vacated stool. Hamid smelled him before he saw him—beer and sweat. Hamid nudged Jess and gestured with his eyes. She shook her head with the same disappointed reaction she had saved for the stoic bartender.

'Scuse me, sir,' Jess said to him. 'That seat's taken.'

Wildhair glanced at her but didn't change the expression on his creased face. 'Do you see me sitting down?' he grunted. 'I'm not sitting down, am I?' His voice was deep and guttural, the sound of jeep tyres revving up on gravel. 'I'm just standing here. I'm not sitting down, am I?'

I walked out of the bathroom, hands and face washed, and that's when I saw him. He looked a little disoriented, hila hua, a little drunk, with puffy cheeks and glassy, blue eyes. He wore a white sweatshirt, unzipped from the middle to reveal a red T-shirt, and grey trackpants. I squeezed back through the crowd, with a little tipsy bounce in my step, moving excitedly to the soundtrack of the hubbub in the bar. Jess looked over and gestured me back to my seat. Back to her.

'Scuse me, sir,' she repeated, this time with more venom.

'Our friend has this seat. Vishnu!' she called out.

'Yo, you gotta move,' said Hamid. 'That's my boy's seat.'

'Fuck off, Mohammad,' Wildhair said.

I got a flashback of that night in Chinatown. Big Silver. Karaoke. Ham-head. I hesitated to speak—for years, I had trained my voice to respond to American ears, to add that something extra, to subtract the unsubtle musicality of my mother tongue. But now, in the face of this sudden affront, I stuttered, and my true voice returned. The full-masala Indian accent. 'Guys, suno,' I said. 'D...Don't worry, I...I don't need a seat. It's okay.'

'No, Vishnu,' Jess said. 'This is your seat. Don't worry. *He* will move.'

Hamid crept up to face Wildhair, and Wildhair sized him up, too, and after a brief, unwavering stare-down, Wildhair's shoulders finally slumped. 'Fucking Mohammads,' he said under his breath, before walking away.

I raised an eyebrow at Hamid and Jess, and then smiled at them as he left. They began to laugh, and then it was over. He was gone, a minor glitch in our perfectly working matrix. We could resume our lives.

We were safe then, safe in each other's company, in the larger company of friendly strangers, in the distracting joy of our beverages, watching the NBA Finals on the big screen, comfortable in the loud freedoms of America that I had grown to love. I bought my friends the next round of drinks, and Jess grabbed my forearm to thank me, and I nodded back, and kasam se, I felt nothing else at that touch. No electricity, no yearning to lean over and kiss her pencil-thin lips again. I saw Hamid slide closer to her, and I remembered what she had told me about them all those months ago, and I thought about how the fatass had left me behind drunken and disoriented in Chinatown. Yaar, jo ho gaya, so ho gaya. But he was here now. I felt strangely at peace to see them sit close together, to see her caress his shoulder when she addressed him, or hear his voice rise in pitch when he spoke to her. I imagined them here without me—a kabab without the haddi—and sach mein, yaar, it was all good.

Wildhair couldn't see this when he returned. He didn't see our little love triangle, or feel the buzz of the ringing phone in my pocket, or feel the sting of the spicy remnants of gravy under Papa's fingernails, or share Hamid's meticulous passion for rolling joints or of Sanjeet who preferred to work with chillums and cotton and gauze, or feel the satisfaction Rishi bhaiya felt when his hands closed around a warm steering wheel, or saw how that bracelet hung loose around Aastha's wrist, or stare at Jess's slightly crooked teeth, or taste the ballpoint pens Mummy chewed on until their plastic ends turned soft and slimy. When Wildhair returned, with the intent to shoot his handgun, with the intent to end lives, he could only see mere shadows of real human beings. He saw two-dimensional characters with no inscapes, no lives beyond what suited him, no backstories. Dead images with no URLs linking to any further information.

There was a mad scramble first, glasses shattering, patrons ducking their heads, and then a clear path—he was less than twenty-five feet away from us. He took aim at Hamid. It was only a second, yaar; a second without any thought or deliberation. Pure blankness, like the vacuum of a nihilist's afterlife, the nirvanic silence that swamis and bodhisattvas yearn for.

I moved into that clear path.

And then he shot.

He reduced me like I had reduced countless others in my life, other colours, other castes, other nationalities, others who sat across from me on cold metal benches in the jail cell, Silver Hair and his friends, innocent pedestrians gunned down indiscriminately by terrorists on cobbled European streets, shivering bodies I saw covered with Hindi newspapers in the dark of Mughalsarai, or that homeless man hugging a toy leopard amidst the pristine white marble of the Union Station. I saw them all as Wildhair would have seen them—shadows of full forms, non-player characters, ideas rather than specific identities.

I was a foreigner to him, an alien microbe invading his place, his country, his family. Hamid, an American-born Muslim, was foreign, too. Jess, a woman who dared to speak back to him, was a foreigner as well. Everyone at Lucky Luke—even those who looked like him and had grown up repeating the same pledge—felt distant. He couldn't comprehend the colleagues he had worked with before he'd lost his job, and had suddenly reached an untranslatable fissure with his own wife. His daughters, for whom he wanted to protect this American sanctity, had also evolved into something foreign, moving in a new dimension of time while he remained in his fixed past.

Family first, he had thought to himself, and family meant home and home meant country, and somewhere between the virtual frustration he shared with a community of angry strangers, the pointy fingers of that orange Gaandu-face, and the demons that haunted him in his nightmares and daydreams, Wildhair had convinced himself that whatever he did to protect this family was the right thing.

I had seen this before. Eight years ago, Papa felt he had been right, too. The riots brought him power, and power brought him stability, and stability led to a bigger factory, and the factory led to comfort. *We did this all for you, Vishnu,* he had said. *We did it all for our family.*

Haan haan, this is what he believed, drinking and scratching himself, paranoid about threats that didn't exist, fearful of those invading alien microbes.

And then a thud, and a shriek, and crashing pint glasses, and the uninterrupted drone of the basketball commentators on TV, and ketchup and blood and salty fries and the smell of my sweat and grease and beer.

Yaar, it would probably not surprise you to know that the Americans can be a little over-systematic about matters of legality and life and death, vagerah. There's always the fear of lawsuits here, hai ki nahi? So, even when a bullet had pierced my forehead and been lodged inside my skull, I was still—for all purposes of the code of the District of Columbia—not dead yet. That determination was made only twenty-six minutes later, not in one place or the other, but in an amorphous quantum space, on the stretcher in the back of the ambulance. An irreversible cessation of all functions of the entire brain including the brain stem. All done.

There is a new scent now. The scent of wet marigolds and sandalwood, of melted hot ghee, and the effluvia of roasting flesh. The smell of cremation, and rose-flavoured incense sticks, criss-crossing agarbattis that Mummy had draped on a photograph of my departed face in Varanasi. The agarbatti became a wormhole, too, a time machine that took me back to an immortal place in my home city, where *all* of time stopped.

My dost, you should spend a little time in this city, too. Your hours will become days and days will turn into years, and years, centuries, between your first cup of chai and your second. Suno, this is why we cremate our dead here, to join this timelessness. Varanasi is a bubble, sheltered from the outside world. From the inception of time to the Buddha to Aurangzeb to the British Raj to Santa Gol Gappa. Bullock carts to drones. This place remains unaffected.

Varanasi, behenchod, is old. It was here before the English sahibs and memsahibs left, and before they arrived. It was here before Amreeka even existed. Before the Mings and the Mughals. Before the goddam Magna Carta, and Guru Nanak, and Jesus Christ, and the Prophet in Mecca. Before Julius Caesar and Socrates and before even the Greeks invented their gods. The city had been around before then and haan, the Ganga had flowed through it.

And besides a bunch of shattered old mandirs and a century-old sewage system and smartphones delivering groceries to your doorstep, little else has changed. It remains in easy equilibrium with the past and the present, with the earthly and the divine. It's the only place where the local residents have the audacity to address the almighties with nonsense, where your rickshawwallah could stroll into a temple, bow before a lingam, and open his paan-reddened mouth to say, 'Aur, ka ho, Shiv Baba? Sab theek? All good?'

Chalo, you must walk with me now. Up the ghat steps, past the temple where Mummy wept, and the chaiwallah's stall where relatives of the dead congregated for a little gup-shup, watching other people burn while sipping sweet, milky tea. Past the women who laid out their blue and yellow and green and red saris on the ghat steps to dry. Past the stacks of wood and trash and through the stone-paved bylanes, the gullies where we'll share the path with a variety of creatures—stray dogs and stray people and cattle and crows and Hindus and Muslims and Christians and others tripping on the local opium. Go past wandering tourists taking photographs of old widows in white saris, their daily suffering exoticized by foreign eyes. Walk past them, past the women who have walked barefoot for so long across the country—for days and for months on dirt, hot gravel, mud—that their toes have begun to fall off their feet. Past tourists taking photographs of ancient wooden doorways hoping to find a way into themselves. Past sizzling hot samosas and bread pakoras. Dekho, how a man hums an old bhajan to himself. How the doodhwallah bicycles down the narrow gully, balancing on the uneven path. A dog yawns, lazing like the humans around him. Stay away from that long-haired baba grinding cannabis leaves at the bhang shop, my dost—your mind has already expanded beyond what any intoxicant could provide. You don't need to worry if what you see now is a hallucination or the real thing. In this mind-state, *everything* is real.

Be careful, open your eyes wide. Dekho, right there, down at the path. There's shit and piss everywhere. Some from buffaloes and dogs, some from other beasts like us. You won't even realize when a dog starts following you and adopts your soul as its own. You hear those pleas, those beggars asking for alms? Oh bhaiya! Hey didi! Just ignore them, because we all ignore them.

The temperature rises, the air getting hotter the closer you get to the burning pyres. The atmosphere feels stuffy, dense with the lost spirits floating as aimlessly as the stray embers in the wind. For some outsiders, it's the most spiritually intense experience of their lives. For us, it's just death.

'Aur, ka ho, Vishnu? Sab theek?'

We're near the calmer parts of the river, the quieter ghats on the outskirts of the city, where you can take a moment to pause and breathe. You can follow the river's path further upstream, through the thousands of kilometres that pass through industrial pollution, spiritual pollution, the chokehold at the Tehri Dam, leading to the cynosure up in Gaumukh—the cow's mouth—its birthplace, way up in the Himalaya among glaciers and crisp cold air, where the river bursts out of the womb, immediately ready to serve as a mother to half of the thirsty nation. Ganga Maiya. There is another legend here that some fraud babas will tell you, that the cow's mouth isn't a mouth at all. It's Vishnu the preserver, who takes possession of all three folds of the universe by treading over the earth, sky, and heaven, and tears through the presidential suites of heaven's highest floor to release the Ganga, and the river flows out to the world through Vishnu's big left toe, descending back to the bhoomi, and moves down from Gangotri to Tehri to Varanasi and further, until it eventually reaches Howrah where it joins the ocean, and is finally free, gaining anonymity among the waters of the world.

For brief stretches, however, the flow of the river changes. In Varanasi, it turns north instead of its usual south-eastern descent, meandering in different directions, going back in time and starting again. You have seen me stroll back here, back to these ghats, ending in the city I had escaped. Once Wildhair's gunshot went off, nothing mattered any more. I had lived without purpose, distracting myself with shots of whisky and buttons on Xbox controllers and obsessing over the way Jess ate her food and whatever I left behind with Jyoti. It was all distraction, all done to avoid thinking about the upcoming abyss. It takes a long time to build a perfect computer application and a simple click to delete it. An instant. *This* instant. This timelessness. On the river, the most riveting of rivers, I expect to hear the final words as promised, the voice of Shiv reaching over and whispering the taraka mantra in my ears, to finally provide that release, a ready-made end to the cycle here in Varanasi, ready-made moksha, packaged like packets of instant noodles. Instead, all I hear is Papa's voice—not his words, but his grunts, his groans, his loud wet slurps as he takes each sip of whisky soda.

So here I am now, not with the body at Lucky Luke but in a place outside of time, a place like Varanasi, and I see all of my lifetime—behenchod all of *every* lifetime—in the same frantic moment. At the speed of light, all the events in the history of time in the universe are experienced this way, and we will all be born and die in the same flash, and only when we slow down will we be able to live this life, to experience it relative to other lives around us.

One of those other lives was my friend Tapiwa the Prince. 'The curtain falling on Othello does not make the play worse,' he had said. 'We may regret death while at the same time knowing that its inevitability is what makes life so valuable in the first place.' Tapiwa was shattered, but he was, strangely, happy, too. Okay, not happy, but theek-thaak. Mostly fine. He played old audio recordings of his mother's voice in his bedroom and giggled to himself. He called his siblings back home to talk and laugh for hours about how she used to embarrass them on family vacations, dancing and flailing among strangers whenever she heard the first hint of a good beat. The play was over but it was still a good experience. Its end didn't negate its existence.

'She'd been a good person, Viz,' Tapiwa had said. 'That's all that matters, no?'

Hai ki nahi? Was I a good person? Or was I a piece of shit?

The curtain had fallen early. Earlier, at least, than Papa expected. When Papa sat in his office with Happy Singh and Sud, allowing the lawyer to flip the pages as he signed his name on his will, he thought that I would have more time, much more time than *he* did. At times in his life, Papa had been happy. At times, he had been sad. When I died, he was nearing fifty. He had beaten the local competition and lost to Chinese machines and ate samosas and seen imaginary worlds in the corridors of the Ram Guest House and inhaled the bloody dust of Muktigarh.

And now, he was doing it alone.

Now, as he stayed up, simmering at night in the glow of the television, Mummy wasn't lying next to him. One evening after my death, he had caught her swaying drunkenly from side to side on the dining table. She began singing an old song, something from a film she remembered watching alone in the movie theatre when she had been a teenager. Shocked that she had raided his precious liquor cabinet, Papa shouted at her. She shouted back. And just as Himanshu strolled in from the kitchen, an innocent witness with a fresh batch of parathas, Papa slapped Mummy—*fataak!*—on her face. The next morning, she packed her bags and left for her brother's house in Delhi, and that's where she lived, and that's where she died.

She got a call two weeks after leaving home, during the twilight hour of the evening when she usually spoke to my sister. But it wasn't my sister on the other line; it was a +1 number from the United States of Amreeka, an international call. Russ cried into the phone as soon as Mummy picked up. He told her he missed her. He apologized for not calling her earlier. She apologized for not calling, too. She told him she'd left Papa. He told her he had called Papa to check on him. Papa had let the phone ring at least twelve long *triiiiiiiiiings* each time. Papa had never answered.

Sakshi called Papa after the separation, too, on a day she sat alone in the balcony of her apartment in Indore, watching fat drops of rain fall from the sky and beat down on the steel shed above her. The rain had a dusty, spicy smell to it, its purity destroyed many hydrological cycles ago. And yet, the rain never failed to soothe her, refresh her mood, break through the stifling humidity of the season. She was ready to hear his voice.

Papa didn't answer.

Papa barely answered the phone nowadays. He preferred the convenience of texts and WhatsApp messages, the freedom to opt into a conversation or to ignore one, forever. He especially didn't respond if he was in one of his particular moods, when he needed silence, when he was angry, when he was mad. Now, in the dark bedroom, when the only light was the TV's glare, Papa had moments of sharp anger. He was angry at how his country was changing, how the minorities were having too many children to run him out, how some rebelled against Punditji and Santa Gol Gappa, how his employees had wanted the same identifying rights as everyone else. 'How can they just *want* these things?' Papa yelled at the TV. 'They have to *earn* it. We earned everything, didn't we?'

After the riots, when Papa had built that newer, better Bhagwan Beads factory, he wanted things to stay as they always had. He wanted to save his family. 'Family first,' he said out loud, but no one was there to hear him.

When he signed those papers with Sud, Papa wanted me to be back home. But nahi yaar, there was no home for me any more. Here I am in this *nowhere notime nonothing* place, a ghost haunted by my own ghosts, by visions of dead bodies battered by cricket bats on hot afternoons, and mindless ATM transactions completed to the joyous sound of money being dipensed *fluff-*

fluff-fluff, and Papa's voice echoing, *Suno, your comfort is someone else's catastrophe.*

Samjhe?

Wildhair pulled his trigger and then I was gone, and Jess fell to her knees, Hamid became speechless, Papa was lost to shock and Mummy to tears, Rishi bhaiya moved further away from his roots, and two nations were pushed into uneasy diplomatic talks.

Mark was charged with first-degree murder when they arrested him. At the police station, one policeman held on to his shoulder, grimacing in disgust at the stench of booze and stale urine emanating from his body, while the other officer filed the charge sheet over the counter. There was public outrage when the news appeared on local morning shows in the DMV area the next day. They called it a hate crime, behenchod; not a crime against me but against the larger community. By that afternoon, the same officer who had been disgusted by Mark's odour knocked on the bars of his cell and smiled. 'You're fucked, buddy.'

Mark's preliminary hearing was scheduled for later in the winter, and then postponed for spring, and finally, in the heat of the next summer, when another round of the NBA Finals was on the cards, he trudged into court. The officer escorting him loosened the shackles around his wrists, but Mark still held his hands together in front of him, arrested forever in the moment.

In bed in Varanasi, Papa was switching channels, searching for news of Mark Tillerman's sentencing. He had bought a brand-new flat screen TV with a remote control that could understand his voice commands, and he was happy that someone had finally made the technology to recognize Indian accents.

'C-N-N,' Papa said into the voice-recognizing remote control, but the TV switched to ESPN and cricket highlights instead.

Papa tutted and tsked and said louder, slower. 'C...N...N.' The TV of the future responded correctly this time. Papa sighed and slumped into the pillow and headboard of his bed, and when his ankles began to itch again, he ignored it. Slowly, he allowed his eyes to close before the bright glare of the TV in the dark. While a young woman narrated the news, Mark's image popped up on the screen behind her, being ushered into the Superior Court in Washington D.C. through the D Street entrance. Papa had seen photographs of Mark before, of course, but now, his hair was longer and wilder than ever before, and he had a messy beard over his rugged face, and wore a clean, white shirt that fit loosely over his broad shoulders.

But Papa and the news cameras couldn't follow him inside the courthouse. Mark went through the automatic glass doors and past dozens of screens of ongoing cases lined up like airline schedules, and up a few flights of escalators, underneath the semi-exposed glass ceiling that bathed the whole structure in the lush natural light of the afternoon sun. To Mark, the whole place had a smell of sterile sickness, like the smell of hospital disinfectant; it numbed him.

When he finally sat in the courtroom, Mark felt small in the cold, crowded chamber. He could hear shoes squeaking, the sounds of many pairs of nervous feet against the floor. The judge sat on a throne behind the bench, flanked on each side with flags—the bars and red mullets of the District of Columbia, and the stars and stripes of the United States.

Mark stood up. He had a steely expression on his face, bilkul steady. His eyes looked beyond the room into a far nothingness somewhere else. But, while he attempted to look as stoic as he could, beads of sweat formed on his scalp within his knotted, heavy hair, and dripped down his forehead and over the sides of his face, and when the judge pronounced his fate, slamming her gavel with a terrifying thump on her desk, Mark—naked to the unbearable heat of our shared pasts and inescapable future—shivered in his spot.

ACKNOWLEDGEMENTS

Thank you Udit Khanna for being the first reader I wrote for, and for being the co-author of so many adventures. Maybe there is still hope for 'UKM Books'.

Thank you to Stephanie Cabot for being a champion of this manuscript from its earliest drafts. To Amish Mulmi for believing in the potential of my work. And to Kanishka Gupta, an absolute legend, who finally turned this dream into reality. I have been blessed with the best damn readers and editors at Aleph—including Aienla Ozukum and Kanika Praharaj—whose expertise helped transform this raw piece of mush into the novel you see today.

I want to thank my professors and coursemates at the American University's MFA Programme, many of whom were the first to set their eyes on this manuscript. To Melissa Scholes Young, David Keplinger, and Dolen Perkins-Valdez, who provided encouragement and direction to help shape me into a better writer.

I am also grateful to Aatish Taseer for being an invaluable reader of this manuscript.

A special shout-out to the 'Blood Library' crew, going strong (somewhat) years after graduation: Bron Treanor, Karen Keating, Lauren Johnson, Matthew Bukowski, Vincent Granata, and Yohanca Delgado. Your honesty and friendship have been invaluable. Reunion at Wok 'N Roll?

Nina: I could never thank you enough for your patience, your love, and your chocolate chip cookies. You and Laila have made me whole, given me purpose. I guess I should probably thank Bilbo 'Backson' Baggins, too.

My parents and my brother: you have always supported me, unquestioningly, illogically, unconditionally, allowing me the privilege to work towards my dream. Your sacrifices have been a lifelong debt; this book is only a miniscule return for the gratitude that I'll always owe you. Thank you.